TOP SECRET

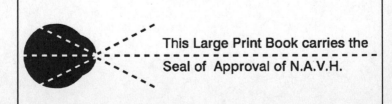

This Large Print Book carries the
Seal of Approval of N.A.V.H.

A CLANDESTINE OPERATIONS NOVEL

TOP SECRET

W.E.B. GRIFFIN
AND
WILLIAM E. BUTTERWORTH IV

THORNDIKE PRESS
A part of Gale, Cengage Learning

GALE
CENGAGE Learning·

LIBRARY OF CONGRESS CATALOGING-IN-PUBLICATION DATA

Griffin, W. E. B.
    Top Secret : a Clandestine Operations novel / W. E. B. Griffin and William E. Butterworth IV.
        pages cm. — (Thorndike Press Large Print Core)
    ISBN 978-1-4104-7142-0 (hardback) — ISBN 1-4104-7142-X (hardcover)
    1. Intelligence officers—Fiction. 2. Cold War—Fiction 3. Spy stories. 4. Suspense fiction. 5. Large type books. I. Butterworth, William E. (William Edmund) II. Title.
PS3557.R489137T725 2014b
813'.54—dc23   2014023234

Published in 2014 by arrangement with G. P. Putnam's Sons, a member of Penguin Group (USA) LLC, a Penguin Random House Company

Printed in the United States of America
1 2 3 4 5 6 7 18 17 16 15 14

26 July 1777
"The necessity of procuring good intelligence is apparent and need not be further urged."

George Washington
General and Commander in Chief
The Continental Army

FOR THE LATE

WILLIAM E. COLBY
An OSS Jedburgh First Lieutenant
who became director of the
Central Intelligence Agency.

AARON BANK
An OSS Jedburgh First Lieutenant
who became a colonel and
the father of Special Forces.

WILLIAM R. CORSON
A legendary Marine intelligence officer
whom the KGB hated more than any
other U.S. intelligence officer —
and not only because he wrote the
definitive work on them.

RENÉ J. DÉFOURNEAUX
A U.S. Army OSS Second Lieutenant
attached to the British SOE
who jumped into Occupied France alone
and later became a legendary
U.S. Army intelligence officer.

FOR THE LIVING

BILLY WAUGH
A legendary Special Forces
Command Sergeant Major
who retired and then went on to hunt
down the infamous Carlos the Jackal.
Billy could have terminated Osama
bin Laden in the early 1990s
but could not get permission to do so.
After fifty years in the business, Billy is
still going after the bad guys.

JOHNNY REITZEL
An Army Special Operations officer
who could have terminated the head
terrorist of the seized cruise ship
Achille Lauro but could not
get permission to do so.

RALPH PETERS
An Army intelligence officer
who has written the best analysis
of our war against terrorists and
of our enemy that I have ever seen.

AND FOR THE NEW BREED

MARC L
A senior intelligence officer,
despite his youth,
who reminds me of Bill Colby
more and more each day.

FRANK L
A legendary Defense Intelligence Agency
officer who retired and now
follows in Billy Waugh's footsteps.

AND

In Loving Memory Of
Colonel José Manuel Menéndez
Cavalry, Argentine Army, Retired
He spent his life fighting Communism
and Juan Domingo Perón

OUR NATION OWES
THESE PATRIOTS A DEBT
BEYOND REPAYMENT.

PROLOGUE

Many in the intelligence community feel that the first American counterfire shot in what became the Cold War occurred even before World War II was over — specifically when Major General Reinhard Gehlen contacted Allen W. Dulles. (Or Dulles contacted Gehlen; the details remain, more than half a century later, highly classified.)

Gehlen was the German intelligence officer who ran Abwehr Ost, which dealt with the Soviet Union. Dulles was the U.S. Office of Strategic Service's man in neutral Switzerland.

Realizing Nazi defeat was inevitable, Gehlen feared both Soviet ambitions for Europe and specifically what the victorious Russians would do to his officers, his men, and their families.

Gehlen struck a deal with Dulles. He would turn over to the OSS all his intelligence and assets. These included the identities of Soviet spies who had infiltrated the Manhattan

Project and of Abwehr Ost agents inside the Kremlin. In exchange, Dulles would place Gehlen, his officers and men and their families — who faced certain torture and death at the hands of the Soviets — under American protection.

Exactly who at the highest levels of the American government knew about Operation Gehlen, and when they knew it, also remains even today highly classified. It is obvious that General of the Army Dwight David Eisenhower, then Supreme Allied Commander in Europe, had to know about it.

It seems equally obvious that President Franklin Roosevelt was not made privy to it. Not only was Roosevelt deathly ill at the time, but he and his wife, Eleanor, had made it clear that they did not regard the Soviet Union and its leader, Josef Stalin, as any threat to the United States. There was wide belief that there were Communists in Roosevelt's inner circle.

There were other problems, too.

Roosevelt's secretary of the Treasury, Henry Morgenthau, was justifiably outraged by the monstrous behavior of the Nazis toward the Jewish people and unable to concede there existed "Good Germans" among the many "Bad Germans." Morgenthau seriously advocated a policy that would have seen senior

German officers executed out of hand whenever and wherever found. It was known that Gehlen was on the list of those German officers to look for.

J. Edgar Hoover, the director of the Federal Bureau of Investigation, posed other problems. Hoover had opposed the very formation of the OSS. He devoutly believed the FBI could do the job better. He made no secret of his loathing for OSS Director William J. Donovan. And vice versa. Hoover had been humiliated before the President when Donovan had turned over the names of Soviet spies in the Manhattan Project that Allen Dulles had turned up, and furious when Dulles had refused to name his source. Dulles of course couldn't, as the source had been Gehlen. Not even Donovan knew of the Gehlen project until after President Roosevelt had died in the arms of his mistress in Warm Springs, Georgia.

So far as Dulles was concerned, if Donovan knew, he would have felt duty bound to inform President Roosevelt. And that would have been the end of the secret; the Soviets would have learned of it within hours.

When, on Roosevelt's death, Vice President Harry S Truman became the thirty-third President of the United States, the former senator from Missouri had seen the President only twice after their inauguration and had never been alone with him.

On Truman's first day in office, Lieutenant General Leslie R. Groves, U.S. Army, went to see him in the Oval Office. Groves headed the Manhattan Project, and told Truman he thought he should know that the United States had a new weapon, the most powerful ever developed, called the "atomic bomb."

It is also known that both Allen Dulles and General Donovan met privately with Truman in the very early days of his presidency. Many believe that Truman was made privy to Operation Gehlen during one of those meetings.

Shortly afterward, in mid-July 1945, Truman met with Stalin in Potsdam, near Berlin. He told the Russian dictator of the atomic bomb. When Stalin showed no surprise, Truman decided this confirmed what Donovan had told him — that J. Edgar Hoover had not been able to keep Russian espionage out of the Manhattan Project.

Truman ordered General George C. Marshall to shut off all aid to the Soviet Union.

Right then. That afternoon.

The OSS — often with the assistance of the Vatican — within days began to send many of "the Gehlens" to Argentina. Others were placed in a heavily guarded OSS compound at Kloster Grünau, a former monastery in

Schollbrunn, Bavaria, which had been provided by the Vatican. These actions could not have happened without Truman's knowledge and approval.

On August 6, 1945, the United States obliterated Hiroshima, Japan, with an atomic bomb. Three days later, a second atomic bomb obliterated Nagasaki.

On September 2, 1945, a formal surrender ceremony was performed in Tokyo Bay, Japan, aboard the battleship USS *Missouri*.

World War II was over.

Argentina, which had declared war on the Axis only in March, was one of the victors, although not a single Argentine soldier or sailor had died in the war and not one bomb or artillery shell had landed on Argentine soil. And now Argentina, as a result of supplying foodstuffs to both sides, was richer than ever.

Argentina's role in World War II, however, was by no means over.

When, as early as 1942, the most senior members of the Nazi hierarchy — as high as Martin Bormann, generally regarded as second in power only to Hitler, and Reichsführer-SS Heinrich Himmler — realized the Ultimate Victory was not nearly as certain as Propaganda Minister Josef Goebbels had been telling the German people, they began in great secrecy to implement Operation Phoenix.

Phoenix would establish refuges in South America — primarily in Argentina and Paraguay — to which senior Nazis could flee should the Thousand-Year Reich have a life shorter than they hoped. National Socialism could then rise, phoenix-like, from the ashes.

Vast sums were sent to Argentina, some through normal banking channels but most in great secrecy by submarine. The U-boats also carried crates of currency, gold, and diamonds and other precious stones. Senior SS officers were sent to Argentina — some of them legally, accredited as diplomats, but again most of them secretly infiltrated by submarine — to purchase property where senior Nazis would be safe from Allied retribution.

The Allies knew of Operation Phoenix and had tried, without much success, to stop it. Their concern heightened as the war drew to a close. They learned that when Grand Admiral Doenitz issued the Cease Hostilities order on May fourth, sixty-three U-boats were at sea.

Five of them were known to have complied with their orders to hoist a black flag and proceed to an Allied port to surrender, or to a neutral port to be interned. There was reliable intelligence that an additional forty-one

U-boats had been scuttled by their crews to prevent the capture of whatever may have been on board.

That left at least seventeen U-boats unaccounted for. Of particular concern were U-234, U-405, and U-977. They were Type XB U-boats — minelayers, which meant that with no mines aboard they could carry a great deal of cargo and many passengers for vast distances.

There was credible intelligence that when U-234 sailed from Narvik on April 16 — two weeks before the German capitulation — she had aboard a varied cargo, some of which was either not listed on the manifest at all or listed under a false description. This included a ton of mail — which of course almost certainly hid currency and diamonds being smuggled. It also included Nazi and Japanese officers and German scientists as passengers. And something even more worrisome: 560 kilograms of uranium oxide from the German not-quite-completed atomic bomb project.

It was only logical to presume that U-405 and U-977 were carrying similar cargoes.

A massive search by ship and air for all submarines — but especially for U-234, U-405, and U-977 — was launched from France, England, and Africa, and by the specially configured U.S. Army Air Forces

B-24 "Liberator" bombers that had searched for submarines since 1942 from bases in Brazil.

The searches of course were limited by the range of the aircraft involved and, as far as the ships also involved in the searches, by the size of the South Atlantic Ocean once the submarines had entered it.

There were some successes. Submarines were sighted and then attacked with depth charges and/or aircraft bombs. While it was mathematically probable that several of the submarines were sunk, there was no telling which ones.

The concern that the U-boats — either certainly or probably — had uranium oxide aboard and were headed for Japan was reduced when the Japanese surrendered on September 2, 1945. But that left Argentina as a very possible destination.

Whether or not the Americans ever located the U-boats allegedly carrying German uranium oxide to Japan or Argentina, or if they did, what happened to them and the uranium oxide is today still classified Top Secret.

I

[One]

National Airport
Alexandria, Virginia

0405 25 October 1945

The triple-tail Lockheed Constellation with HOWELL PETROLEUM lettered on its fuselage came in low over the Potomac River, lowered its gear, put down its huge flaps, and touched smoothly down at the very end of the main north-south runway.

Her four engines roared as the pilot quickly moved the propellers into reverse pitch and shoved her throttles forward. When the Connie finally stopped, she was very uncomfortably close to the far end of the runway and her tires were smoking.

The pilot radioed: "National, Howell One on the ground at six past the hour. Request taxi instructions."

"Howell One, turn and take Taxiway One

on your right. Hold there."

"Howell One understands hold on Taxiway One."

The Constellation was the finest transport aircraft in the world. It was capable of flying forty passengers in its pressurized cabin higher — at an altitude of 35,000 feet — and faster — it cruised at better than 300 knots — and for a longer distance — 4,300 miles — than any other transport aircraft in the world. When National Airport had opened in June 1941, it had been not much more than a pencil sketch in the notebook of legendary aviator Howard Hughes, who owned, among a good deal else, the Lockheed Aircraft Company. Hughes, who had designed the Lockheed P-38 "Lightning" fighter plane, had decided that if he took his design of the P-38's wing, enlarged it appropriately, put four engines on it, and then married it to a huge, sleek fuselage with an unusual triple-tail design, he would have one hell of an airplane.

"Build it," Hughes ordered. "The Air Corps will buy it once they see it. And if they don't, I know at least one airline that will."

Although the Congress, in its wisdom, had decreed that airlines could not own aircraft manufacturing companies, and vice versa, it was widely believed that Hughes secretly owned TWA, then known as Transcontinental & Western Airlines, and later as Trans-World Airlines.

No sooner had Howell One stopped on Taxiway One than a small but impressive fleet of vehicles surrounded it. There were four Ford station wagons and two large trucks. On all their doors was the insignia of the Federal Bureau of Investigation. There was also a third truck with a crane mounted in its bed, and a black 1942 Buick Roadmaster. Neither was marked. The Buick had a large chrome object housing a siren and a red light mounted on its left front fender. Finally, there was a truck carrying the logotype of National Airport. It had a stairway mounted in its bed.

A dozen or more men in business suits and hats and carrying Thompson submachine guns erupted from the station wagons as the truck with the stairs backed up against the Constellation's rear door.

Two men in business suits got out of the Buick and quickly climbed the stairs up to the fuselage.

They stood waiting at the top until the door was finally opened.

A handsome young officer — blond, six-foot-one, 212 pounds — stood in the doorway. He was wearing an olive drab woolen "Ike" jacket and trousers. The jacket's insignia identified him as a second lieutenant of Cavalry. The jacket was unbuttoned, and his necktie pulled down.

The two men in suits flashed him looks of surprised disapproval as they pushed past him and entered the cabin.

The cabin looked more like a living room pictured in *Architectural Digest* than the interior of a passenger aircraft. Instead of rows of seats, there were leather upholstered armchairs and couches scattered along its length. There was a desk and two tables. A full bar was at the front of the cabin. The floor was lushly carpeted.

Seated in armchairs were three people: a tall, sharp-featured, elegantly tailored septuagenarian; a stocky, short-haired blond woman in her late forties; and an attractive, tanned, and athletic-looking young woman of about twenty.

They were, respectively, Cletus Marcus Howell, president and chairman of the board of the Howell Petroleum Corporation; his daughter-in-law, Martha Williamson Howell; and her daughter — the old man's granddaughter — Marjorie.

"I'm Assistant Deputy Director Kelly of the FBI," the older of the two men who had come into the cabin announced. He was in his fifties, wore spectacles, and had a short haircut. "Welcome to Washington."

No one responded.

"Where is the officer-in-charge?" Kelly asked.

The old man pointed to the young officer standing at the door.

"You just walked past him," he said.

"I asked for the officer-in-charge, sir," Kelly snapped.

"Sonny," the old man said, "I hate to rain on your parade, but if that FBI army you have with you was intended to dazzle me, it has failed to do so."

"Dad!" the older woman said warningly.

Her daughter smiled.

There came the sound of a siren, and then the squealing of brakes, and finally the faint sound of car doors slamming closed.

A moment later, three men came into the cabin.

One wore the uniform of a rear admiral. Another, an Army brigadier general, was in "pinks and greens" — a green tunic with pink trousers. The third, a colonel, wore an Army olive drab uniform.

The colonel stopped just inside the door to both shake the hand of the young officer, then affectionately pat his shoulder.

"You done real good, Jimmy," Colonel Robert Mattingly said.

"Thank you, sir," Second Lieutenant James D. Cronley Jr. replied.

"Admiral," Kelly said.

"What are you doing here, Kelly?" Rear Admiral Sidney W. Souers, U.S. Navy, demanded coldly.

"Self-evidently," Kelly announced, "the FBI is here to guarantee the security of the cargo aboard this aircraft until it can be placed in the hands of the Manhattan Project."

The door to the cockpit opened and a man wearing an airline-type uniform stepped into the cabin. His tunic carried the four golden stripes of a captain.

Admiral Souers turned to him.

"Any problems, Ford?"

The "captain," who was in fact U.S. Navy Commander Richard W. Ford, came to attention.

"None, Admiral," he said.

Souers turned to Kelly.

"Thank you for your interest, Mr. Kelly. You and your people may go."

"Admiral, the FBI will stay here until the cargo is in the hands of the Manhattan Project."

Souers gestured toward the man in pink

and greens.

"This is General Tomlinson of the Manhattan Project, Mr. Kelly. You may report to Mr. Hoover, if you are here at his orders, that you witnessed my turning over of the cargo to the Manhattan Project."

Kelly, white-faced, didn't reply.

"Are you going to leave, taking your people with you, Mr. Kelly? Or am I going to have to go down to my car, get on the radio, wake the President up, explain the situation to him and ask him to call Director Hoover and tell him to tell you your presence here is not required?"

Kelly turned on his heels, made an impatient gesture for the man with him to follow, and left the cabin.

Souers shook his head as he looked away from the door.

"How did those sonsofbitches manage to beat us here?" he asked rhetorically. He then quickly added, "Pardon the language, ladies."

"My daughter-in-law and granddaughter have heard the word before," Cletus Marcus Howell said.

"Mattingly, do you think Hoover has someone in my office?" Souers asked.

Mattingly shrugged. "Sir, I would not like to think so. But . . ."

"Admiral," Commander Ford said, "the FBI must have had people at the airport in Miami . . ."

"Where you refueled," Souers instantly picked up his thought. "With orders to keep an eye out for a civilian Constellation coming from South America."

"And they called Washington," Mattingly added. "When they learned you had filed a nonstop flight plan to National."

"And instead of calling me," Souers concluded, "the FBI — probably J. Edgar himself — decided to meet the plane here."

"Why?" General Tomlinson asked.

"J. Edgar is very good at turning any situation so that it shines a flattering light on the FBI," Souers said.

He turned and walked back to Second Lieutenant Cronley.

"I have a message for you, son, from President Truman," he said.

"Yes, sir?"

"Quote Well done unquote."

"Thank you, sir."

"The President also said he wants to see you. That won't happen today, but when it does, I wouldn't be surprised if he said you can replace your golden bar with a silver one. But . . ."

Souers stopped as a colonel in an olive

drab uniform with Corps of Engineers insignia appeared in the doorway.

"Good morning, Broadhead," General Tomlinson said. "Come in."

"Good morning, sir."

"Admiral Souers," Tomlinson said, "this is Colonel Broadhead, who will take charge of the cargo."

Souers nodded, and then asked of Cronley, "Where is it, son?"

"In the cargo hold, sir."

"How hot is it?" Colonel Broadhead asked.

Commander Ford answered for him.

"There are six packages, Colonel. Each weighing a little over two hundred pounds. They're roped so as to be manhandle-able. Each came with two lead blankets, each weighing about a hundred pounds. With the blankets off, my Geiger counter indicated significant, but not life-threatening, radiation within a two-hour period. With the lead blankets in place, the counter shows only insignificant radiation."

"You are?" Broadhead asked.

Ford looked to Souers for permission to answer the question. Souers nodded, just perceptibly.

"Commander Richard Ford, sir."

Broadhead then said, "Where did you first

27

put the Geiger counter to it, Commander? On the submarine?"

"Colonel," Souers snapped, "who told you anything about a submarine?"

"Admiral," General Tomlinson put in, "Colonel Broadhead has worked for me in the Manhattan Project for three years. He has all the necessary security clearances."

"That's very nice, General," Souers said unpleasantly. "But my question to the colonel with all the necessary security clearances was 'Who said something — *anything* — to him about a submarine?' "

"Sir," Broadhead said, "one of my duties at the Manhattan Project was to keep an eye on the German efforts in that area. I knew they had some uranium oxide — from the Belgian Congo — and I heard about the missing German U-boats. When I heard that the OSS was about to turn over to us a half ton of it that they'd acquired in Argentina, it seemed to me the most logical place for the OSS to have gotten it was from one of the missing U-boats."

Souers went on: "And did you share this assumption of yours, Colonel, with a bunch of other colonels — all with the necessary security clearances — while you were sitting around having a beer?"

Broadhead, sensing where the line of

28

questioning was headed, replied, "Yes, sir. I'm afraid I did."

"Not that it excuses you in any way, Colonel," Souers said icily, "but you're just one of a great many stupid senior sonsof . . . officers with all the necessary security clearances who think it's perfectly all right to share anything they know with anyone else who has such clearances. Now do you take my point? Or do I have to order you not to share with anyone anything you've seen or heard here today or any assumptions you may make from what you have seen or heard?"

"Sir, I take your point."

Souers let the exchange sink in for a very long twenty seconds, and then ordered, "Ford, answer the colonel's question."

"When Cronley seized the cargo, sir," Ford said, "he did not have a Geiger counter device."

"May I ask who Cronley is? And why he didn't have a radiation detection device?"

Admiral Souers turned to Cronley. "Son, I'm going to give Colonel Broadhead the benefit of the doubt, meaning I am presuming that he has a reason beyond idle curiosity in asking it. Therefore, you may answer those questions."

"Yes, sir," Cronley said, then looked at

Broadhead. "Sir, I'm Second Lieutenant James D. Cronley Junior. The first Geiger counter I ever saw was the one Commander Ford used on the . . . packages that I took off . . . wherever they were and gave to him."

"I predict a great military career for this fine young officer," Admiral Souers said. "I'm sure everyone noticed that he didn't say 'submarine' or 'U-boat' or 'uranium oxide' even once."

Souers let that sink in for another ten seconds, and then went on: "Now my curiosity is aroused. Why did you want to know, Broadhead, if the Geiger counter had been used on . . . wherever these packages were when Cronley seized them?"

"Sir, I was hoping that someone looked for radiation that might have leaked from the packages while they were on the sub —" He stopped.

"Now that the cat's out of the bag, Colonel," Souers said, "you can say 'submarine.' You can even say 'U-boat' and 'uranium oxide.' "

"Yes, sir."

Souers looked at Cletus Marcus Howell, who was grinning widely.

"Please don't think this is funny, Mr. Howell," he said.

"That was a smile of approval, Admiral.

From one mean sonofabitch to another."

"Dad, for God's sake!" Martha Howell said.

"I will take that as a compliment, Mr. Howell," Souers said.

"It was intended as one," the old man said.

Souers turned to Broadhead.

"You think the submarine may be hot, Broadhead?"

"I think it's possible, sir. The uranium oxide was on the submarine for a couple of months, maybe even longer."

"Mattingly, get that word to Frade just as soon as we're finished here," Souers ordered. "We don't want to sterilize half the brighter officers of the Armada Argentina, do we?"

"Yes, sir," Colonel Mattingly said, smiling. "And no, sir, we certainly wouldn't want to do that."

Second Lieutenant Cronley chuckled.

"I don't understand that," Cletus Marcus Howell said.

"Possibly, Dad," his daughter-in-law said, "because you're not supposed to. It's none of your business."

"Actually, with apologies to the ladies, I was being crude in order not to have to say 'suffer radiation poisoning,' " Souers said. "And, ma'am, the President ordered me to

31

answer any questions Mr. Howell might have."

"I thought I told you, Martha," the old man said, "that ole Harry and I have the honor to be Thirty-third Degree Masons. We can trust one another."

"May I ask who 'Frade' is?" Broadhead said. "And if he's qualified to conduct an examination of this kind?"

"No, Colonel, you may not. You don't have the Need to Know," Souers said. "Are you and General Tomlinson about ready to get the cargo moving?"

"At your orders, Admiral," Tomlinson said.

"Then may I suggest you get going?"

"Yes, sir."

"Show them how to get into the cargo bay, Ford."

"Aye, aye, sir."

Cronley made a move suggesting he was going with them.

Souers held up his hand. "Unless the commander can't find the cargo without your help, son, you stay here."

"Yes, sir," Cronley said.

Souers waited until enough time had passed for Tomlinson, Broadhead, and Ford to have gone down the stairway, then walked to the door to make sure they had.

He turned to Cronle~

"The next proble~
to do with you. ~
first heard of ~
that you we~
oxide."

"For Christ's sa~
cus Howell explode~
that goddamned radio
for Jimmy! It seems to ~
is in order. Starting with a~
can go to Texas and see ~
mother."

Souers ignored him.

"In the best of all possible worlds,~
went on, "you would already be ba~
Germany. But the worst-case scenario ~
happened. Hoover now knows your name
and that you have had something to do with
the uranium ore. He will now be determined
to learn that precise relationship."

"And Truman can't tell him to mind his
own business?" the old man asked. "I think
he will if I ask him. And I goddamned sure
will. I figure ole Harry owes me a little favor
— hell, a large favor. You know what it costs
by the hour to fly this airplane? And I don't
mind at all calling it in."

"I hope I can talk you out of doing that,
Mr. Howell. The problem there is that if the

s Hoover to mind his own
that will do is whet Hoover's
d we have to keep in mind that
t the only thing Cronley knows

ean the Germans we sneaked into
a?"

s nodded. "That whole operation."

d you don't trust Jimmy to keep his
h shut, is that it? That's insulting!"

he less he tells the FBI agents that
over certainly is going to send to
terview' him, the greater their — Hoo-
er's — curiosity is going to be. I don't want
— can't permit — the ax of Hoover learning about the Gehlen operation to be hanging over the President."

"I understand this, Mr. Howell," Cronley
said, then met Souers's eyes. "Sir, I'm
perfectly willing to go back to Germany
right away."

"And then where do we get married?"
Marjorie Howell demanded. "In the ruins
of Berlin? Maybe we could get married in
that bunker where Hitler married his mistress the day before he shot her. That would
be romantic as hell, wouldn't it?"

"Chip off the old block, isn't she, Admiral?" the old man said, smiling with obvious
pride. "She's got my genes. I advise you not

to cross her."

"Squirt," Cronley said. "This is important stuff."

"So far as I'm concerned, getting married is pretty important stuff," she said.

"Not that I think the admiral is at all interested," Martha Howell said, "but I thought you and Beth wanted a double wedding. And I can't set up something like that in less than three months."

"You wanted the double wedding, Mother," Marjorie said. "Let's get that straight. Beth would like to get married today. And so, goddamn it, would I, now that I think about it."

"I'm afraid your marriage plans are going to have to be put on hold until we get this straightened out, Miss Howell," Souers said.

"On hold for how long?" Marjorie demanded. "Or is that another classified secret?"

"Yes, it is classified," Souers said. "Highly classified. Lieutenant Cronley is right, Miss Howell. This is very important stuff."

"So you're going to send him right back to Germany?" Marjorie said. " 'Thank you for all you've done, Lieutenant. Don't let the knob on the airplane door hit you in the ass as you get on board.' "

"That's quite enough, Marjorie!" her

mother announced.

"Cool it, Squirt," Cronley said. "I'm a soldier. I obey my orders."

"I would like to send him back to Germany immediately, Miss Howell," Souers said. "But unfortunately, that's not possible. President Truman wants to see him before he goes back, and that's it."

"You're going to explain that, right?" Cletus Marcus Howell said.

"What Colonel Mattingly suggested, and what we're going to do, is put Lieutenant Cronley on ice, so to speak, until the President's schedule is such that he can see him."

"What does 'on ice, so to speak' mean, Admiral?" Marjorie said.

"Well, since we can't put him in a hotel, or at Fort Myer, because J. Edgar's minions would quickly find him, what we're going to do is put him in the Transient Officers' Quarters at Camp Holabird. That's in Baltimore. Mattingly tells me junior CIC officers passing through the Washington area routinely stay there — it's a dollar and a half a night — so he won't attract any attention. Mattingly will arrange for them to misplace his registry card, so if the FBI calls for him they can say they have no record of him being there."

"And how long will he be there?" the old man asked.

"Just until he sees the President. And on that subject, Mr. Howell, the President would like to see you there at the same time. And he would be furious with me if he later learned that your granddaughter and Mrs. Howell were here and I hadn't brought you along to the White House for his meeting with Lieutenant Cronley."

"And after he meets with the President, he gets on the plane to Germany?" Marjorie said.

Souers nodded.

"If Jimmy goes to Germany, I'm going to Germany," Marjorie then announced.

"We'll talk about that, dear," Martha Howell said.

"If Jimmy goes to Germany, I'm going to Germany. Period. Subject closed."

[Two]

The Officers' Club
U.S. Army Counterintelligence Center &
  School
Camp Holabird
1019 Dundalk Avenue, Baltimore 19, Maryland

1730 25 October 1945

The artwork behind the bar at which Second Lieutenant Cronley was sipping at his second scotch was more or less an oil painting. It portrayed three soldiers wearing World War I–era steel helmets trying very hard not to be thrown out of a Jeep bouncing three feet off the ground.

Rather than an original work, it was an enlargement of a photograph taken at Camp Holabird in 1939. The U.S. Army Quartermaster Corps, which had then reigned over Camp Holabird, was testing the new Willys-designed vehicle. Some GI artist had colored the photograph with oil paints.

Cronley had heard the rumor that it was at Camp Holabird that the vehicle — officially known as "Truck, 1/4 Ton, 4×4, General Purpose" — first had been dubbed "Jeep," from the G and P in General Purpose.

He wasn't sure if this was true or just lore. Or bullshit, like the rumors circulating among the student officers and enlisted men about My Brother's Place, the bar directly across Dundalk Avenue from the main gate. That lore, or bullshit, held that an unnamed "foreign power" had a camera with a long-range lens installed in an upstairs window with which they were taking photographs of everyone coming out the gate.

That, the lore said, would of course pose

enormous problems for the students when they graduated and were sent "into the field."

His thoughts were interrupted when a voice beside him said, "Cronley, isn't it?"

He turned and saw the speaker was a major.

"Yes, sir."

The major offered his hand. "Remember me, Cronley? Major Derwin? 'Techniques of Surveillance'?"

"Yes, sir, of course. Good to see you again, sir."

"So they sent you back, did they, to finish the course?"

"Just passing through, sir."

"From where to where, if I can ask?"

"Munich to Munich, sir. With a brief stop here. I was the escort officer for some classified documents."

That bullshit came to me naturally. I didn't even have to wonder what cover story I should tell this guy.

"Munich? I thought you'd been sent to the Twenty-second in Marburg."

"Yes, sir. I was. Then I was transferred to the Twenty-seventh."

Counterintelligence Corps units were numbered. When written, for reasons Cronley could not explain — except as a manifes-

39

tation of the Eleventh Commandment that there were three ways to do anything, the Right Way, the Wrong Way, and the Army Way — Roman numerals were used. For example, the XXVIIth CIC Detachment.

"I'm not familiar with the Twenty-seventh. Who's the senior agent?"

Is that classified? No. It's not.

The XXIIIrd CIC Detachment and what it does is classified — oh, boy, is it classified! — but not the XXVIIth. The XXVIIth is the cover for the XXIIIrd.

"Major Harold Wallace, sir."

"Wallace? Harold Wallace?"

"Yes, sir."

"I don't think I know him."

"I'm not sure if this is so, sir, but I've heard that Major Wallace was in Japan, and sent to Germany because we're so under strength."

Actually, before President Truman put the OSS out of business, Wallace had been deputy commander of OSS Forward. I can't tell this guy that; he doesn't have the Need to Know. And if I did, he probably wouldn't believe me.

And, clever fellow that I am, I learned early this morning from Admiral Souers — who really knows how to eat someone a new anal orifice — that sharing classified information one has with someone who also has a security clearance is something that clever fellows such as myself just should not do.

"That would explain it," Major Derwin said. "The personnel problem is enormous. They scraped the bottom of the Far East Command IC barrel as they scraped ours here."

"Yes, sir."

As a matter of fact, Major, the morning report of the XXIIIrd CIC Detachment shows a total strength of two officers — Major Wallace and me — and two EM — First Sergeant Chauncey L. Dunwiddie and Sergeant Friedrich Hessinger. And we really see very little of Major Wallace of the XXVIIth.

"No offense, Cronley," Major Derwin said.

"Sir?"

"It certainly wasn't your fault that scraping the barrel here saw you sent into the field before you were properly trained. Did you find yourself in over your head?"

"Sir, that's something of an understatement. No offense taken."

On the other hand, this morning Colonel Mattingly patted my shoulder and said, "You done good, Jimmy."

Their conversation was interrupted by the bartender, a sergeant who was earning a

41

little extra money by tending bar. He inquired, "Is there a Lieutenant Crumley in here?"

Speaking of the devil, that's Colonel Mattingly, calling to tell me the President can't find time for me and that he's sending a car to take me to the airport for my flight back to Germany.

And I probably won't even get to say goodbye to the Squirt.

Shit!

"There's a Lieutenant Cronley," Jimmy called.

The bartender came to him and handed him a telephone on a long cord.

Jimmy said into it: "Lieutenant Cronley, sir."

"Sergeant Killian at the gate, Lieutenant," the caller replied. "There's a civilian lady here wanting to see you. A Miss Howell. Should I pass her through?"

Cronley's heart jumped.

"After first giving her directions to the officers' club, absolutely!"

"Yes, sir."

Cronley handed the phone back to the bartender.

"My date has arrived, sir," Cronley said to Major Derwin.

We never had a date, come to think of it.

One moment, Squirt was Clete's annoying little sister, and the next we were . . . involved.

"Ah, to be young!" Major Derwin said. "You just got here, and already you're playing the field."

Cronley smiled but didn't reply.

Derwin had a helpful thought and expressed it.

"Perhaps you should go outside and wait for her. The club's sign is poorly lit."

"She's a very resourceful young woman, sir. She'll find me."

Five minutes later, the Squirt did.

She stopped at the door to the bar just long enough for Jimmy to see her, which caused his heart to thump, and then walked to him.

"Hi," she said.

"Hi, yourself." Jimmy then turned to Derwin. "Major Derwin, may I introduce Miss Marjorie Howell?"

Please, Major, say "Nice to meet you" and then leave us alone.

"A great pleasure, Miss Howell. When the lieutenant was a student here, I was his instructor in the techniques of surveillance. Obviously, I taught him well. Look what he found."

Miss Howell gave him an icy look.

43

Please, Squirt, don't say what you're thinking!

"Oh, really?" she asked. Then, "Jimmy, why don't you pay your tab? I'm pressed for time."

"Well, there's a small problem there," Cronley said. "All I have is Funny Money — Army of Occupation Scrip — and they won't take that here. I don't suppose you'd loan me a few dollars?"

She looked at him, saw on his face that he was telling the truth, and reached into her purse. She came out with a thick wad of currency, folded in half, that seemed to be made up entirely of new one-hundred-dollar bills.

She unfolded the wad and extended it to him. He took three of the hundreds.

"Thank you," he said, and then curiosity got the better of him. "What are you doing with all that money?"

"I thought I might need it in Germany, so I cashed a check."

"You're going to Germany, Miss Howell?" Major Derwin asked.

"Yes, I am," she said. "Pay the bill, please, Jimmy."

"Oh, you're from an Army family?"

"Not yet," Marjorie said. "Thank you for

entertaining Jimmy until I could get here, Major."

[Three]

Marjorie took Jimmy's hand as they left the officers' club and led him to a bright yellow 1941 Buick convertible.

"I'll drive," she said. "You've been drinking."

He got in beside her.

"Where the hell did you get the car?"

"On a lot on Ninth Street. One look and I had to have it."

"You bought it?" he asked incredulously.

"And since it was parked right in front of the lot, I thought I could buy it quicker than anything else they had. I didn't know how long it was going to take me to get here."

"What are you going to do with it when you go to Midland?"

"I'm not going to Midland. Weren't you listening? I'm going to Germany."

"We have to talk about that," he said.

"I don't like the way you said that."

She turned to face him. Their eyes met.

"Jimmy, you sound like my mother trying to reason with me . . ."

Their conversation was interrupted when the proximity of their faces caused a mutual involuntary act on both their parts.

A minute or so later, Jimmy said, "Jesus H. Christ!" and Marjorie said, a little breathlessly, "Don't let this go to your head, but as kissers go, you're not too bad."

A moment after that, she said, "No! God, Jimmy, not in the car!"

"Sorry."

"Let's go to a motel," she said. "God, I can't believe I said that!"

He put his hands on her arms and moved her back behind the steering wheel.

"About you coming to Germany," he then said. "Do you remember what the major said, that he asked, 'Oh, you're from an Army family?' "

"What's that got to do with anything?"

"The only way you're going to get into Germany, Squirt, is as a member of an Army family. The Army calls them 'dependents.' "

"I'll get into Germany. Trust me."

"If you did, we couldn't get married. There's a rule about that, too. You can't get married in Germany without permission, and they won't give you permission to marry unless you have less than ninety days to serve in the theatre."

"In the theatre?"

"That's what they call it, the 'European Theatre of Operations.' The rules are de-

46

signed to keep people from marrying Germans."

"How do you know so much about this subject?" Marjorie asked suspiciously.

"Professor Hessinger delivered a lecture on the subject to Tiny and me one night when we were sitting around with nothing else to do."

"Who the hell are they?"

"They are my staff," he said, chuckling. "If you're going to be an Army wife, Squirt, you'll have to learn that all officers, including second lieutenants, have staffs. Hessinger and Tiny are mine."

"If you're trying to string me along, Jimmy, you're never going to get to do what you tried to do a moment ago."

"Hessinger is a sergeant. Tiny Dunwiddie is a first sergeant. Interesting guys."

"I will play along with this for the next thirty seconds."

"Hessinger is a German Jew who got out of Germany just in time, went to Harvard, and then got drafted. They put him in the CIC because he speaks German. He's still got an accent you can cut with a knife."

"Fifteen seconds."

"Tiny is an enormous black guy. Two-thirty, six-three. He went to Norwich University in Vermont."

"Where? Ten seconds."

"Norwich is a private military college in Vermont, the oldest one," Cronley said, now speaking so rapidly it was almost a verbal blur.

Marjorie giggled, which he found surprisingly erotic.

"Slow down," she said. "You've got another thirty seconds."

". . . from which, rather than waiting to graduate and get a commission, he dropped out and enlisted so he could get into the war before they called it off. He's from an Army family. His ancestors were the Buffalo Soldiers who fought the Indians. Two of his great-grandfathers were in the Tenth Cavalry, which, Tiny has told me at least twenty times, beat Teddy Roosevelt up San Juan Hill in Cuba during the Spanish American War."

"And did he manage to get in the war before they called it off?" Marjorie asked, and then added: "Damn you. You've got me. You're as good at that as my mother. But there better be a point to this history lesson."

"Yeah, he got in the war. Silver Star, Bronze Star, and two Purple Hearts serving with a tank destroyer battalion in the Second Armored Division. Plus first sergeant's stripes when all the sergeants senior to him got killed or wounded. He's one hell of a soldier."

"But they still didn't give him a commission? Why, because he didn't finish college? Or because he's Negro?"

"No. Because he was needed to run the company of black troops Colonel Mattingly has guarding the Gehlen compound. I said he's a hell of a soldier. He takes that duty, honor, country business very seriously. He knows guarding General Gehlen and his people is more important than being one more second lieutenant in a tank platoon somewhere."

"I get the feeling you really like this guy."

"Yeah, I do."

"So what about the Jewish sergeant with an accent you can cut with a knife?"

"Freddy's hobby is reading. You never see him without a book of some kind in his hand. Including Army Regulations. And he remembers every last detail of anything he's ever read. That's why we call him 'the professor.' "

"His hobby is *reading*? You're suggesting he's a little funny?" Marjorie waved her hand to suggest there might be a question of his sexual orientation.

Jimmy laughed.

"That's not the professor's problem. I should have said, 'You never see him without a tall, good-looking German blond — or two — on his arm, and a book in the other hand.' "

"And what did this Jewish Casanova with an accent remember Army Regulations saying about us getting married in Germany?"

Jimmy told her again: The bottom lines were (a) she could not get into Occupied Germany unless she was a dependent, and (b) even if she did somehow get into Occupied Germany, they could not get permission to marry there.

When he had finished, she said without much conviction, "There has to be a way."

"I've been thinking about that. Are you open to a wild idea?"

"Try me."

"When I was here before, I learned that Elkton, Maryland, up near the Pennsylvania border, is where people go when they're eloping. Justices of the peace there will issue a marriage license, then marry you, and have you on your way in about an hour."

"Huh," Marjorie said.

"What I was thinking was that, since they're going to send me —"

"Where did you say Elkton, Maryland, is?"

"On U.S. 1 up near the Pennsylvania border."

"I came from Washington on U.S. 1," Marjorie said. "I know how to find it."

She reached to the dashboard, turned the ignition key, and then pressed the starter button.

[Four]

The Lord Baltimore Hotel
20 West Baltimore Street, Baltimore 21,
  Maryland

2325 25 October 1945

"Yes, sir? May I be of assistance?" the assistant manager of the hotel inquired of Second Lieutenant Cronley.

"We'd like a room, please. A nice room."

"Have you a reservation, sir?"

"No. I don't."

"And your luggage, sir?"

"No luggage."

The assistant manager adjusted his necktie knot, then said, "Sir, the Lord Baltimore might not be appropriate for you and the lady. May I suggest —"

"If you're about to suggest we try some sleazy motel down the street," Mrs. Marjorie Howell Cronley interrupted, "I would be

51

forced to conclude you have an evil mind, sir."

She pulled from her purse a certificate of marriage and held it up for the assistant manager's edification.

He forced a big smile. "I was about to suggest, madam, one of our junior suites."

"Do you have a senior suite? If so, we'll take it," she said.

"Well," Jimmy asked not more than fifteen minutes later, as Marjorie laid her head on his chest, "now that our marriage has been truly consummated, what do we do now?"

"What do you mean 'truly consummated'?"

"You have to do what we just did or you're not really married."

"Professor Freddy told you that, right?"

"Sergeant Hessinger is a fountain of information, most of it useful."

"So, what did he have to say about the Army and lieutenants whose marriage has been truly consummated?"

"As much as I remember — this took place of course before you seduced me, and I wasn't all that interested in the subject at the time —"

He yelped when she bit his nipple.

"*I* seduced *you?*"

"As I remember it, that's what happened."

"We'll fight later. Tell me what he said."

"Presuming you're married, as we are now, the sponsor — that's me — goes to his commanding officer and requests that his dependent — that's you — be allowed to join him in Germany."

"Requests? He could turn you down?"

"Commanding officers can do anything. But he won't. Major Wallace is a good guy. Then, once quarters are assigned — that's what the Army calls houses — you will get what they call 'invitational orders' which will allow you to get on a transport — a Navy ship — and sail to Germany. Bremerhaven, Germany. Sponsors usually meet the incoming dependents on the dock. There will be several hundred of us, but you will be able to spot me from afar. I will be the sponsor with the biggest boner, the painful result of my having been separated from my dependent for six weeks or so."

"This thing, you mean?" Marjorie grabbed his male appendage.

"That's it. That's what I had in mind when I endowed you with all my worldly goods."

"And you had better not forget who it belongs to now."

"Indeed."

"Wait. Why can't I fly over there?"

"I don't know, but I will damned sure ask Freddy to look into it. Dependents of senior officers — colonels and generals — sometimes get to fly. But I am the exact opposite of a senior officer. I'll see what I can find out. Maybe I could say you live in France or England. I just don't know. I'll ask Freddy."

She sighed. "Six weeks or so seems like a very long time."

"When I asked before, 'What do we do now?' I meant right now. Tonight."

"Re-consummating our marriage is the first thing that pops into my mind," Marjorie said.

"Keep that thought. But what I was wondering is what do we tell your mother?"

"Nothing," she replied immediately, which told him that she had already given the problem some thought. "Let her go ahead with her plans for a double wedding."

"I don't think Colonel Mattingly would let me come back here now. And I understand."

"I was afraid of that. I still don't want to tell her until I have to. You don't have to tell your parents either. We can wait until we see what's going to happen."

"What are you going to tell her about tonight?"

"I'm sure she thinks we're doing what we've been doing. Out of the bounds of holy matrimony. She knows there's nothing she can do about it. She feels sorry for us that you're being sent back to Germany right away."

"So you can spend the night?"

She grunted. "Mom doesn't feel that sorry. After a while, I'll take you back out to Camp Holabird and then drive back to Washington. After breakfast tomorrow, I'll tell her I'm going to quote visit unquote with you again, and come pick you up and we'll come back here."

"Here?"

"Our first home. More than that. I'll get an historical sign made. 'On this site on October 25, 1945, the marriage of Lieutenant and Mrs. J. D. Cronley Junior was consummated at least twice.' "

He laughed.

"I'll get a cab back to Holabird. It's a long way out there."

"No. I am now a wife. A good wife drops her husband off at work, and I want to be a good wife."

"Is that before or after consummation?"

"During," she said.

[Five]

The Officers' Club
U.S. Army Counterintelligence Center &
  School
Camp Holabird
1019 Dundalk Avenue, Baltimore 19, Maryland

1120 26 October 1945

Lieutenant Cronley drained his Coca-Cola and set the glass on the bar. In an hour, he could call room service at the Lord Baltimore and order up something a little stronger. But Coke was it for now.

I wouldn't want my bride to think I'm a boozer.

The Squirt said she would be here between eleven-thirty and noon. That gives me ten minutes to walk to the gate so I can be waiting for her.

He almost made it to the door when the bartender called his name. Jimmy turned to see he was holding up the handset of a telephone. He walked quickly to take it.

"Lieutenant Cronley, sir."

"Colonel Mattingly, Jimmy. A car is being sent for you. It should be there within the hour. Collect your stuff and be waiting for it. You're to be at the White House at fifteen hundred hours."

"Shit!"

"Excuse me, Lieutenant?" Mattingly said coldly.

"Sorry. That slipped out."

"Make sure nothing slips out when you're with the President."

"Yes, sir."

"The car will be a Chevy station wagon. Civilian plates. The driver and his assistant are fellow alumni of Holabird High."

"Yes, sir."

"They will bring you to the Hay-Adams. Your parents are there."

"My parents? How did they get there?"

"How would you guess? Your girlfriend's grandfather sent the Connie for them. They'll be going to the White House with us."

She's not my girlfriend. She's my wife.

When do I tell Mattingly?

"And afterward?"

"You're on the twenty-one hundred MATS flight . . . *we're* on the twenty-one hundred MATS flight . . . from Bethesda to Frankfurt."

"Shit!"

"That one I understand," Mattingly said. "It's out of my hands, Jim."

"Yes, sir. I understand."

"See you shortly."

57

[Six]

Main Gate
U.S. Army Counterintelligence Center &
  School
Camp Holabird
1019 Dundalk Avenue, Baltimore 19, Maryland

1132 26 October 1945

Marjorie kissed him when he got into the Buick.

"Well," she said, "whatever should we do now to pass the time?"

"They called. We all have to be at the White House at three."

She didn't reply.

"My folks are there," he said. "At the Hay-Adams."

"I know. I thought I was going to have to break your mother's legs to keep her from coming here with me. Grandpa saved me. He said, 'Well, Virginia, I guess you are too old to remember that when you're in love, you don't want your mother hanging around.' "

"And then I'm on a plane at nine tonight for Frankfurt."

"I didn't know that. Oh God, Jimmy!"

"Yeah, oh God!"

"Well, maybe we can find a five-dollar

58

motel between here and Washington," Marjie said. "For a quickie."

"They're sending a car for me."

"Wonderful!" she said, thickly sarcastic. Then she had a second thought. "I can't go to the White House dressed like this. I'll have to change!"

"Yeah. I guess."

They locked eyes.

"I don't know how yet," Marjorie said, "but we're going to find time between now and when you get on the plane."

"God, I hope so!"

"Kiss me quick, Jimmy, before I start saying a lot of dirty words."

He watched the Buick drive down Dundalk Avenue, and then he went inside the fence and walked to the goddamned Transient Officers Quarters to wait for the goddamned Chevrolet station wagon with goddamned civilian plates driven by a goddamned fellow alumnus of goddamned Holabird High.

[Seven]

The Hay-Adams Hotel
800 Sixteenth Street, N.W.
Washington, D.C.

1345 26 October 1945

Jimmy saw his mother and father standing

with Cletus Marcus Howell and Colonel Mattingly the moment he walked into the hotel lobby.

His mother was wearing an ankle-length Persian lamb coat. His father had on a Stetson and western boots, and between them a Brooks Brothers suit, button-down collar shirt, and a rep-striped necktie. Both parents fit — as did their son — the description "lanky and tanned Texan." But only his father had been born in Texas. His mother was from Strasbourg, a "war bride" from the First World War.

His mother went to him quickly and wrapped him in an embrace.

"My baby," she said. "My poor, poor baby."

She seemed to be on the edge of tears, and, he realized a moment later, had spoken in German, which he'd learned from his mother.

Jimmy then wondered what the hell that was all about, but asked the question that was foremost in his mind.

"Mama, wo ist der Squirt?"

His mother started to sob.

He partially freed himself from her embrace.

"Mama, was ist los?"

A visibly upset Cletus Marcus Howell

walked up to them, tears streaming down his sheeks.

"Marjie's gone, Jimmy," he said. "Some drunken sonofabitch in a goddamned sixteen-wheeler hit her Buick head-on on U.S. 1 just inside the District and she's gone."

[Eight]

The Marquis de Lafayette Suite
The Hay-Adams Hotel

1505 26 October 1945

When the President of the United States came into the sitting room of the suite, Second Lieutenant James D. Cronley Jr. was sitting on a couch, holding a glass dark with whisky. To his left was Mrs. Martha Howell, and to his right, Mrs. Virginia Cronley, his mother. Cletus Marcus Howell and James D. Cronley Sr. were sitting on a matching couch across a coffee table from them.

The coffee table held a silver coffee service, a bottle of Collier and McKeel Handcrafted Tennessee Sour Mash Whiskey, a bottle of Haig & Haig Pinch scotch, and a silver bowl of ice.

Leaning against the wall, and wearing a starched white jacket, was Thomas Jefferson

"Tom" Porter, a silver-haired black man in his late sixties. He had been Cletus Marcus Howell's butler/chauffeur/confidant and close and loving friend for as long as anyone could remember.

In an armchair pulled up to the end of the coffee table was an elegantly dressed Irishman in his early sixties. His name was William Joseph Donovan. Until it had been disbanded by Presidential Order about three weeks before — on October 1, 1945 — he had been director of the Office of Strategic Services. Pulled up in another armchair at the other end of the coffee table was Colonel Robert Mattingly.

The First Lady followed the President into the room. She was followed by Rear Admiral Sidney William Souers.

All the men stood.

"The admiral tells me he thought it would be all right if Bess and I came to express our sympathy," President Truman said.

"Very kind of you both, Harry," Cletus Marcus Howell said. "Tom, fix the President a little taste of the Collier and McKeel while I make the introductions."

The President ignored him and walked to Jimmy Cronley.

"Son, I can't tell you how sorry Bess and I were when Admiral Souers told us what happened to your girlfriend."

"She wasn't his girlfriend, Mr. President," Jimmy's mother said. "They eloped yesterday."

"Oh my God!" Mrs. Truman blurted.

Jimmy's mother put her hands over her face and began to sob. Bess Truman went to the couch, dropped to her knees, and put her arms around her.

"That's Jimmy's mother, Mrs. Truman," Cletus Marcus Howell said. "The other lady is — was — Marjorie's mother."

"Thank you, Mr. President," Jimmy said. "And thank you for not making . . . for excusing me from reporting to you at the White House."

The President didn't reply. He looked around and then took the glass Tom was extending on a silver tray. He took a healthy swallow, then looked around.

"General," he said to Donovan. And then he said, "Colonel," to Mattingly.

"Mr. President," they replied just about simultaneously.

"And that's Jimmy's dad, Harry," Cletus Marcus Howell said. "James D. Cronley Senior."

The two shook hands.

"You can take a lot of pride in your son, Mr. Cronley," President Truman said.

"I do, Mr. President. I'm very . . ." His voice broke, and then he found it and continued, ". . . I'm very proud of Jimmy."

The President took another sip of the Collier and McKeel.

"I'd forgotten, Mr. Cronley," he said, "that you and General Donovan served together in the First War."

"Yes, sir. We did."

President Truman scanned the room, then gestured. "Everybody please sit down," he ordered. He turned to Tom Porter. "Could you get chairs for my wife and me, please? And Admiral Souers?"

The President helped his wife to her feet and installed her in a chair and then sat down himself. He looked at Jimmy.

"Son, the reason I asked the admiral to bring you to the White House was that I was going to make you a first lieutenant and give you the Bronze Star for what you did. That was General Marshall's recommendation. He said he thought the Bronze Star was appropriate, but that since the war was over, the Bronze Star could not have the *V* for Valor device on it. And he said he would 'look into' making you a first lieutenant even though you don't have the time in grade.

"This was before, I think I should men-

tion, Admiral Souers t⌐
pened on U.S. 1. I d⌐
that what's going t⌐
I pity you, thougʰ
happened to you thⁱ
worst kick in the ba—
can imagine.

"What happened was I g⌐
Bronze Star without the *V* ⁱ
wasn't 'appropriate.' And as faⁱ
Marshall 'looking into' whether ⌐
be promoted early or not, I remⁱ
when my National Guard outfit got
up for the First War, I went from ⌐
sergeant to captain overnight. And finally,
remembered I'm commander in chief of the
Armed Forces of the United States of
America."

The President drained his Collier and Mc-
Keel, handed the glass to Tom, and said,
"I'll have another of those, but hold off a
minute, please."

"Yes, sir."

"Stand up, son," the President ordered as
he rose from his own chair. "We'll get to
what was supposed to happen in the White
House."

Jimmy stood.

"Okay, Sid," the President ordered.

"Attention to orders," Admiral Souers

Donovan and Colonel Mattingly
o their feet and came to attention.
Marcus Howell got to his feet next,
immy's father, and finally all the
h.
r Department, Washington, D.C.,
ty-sixth October 1945," Admiral
ers read from a sheet of paper. "Extract
General Orders. Classified SECRET.
aragraph one. Second Lieutenant James D.
Cronley Junior, Cavalry, Army of the United
States, with detail to Military Intelligence,
is promoted to Captain, Cavalry, with detail
to Military Intelligence, with date of rank
twenty-six October 1945. Authority, Verbal
Order of the President of the United States."

Two men entered the sitting room. One
was a photographer and the other a full
colonel, from whose epaulet hung the heavy
golden cords that identify the military aide
to the President.

He handed a small box to the President.
He took it and walked to Jimmy's mother.

"Would you like to pin these onto Captain
Cronley's epaulets, Mrs. Cronley?"

She started sobbing again, and Mrs.
Truman again put her arms around her.

"Maybe you'd better do it, Mr. Cronley,"
the President suggested.

When he had done so, he hugged his son.

"Thank you, Mr. President," Jimmy said.

"Right now you're probably thinking 'So what?' " the President said. "But that will change, Captain Cronley — believe me, based on my own experience — when some other soldier calls you 'Captain' for the first time."

"Yes, sir," Jimmy said, chuckling. "Thanks again, sir."

"We're not finished," the President said. "Sid?"

"Attention to orders," Admiral Souers proclaimed. "The White House, Washington, D.C., twenty-sixth October 1945. Award of the Distinguished Service Medal. By order of the President of the United States, the Distinguished Service Medal is presented to Captain James D. Cronley Junior, Cavalry, Detail Military Intelligence, Army of the United States. Citation: Captain Cronley, then second lieutenant, while engaged in a classified operation of vital importance to the United States demonstrated great courage and valor and a willingness, far above and beyond the call of duty, to risk his life in the completion of his mission. In doing so, he also demonstrated a level of professional skill and knowledge far above that which could be expected of someone of his rank, youth, and experience. His actions and valor reflect great credit upon the U.S. Army. Entered the military service from Texas. Signed, George C. Marshall, general of the Army."

The aide extended to Truman an oblong blue box from which he took the DSM. He then pinned the medal to Jimmy's uniform.

The photographer went into action.

"You understand," the President said to the photographer, "that those photos are not to be given to the press?"

"Yes, sir. Admiral Souers made that quite clear, Mr. President."

"You'll be given copies, of course," the President said to the room in general. "But I'm going to have to ask that you, at least for the time being, regard them as secret."

He waited until he got acknowledgment from everyone, and then he said, "Bess and I will be leaving now. Please forgive our intrusion on your grief."

II

[One]

Arriving Passenger Terminal
Rhine-Main USAF Base
Frankfurt am Main
American Zone, Occupied Germany

0825 28 October 1945

"Captain," the sergeant called.

And then he called "Captain!" again, this time a little louder.

Captain James D. Cronley Jr. belatedly realized he was the subject of the sergeant's interest.

"What?"

"I think that's yours, and the colonel's, stuff over there," the sergeant said, pointing. "You must have been the last people to get on the plane and they didn't have time to put your stuff in the cargo hold with the other luggage."

Jimmy looked and saw their luggage against the wall. Until just now, he and Colonel Mattingly had been worried that it had been left behind in Washington.

"That's it, thanks," Cronley said, and then raised his voice and called, "Colonel!"

Mattingly was across the huge room, looking at stacks of luggage. When he turned, Cronley pointed. Mattingly nodded and started toward their luggage.

When they had carried their luggage into the main terminal, Mattingly said, "The problem now is how to get you to Munich. In the good old days, one of our puddle jumpers would be waiting here."

The Piper Cub aircraft, known as the L-4 in the U.S. Army, was universally referred to as a puddle jumper. A dozen of them had been assigned, primarily for personnel transport, to the now out-of-existence organization known as OSS Forward.

Cronley didn't reply.

"But let me get on the horn and see if I can get a puddle jumper from the United States Constabulary," Mattingly said.

"From whom?"

"The newly formed police force of the American Zone."

Mattingly walked to a desk, where he commandeered a telephone. Ten minutes later, he walked back to Cronley.

"You got lucky, Jimmy," he said. "They loaned me one. You will be spared that long ride down the autobahn to Munich. And I called Tiny and told him to meet you there at the Vier Jahreszeiten."

The luxury hotel had been requisitioned

by the Army. The XXVIIth CIC Detachment had space in the building.

"Thank you, sir."

"You okay, Jimmy?"

"I'm fine, sir."

"Forgive me, Captain, for not thinking so."

"I'm really okay, sir. But thanks for getting me a ride."

"They said within thirty minutes. We can get a cup of coffee over there" — he pointed to a PX coffee bar — "while we wait."

"Colonel, you don't have to wait with me."

"Captains don't get to tell colonels what they don't have to do. And I just realized I have some questions for you."

"Should I be worried?"

"That would depend on the answers I get."

Mattingly pointed again toward the coffee bar. They walked to it and ordered coffee and doughnuts — it was all that was available — and sat at a small table.

"When Admiral Souers told me that you had found that stuff everybody was looking for, I naturally wondered how you had found it," Mattingly began his interrogation. "When I asked him, he said something to the effect that Cletus Frade had told him that after you had come up with a pretty good idea where that vessel was, you and

71

two of our Germans got into Clete's Fieseler Storch and a Cub, and went looking for it."

"Yes, sir. The Germans were Willi Grüner — he's the Luftwaffe buddy of Clete's buddy von Wachtstein. They found him in Berlin and took him to Argentina — and Kapitän von Dattenberg. He's the guy who surrendered U-405 to the Argentines. He and the captain of U-234 . . . Sorry. He and the captain of the *vessel* we were looking for were friends, and Clete thought that might be useful — and it was — if we found what we were looking for."

Mattingly made a *Keep talking* gesture with his hands.

"Well, the first thing Clete did when I figured out where U-2 . . . *the vessel . . .* probably was, was to take the wings off his Storch and one of his Cubs. Then he had them loaded onto flatbed trucks and trucked them down to a place called Estancia Condor. He sent Grüner along to make sure the mechanics put the wings back on right. And Grüner had a lot of experience flying Storches in Russia."

"What was that all about?"

"Well, when I say I figured out where the vessel was, I mean that I thought it was way down south, within fifty miles of the mouth

72

of the Magellan Straits. There's not much but mountains and snow and ice down there. To find anything, we knew we would have to fly low and slow. The only way to do that was with little airplanes — you can't do that in, say, a Lodestar."

"Souers said that Commander Ford told him the material was brought to Mendoza, where it was transferred to the Constellation, on a Lodestar."

"Yes, sir. That's right."

"The Lodestar was flown by Cletus?"

"No, sir. If Cletus had left Buenos Aires to fly the Lodestar, the wrong people would have asked questions. So Clete didn't go down south."

"Getting to the heart of our little chat, Captain Cronley: If Colonel Frade didn't fly the Lodestar during this exercise, who did?"

After a long moment, Cronley said, "I did."

"And you were flying what when you found U-234? It was you who found her. Correct?"

"Yes, sir. I was flying the Cub."

"I wasn't aware that you were a pilot."

Cronley didn't reply.

"You want to explain this?" Mattingly said.

Again Cronley didn't reply.

"That was more in the nature of an order for an explanation, Captain, than an idle question."

"Yes, sir. Clete is like my big brother, Colonel."

"Would it surprise you to hear I have already come to that conclusion? *And . . . ?*"

"I followed him all my life. Into the Cub Scouts. Into the Boy Scouts. Into Texas A&M. I was about to follow him into the Marine Corps when I decided I had had enough of following him."

"Was this before or after you became a pilot?"

"I've been flying since Clete taught me when I was fourteen."

"So, passing up the glory of becoming a Marine fighter pilot, you joined the Army instead? On behalf of the officer corps of the U.S. Army, let me say how pleased we are that you're slumming amongst us."

Jimmy didn't reply.

"I gather you did not qualify for the Army's aviator training program? Why not?"

"I never applied for it."

"Why not?"

"I didn't want to spend four years as an aerial taxi driver."

"Had you applied, would you have been

qualified? What sort of a license to fly do you hold? How experienced a pilot are you?"

When Jimmy hesitated, Mattingly said, "That, too, was not a question born of idle curiosity as we wait for *your* aerial taxi driver to appear, Captain Cronley."

"I've got eleven hundred hours, sir, and hold a commercial ticket, with instrument and multi-engine ratings."

"This secret talent of yours comes as something of a surprise. I'll have to think about it."

"Life is just full of surprises, isn't it, Colonel?"

Mattingly looked at him for a moment.

"Under the circumstances, Captain," he said, "I'll choose not to consider that a smart-ass remark."

Five minutes later, a first lieutenant whom Cronley could not remember having seen before walked up to their table and saluted. He wore a zippered "Tanker Jacket" to which were sewn Liaison Pilot wings and a shoulder insignia — a circle of Cavalry yellow, in which was the letter "C" with a diagonal lightning bolt through it.

"Sir, Colonel Wilson said you need a ride."

"Not me," Mattingly said as he quickly — and Cronley belatedly — returned his salute. "The captain here needs a ride to Munich."

"Yes, sir. Not a problem. It's right on my way. I'm headed to Sonthofen."

"Be gentle with him, Lieutenant," Mattingly said. "The captain doesn't like to fly."

The lieutenant, looking a little uneasy, said, "Yes, sir. If you'll come with me, sir?"

Jimmy stood and looked down at Mattingly, wondering if he was supposed to salute.

Mattingly answered the question by getting to his feet and putting out his hand.

"If I somehow forgot to say this earlier, Jimmy, I'm very sorry for your loss and greatly admire the way you're handling it."

"Thank you, sir."

[Two]

Supreme Headquarters, Allied European Forces
I.G. Farben Building
Frankfurt am Main, American Zone, Occupied Germany

1045 28 October 1945

Colonel Robert Mattingly returned the salute of the two natty paratroopers of the 508th Parachute Infantry Regiment on ceremonial guard at the entrance of the building and entered the lobby. He walked past the sea of red general officers' personal flags — in the center of which was the red flag with five stars in a circle of General of the Army Dwight D. Eisenhower — and stepped onto the right of the two devices he thought of as the dumbwaiters.

He had no idea of the proper nomenclature of the devices that moved people up (the right one) and down (the left one) in the largest office building in Europe. They functioned by constantly moving small platforms onto which passengers stepped on and off.

In 1941, I.G. Farben G.m.b.H. had been the fourth largest corporation in the world, after General Motors, U.S. Steel, and Standard Oil of New Jersey. Eisenhower had decided, early on, that he wanted the building as his headquarters. With great difficulty, the enormous structure had been spared damage by the thousand bomber raids that had reduced most of Frankfurt to rubble.

Mattingly, ascending upon what he now idly thought could probably be called the "vertical personnel transport device," arrived at the fifth floor. It was his intention to call upon Brigadier General H. Paul Greene, chief, Counterintelligence, European Command, whom he hoped to deceive sufficiently to get him off the backs of the XXIIIrd and XXVIIth CIC detachments — and off himself personally.

The last time Mattingly had seen Greene, who was *de jure* but not *de facto* his immediate superior, Greene had ordered him to consider himself under arrest for disobedience of a direct order. The one-star released him from arrest only after Mattingly had threatened to bring their disagreement to the personal attention of General Eisenhower.

There was a very good chance, Mattingly understood, that he would again find himself under arrest today. But that chance had to be taken.

He stepped off the dumbwaiter and marched purposefully down the marble-floored corridor to General Greene's suite of offices.

When he entered the outer office, a major and a master sergeant looked up from their desks. The master sergeant then stood.

"Good morning," Mattingly said. "I'm here to see General Greene."

"I'll see if the general is free, sir," the major said, and reached for his telephone.

"Just to clear the air between us, Major: That was an announcement of intention. As deputy commander, CIC, I don't need your permission to see the general. Perhaps you might wish to write that down."

Mattingly marched to, and through, the doorway to General Greene's office, then up to his desk. The major hurriedly followed him to the doorway.

Mattingly came to attention and saluted.

General Greene's face whitened and he glared at Mattingly for a long moment before returning the salute.

"Good morning, General," Mattingly said.

General Greene did not immediately reply.

"General," the major began, "he just walked in —"

Mattingly turned to him. "That will be all, thank you, Major. I'm afraid you're not cleared for the matter the general and I will be discussing."

The major looked to General Greene for guidance. After a moment, Greene waved his hand, telling him to leave.

"Please close the door tightly, Major," Mattingly ordered.

When the door was closed, General Greene said, "You better have a good explanation for this, you arrogant sonofabitch!"

"With the general's permission, I have several documents, classified Top Secret–Presidential, I would like the general to peruse."

After a moment, still white-faced and tight-lipped, General Greene made another hand gesture — *Let's see them.*

Mattingly opened his briefcase, took from it a thin sheath of papers and photographs, and laid them before General Greene.

On top was an eight-by-ten-inch glossy photograph of Captain James D. Cronley Jr. with, on his right, the President of the United States and, on his left, Rear Admiral Sidney William Souers. To their left and right were James D. Cronley Sr., Major General William J. Donovan, and Colonel Robert Mattingly.

"What am I looking at?" General Greene asked, more than a little unpleasantly.

"Forgive me, sir, but I must have your confirmation of your understanding that this material is classified Top Secret–Presidential."

"I'm not deaf, Mattingly," Greene snapped. "I heard you the first time."

"That photograph was taken the day before yesterday, General, immediately after President Truman promoted Captain Cronley to that grade and awarded him the Distinguished Service Medal."

"Who the hell is he?"

"He's the officer I placed in charge of the

Twenty-third Detachment's —"

"Twenty-third Detachment?" Greene interrupted. "We don't have a Twenty-third Detachment!"

"I formed it, sir, under the Twenty-seventh, to run the operation at Kloster Grünau, sir, to further shield it."

Green stared at him a long moment. "Tell me more about this Captain Cronley."

"I think you're asking if he's the officer who had the misunderstanding with Colonel Schumann at Kloster Grünau. Yes, sir, he is."

" 'Misunderstanding'? You call blowing the engine out of Tony Schumann's car with .50 caliber machine gun fire a *misunderstanding*? Jesus, Mattingly!"

"Sir, that was regrettable. Sir, I have been authorized to make you privy to some of the details of Operation Ost. With the caveat that you are not to share anything I tell you with anyone absent my express permission in each instance. May I have your assurance, General, that you understand?"

Greene glared at him again, but finally said, "You have my assurance, Colonel."

"Thank you, sir. Sir, the use of deadly force has been authorized if necessary to preserve the security of Operation Ost."

"You're telling me that this operation of

yours is so important that that young officer could have killed Colonel Schumann to keep him from finding out about it?"

"Yes, sir. That is indeed the case. Colonel Schumann or anyone else posing a threat to the operation. Or anyone who might threaten to compromise the security thereof."

"Jesus Christ!" Greene said, looking past Mattingly and shaking his head slowly.

Mattingly decided Greene was now convinced he was being told the truth.

Greene then said in a tone of reason: "I would be grateful, Colonel, if you told me as much as you're able about this operation of yours."

Mattingly began to do so.

"So those rumors are true," Greene said five minutes later. "We are sneaking people, Nazis, into Argentina."

"Yes, sir."

"And Eisenhower knows about this?"

Mattingly did not reply directly.

"General, outside the Twenty-third and Twenty-seventh CIC detachments, there are four people — now that I've told you, five — in the European Theatre who are privy to Operation Ost. I am not at liberty to tell you who they are."

"I can understand why," Greene said,

thinking out loud. "Can you tell me why this Cronley fellow was promoted and given the DSM?"

"Some of it, sir. Using intelligence obtained from General Gehlen, Captain Cronley located the submarine — U-234 — in Argentina and recovered the half ton of uranium oxide she was carrying. The operation was not carried out perfectly. SS-Oberführer Horst Lang and a detachment of SS personnel were onboard the U-234 to guard the material. We have reason to believe Lang intended to sell it to the Soviet Union. It was necessary for Captain Cronley to terminate Lang, despite our hope that we would be able to keep him alive for questioning."

"By 'terminate' I presume you mean Cronley had to kill him?"

"Yes, sir."

"Do you know why you have been authorized to bring me into this?"

"Yes, sir. You have a reputation for being very good at what you do. You — and your inspector general — came very close to compromising the security of Operation Ost."

"And it was decided that I be told what's going on so that I'll understand why I'm now to keep my hands off — keep my nose out of — your business?"

"Yes, sir. That and to provide assistance . . ."

"What kind of assistance?"

"Whatever we might need at some future date."

"I don't suppose I'm authorized to tell Schumann about this?"

"No, sir, you are not."

"Does General Seidel know?"

"I'm not at liberty to answer that, sir. I can only repeat that you are not authorized to — you are forbidden to — tell anyone anything at all about what I have just told you."

"Can I have that in writing?"

"Sir, the policy is to put nothing on paper."

"That figures." He grunted. "Okay. I'll tell Schumann to back off."

"Thank you, sir."

"Mattingly, I'm sure you appreciate that when I began to nose around, I was doing what I considered my duty."

"Yes, sir. I fully understand that."

"Unaware that you had — how do I say this? — friends in high places and were involved in anything like this, I gave you a hard time when over my objections you were appointed my deputy. And I was prepared when you burst in here just now to double down on giving you a hard time. No hard feelings?"

"Absolutely none, sir."

"One last question. Who's that admiral in the picture?"

Mattingly didn't reply for a long moment. Finally he said, "General, when you hear, sometime in the next few months, that President Truman has established a new organization, working title Central Agency for Intelligence, and has named Rear Admiral Sidney William Souers to be its head, please act very surprised."

Greene grunted again. He then stood and offered his hand.

"I didn't hear a word you just said, Colonel. I imagine we'll be in touch."

"Yes, sir, we will."

Mattingly raised his hand to his temple.

"Permission to withdraw, sir?"

Greene returned the salute, far more crisply than he had previously, and said, "Post."

Mattingly started for the door.

"You forgot your pictures and the general orders," Greene called after him.

"I thought the general might wish to study them closely before he burns them, sir."

"Thank you."

As Mattingly went through the doorway, he thought, *He's not going to burn any of that material. It's going into his personal safe, in case he needs it later.*

That doesn't matter. Nothing in that stuff touches on Operation Ost.

And I think even Admiral Souers would understand why I thought I had to show it to him.

He had another tangential thought.

I wonder where Hotshot Billy Wilson is on this miserable German morning?

That's next.

[Three]

Hotel Vier Jahreszeiten
Maximilianstrasse 178
Munich, American Zone of Occupation,
  Germany

1215 28 October 1945

First Sergeant Chauncey L. Dunwiddie and Sergeant Friedrich Hessinger had been waiting for Cronley at the Munich airfield. Both had been wearing uniforms identifying them as civilian employees of the U.S. Army. Dunwiddie wore an olive drab woolen Ike jacket and trousers, with an embroidered insignia — a blue triangle holding the letters "US" — sewn to the lapels. Hessinger was more elegantly attired, in officer's pinks and greens with similar civilian insignia sewn to its lapels.

Jimmy remembered there were rumors that the pudgy German was making a lot of money somehow dealing in currency.

"Welcome home," Tiny Dunwiddie had said, as he reached in the Piper Cub and effortlessly grabbed Cronley's Valv-Pak canvas suitcase from Jimmy's lap.

Jimmy then climbed out, turned to the pilot, and said, "Thanks for the ride."

"My pleasure, sir," the lieutenant said, and saluted.

Neither Tiny nor Freddy had commented on the twin silver bars of a captain pinned to Cronley's epaulets at the airfield — the reason the puddle-jumper pilot had saluted him — or in their requisitioned Opel Kapitän on the way to the hotel or during lunch in the elegant officers' mess.

It was only after they had gone upstairs — and into Suite 507, above the door of which hung a small, neatly lettered sign, XXVIITH CIC DET. — that there was any clue that anyone had noticed the insignia.

There, Tiny had produced bottles of Löwenbräu and passed them out. As Freddy was neatly wiping gold-rimmed lager glasses, Tiny said, "When Mattingly called, he said 'no questions.' He said you could tell us some of what's happened to you, or all of it, or none of it. He said he was going to call Major Wallace and tell him the same thing. So it's your call, Jim. If I can still call you by your first name, Captain, sir."

Despite Cronley's clear memory of Admiral Souers giving the Engineer colonel a very hard time for sharing intelligence that should not be shared, he told Tiny and Freddy everything that had happened in Argentina and Washington.

"I'm not surprised that President Truman came to offer his condolences," Freddy said when he'd finished. "From what I know of him, he is a fine gentleman."

That came out in such a thick accent that Jimmy had to work hard not to smile. Or giggle.

Tiny said, "Sonofabitch! And the bastards sent you back before you could even go to her goddamned funeral!"

Jimmy was touched by Tiny's emotional response; it was clear he really shared his grief.

"I stopped at the funeral home on the way to the airport," Jimmy said softly. "I asked if I could see her. The funeral director guy . . . whatever the hell they call those people . . . said 'No,' and I said, 'Fuck you, I want to see her,' and he said, 'No, you don't. The remains were so torn up from the accident that there couldn't possibly be open casket services, so the coroner didn't sew the remains up after the autopsy. You don't want to see her like that, believe me. Remember her as she was when she was alive.' "

"So, what did you do?" Tiny asked.

"I broke down is what I did. Cried like a fucking baby."

And then, without warning, he broke down and cried like a baby.

Tiny wrapped his massive arms around him and held him until Jimmy managed to control his sobbing and shook himself free of Tiny's embrace.

When he finally got his eyes to focus he saw that Freddy Hessinger was looking at him through incredibly sad eyes.

"What do you say we get in the Kapitän and go home?" Tiny asked gently.

Cronley nodded, and then followed Dunwiddie out of the room.

[Four]

Kloster Grünau
Schollbrunn, Bavaria
American Zone of Occupation, Germany

1630 28 October 1945

When Cronley and Dunwiddie reached the

compound, instead of driving through the gate, Dunwiddie had driven the Kapitän completely around the double barbed wire barriers around the perimeter.

Cronley wondered what that was all about but, before they had completed the round, decided Dunwiddie wanted both to show the troops that their commanding officer now had twin silver bars on his epaulets and to remind them once again that their first sergeant checked the security of the compound frequently and without advance warning.

Cronley had learned that behind his back the troops guarding Kloster Grünau referred to their first sergeant with the motto of the 2nd Armored Division, from which they had come — "Ole Hell on Wheels."

When they finally entered the headquarters building — which also housed the officers' mess and, on the second floor, the American officers and the senior German officer prisoners — General Reinhard Gehlen and Oberst Ludwig Mannberg were sitting in the foyer.

Gehlen was in an ill-fitting civilian suit. Mannberg, previously and now Gehlen's Number Two, was wearing a superbly tailored Wehrmacht uniform from which all insignia had been removed. Only a wide red stripe down the trouser leg, signifying membership in the General Staff Corps, remained.

Both stood up when they saw Cronley and Dunwiddie.

"Captain," Gehlen said. "I hope that you will have a few minutes for Mannberg and myself."

"Certainly, sir," Cronley said. He gestured toward the door of the mess.

There was no bartender on duty. Tiny went behind the bar, and in perfect German asked, "May I offer the general a scotch?"

"That would be very kind."

"Oberst Mannberg?"

"The same, thank you."

"Captain?"

"Jack Daniel's, please."

Dunwiddie made the drinks, taking a Haig & Haig for himself, and delivered them.

Gehlen raised his to Cronley.

"In addition to offering our congratulations on your well-deserved promotion," the general began in a solemn tone, "Mannberg and I would like to offer our condolences on your loss." He paused, then as if he had read Cronley's mind, added, "Colonel Mattingly telephoned earlier."

As everyone took a sip of drink, Cronley

thought, *That's not surprising.*

But what all did Mattingly tell you, General?

That we had found U-234 and the uranium oxide?

And that I'd been promoted? But not why or by whom?

And that my girl — my wife — had been killed in an auto accident?

Why the hell didn't Mattingly tell me what he was going to tell you?

Or tell me what I could tell you?

Admiral Souers made it pretty goddamned clear that the Eleventh Commandment is "Thou shalt not share classified material with people who don't have the Need to Know."

Technically, you're both prisoners of war. POWs by definition do not have the Need to Know.

But you're only technically POWs, as we all know.

And I wouldn't have found U-234 had it not been for you giving me what intel you had about her.

This is one of those situations where I have to choose between two options, both of which are the wrong one.

So, what do you do, Captain Cronley, you experienced intelligence officer with two whole days in grade?

You follow the rules and tell them nothing.

Or as little as possible.

I can't follow the rules.

In this Through the Looking Glass World we're in, the jailer has to earn and hold the respect of the prisoners. Or at least these two prisoners.

"Thank you," Cronley then said. "I'm still trying to get used to both situations. So let me begin by giving you, Oberst Mannberg, the best wishes of Fregattenkapitän Wilhelm von Dattenberg."

Cronley had spoken in German. He spoke it so well that most Germans thought that he was a Strasbourger, as his mother was.

"It's good to hear he survived," Mannberg said.

"He was with me when we found the U-234. He persuaded her captain —"

"That would be Schneider, Alois Schneider?" Mannberg put in.

"Yes, sir."

I'm being interrogated. That's not the way it's supposed to be.

And I don't think I'm supposed to call him "sir."

Oh, what the hell! He was a colonel and I'm a captain who two days ago was a second lieutenant.

Cronley went on: "Schneider was at Philipps University in Marburg an der Lahn

93

with von Dattenberg. And with von Wacht-stein, too, come to think of it."

"That's correct," Mannberg said.

"When we got to the U-234, von Datten-berg told Schneider the war was over, and surrender therefore honorable. He just about had him convinced when SS-Oberführer Horst Lang appeared. He pulled a pistol from his pocket and was shot."

"Von Dattenberg shot him?" General Gehlen asked. "Or Schneider?"

"I shot him," Cronley said.

He saw Tiny's eyebrows go up at that, and realized he had left that out when he'd told Tiny and Hessinger what had happened.

"Wounded or killed?" Gehlen asked.

"Killed. I had a Thompson."

"I'm sorry that was necessary," Gehlen said.

"I thought it was necessary," Jimmy said a bit defensively. "There were other SS types, armed with Schmeissers, standing with him. I couldn't take the risk that things would get out of control."

"I'm sure it was, Captain Cronley," Geh-len said. "I regret the death of that swine only because there's a good deal he could have told us. Is Colonel Mattingly aware of this?"

"I didn't have the chance to tell Colonel

94

Mattingly. But Colonel Frade knows about it."

"Well, if there is anything to be learned from the rest of them — either the SS swine or the crew of U-234 — Oberst Frade will learn it," Gehlen said with certainty.

Clete was just complimented by Gehlen, one of the best intelligence officers in the world. I'm sorry he didn't get to hear that.

"Well, that leaves U-977," Mannberg said. "Did you get anything on her at all?"

"Von Dattenberg and Schneider seemed to agree there are only two credible scenarios," Cronley said. "Worst: that, despite what we thought — that she was headed for Argentina or Japan — U-977 either went to Russia directly from Norway, or met a Russian ship on the high seas. Best scenario: that she was sunk while trying to get through the English Channel, or shortly after entering the Atlantic Ocean."

Gehlen nodded thoughtfully. "I've heard nothing — nothing at all — about either scenario, or about U-977 itself from our people in Moscow. That's not surprising, and I will of course order them to keep trying. But I think we are going to have to presume the Soviets now have the uranium oxide loaded onto U-977."

He exhaled in disappointment or resignation or both.

"Well, we tried," Gehlen went on. "And, largely due to your efforts, Captain Cronley, we did better than I expected we would."

Is Gehlen soft-soaping me, or does he mean that?

Gehlen looked at Tiny. "Would you agree, Dunwiddie, that we should now turn to what has happened here?"

"Yes, sir."

Gehlen met Cronley's eyes. "Two nights ago, Dunwiddie's diligent troops apprehended a man as he attempted to pass outward through the outer barbed wire. He was found to be in possession of a nearly complete roster of my people here in Kloster Grünau, a nearly complete roster of those who have been moved to Argentina, and, finally, an equally nearly complete roster of my people we hope have made it out of the Russian Zone but have not been located yet."

"Jesus!" Cronley exclaimed. "Who was he?"

"There seems little question that he is an NKGB agent," Mannberg said.

Dumb question!

Who else would it be? The German census bureau?

96

My ignorance is showing. And why n
year ago, I'd never heard of the NKGB.

But now that I am, as of the day be
yesterday, a captain, of military intelligen
of course know that's the acronym for
People's Commissariat for State Security,
Soviet secret police, intelligence, and count
intelligence organization.

Am I really sitting here, discussing an NKG
agent with a German general who used to rur
the German intelligence organization dealing
with the NKGB?

And have I just told him that it was "neces-
sary" for me to shoot an SS-Oberführer so
that he wouldn't get in the way of my grab-
bing a half ton of the dirt from which atom
bombs are made?

This would be surreal if I didn't know it was
real.

A year ago, I hadn't even heard of the atom
bomb, and the only thing I knew about the SS
was what I learned from the movies.

I wonder if the writers of those Alan Ladd
Against the Nazis movies knew that the way it
works in real life is that when you shoot a real
Nazi sonofabitch you want to throw up when
you see the life going out of his eyes and his
blood turning the snow red?

What did Major Derwin ask me in the O Club
bar at Camp Holabird? "Did you find yourself

97

in over your head?"

Oh, boy, am I in over my head!

"Does Colonel Mattingly know about this?" Cronley asked.

Tiny said, "He asked if I thought we could handle it, and I told him yes. He said, 'Take care of it, and let me know what happens.' "

"There is a small chance," Mannberg said, "that we will be able to determine whom the NKGB has turned before the move to Pullach. But we don't have much time."

What the hell is he talking about? "Determine whom the NKGB has turned"? Turned how?

Jesus Christ, he's talking about his own people!

"Turned" means "switched sides." He knows that there's a traitor among them.

But then Gehlen has agents in the Kremlin, so why should the Soviets having agents inside Abwehr Ost be so surprising?

"How's that going?" Cronley asked. "The move to Pullach?"

The U.S. Army Military Government had requisitioned Pullach, a village south of Munich, and moved out all of its occupants. The Corps of Engineers was preparing it for use by what they had been told was the South German Industrial Development Organization.

The engineers had been naturally curious about why a bunch of Krauts who were going to try to restart German industry needed a place surrounded by barbed wire, motion detectors, and guard towers. But when they asked, they were either ignored or told, "Who knows? USFET wants it built, so build it."

The engineers did not have the Need to Know that when they were finished Operation Ost — now renamed the South German Industrial Development Organization — would move in.

"They're ahead of schedule," Dunwiddie answered. "Maybe we better start to think of not moving until we find out more about who the NKGB has in here."

Cronley looked at Gehlen. "You have no idea who he might be?"

"No," Gehlen said. "And it might be, almost certainly is, more than one."

"I'm not sure we can break the Soviet," Mannberg said. "Obviously we have to continue his interrogation until we know that it's fruitless."

Cronley had a quick mental image, from the Alan Ladd movies, of a bare-chested man tied to a chair, his body bloody and bruised, and his face bleeding from multiple cuts inflicted by the riding crop in the hands of a man wearing a black SS uniform.

"With respect, Herr Oberst," Dunwiddie said, smiling, "I think you may have to reconsider your boiling pot and the beat of drums."

Gehlen smiled. Mannberg laughed.

"Perhaps later," Mannberg said. "There's still time for us to see if the disorientation is working."

"What the hell are you talking about, Tiny?" Cronley demanded.

"This guy is terrified of Tedworth, Jim," Dunwiddie said. "I suggested to Colonel Mannberg that we use this."

"What did Tedworth do to this guy?" Cronley said.

Cronley had another mental image of a bloody and battered man in a chair being beaten, this time by Technical Sergeant Abraham L. Tedworth. Even more massive than Dunwiddie, he was Dunwiddie's first field sergeant, his Number Two.

"Captain Cronley," Gehlen explained, smiling, "there are very few Negroes in Russia — very few Russians have ever seen someone of Herr Dunwiddie's and Stabsfeldwebel Tedworth's complexion. Or size. When I commented to Dunwiddie that this chap obviously expected to be put in a pot, boiled, and served for dinner, Dunwiddie said he knew there was such a pot — used to process slaughtered pigs — in one of the buildings. He suggested we fill it with water and build a fire under it, let this chap see it, and see if that didn't produce the cooperation we needed. I told him, 'Perhaps later, if the disorientation fails.' "

Gehlen, Mannberg, and Dunwiddie chuckled.

Is that what they call torturing a guy in a chair, "disorientation"?

And now that I think about it, I'm sure Tiny heard from his great-grandfathers, the Indian-fighting Buffalo Soldiers, that the Apaches hung their prisoners head-down over a slow fire to get them to talk. Or just for the hell of it. I'm surprised he didn't suggest that.

Hell, maybe he did. He's the professional soldier and I'm the amateur.

"Disorientation?" Cronley said.

"Disorientation," Mannberg confirmed. "We learned over time that causing pain is more often than not counterproductive. Especially with skilled agents, as we believe this fellow has to be. Disorientation, on the other hand, very often produces the information one desires."

How about pulling out his fingernails? That would certainly disorient somebody.

"What we did here," Mannberg went on,

"was put this fellow in a windowless cell, in the basement of what was the church when this was an active monastery. We took all his clothing except for his underwear, and provided him with a mattress, a very heavy blanket, and two canvas buckets, one filled with water and the other for his bodily waste. And a two-minute candle." He held fingers apart to show the small size of a two-minute candle. "Then we slammed the door closed and left him."

"For how long?"

"At first, long enough for the candle to burn out, which left him in total darkness. And then for several hours. Each time, suddenly, his door burst open, and there he could see — momentarily and with difficulty, his eyes trying to adjust to the bright light — Stabsfeldwebel Tedworth. Then the lights — we improvised the lights using jeep headlights — went out and the door slammed closed again.

"The next time the door opened, he was given his dinner. It was time for breakfast, but we served him what the officers were going to have for dinner. And another two-minute candle. By the time his eyes adjusted to the candlelight, it was pretty well exhausted and went out. He had to eat his dinner in absolute darkness and without any utensils. And, pardon the crudity, but can you imagine how difficult it is to void one's bladder, much less one's bowels, into a soft-sided canvas bucket while in total darkness? Are you getting the idea, Captain Cronley?"

Cronley nodded. "How long are you going to keep this up?"

"For another twenty-four hours. Perhaps a bit longer."

"And then?"

"The interrogation will begin."

"By who?"

"We're trying to decide whether it should be Dunwiddie or myself. One or the other. Dunwiddie's Russian isn't perfect, but on the other hand, he is an enormous black man."

"Would me getting a look at this guy interfere with your interrogation of him?"

Cronley saw that Mannberg didn't like the question.

"I'll keep my mouth shut," Cronley said. "I just want a look at him."

Mannberg looked at his watch.

"We're going to feed him his breakfast in about an hour. That will give you time to have your supper before you have your look."

"I'll take you," Dunwiddie said.

[Five]

When he'd gone to bed, Cronley had had a very difficult time falling asleep. His mind insisted on replaying — over and over — everything that had happened in the past ten days. But eventually, at about one in the morning, fatigue had finally taken over.

When the telephone rang, he was in a deep sleep, and he took a long time to awaken and reach for it.

"Twenty-third CIC, Lieutenant Cronley speaking, sir."

"That's Captain Cronley, actually," the voice of Colonel Robert Mattingly informed him. "You might wish to write that down."

"Sorry, sir. I was really out."

"Well, rise and shine, Captain Cronley. A new day has dawned. Duty calls."

"Yes, sir."

"Get dressed, have a shower, a shave, and a cup of coffee. Then go out to the road. Order the jeeps sitting there blocking it to move off the road. Whereupon, the road will

104

now resume its covert role as a landing strip. With me so far, Captain? Or do you wish to find a pencil and paper and write this all down?"

"I'm with you, sir."

What the hell is going on?

"Within the hour, an aircraft will land on the road. You will get in said aircraft and do whatever Lieutenant Colonel William W. Wilson, who will be piloting the aircraft, tells you to do. Got it?"

"Yes, sir. What —"

"It would behoove you to treat Colonel Wilson with impeccable military courtesy, Captain Cronley. He has the reputation for being a crotchety Old Regular Army sonofabitch. Speak only when spoken to. Do not ask questions. Understand?"

"Yes, sir."

The line went dead.

Forty minutes later, Captain Cronley — having showered, shaved, and donned a fresh uniform — stood at the end of the road that, in a pinch, could be used as a landing strip for light aircraft. The two jeeps, both with pedestal-mounted .50 caliber Browning machine guns, which had had the dual mission of protecting the compound perimeter and blocking the use of the road as a landing strip, were now half in the ditch beside the road.

Cronley heard the sound of an aircraft engine, and just had time to identify it as the Argus 240-hp air-cooled inverted V8 engine of a Fieseler Storch, when a Storch appeared. Not from above, but from below. It had to pull up before the pilot could lower the nose and put his gear down on the road.

Kloster Grünau sat atop a hill in what Cronley had decided were probably the foothills of the Alps.

Jesus, this guy must have been chasing cows around the fields!

The Storch, which had U.S. ARMY painted on the fuselage and the Constabulary insignia on the vertical stabilizer, slowed quickly and stopped just past where Cronley was standing. It turned and taxied back down the "runway" to the end — where the road curved — where it stopped again, turned again, and stood there with the engine idling.

Conley realized that the pilot, the lieutenant colonel whom Colonel Mattingly had described as "a crotchety Old Regular Army sonofabitch," was waiting for him, and probably impatiently.

He trotted down the road, rehearsing in his mind what he was going to do now:

come to attention, salute (holding the salute until it was returned), and bark, "Sir, Captain Cronley, James D., reporting to the colonel as ordered, sir!"

He got as far as coming to attention and raising his hand in salute when he saw the pilot's face. Cronley instantly concluded that the crotchety Old Regular Army sonofabitch lieutenant colonel wasn't flying the Storch.

The guy in the front seat had the bright unlined face of a newly commissioned second lieutenant.

He looks younger than me. He has to be a second lieutenant.

Cronley dropped the salute, walked up to the aircraft, put his foot on the step on the main gear, hoisted himself up into the cockpit, and said with a smile, "Hi, where'd you get the Storch?"

The words were out of his mouth before he noticed the three silver oak leaves — one on each shoulder and a third on his collar point — pinned to the uniform of the guy who had the bright unlined face of a newly commissioned second lieutenant.

"Shit!" Cronley said.

"I have been led to believe, Captain," Lieutenant Colonel William W. Wilson said, "that you have had some experience with

Storch aircraft."

"Yes, sir."

"Sufficient experience for you to be able to get into the backseat without assistance?"

"Yes, sir."

"Please do so."

Cronley climbed into the backseat and closed the window-door. He had just located the seat belt and was putting it on when the Storch began to move.

Moments later it was airborne.

Jimmy looked around where he was sitting. The rear seat had the basic controls — stick, rudder pedals, throttle, airspeed indicator, altimeter, and artificial horizon. There was a small panel holding an Army Air Corps radio of a type he had never seen. A headset and a microphone hung to the side.

Suspecting that the colonel was anxious to use the intercom to say a few words about the unusual greeting he had received, Cronley put on the headset.

He rehearsed his reply, drawing on his military courtesy training at Texas A&M. "Sir," he would say. "Sorry, sir. No excuse, sir."

Nothing but an electronic hiss came over the earphones for perhaps ten minutes.

Cronley became aware that they were at

an altitude of about 2,000 meters, making, according to the airspeed indicator, about sixty knots.

That was cause for concern. In his lengthy flight training in the Storch — almost two hours — Willi Grüner had told him that the Storch tended to stop flying somewhere between forty-five and fifty-five knots.

Unless the colonel watches himself, he's going to put us into a stall.

The engine coughed and stopped.

Jesus Christ, now what?

The airspeed needle rapidly unwound.

As the Storch stopped flying and went into a stall, the earphones came to life.

"You have the aircraft, Captain," Lieutenant Colonel William W. Wilson announced.

Cronley saw that the colonel was demonstrating this by holding both his hands above his head.

"Holy shit!" Cronley said, and then Pavlovian reaction took over.

He shoved the stick forward.

If I can get this sonofabitch back up to sixty, maybe it'll fly!

When he first felt a little life come into the controls, they were at 500 meters, and the needle was indicating 350 when he felt confident enough to try to pull out of the stall.

He came out of the stall moments later and was desperately looking around for someplace where he could — very quickly — make a dead stick landing when the starter ground, the engine started, and the propeller began to take a bite out of the air.

"Why don't you pick up a little altitude," Lieutenant Colonel William W. Wilson suggested conversationally over the earphones, "and take up a heading of two-seventy?"

Five minutes later, they were indicating 150 knots at 3,000 meters on a heading of 270.

Cronley took the microphone from its hook.

"Sir, may I inquire where we're going?"

"Sonthofen. It's about thirty miles. You'll know we're close when I get on the radio."

Sometime thereafter, Lieutenant Colonel William W. Wilson suggested, "Why don't you start a gentle descent to five hundred meters?"

Several minutes after that, he announced, "Sonthofen, Army-Seven-Oh-Seven. About three miles out. Request straight-in approach to Twenty-seven."

"Sonthofen clears Army Seven-Oh-Seven as Number One to land on Two-seven. We have you in sight. Welcome home, Colonel."

"Tell the man you understand, Captain,"

Colonel Wilson ordered.

"I'm supposed to land this thing?"

"Without breaking anything, if possible. Talk to the man."

Cronley dropped the nose so that he could make out what lay ahead. He saw they were more or less lined up with a runway, around which was a fleet of L-4s, plus two C-47s and some other aircraft Cronley didn't recognize.

"Sonthofen, Seven-Oh-Seven understands Number One to land on Two-seven," Cronley then said into the microphone.

"There are two hangars," Wilson announced. "If you manage to return us to Mother Earth alive, taxi to the one on the right."

"Yes, sir."

When Cronley had parked the Storch on the tarmac before the hangar, Lieutenant Colonel Wilson climbed out of the front seat and motioned for Cronley to follow him.

A master sergeant approached them and saluted.

"Say hello to Captain Cronley, Sergeant McNair," Wilson said. "And then get out the paint and obliterate our beloved insignia that's on the vertical stabilizer. Our bird has a new master."

"I hate to see her go," Sergeant McNair said.

He offered his hand to Cronley and said, "Captain."

"I am taking some solace in knowing that she has found a new and loving home," Wilson said, and turned to Cronley. "Let's go get a cup of coffee. It will take half an hour for the obliteration to dry."

He led Cronley to an office inside the hangar.

"Close the door, please, Captain," Wilson said. "I wouldn't put it past the Air Force to have a spy in here, and we wouldn't want them to hear what I have to say, would we?"

He added, "Sit," and walked to a coffee-maker.

There was a framed photograph on the wall, showing an L-4 about to touch down beside the Coliseum in Rome.

Cronley blurted, "I saw that in the news-reels."

Wilson glanced at the photograph. "Ah, yes. The triumphal entry of General Markus Augustus Clark into the Holy City. I had the honor of being his aerial taxi driver."

When Wilson saw the look on Cronley's face, he added, "Oh, yes, Colonel Mattingly told me what you think of Army Aviators. You're wrong, of course, but young officers often are."

He let that sink in a moment, and then added, as he handed Cronley a coffee cup on a saucer, "Yes, Captain Cronley, I know a good deal about you — and knew you were out of the mold even before I saw you running up to the Storch in your cowboy boots."

Shit, I shouldn't have put my boots on.

After all, Mattingly did warn me he was a crotchety Old Regular Army sonofabitch.

"And while we're on the subject of being out of uniform," Wilson said, as he pulled from a metal locker a zippered tanker jacket, to the breast of which were sewn pilot's wings. "This is one of your prizes for having successfully completed the William W. Wilson course in the operation of the Storch aircraft. The other prizes being two Storches. Treat them kindly, Captain. I have grown very fond of them."

"Colonel, I'm not entitled to wear those wings."

"That may be true. On the other hand, as Colonel Mattingly and I discussed, there is very little chance of someone rushing up to you when you land someplace and demanding to see your certificate of graduation from flight school. No one has ever asked me for such proof. And even if the unexpected happened, you could dazzle him with your CIC credentials, couldn't you, Special Agent Cronley?"

Cronley chuckled.

"Jim — may I call you 'Jim'?"

"Yes, sir. Of course."

"And you may call me 'sir' or 'Colonel,' whichever comes easiest."

"Yes, sir."

"Jim, Bob Mattingly and I go back a long ways. We share a mutual admiration for Major General I. D. White, who will shortly return to Germany and assume command of the U.S. Constabulary. When it is activated, I will become Aviation Officer of the U.S. Constabulary.

"The Air Force, always willing to share its superior knowledge with we lesser birdmen, volunteered to have a look at the proposed Table of Organization and Equipment, came to item Number So and So, two each Fieseler Fi 156 Storch aircraft, and promptly wet its panties. They could not in good conscience approve the use of captured enemy aircraft, as the reliability of such aircraft was unknown, and they didn't want to be responsible for some Army Liaison pilot of limited skills injuring himself.

"Over the years, I've provided Bob Mattingly — that is, provided the late and lamented OSS — with all sorts of aircraft. So I mentioned this to him, wondering if he had use for the Storches. His response was he'd love to have them, but would have to look around for a pilot or pilots and that would be a problem.

"Yesterday, he called me. A benevolent Deity had just dropped a pilot in his lap. There was a small problem: Although this chap had a commercial ticket, with multi-engine and instrument ratings, he had not wanted to be an aerial taxi driver and had concealed these ratings from the Army. In spite of that, he had just returned from flying a Storch, a Cub, and a Lodestar around the mouth of the Magellan Strait in connection with some activity Mattingly didn't wish to share with me but which had caused President Truman to jump him from Second John to Captain and pin the DSM on his manly chest.

"So here we are," Wilson went on. "That was a nice recovery from the stall, by the way. Most people would have tried — and suffered a possible fatal mistake at that altitude — restarting the engine."

"Thank you."

"So, what you get is two Storches, a decent supply of parts, and, if you think they would fit into Kloster Grünau, a former Luftwaffe Storch pilot and three mechanics."

Cronley's first reaction was: *Great! I barely know how to fly a Storch, and I know zilch about maintaining one.*

That was immediately followed by: *And what is Major Harold Wallace, not to mention Colonel Robert Mattingly, going to say when they hear I've moved four Germans into Kloster Grünau, thereby posing a threat to the secrets of Operation Ost?*

And that was immediately followed by: *Stop thinking like a second lieutenant, Captain Cronley. You command Kloster Grünau. If Mattingly told Tiny "to handle" the problem of the Russian he caught, and you ask him, "Colonel, what should I do?" he's going to have one more confirmation of his suspicions that giving you responsibility for Kloster Grünau, considering your youth and inexperience, was one of the dumbest decisions he ever made.*

"Colonel, what can you tell me about the Germans?"

"The former Luftwaffe captain — his name is Kurt Schröder — showed up a couple of days after I brought in the Storches. I found them, loaded them on trucks, and brought them here. Schröder

116

said that he had just been released from a POW enclosure, and as he walked home — he lives near here — he saw the Storches being trucked here. He thought we might need someone to work on the planes. And he needed a job to feed his family. He also said he knew where to find the Storch mechanics. So I hired him. Them. They've worked out well. Schröder checked me out in the airplane, and his men do a fine job maintaining them. Even Sergeant McNair approves."

"Sounds great, sir. I'll take them. Thank you."

"There are several problems, starting with paying them. The German currency is useless. What Schröder and his people had been working for is food. That isn't a problem for me here. It's not hard to find extra food for twenty-odd mouths when Sonthofen is drawing Quartermaster rations for about sixteen hundred people. But how would you handle that at Kloster Grünau?"

"Not a problem, sir."

Wilson's eyebrows went up questioningly.

"We draw standard GI rations for our prisoners, sir, as well as for our guard company."

"Okay," Wilson said, his tone making it

clear that he didn't believe that was the complete answer.

And it wasn't.

First Sergeant Chauncey L. Dunwiddie had explained that what was almost certainly a fraud committed daily upon the U.S. Army had begun as a solution to a deadly serious problem concerning the secrecy of Operation Ost. The solution had been proposed by Sergeant Friedrich Hessinger and approved by Colonel Robert Mattingly.

As long as General Gehlen and the members of Abwehr Ost had been prisoners of war, they had been entitled under the Geneva Conventions to the same rations as their U.S. Army captors.

It was important that everybody in Abwehr Ost be run through a De-Nazification Court, declared to be Non-Nazis, and released to civilian life as quickly as possible.

And this was done. All members of Abwehr Ost, including a substantial number of Nazis, were run through De-Nazification Courts, adjudged to be Non-Nazis, and released from POW status.

This permitted Headquarters, European Command, when the Russians demanded to know if EUCOM had in its POW enclosures any former members of Abwehr Ost, whom they wished to interrogate, to truthfully state that they did not.

The problem then became how to draw rations for Gehlen and his men, now that they were not POWs and had been returned to their civilian pursuits.

Sergeant Hessinger's suggestion, which after serious consideration Colonel Mattingly ordered put into execution, was to have the XXIIIrd CIC Detachment accept the surrender of a number of German officers and soldiers and place them into its POW enclosure at Kloster Grünau. The number of prisoners equaled that of the Abwehr Ost prisoners, plus ten percent as a cushion.

Names of the prisoners were compiled from a copy of the Munich telephone book, and their organizations from the USFET G-2 Order of Battle. Once this compilation had been made, it was checked against the roster of Operation Ost to make sure that no name on the latter appeared on the Roster of Prisoners.

The vetted list was classified Secret and then presented to the U.S. Army Quartermaster Depot in Munich, which accepted it without question — it was signed by the deputy chief, CIC, European Theatre of Operations — and began its daily issue of rations to feed the prisoners.

Sergeant Hessinger had also been tasked by Colonel Mattingly to acquire the "goodies" the XXIIIrd CIC was going to need. Goodies were loosely defined as those things CIC agents needed to bribe people in the acquisition of intelligence.

Money was one such goody. Mattingly — and only a few other senior officers — could acquire U.S. dollars from a U.S. Army Finance Office and then sign a sworn statement that those dollars had been expended in the service of the United States. But as the reichsmark was just about useless — there was nothing to buy — and U.S. Army Occupation Scrip not much better for intelligence purposes, other things — coffee, cigarettes, candy bars, and spirits (the latter being called "Class Six Supplies") were necessary.

There were two ways to get such supplies out of Army warehouses and into the hands of the XXIIIrd CIC Detachment and thus into the hands of the men of Operation Ost. One was to go through proper channels and request they be issued. This would inevitably result in all sorts of questions that couldn't be answered without bringing attention to the function of the XXIIIrd CIC Detachment and Operation Ost.

The second way — the one Sergeant Hessinger put into execution — was to prepare two Morning Reports every day. One was bona fide. It was sent upward through channels. It showed the strength of the XXIIIrd CIC Detachment as two officers — Major Wallace and Captain Cronley — and two enlisted men — First Sergeant Dunwiddie and Sergeant Hessinger.

The second Morning Report was shown only to Munich Military Post and the Munich Quartermaster Depot. It showed a personnel strength of eleven officers and forty-three enlisted men — typical CIC detachment strength — physically present at Kloster Grünau.

Hessinger had created a phantom force within the Twenty-third. And because only the deputy commander USFET CIC, Colonel Robert Mattingly, was authorized to visit Kloster Grünau or would be authorized to visit the Pullach facility when that was opened, detection of the deception was very unlikely.

Sergeant Hessinger had further refined his solution for obtaining the necessary goodies. Not only was each member of the phantom force issued a EUCOM PX ration card (which authorized the weekly purchase of, among other things, 1.5 cartons of cigarettes, a pound of coffee, and a box of Hershey bars) but because of its remote location, Kloster Grünau was authorized a "Mini-PX" under the Munich Military Post PX.

One Sergeant F. Hessinger was assigned as Mini-PX manager.

Further, to accommodate the officers and non-commissioned officers of the XXIIIrd CIC and the enlisted men of Company C, 203rd Tank Destroyer Battalion, which guarded Kloster Grünau, both an officers' open mess and an NCO club were authorized. At the time of the authorization, Second Lieutenant Cronley was appointed officers' open mess officer and Technical Sergeant Tedworth NCO club manager. The Kloster Grünau officers' open mess graciously agreed to give the NCO club access to the Class VI Store it would operate.

"There is another problem," Colonel Wilson went on. "If I try to truck the second Storch, the parts, and Schröder's mechanics to Kloster Grünau, that would cause the Air Force to wonder what's going on."

"But," Captain Cronley offered, "the Air Force could be run off by my people?"

"Some of your people — Tiny and Sergeant Tedworth come to mind — can run people off by just baring their fangs. Couple that with those dazzling CIC credentials."

"Yes, sir."

"And if the Air Force gets really curious, Bob Mattingly can cut them off at the Farben Building."

"As soon as I get back, I'll send our trucks here."

"Good. Any questions?"

Cronley's face showed both that he had one and that he was reluctant to ask it.

"Go ahead."

"Colonel, can I ask how old you are?"

"Thirty-two," Wilson said, paused, and then went on: "That's what I usually tell people who ask. Actually, I'm almost twenty-five. Class of 'forty at the Academy. And you're 'forty-five at A&M?"

"Yes, sir."

"And Tiny is — or would have been — 'forty-five at Norwich. The next time we get together we'll have to knock rings and sing 'Army Blue' and 'The Aggie War Hymn' and whatever the hell they sing at Norwich."

"Tiny didn't mention you knew each other."

"Tiny, like you and General White, is Cavalry. I've always thought you Horse

Soldiers had odd senses of humor." He paused, and then said, "Your boss is a University of the South — Sewanee — graduate. I think their school song is 'Jesus Loves Me.' "

Cronley laughed. And then he had a series of thoughts.

He's now treating me as an equal.

Well, maybe not as an equal.

But as a fellow professional soldier.

What did he say about "knocking our rings"?

Maybe this is what this is all about.

Maybe I am destined to be a professional soldier.

God knows with the Squirt gone — Jesus Christ, she's probably being buried today! — I can never go back to Midland.

"Well, put your new jacket on, and I'll get Kurt Schröder in here," Wilson said.

"My new jacket?" Cronley asked, and then understood. "The jacket with the wings."

"Affirmative. I don't want Kurt to think I'm turning the Storches over to someone who can't fly."

"Yes, sir."

I'll put the jacket on as ordered, but as soon as I get back to Kloster Grünau and can find a razor blade, the wings come off.

III

U.S. Army Airfield B-6
Sonthofen, Bavaria
American Zone of Occupation, Germany

1105 29 October 1945

A short, muscular blond man in his late twenties came into Wilson's office. He looked very much, Cronley thought, like Willi Grüner. Even though this man was wearing baggy U.S. Army mechanic coveralls, which had been dyed black, it was easy for Cronley to imagine him in a Luftwaffe pilot's uniform, with a brimmed cap jauntily cocked on his head.

"You sent for me, Colonel?" he asked, in heavily accented but what seemed like fluent English.

"This is the officer who'll be taking over the Storches," Wilson announced, and then added, "Kurt, I told you that was almost certainly going to happen."

"Yes, sir."

"Cronley, this is Kurt Schröder, the man I've been telling you about."

Schröder bobbed his head courteously at Cronley.

"Cronley may be able to use you and your men," Wilson said. "Why don't you tell him something about yourself and them?"

"Yes, sir. Sir, I was a pilot in the Luftwaffe, where I flew the Fieseler Storch. The men —"

"Das ist alles?" Cronley interrupted.

"Wie, bitte?"

"The Storch was the only aircraft you flew in the Luftwaffe?" Cronley continued in German.

Schröder's surprise at Cronley's fluent German showed on his face.

Good, Cronley thought. *What I want to do is get you off-balance.*

"No, sir. I was primarily a fighter pilot. I flew mostly the Messerschmitt BF-109, but also the Focke-Wulf Fw-190."

"Does the name Major Hans-Peter Freiherr von Wachtstein ring a bell with you, Schröder?"

Schröder's face showed he recognized the name, but was afraid of the ramifications of any answer he might give.

"The Focke-Wulf Fw-190 pilot who received the Knight's Cross of the Iron Cross from the hands of Der Führer himself?" Cronley pursued.

Schröder, now visibly off-balance, exhaled audibly and told the truth.

126

"Sir, I had the honor of serving in Baron von Wachtstein's squadron in the defense of Berlin."

Well, that should be recommendation enough, but as soon as I get back to Kloster Grünau, I'll get on the radio and ask ole Hansel about him.

"Schröder, I may have use for you and your men," Cronley said. "But before I can offer you the job, you'll have to be vetted by another officer. What I propose to do now, with Colonel Wilson's permission, is take you to see him."

"Kurt," Wilson said, "I've explained our pay arrangements. Cronley is willing to do the same."

"Yes, sir. May I ask where we'll be going?"

"No," Cronley said simply.

"We'll be going in the Storch?"

"Yes."

"Excuse me, but how can I fly you any-where if I don't know where we're going?"

"I will be flying the Storch," Cronley said. "Why don't you top off the tanks while I have a final word with Colonel Wilson?"

"Yes, sir."

"And while you're at it, put two or three jerry cans of avgas in the backseat."

"Yes, sir."

■ ■ ■

"Jim, who was that Luftwaffe hero you brought up?" Wilson said when they were alone. "Or is that classified?"

"Yes, sir, probably. I met him in Argentina. Good guy. He's now flying South American Airways Constellations between here and Germany. I'm going to check out Schröder with him and an officer back at Kloster Grünau."

"And the name of this other officer? Or is that classified, too?"

"That's probably classified, too, sir. Will you settle for 'a former senior officer of Abwehr Ost'?"

"That's likely Oberst Ludwig Mannberg. Or maybe General Gehlen himself."

When Cronley didn't reply, Wilson added, "Apropos of nothing, I was the aerial taxi driver who flew Major Wallace to accept General Gehlen's surrender."

Cronley nodded. "That being the case, sir, I'm going to run Schröder past Mannberg first, and then maybe past the general, too."

"You're good, Cronley. I now understand why Mattingly put you in charge of Kloster Grünau."

"He put me in charge because he had no one else, sir, and because the guy who should be running it, Tiny, passed up a commission for the good of the service."

"Modesty becomes you, but that's not the way it was. What I said before, that you're good, was a sincere compliment. Now comes the fatherly advice of a senior officer, welcome or not."

"Yes, sir?"

"Prefacing this with the immodest announcement that I am, by thirteen months, the senior officer of the Class of 1940 — in other words, I got my silver oak leaves thirteen months before the second guy in 'forty got his — and thus know what I'm talking about . . ."

He stopped, collected his thoughts, and then went on: "The disadvantages of getting rank and or authority and responsibility before your peers get it are that it (a) goes to your head, and (b) makes people jealous, which (c) causes them to try like hell to knock you back to their level by fair and — more often — foul means.

"The advantages of getting rank, et cetera, mean that you can do things for the good of the service that otherwise you could not do. And that's what we professional soldiers are supposed to do, isn't it? Make contributions to the good of the service? Lecture over."

"Thank you, sir," Cronley said softly.

"Get out of here, Cronley. Hie thee to thy monastery!"

Cronley came to attention and saluted crisply. Wilson returned it as crisply. Cronley executed an about-face movement and marched to the office door.

[Two]

Kloster Grünau
Schollbrunn, Bavaria
American Zone of Occupation, Germany

1235 29 October 1945

Two machine gun jeeps were blocking the road, and Cronley had to make two low-level passes over what was to be his runway — very low and very slow passes, with the window open so they could see his face — before the jeeps started up and moved out of the way.

He put the Storch down smoothly, taxied to the end of the "runway," and shut down the engine.

"It would appear that I have cheated death once again," he said to Schröder.

Schröder's expression did not change.

"May I ask where we are?" Schröder said.

"No."

Tiny walked toward the airplane. Cronley made a slight hand signal to him, which he hoped would make Dunwiddie salute him and — more important — play the respectful role of a non-com dealing with an officer.

Dunwiddie understood. He saluted crisply and Cronley returned it.

"Two things, Sergeant," Cronley ordered. "Have your men push the aircraft off the strip, and then have them put a tarpaulin over it. And then get someone to escort this gentleman while he's here."

"Yes, sir," Dunwiddie said, and gestured for one of the jeeps to come to them.

When the jeep stopped before him, Dunwiddie pointed to the machine gunner, a corporal, and ordered: "You will escort this gentleman until you are relieved."

"You got it, First Sergeant."

Dunwiddie pointed to the driver.

"You go to the barracks and get enough men to push this airplane up beside the chapel. Then put a tarp over it so it'll be hard to see from the air."

The jeep driver, a sergeant, nodded, and the moment the corporal had tied down his Browning and jumped free of the jeep, turned it around and drove off.

"You can get out now, Herr Schröder," Cronley said in German.

They set out for the headquarters building, Cronley and Dunwiddie walking side by side. Schröder walked behind them as the corporal, now cradling a Thompson submachine gun like a hunter's shotgun, followed him.

As they approached the building, Cronley saw General Reinhard Gehlen and Oberst Ludwig Mannberg standing just outside. That made moot the question he had had in his mind about how he was going to get one or the other of them out of the mess in order to explain the situation.

Cronley also saw on Schröder's face that he recognized one of them. Or both.

"Good afternoon, Herr Cronley," Gehlen said courteously.

"I hope my arrival didn't disturb your lunch, sir."

"It did, but the sound of a Storch coming in here caused my curiosity to overwhelm my hunger." He looked closely at Schröder. "We know one another, don't we?"

Schröder snapped to rigid attention, clicked his heels, bobbed his head, and said, "Herr General, I had the honor of flying the general on many occasions. In Poland and the East, Herr General."

"I thought you looked familiar," Gehlen said. "Schröder, isn't it?"

Schröder bobbed his head and clicked his heels again.

"Herr General, I am flattered that the general remembers."

"We don't do that here, Schröder," Mannberg said. "The war is over and we are no longer in military service."

"Jawohl, Herr Oberst."

"And," Mannberg added, drily sarcastic, "it would follow that since we are no longer in military service, neither do we have military rank."

"Corporal, take our guest around the corner, please," Cronley said, "while I have a word with these gentlemen."

Schröder went around the corner of the building with the corporal three steps behind him.

Gehlen looked expectantly at Cronley to see what he wanted.

"General, how would you feel about Schröder joining us here?"

"In connection with that Storch he just flew in here, you mean?"

Cronley nodded.

"The Storch, and another one, is now ours," he said.

"I think he could prove quite useful. But I

133

suspect you have some doubt?"

"Yes, sir. You think he can be trusted?"

"Oh, yes."

"Could you tell me why?"

"Because right now he's wondering whether he's going to be put to work, or be shot for having seen too much," Gehlen explained.

Cronley thought there was a hint of sarcasm in his tone.

"Exactly what has he seen?"

"Mannberg and myself," Gehlen said, more than a little condescendingly.

Cronley felt a wave of anger rise. He recognized it and waited until he felt he had it under control before he replied.

"General, keeping in mind that three days ago I was a second lieutenant, you're going to have to have a little patience when I ask what you and Oberst Mannberg, with your far greater experience, consider to be dumb questions."

"The general meant no disrespect, Hauptman Cronley," Mannberg said.

"Actually, quite the opposite, Hauptman Cronley," Gehlen said. "My problem with you is that I've seen — and I mean seen here, not what you did in Argentina, but that also obviously applies — what a competent intelligence officer you are, and I sometimes forget there probably are . . . how do I say this? . . . certain gaps in your professional experience."

"My professional experience can be written inside a matchbook cover with a thick grease pencil," Cronley said. "And the gaps in it make a hole somewhat larger than the Grand Canyon. And I think you both are fully aware of that."

Mannberg laughed.

"Is something funny?" Cronley snapped.

"Yes," Mannberg said. "That colorful expression of annoyance, I'm afraid, did not translate very well into German."

"I was speaking German?" Cronley blurted.

So I didn't have my temper firmly in hand.

"You sounded like a Strasbourger on his fourth liter of beer," Mannberg said.

"That's bad."

"But you made your point," Gehlen said, "and it was taken, Hauptman Cronley. I apologize for not understanding. You were — as you should have been — concerned that taking Schröder here might pose security problems. When I so quickly suggested I didn't think it would be a problem, you wondered — as you should have — how quickly I had made that decision. I thought it should have been obvious to you. My mistake. One of the gaps in your experience is that you have had no experience in the East."

By East he means Russia.

Why are these guys so reluctant to say Russia?

Gehlen met his eyes a long moment, then went on: "Let me tell you what it was like in the East when Schröder was flying me and Mannberg around at the front. It was understood that under no circumstances could we fall into the hands of the Red Army. Specifically, Schröder knew that when we took off, there was an explosive charge aboard the Storch that I would detonate, or he would, if it appeared there was any chance at all that we were going to go down behind the Red Army's lines.

"Even after the flight, or flights, Schröder understood that it was unacceptable for him to be captured with knowledge of the location of any Abwehr Ost detachment or the like. He gave his word as an officer to die honorably by his own hand in that circumstance."

"Jesus Christ!" Cronley said softly.

"When you brought him here, and he saw Mannberg and me, he naturally assumed the same security protocol would be in place here. And I'm sure he knows the Red Army is looking for any former member of Abwehr Ost.

"Schröder knew the moment we saw and recognized one another that he would not be allowed to leave in possession of such intelligence. I had those facts, plus my knowledge that he was a courageous and trustworthy officer — as well as a very good pilot — in mind when I made what appeared to you to be a casual decision about whether he would be useful here."

Gehlen let that sink in a moment, and after Cronley nodded, went on: "My mistake, Hauptman Cronley, was to forget about those gaps in your experience, and again, for that I apologize."

"There's no need to apologize, General," Cronley said. "The problem as I see it is that I'm afraid we've only begun to learn how large those gaps, those many gaps, in my experience are."

"And your decision about Schröder?" Gehlen asked.

"I suggest we take him inside, give him lunch, and welcome him to Kloster Grünau."

Gehlen nodded, and then smiled.

"An expression Colonel Mattingly uses frequently seems appropriate here," he said, and then quoted, " 'The true test of another man's intelligence is to what degree he agrees with you.' "

"I'm flattered, sir," Cronley said, and then raised his voice: "Corporal!"

The corporal appeared around the corner of the building a moment later, prodding Schröder ahead of him with the muzzle of his Thompson.

"Lower that muzzle, Corporal," Cronley ordered. "Herr Schröder has been declared one of the good guys."

A look of enormous relief flashed over Schröder's face.

Not that I doubted what Gehlen said about Schröder wondering if he was about to be shot, but if I needed proof, there it was on Schröder's face.

"Pass the word," Cronley continued. "And then find First Sergeant Dunwiddie and ask him if he's free for lunch."

"Yes, sir," the corporal said.

"Come with us, Schröder," Gehlen said. "And while we have lunch, I'll try to determine where you'll be most useful around here."

"So, what we're going to do now," Dunwiddie said, as the discussion about the airplanes and Schröder and his men died down, "is send a couple of trucks — probably it would be better to send four — to Sonthofen to pick up the other airplane, the mechanics, and the parts. Right?"

Cronley made a *Time out* signal with his hands and announced, "I've been thinking."

"That's always dangerous," Tiny said.

"Kurt, now that you know what's going on here, what about your men?" Cronley asked.

"What Hauptman Cronley is asking, Schröder," Mannberg said, "is (a) whether you trust them to keep their mouths shut about what they might see here, and (b) whether they understand what will happen to them if they talk. We simply cannot have them talking, even to their wives."

It took Schröder a good fifteen seconds to frame his reply.

"Two of them served with me in the East," he began. "When I tell them the same security protocol we had there will apply here, they will understand. If they don't wish to subject themselves to that protocol, I won't bring them here."

"And the third man?" Mannberg asked.

"He is a brother of one of the men who was with me in the East. If he is reluctant to accept the protocol, then I will not bring either of them here."

"How long would it take you to hold this

conversation, *conversations*, with them?" Cronley said.

"Do I understand that I am to return to Sonthofen with the trucks?"

"Answer my question, please."

"Thirty minutes or so. No longer than that."

"And how long would it take to tell them, 'Say nothing to anyone, I will return here shortly'? With confidence that they would obey that order?"

"You've lost me, Jim," Dunwiddie said.

"It would take me twice as long to say that than it did for you to say it. Because I would say it twice, to make sure they understood."

Cronley nodded, then turned to Tiny.

"What's going to happen now is that Schröder and I are going to fly back to Sonthofen. When we land, Schröder will deliver that little speech to his men. I will then get out of Storch One, and Schröder will immediately get in Storch One and fly back here. I will then get in Storch Two and fly it back here. When I land, you and Schröder and four trucks will go to Sonthofen, pick up the mechanics and the parts, and drive very slowly and carefully back here."

When he saw that everyone was considering his remarks with what appeared to be

140

little enthusiasm, Cronley provided amplification.

"If we fly Storch Two back here, that will (a) get it out of Sonthofen immediately, (b) eliminate the risk of it getting damaged while moving it by truck, and (c) questions will not be raised by anyone about a Storch with U.S. Army markings being driven down the roads to here."

Gehlen and Mannberg nodded their understanding and acceptance. Schröder's face remained expressionless.

Tiny asked, "And I'm going with the trucks? Why?"

"Because, Marshal Earp, you have your marshal's badge with which you can dazzle anybody who wants to ask you about anything."

"Marshal Earp?" General Gehlen asked.

"He was a famous American cowboy, General," Mannberg said.

"A U.S. Marshal," Cronley corrected him. "In the Arizona Territory before it became a state. He and his brothers and a dentist named Doc Holliday were involved in — I should say won — a famous gunfight in the O.K. Corral in Tombstone."

"Actually, it wasn't *in* the O.K. Corral, but near it," Tiny further clarified.

Gehlen, Mannberg, and Schröder obviously had no idea what they were talking about.

"Ready to go flying, Kurt?" Cronley said.

Schröder stood.

Cronley handed him the zipper jacket Lieutenant Colonel Wilson had given him.

"Put this on," he ordered. "If we find ourselves in the hands of the MPs or anyone else asking questions, your answer is you are under orders to answer no questions without the permission of Colonel Robert Mattingly, deputy commander, Counterintelligence, European Command. Got it?"

Schröder nodded, and then repeated, as if to fix it in his memory, "Colonel Robert Mattingly, deputy commander, Counterintelligence, European Command."

"That's it," Cronley confirmed, and then turned to General Gehlen. "When I get back, I want to see our guest."

Gehlen nodded.

[Three]

Kloster Grünau
Schollbrunn, Bavaria
American Zone of Occupation, Germany

1705 29 October 1945

The machine gun jeeps were already moving off the road when Cronley made his first pass over Kloster Grünau. He decided they had seen — or heard — the Storch approaching.

When he turned and made his approach, he saw that a small convoy — a lead machine gun jeep, the Opel Kapitän, two GMC 6×6 trucks, and a trailing machine gun jeep — was lined up on the road from Kloster Grünau.

Tiny's ready to go, he thought. *Why not? It's a long ride to Sonthofen and back.*

Only two trucks; Schröder must have told him he wouldn't need four.

And then his attention was abruptly brought back to what he was doing — flying.

He was far to the left of the runway; winds had blown him off his intended track.

Well, I guess we're going to need a windsock.

He corrected his approach and touched gently down where he had originally intended to land.

Not bad, Eddie Rickenbacker!

Especially for someone who professes to hate flying.

Who are you kidding? You love flying and really missed it.

He completed the landing roll, turned the Storch, and taxied to the convoy at the end of the runway. He saw Tiny and Schröder get out of the Kapitän.

Cronley shut down the engine and opened the window.

Schröder, smiling, made a gesture with his hand demonstrating Cronley's last-second efforts to line up with the runway.

"I was thinking we might need a wind-sock," Cronley said.

"I think that's a very good idea."

"On the way to Sonthofen, why don't you tell Sergeant Dunwiddie here how to make one?"

"Why don't you tell Tedworth how to make one," Dunwiddie challenged, "while Herr Schröder and I are bouncing down the bumpy roads in the dark?"

"Because as an officer I am dedicated to preserving the privileges of rank," Cronley said piously.

Dunwiddie smiled and shook his head.

"Speaking of officers," he said, "Mattingly called. I didn't think you wanted him to know what you were really doing, Charles Lindbergh, so I told him you were off in a jeep somewhere, and I would have you call him when you got back. That was about an hour ago."

"Okay. Thanks. I'll call him. Have a nice ride."

I'll call him after I see the Russian NKGB agent.

He nodded and smiled at Schröder, then in a loud voice called out "Clear!" and started the engine. He taxied back down the runway to where a dozen soldiers were waiting to push the Storch off the runway and out of sight.

Cronley found Mannberg in the officers' mess bar. He was reading *Stars and Stripes,* the U.S. Army newspaper, over a cup of coffee.

Cronley sat beside him and said, "When you're through with the *Stripes,* I'd like to see the NKGB agent."

"Of course," Mannberg replied, and laid the newspaper down.

Cronley could see that Mannberg was unhappy.

"I don't want to interfere in any way with your interrogation," Cronley said. "I just want to see him."

"May I ask why?"

"I think I should."

"Of course," Mannberg said, and stood.

As they walked out of the bar, Cronley saw the zipper jacket Lieutenant Colonel Wilson had given him. It was hanging from a peg by the door.

Schröder must've left it there — returning it to me — when he came back from Sonthofen. It still has the Liaison Pilot's wings.

To which neither of us is entitled.

Cronley took the jacket and put it on as they walked to what had once been the monastery's chapel.

At least it'll cover my captain's bars, and if I speak German, the NKGB guy will think I'm another German.

Why is that important?

Because, on the rank totem pole, a U.S. Army captain is far down from Gehlen and Mannberg.

Unless he already knows Kloster Grünau is being run by me. Which he probably does.

Which means — Tiny's people grabbed him before I returned from the States with my brand-new captain's bars — that if he does know who I am, he thinks I'm a second lieutenant, which is really at the bottom of that totem pole.

To hell with it. My gut feeling is to wear the jacket; go with that.

There were four of what Cronley thought of as "Tiny's Troopers," plus two of Gehlen's men, just inside the foyer of the former chapel. They were seated around a card table playing poker. Packs of cigarettes and

Hershey chocolate bars were used as chips.

It was less innocent than it seemed. Cigarettes and Hershey bars were the currency of the land when dealing with the Germans, and could be used to purchase what little the Germans had to sell, including very often the sexual favors of the women.

Everybody quickly rose to their feet when the senior non-com among them, a staff sergeant, barked, "Ten-hut!"

The sergeant — who was uncommonly small for a trooper, not much over five-feet-two, the Army minimum height — casually held an M-3 .30 caliber carbine in his hand. The others were holding Thompson .45 caliber submachine guns.

"At ease," Cronley said. "I'm here to investigate rumors that gambling is taking place on the premises."

"Ah, Lieutenant, you know we wouldn't do nothing like that," the sergeant said.

One of the troopers hissed, "That's *Captain,* asshole!"

"Excuse me, *Captain,*" the sergeant said. "Sorry, sir."

"You have an honest face, Sergeant. So I will believe you when you say you wouldn't even think of gambling," Cronley said. "And as far as that Captain business is concerned,

I've only been a captain for a couple days. If you had called me Captain, I probably would have looked around to see who you were talking to."

The troopers smiled and chuckled.

"I came to have a look at our guest," Cronley said. "How is he?"

"He's all right. I've got another two guys down there who peek at him every five or ten minutes or so," the sergeant said.

And then he came to attention.

"Permission to speak, sir?"

Another Regular Army old soldier.

Why am I not surprised? Tiny would be very careful who he put in charge.

"Granted."

"Sir, my orders from First Sergeant Dunwiddie are to do what Konrad here says about keeping that guy in the hole."

He nodded toward one of the Germans, a pink-skinned man in his thirties.

Cronley looked at Mannberg, who said, "Konrad Bischoff, Hauptmann Cronley, former major. Interrogation specialist."

Bischoff bobbed his head to Cronley.

"And . . . ?" Cronley said to the sergeant.

"And, Captain, ever since I put that guy in the hole, he's been . . . doing his business . . . in a canvas bucket. It smells to high heaven in there. Konrad says, 'That's part of the process,' and not to change it. I'm really starting to feel sorry for that Communist sonofabitch, sitting there in the dark and —"

Cronley held up his hand to stop him.

What do I do now?

Say, "Fuck the Russian" or "Tough shit"?

That'd be the same thing as admitting the Germans are running Kloster Grünau, running Operation Ost.

They're not. Or at least they're not supposed to be running it.

If I override the order, I'm not only going to confirm Mannberg's opinion that I'm getting a little too big for my britches, challenging the superior knowledge and the decisions of his "interrogation specialist," but piss him off. And if I piss him off, I piss off Gehlen.

Bottom line, I'm supposed to be running Kloster Grünau.

"Let's go see what you're talking about," Cronley said. "You, me, Herr Mannberg, and Herr Bischoff. Tell me how that works, Sergeant."

"Yes, sir. What Konrad got us to do is rig up a floodlight — six jeep headlights mounted on a piece of plywood, hitched to a jeep battery. We turn the lights on, then open the door. The Russian, who's been sitting there in the dark since his candle went

149

out . . . you know about the candles, Captain? They last about two minutes —"

"I know about them," Cronley interrupted.

"Yes, sir. Well, the Russian, who's been there in the dark for an hour at least, is blinded when the lights shine in his eyes. We can see him, but he can't —"

"Okay, Sergeant," Cronley interrupted again. "Let's go."

The sergeant led the way through the former chapel to a room behind what had been the altar, past crates of supplies where once, presumably, there had been pews full of hooded priests and monks.

Two troopers, both armed with Thompsons, were in the room. They popped to attention.

"What's he doing?" the sergeant asked.

"Ten minutes ago, he was sitting with his back against the wall," one of them, a sergeant, replied.

"Open the door," the sergeant ordered.

He took two flashlights from a shelf, handed one to Cronley, and waited until the door had been opened. Then he started down the stairway. Cronley followed.

At the foot of the stairway, Cronley found himself in a small area, perhaps six feet by eight. To the left was a single heavy wooden door. It was closed with a piece of lumber jammed against it. Across from the door, the improvised floodlights rested against a brick wall.

The sergeant pointed to one of the men who had followed them down the stairs, gesturing for him to take the floodlights, and then to another man, ordering him to be prepared to remove the timber that held the door shut.

Then he stood by the door, unslung the carbine from his shoulder, and held it as if he expected to use it as a club if the prisoner tried to burst out of the room.

"Now!" he ordered.

The man with the floodlights moved to the door and turned them on. The man on the timber kicked it free and then jerked the door open.

Cronley could now see the cell and the man in it.

And he smelled the nauseating odor of human waste.

The NKGB agent, who had been sitting on a mattress, shielded his eyes from the light as he rose, sliding his back against the wall.

"Take your hand away from your face!" Cronley barked in German.

The man obeyed but closed his eyes.

That was involuntary, Cronley decided. *That light really hurts his eyes. He's not being defiant.*

He could now see the NKGB agent's face.

He was surprised at what he saw: a slight man, fair-skinned and blond, who appeared to be in his twenties.

A nice-looking guy.

What the hell did you expect? Somebody who looks like Joe Stalin? Or Lenin?

The NKGB agent finally managed to get his eyes into a squint. His eyes were blue.

"Get another waste bucket in there," Cronley ordered in English. "And get that one out of there. This room smells like a latrine!"

The trooper who had kicked the timber out of the way said, "Sir, we were told —"

"Don't argue with me, Corporal!" Cronley snapped. "Get that bucket out of there, and do it now. We're not savages!"

"Yes, sir."

"What's your name?" Cronley demanded, first in English, then in German.

The NKGB officer didn't reply.

"We believe him to be Konstantin Orlovsky," Mannberg said softly from behind Cronley.

"Major Konstantin Orlovsky of the

Peoples Commissariat for Internal Affairs at your service, sir," the NKGB officer said in fluent English. "And you are?"

That's not English English, but it's not American English, either.

"My name is Cronley, Major. We'll talk again."

He turned to the sergeant.

"Major Orlovsky's waste bucket will be replaced at regular intervals. The next time I come down here, I want to smell roses. Got it?"

"Got it, sir."

"Thank you," Orlovsky said.

Cronley turned from the door and went quickly back up the stairs. Mannberg and Bischoff followed him.

As soon as they reached the room behind the altar, Bischoff asked, "Am I to assume, Herr Hauptman, that you are taking over the interrogation?"

You're really pissed that the naïve young American countermanded your orders, aren't you?

And, Mannberg, to judge from the look on your face, you're pissed that I countermanded the orders of your "interrogation specialist" and did so in front of the black American enlisted men.

Too fucking bad!

"The assumption you should be working under, Herr Bischoff, is that you are conducting the interrogation under my direction. So far as what happened down there just now, vis-à-vis Orlovsky's waste bucket, what I had in mind was something Herr Mannberg told me, something to the effect that causing pain — and I think making Orlovsky sit in a blacked-out cell forced to smell his own waste caused him pain — is usually counterproductive.

"And if memory serves, Herr Mannberg, you also said that's even more true when the person being interrogated is a skilled agent. I think we agree that Orlovsky is a skilled agent. I think that before he sneaked in here, he knew Kloster Grünau was commanded by a very young American. With that in mind, I told him my name. What good would it do to pretend otherwise?"

"Your points are well taken," Mannberg said.

He means that.

But he is also surprised.

"And now, you'll have to excuse me, I have to get on the phone."

And I want to get away from you while I'm still ahead.

In other words, before I say something else stupid.

154

[Four]

Kloster Grünau was connected to a secure radio network that had originally been established by the OSS during the war. It used equipment — primarily Collins Radio Corporation Model 7.2 transceivers coupled with SIGABA encryption devices — acquired from the Army Security Agency's Secret Communications Center at Vint Hill Farms Station in Virginia.

During the war, the network had provided secure communications between OSS headquarters in Washington and important OSS stations around the world. Deputy OSS Director Allen Dulles had had one when he had been stationed in Berne, Switzerland. David Bruce, who had run the OSS organization attached to Eisenhower's Supreme Command in London, had had another. Lieutenant Colonel Cletus Frade, who commanded Team Turtle, the OSS operation covering the "Southern Cone" — Argentina, Chile, and Uruguay — had another. And there had been a very few other stations in the network.

Despite the demise of the OSS, parts of the network remained "up." Instant, secure communication between Germany and Vint Hill Farms was still possible, but since the

OSS had been "disestablished" was never used.

There were now two stations in Germany. One had been set up immediately after the war by Colonel Mattingly in what had been Admiral Canaris's home in the Berlin suburb of Zehlendorf. Mattingly had moved the station he had had with OSS Forward to Kloster Grünau the day before the OSS had ceased to exist.

Communications between Germany and Argentina, because of Operation Ost, were frequent.

There were no secure communications links between Colonel Mattingly's office in the I.G. Farben Building in Frankfurt, Major Harold Wallace's office in the Vier Jahreszeiten Hotel in Munich, and Kloster Grünau. Or between any of them.

One of the reasons was the "antenna farm" that the Collins transceiver needed. Since Mattingly did not want anyone to know the radio network even existed, he could not order that antennae be set up on the roofs of either the Farben Building or the Vier Jahreszeiten.

And since the less known by anyone about Kloster Grünau the better, he could not go to the Signal Corps and tell them to install a secure — encrypted — telephone line there. They would want to know why one was needed. And even if he told them why he needed one and pledged — or threatened — them to silence, a platoon of Signal Corps telephone linemen installing the heavy lead-shielded cable necessary for encrypted secure lines would cause questions to be asked about what was going on at the supposedly deserted former monastery.

These problems would go away when the South German Industrial Development Organization moved to Pullach. But for the time being, telephone calls had to be conducted in the presumption that someone was listening to what was being said.

"Mattingly."

"Cronley, sir."

"Thank you for returning my call so promptly, Captain. It can't be more than two or three hours since I asked Dunwiddie to have you call me immediately."

"Yes, sir."

"I hope you had a pleasant joyride through the countryside?"

"Colonel, I need to talk to you."

"Odd, when I called before, I needed to talk to you."

"Yes, sir."

"Among other things, I was curious how your flying lesson went."

"I think it went well, sir."

"And then I can hope that sometime in the near future, we may look forward to having our own aerial taxi service?"

"Yes, sir."

"Can you give me an idea, just a ballpark estimate, of when that might be? In, say, two weeks?"

"Sir, the planes are at the monastery."

"Excuse me?"

"Sir, I have the planes here now."

"How did they get there?"

"I flew one of them and Schröder flew the other."

"I don't believe I know anyone by that name."

"He and three mechanics came with the planes, sir."

"Are you telling me you flew a German national to the monastery?"

"I wanted to run him past the general, sir. The general vouched for him. They were in the war together."

"I'm tempted to say, 'Well done,' but I'm afraid of the other shoe that's sure to drop."

"We have the planes, sir. No problem. Tiny is on his way to Sonthofen to pick up the mechanics and the spare parts."

"With great reluctance, I am going to give you the benefit of the doubt. My friend said it would probably take six or eight hours for him to properly instruct you. I'm finding it hard to understand how."

"What he did, Colonel, was take me up, and put it into a stall and took his hands off the stick. When I recovered from it, I guess I passed his test."

"I have no idea what you're talking about, Captain Cronley. But if you have the airplanes . . ."

"I have them, sir."

"What's on your mind?"

"Our guest, sir."

"What guest is that?"

"The one Sergeant Tedworth brought home."

"I told Sergeant Dunwiddie to deal with that. Didn't he tell you?"

"That's what I want to talk to you about, sir."

There was a significant pause before Mattingly replied.

"Yeah," he said, finally and thoughtfully slow. "I think we should have — have to have — a little chat about that situation. And similar ones that will probably crop up in the future."

Mattingly paused again, then continued,

159

now speaking more quickly, as if he had collected his thoughts.

"What I'll do, Cronley, is ask my friend if he can fly me into there for an hour or two. Him personally. We don't want any of his pilots talking about monasteries, do we? Which means he'll have to fit me into his schedule, which in turn means it's likely going to be a day or two before we can have our chat."

"Or I could fly into Eschborn first thing in the morning," Cronley said.

"Eschborn?"

"Isn't that the name of that little strip near the Schlosshotel Kronberg?"

The Schlosshotel Kronberg in Taunus, twenty miles from Frankfurt, was now a country club and hotel for senior officers. It had been, before the demise of the OSS, home to Colonel Mattingly's OSS Forward command.

It was there that Second Lieutenant Cronley had been drafted into the OSS. At the time, he had been the newest, least qualified and thus least important agent in the XXIInd CIC Detachment in the university town of Marburg an der Lahn. His sole qualification for the CIC had been his fluent German. His sole qualification for the

160

OSS, aside from his fluency in German, had been that it had come out that his father had served in World War I with OSS Director Major General William J. Donovan, who had told Mattingly he remembered Cronley to be a "nice, smart kid."

Mattingly had frankly told Cronley that his being taken into the OSS was less nepotism than a critical shortage of personnel. There were few officers left to scrape from the bottom of the barrel for OSS service — the war was over and the wartime officers had gone home — and an officer was needed for a unique position Mattingly had to fill that would require no qualifications beyond his second lieutenant's gold bar, his Top Secret security clearance, and the color of his skin.

Major General Reinhard Gehlen and what had been Abwehr Ost were being hidden from the Soviets in a former monastery — Kloster Grünau. They were being guarded by a reinforced company of 2nd Armored Division soldiers. They were all Negroes. They had no commanding officer, and one was needed. There were no Negro officers in the "intelligence pool" who spoke German, and the white officers in the pool who did were needed for more important duties.

At the time, Cronley thought that he was

about to spend the foreseeable future in the middle of nowhere as the cushion between 256 black soldiers and about that many German intelligence officers and non-coms. The one thing he could be sure of, he had thought, was that for the rest of his military service — he was obligated to serve four years — he would be doing something even less exciting than washing mud off the tracks of tanks in a motor pool somewhere.

He had quickly learned how wrong his prediction was.

"You would feel safe flying a Storch there?" Mattingly asked.

"Yes, sir. No problem."

"I seem to recall hearing my friend say that 'there are old pilots and bold pilots, but no old bold pilots.' "

"I'm a young, very cautious pilot, sir. I can get into Eschborn with no trouble."

"Okay. I'll meet you at Eschborn at half past eleven tomorrow morning. Come as a civilian."

"Yes, sir."

[Five]

When Cronley went from his quarters to the senior officers' dining room, he saw that only one place was set at the table. Dunwiddie was on his way to Sonthofen, which meant he wouldn't be here for supper. No plates for Gehlen and Mannberg meant they had already eaten.

Without waiting for me, and thus expressing — without coming right out and saying anything — their displeasure with me for countermanding Bischoff's order about not changing Orlovsky's shit bucket.

And probably conferring on how they can tactfully remind Major Wallace and Colonel Mattingly of my youth and inexperience in the hope he will tell me to pay attention to my elders.

Well, fuck both of them!

Cronley went into the bar, found the *Stars and Stripes* where Mannberg had left it earlier, went back into the dining room, and ate alone. He refused the offer of a drink, or a beer, as he would be flying first thing in the morning.

The mess was run by Tiny's mess sergeant and two of his assistants. Tiny's mess sergeant supervised — declared — the menu, and his two sergeants drew the rations from the Quartermaster, divided them between what would be eaten in the two messes, and those to be given to the families of Gehlen's men.

Gehlen's men did the actual cooking and

163

all the other work connected with the two messes and the NCO club, including the bartending.

The only news that Cronley found interesting in *Stars and Stripes* as he read it over his grilled pork chops, applesauce, mashed potatoes, and green beans was that the PX was about to hold a raffle, the winners of which would be entitled to purchase jeeps for $380. The vehicles, the story said, had been run through a rebuild program at the Griesheim ordnance depot and would be "as new."

The first thing Cronley thought was that he would enter the raffle. A jeep would be nice to have on the ranch outside Midland, if he could figure a way to get one from Germany to Texas.

That thought was immediately followed by his realization that he was never going back to the ranch in Midland.

Not after what happened to the Squirt . . .

He realized he had to put the Squirt, the jeep, and Midland out of his mind.

The first thing he thought next was that while he knew he had seen a chart case in Storch Two, which meant there was probably also one in Storch One, he hadn't actually seen a chart, and a chart would be a damned good thing to have when trying to fly to Eschborn.

The first time he'd flown into Sonthofen he had made a straight-in approach on a heading of 270, the course Colonel Wilson had ordered him to fly. The first time he'd flown back to Kloster Grünau, he'd had Schröder with him, and since that was before Schröder had been vetted by General Gehlen and he hadn't wanted Schröder to know where they were going, Cronley simply had taken off and set a course of 90 degrees, the reciprocal of 270, and flown that until he saw Schollbrunn ahead of him. He knew where Kloster Grünau was from there. On his second flight from Sonthofen, he'd done the same thing; the second time it was easier.

Flying to Eschborn is not going to be so simple. I am going to need a chart of the route showing, among other things, the available en-route navigation aids and the Eschborn tower frequencies so I can call and get approach and landing instructions.

Come to think of it, I have never seen an Air Corps chart.

Are there Air Corps charts and Army charts? Or does the Army use Air Corps charts? And what's the difference, if any, between military charts and the civilian ones I know?

Jesus, am I going to have to call Mattingly

back and tell him that on second thought I've decided to put off flying into Eschborn until I think I know what I'm doing?

He got up quickly from the table and walked out of the room and then the building. He saw one of the machine gun jeeps making its rounds and flagged it down.

"Take me to the Storches," he ordered.

"The what, sir?" the sergeant driving asked as the corporal who had been in the front seat scurried into the back.

"The airplanes," Cronley clarified.

Getting to the map cases in the airplane turned out to be a pain in the ass. The troopers had done a good job putting them under tarpaulins so they would be less visible from the air. Untying the tarpaulins so that he could get under them was difficult in the dark, and once he got to the chart case and looked inside, he knew that he would not be able to examine what it contained in the light of his flashlight. Sticking the nose of the jeep under the tarpaulin to use the jeep's headlights proved to be difficult and then ineffective.

Finally, he stuffed the charts back into the case, removed it from the Storch's cockpit, and made his way out from under the tarpaulin.

"You want us to take the tarpaulin all the

166

way off, Captain?"

"No, thanks. Just take me back to the mess."

"Yes, sir."

"No. Take me to the chapel," he said. He thought: *So I can see if they changed the shit bucket in Orlovsky's cell, or whether Bischoff told them to ignore me.*

Bischoff and the small, tough sergeant who had been in the room behind the altar were again sitting at the card table, playing poker with packs of cigarettes and Hershey bars for chips. There were two others at the table, both soldiers, neither of whom Cronley had seen.

The sergeant stood.

He nodded politely and said, "Captain."

"What does it smell like down there?" Cronley asked.

"Well, Captain, it don't smell like roses," the sergeant said. "But it smells better . . . scratch that. It don't smell near as bad as it did."

"Show me," Cronley said, and then added, "We won't need you down there, Herr Bischoff."

Major Konstantin Orlovsky of the Peoples Commissariat for Internal Affairs reacted to the opening of his cell door as he had the first time. Shielding his eyes from the headlights, he slid his back up the wall until he was standing.

"Take the light out of his eyes," Cronley ordered, and then, "If you can, turn all but one of those headlights off."

"I'll have to rip them loose," the sergeant said.

"Then do it."

"Yes, sir."

"Everybody out of here but you and me, Sergeant, and then close the door."

"Sir?"

"You heard me."

"Yes, sir."

"Thank you," Orlovsky said.

Cronley didn't reply.

When the door had creaked closed behind them, Cronley looked at the sergeant.

"I'm sorry, I don't know your name."

"Staff Sergeant Lewis, Harold Junior, Captain."

"If I hear that you have repeated to anyone but First Sergeant Dunwiddie one word of what I'm about to say in here, Staff Sergeant Harold Lewis Junior, you will be Private Lewis, washing pots and pans for the Germans in the kitchen until I decide whether or not to castrate you with a dull bayonet before I send you home in a body bag. You understand me?"

"Yes, sir, Captain."

"Okay. Now the question, Major Orlovsky, is, 'What do I do with you?' "

Orlovsky didn't reply.

"What the Germans want from you are the names of the people here who gave you those rosters Sergeant Tedworth took away from you. Once you give them the names, you'll all be . . . disposed of."

"That's the scenario I reached, Captain Cronley."

"It doesn't seem to worry you very much."

"Are you familiar with Roman poet Ovid, Captain?"

"I can't say that I am. I'm just a simple cowboy. We don't know much about Roman poets — for that matter, about any poets — in West Texas."

Orlovsky smiled.

"Ovid wrote, 'Happy is the man who has broken the chains which hurt the mind, and has given up worrying once and for all.' "

"Which means what? That you're happy to be locked up in the dark, waiting to be shot?"

"Which means that my only worry is that I will be subjected to a painful interrogation — for you a useless interrogation — before

I am shot. That I will be shot is a given."

"Why useless? And why is you being shot a given?"

"So far as your first question is concerned, since I know I'm to be shot, why should I give you those names? And how could you be sure, if I gave you a name, or names, that they would be the names of the people you want? As to the second, what alternative do you have to eliminating me? You can't free me, and you can't keep me here for long."

Cronley didn't reply. He instead asked, "Where'd you learn your English?"

"In university. Leningrad State University. Why do you ask?"

"You speak it very well. I was curious."

"And you speak German very well," Orlovsky said, his tone making it a question.

"My mother taught me — she's German. I'll tell you what, Major: You think some more. Think of some way that you can give me the names I want in exchange for your life. And I'll do the same. Maybe we can make a deal."

"Why should I believe you have the authority to 'make a deal'?"

"Because I'm telling you I do."

"And what would Major Bischoff have to say about you making a deal?"

"I don't know, and I don't care. The Germans lost the war. I'm the honcho here. 'Honcho' is West Texas talk for 'the man in charge.' "

"That's a good deal of authority for a simple West Texas cowboy to have. Why should I believe you?"

"I don't see where you have another option."

He nodded at Orlovsky and turned to Staff Sergeant Lewis.

"I'm going, Sergeant. Bring people in here and make absolutely sure Major Orlovsky doesn't have the means to pull the plug on himself."

"Bischoff already thought of that, Captain."

"Look again. And keep Bischoff out of here."

"Yes, sir."

"Good night, Major Orlovsky. We'll talk again."

"Good evening, Captain Cronley."

[Six]

When he had taken the chart case to his room and laid its contents out on his desk, Cronley quickly saw that Army Aviators used Air Force aerial charts, and that Air Force charts were essentially identical to

171

the civilian charts with which he was familiar.

The case also contained a "knee-pad" — a clipboard onto which a chart could be fitted under a sheet of plastic. It had a spring clip on its underside so the board could be clipped to his pant leg — and not fall off — in flight.

He spent the better part of an hour planning his flight to Eschborn, using a grease pencil to write the critical data on the plastic over the chart, and then very carefully checking everything twice.

Then he took a shower and went to bed.

He went to sleep wondering what to think of his last conversation with Orlovsky. Was he really so resigned to being shot? Or was it a case of a skilled NKGB officer being able to use that to put a young and inexperienced officer in his pocket?

That raised the question of why he was putting his nose into something that could be — and more than likely should be — handled by Gehlen, Mannberg, and Bischoff without his interference.

The Squirt was lying asleep on her side on the couch along the right side of the Beech Model 18's cabin. She was wearing Western boots with a skirt that had come pretty high up as she moved in her sleep.

Jimmy had always found boots on girls in skirts very erotic.

He dropped to his knees and touched the Squirt's face tenderly with his fingertips.

Her eyes opened.

"What are you doing back here and not flying?" she said.

"I have designs on your virginal body."

"Not so virginal anymore, thanks to you. Who's flying the plane?"

"We're at ten thousand feet over Midland making five-minute circles on autopilot."

"You're crazy."

"I'm horny, is what I am."

She sighed. "Me too, now."

They kissed.

He put his hand up her skirt.

She put her hand to the front of his trousers.

"Well, look what I found!" the Squirt said, smiling.

"Shit! Shit! Shit!" he said furiously as he awoke.

And then he wailed, "Oh, God!" in anguish.

And then he wept.

For a long time.

And then he went to sleep again.

173

IV

[One]

Kloster Grünau
Schollbrunn, Bavaria
American Zone of Occupation, Germany

0715 30 October 1945

First Sergeant Chauncey L. Dunwiddie, easily holding two large china mugs in his massive left hand, knocked at the door to Captain James D. Cronley Jr.'s bedroom with the knuckles of his right fist.

"Come!"

Cronley was sitting on his bed, pulling on his pointed-toe boots.

"Coffee?" Dunwiddie asked.

"Oh, yeah. *Danke schön.*"

Dunwiddie handed him a mug.

"You all right, Jim?"

"Why do I think you have a reason for asking beyond a first sergeant's to-be-expected concern for his beloved commanding officer?"

Dunwiddie hesitated momentarily, then said, "I've been wrong before. But when I got back at oh-dark-hundred and walked past your room, I thought I heard you crying in your sleep. I almost came in then, but my back teeth were floating, so I took a leak.

174

When I came back, you'd stopped."

Cronley hesitated momentarily, too, before replying.

"I wasn't crying in my sleep. I was wide awake. I had what is politely called 'a nocturnal emission.' I started crying when I woke up and realized that wet dream — and every goddamned thing associated with it — was never going to come true."

Dunwiddie didn't reply.

"Am I losing my mind, Tiny?"

Dunwiddie hesitated again before replying, and when he did it wasn't a reply, but a question. He pointed at the chart case. "What's that?"

"That's an aviation chart case. Experienced pilots such as myself use them to carry maps — aviation navigation charts — around."

"You're going somewhere?"

"Eschborn. As soon as I have breakfast."

"Mattingly sent for you?"

"I told him I needed to talk to him."

"You going to tell me what about?"

"Orlovsky."

"He told me to deal with Orlovsky, Jim."

"That's what I want to talk to him about."

"I heard you went to see our Russian friend. Twice."

"Sergeant Lewis told you?"

"Sergeant Lewis waited until I got back from Sonthofen to tell me."

"I gather he didn't approve?"

"Actually, he began the conversation by saying, 'You know, our baby-faced captain isn't really a candy-ass. He told Bischoff to fuck off, and then he told me if I told anybody but you what he said to Orlovsky he'd cut off my dick with a dull bayonet.' Or words to that effect."

"That's close enough."

"Mattingly doesn't want to know what Gehlen does with the Russian. That's why he told me to deal with it."

"And you're happy with that?"

"Do I have to point out that first sergeants — and brand-new captains — do not question what full bull colonels tell them to do?"

"Do first sergeants question their orders from brand-new captains?"

Dunwiddie didn't reply.

"Let's try one and see. Sergeant, if the prisoner Bischoff attempts to talk to Major Orlovsky, you will place him under arrest."

"You're crazy, Jim. He'll go right to General Gehlen —"

"I'm not finished," Cronley interrupted. "You will immediately assign enough of our men to protect Major Orlovsky around the clock from any attempt by any of the Germans to kill him. The use of deadly force is authorized to protect Major Orlovsky. The foregoing is a direct order."

"Jesus, Jim!"

"The answer I expect from you, Sergeant, is 'Yes, sir.' "

Dunwiddie looked at Cronley for ten seconds before coming to attention and saying, "Yes, sir."

"Thank you."

"Permission to speak, sir?"

"Granted."

"Mattingly is not going to like this."

"Probably not. On the other hand, I don't like the way he's trying to cover his ass about the Russian. If he wants to let the Germans shoot him — or, for that matter, torture him — I don't know right now what I can do about that. But I do know I'm not going to let him get away with saying, 'I didn't know anything about what happens at Kloster Grünau,' and then blame whatever happens on you and me."

"You really think that's what Mattingly is doing?"

"It may not have started out that way, but yeah, I think I damned well *know* — that's what he's doing. He considers you and me expendable, Tiny."

"Operation Ost is really important, Jim."

"So important that Mattingly is perfectly willing to throw you and me to the hungry lions to keep it going. That's the point. But I'm not willing to be fed to the lions."

"You realize the spot you're putting me in?"

"Are you going to obey the direct order I gave you?"

"You heard me say 'Yes, sir.' "

"Then you're off the spot. I just moved onto it."

Dunwiddie threw up his hands in resignation.

"Let's go get some breakfast," Cronley said.

[Two]

U.S. Army Airfield H-7
Eschborn, Hesse
American Zone of Occupation, Germany

1120 30 October 1945

"Eschborn, Seven-Oh-Seven understands Number Two to land on Niner-zero behind the C-47," Cronley said into the microphone.

He looked at his wristwatch and saw that he was ten minutes early.

A minute later, he saw that Colonel Robert Mattingly was also ten minutes early; he

178

was leaning against the front fender of his Horch, which was parked next to what had to be Base Operations.

Did he come early to be a nice guy?

Or has Gehlen called him and complained about my behavior — and he can't wait to put me in my place?

A minute after that, the Storch was on the ground. A *Follow me* jeep led it to the visitors' tarmac in front of Base Operations.

As he was shutting down the Storch, Mattingly walked up to the airplane and waited for him to climb down from it.

He smiled and offered his hand.

"Right on time, Jim. Ready to go?"

I guess Gehlen did not complain.

"Sir, I have to see about getting it fueled, and I want to check the weather." He pointed to the Base Operations building. "It won't take a minute."

"Fine," Mattingly said with a smile, but Cronley sensed he was annoyed.

There were two signs over the Flight Briefing Room. One read FLIGHT PLANNING/WEATHER. The other read PILOTS ONLY.

Mattingly nevertheless followed Cronley into the room.

Why not? Full bull colonels get to go just about anyplace they want to.

179

Cronley studied the weather map, and then caught the eye of an Air Force sergeant.

"It doesn't look good for the south this afternoon, does it?"

"Not good unless you're a penguin. Penguins don't fly."

"When do you think that front will move through southern Bavaria?"

"Very late this afternoon."

"You think it will be clear in the morning?"

"Probably."

"Who do I have to see to get fuel?"

"Me," the sergeant said, and produced a clipboard with a form on it. "Name, organization, type of aircraft, tail number, and fuel designation. And signature."

Cronley filled in the blanks and the sergeant examined the form.

"Twenty-third CIC, huh?" the sergeant said, pronouncing it "Ex Ex Eye Eye Eye See Eye See."

"Guilty," Cronley said.

"And what the hell is a Fieseler Storch?"

Cronley pointed out the window.

"Funny-looking," the sergeant opined.

"It flies that way, too."

"Kraut?"

"Not anymore."

"I'll have your tanks topped off in half an hour."

"No rush. I'm not going to fly into that weather. I'll try to get out in the morning. Thanks."

"You're welcome."

Cronley looked at Colonel Mattingly and gestured toward the door.

When they were out of the building, Mattingly said, "I gather you have to spend the night?"

"Yes, sir. There's a front moving across Bavaria that I don't think I should fly into."

"I defer, of course, to your airman's judgment. But what I had in mind was that I don't like leaving that airplane here overnight. Questions might be asked."

"What would you like me to do, sir?"

"Well, if you can't control something, don't worry about it. You might wish to write that down."

He saw Cronley smile. "Did I say something funny, Captain?"

"No, sir. But that's a paraphrase of what Major Orlovsky said to me. He quoted a Roman poet named Ovid. 'Happy is the man who has given up worrying.' Something like that."

"You've been discussing Roman poets with an NKGB officer?" Mattingly asked incredulously.

"It came out during my interrogation of him, sir."

"*Your* interrogation of him?" Mattingly asked even more incredulously.

"Yes, sir."

They were now at the Horch.

"Get in," Mattingly ordered.

"Sir, where am I going to stay tonight?"

When Mattingly didn't immediately reply, Cronley said, "I've got an overnight bag in the plane. Should I get it now?"

"Get your bag," Mattingly ordered.

Immediately after they had left the airfield, Mattingly explained what was going to happen.

"We're going to the Schlosshotel, which is now a field grade officers' facility. We're going to get you a room. After lunch, we will have our little chat in the privacy of that room. Following that, I will go back to my office, and you will stay in the room, leaving it only for supper and breakfast. You will not, in other words, take advantage of the golf club, nor whoop it up tonight in the bar. Got it?"

"Yes, sir."

"I will arrange for a car to take you from the hotel to the airport after you've had your

182

breakfast."

"Yes, sir."

"The fewer people who see you in the hotel, the better. Questions would be asked. Understand?"

"Yes, sir."

[Three]

Schlosshotel Kronberg
Kronberg im Taunus, Hesse
American Zone of Occupation, Germany

1150 30 October 1945

Mattingly and Cronley had taken perhaps ten steps into the lobby when they were intercepted by an attractive American woman. Cronley noted that she had a shapely figure, a full head of black hair, and appeared to be in her early thirties.

"Well, I didn't expect to see you here, Colonel," she said. "But you're very welcome!"

"Mrs. Schumann," Mattingly said, turning on the charm. "What an unexpected pleasure."

"And have you brought us a newly arrived?"

"Excuse me?"

"Well, he's wearing the triangles," she said. "And he doesn't look old enough to

183

be a major. And he's with you. So I have leapt to the conclusion that he's one of us."

"Mrs. Schumann, this is Special Agent Cronley."

She offered Cronley her hand. He took it. She didn't let go.

"I've so wanted to meet you," she said.

"Excuse me?" Cronley said.

"You are the young man who shot the engine out of my husband's car, right?"

"He told you about that?" Mattingly blurted.

"Well, Tony is pretty sure I'm neither a Nazi nor a member of the NKGB, and we *are* married. So why not?"

Mattingly gathered his thoughts.

"Well, are you or aren't you?" she pursued, still hanging on to his hand and looking into Cronley's eyes.

He thought she had very sad eyes, not consistent with her bubbly personality.

"There was a misunderstanding," Cronley said.

"About which the less said, the better," Mattingly said.

"My lips are sealed," she said, letting loose of Cronley's hand so that she could cover her mouth with it.

"Is Colonel Schumann here?" Mattingly asked. "And what's going on here?"

"He arranged to be in Vienna so he wouldn't have to be here," she said, and then pointed toward the entrance to the main dining room.

Cronley followed her gesture. He saw a brigadier general walking toward them. And then read a sign mounted on a tripod:

**CIC/ASA WELCOME TO EUCOM
LUNCHEON
MAIN DINING ROOM
1200 30 OCTOBER 1945**

"Shit," Colonel Mattingly said under his breath, and then he said, "Good afternoon, General."

"Rachel," the general said, "may I say how lovely you look?"

And how very sad, Cronley thought. *I wonder what that's about?*

And who's the general?

"Colonel," the general said, "I'm more than a little surprised to see you here."

"Truth to tell, sir, I forgot about the luncheon. I'm here on other business."

"Really?"

The general put out his hand to Cronley.

"I don't believe we've met. I'm General Greene."

"General, this is Captain Cronley," Mat-

185

tingly said.

"I thought it might be. I've heard a good deal about you, Captain."

"How do you do, sir?"

A captain wearing the aiguillette and lapel insignia of an aide-de-camp walked up to them.

"I think, Jack," General Greene said, "that you know everybody but Captain Cronley."

"Yes, sir," the captain said. "Ma'am, Colonel." He put out his hand to Cronley and said "Captain" as he examined him very carefully.

"Colonel Mattingly has brought Captain Cronley as his newly arrived," General Greene said. "So, what you're going to have to do, Jack, is rearrange the head table so there's a place for them."

"General," Mattingly said, "as I said, Captain Cronley and I are here on business —"

"So you said," Greene interrupted. "But you have to eat, and if you eat with us, all the newly arrived will get to see the deputy commander of EUCOM CIC sitting right up there beside the president of the CIC Officers' Ladies Club at the head table, won't they?"

"Yes, sir," Mattingly said.

This general is sticking it to Mattingly.

Ordinarily, I'd be delighted, but Mattingly is already pissed at me, and this is likely to make that worse.

"And we wouldn't want to deny the newly arrived that, would we?" Greene went on. "So, Jack, you rearrange the head table while Mrs. Schumann, Colonel Mattingly, Captain Cronley, and I slip into the bar for a little liquid courage. When everything's set up, you come fetch us, and we'll make our triumphant entry."

"Yes, sir," the aide-de-camp said.

"How may I serve the general?" the German bartender asked, in British-accented English.

"Well, since Colonel Mattingly has so graciously asked us to join him for a little nip, I'll have a taste of your best scotch, straight, water on the side. Better make it a double."

This Greene is really sticking it to Mattingly. And enjoying it.

"Yes, sir. And you, madam?"

"I'll have a martini, please," Mrs. Schumann said.

"As before, madam? Vodka, no vegetables?"

A vodka martini, no vegetables? "As before"?

187

Lady, you don't look like somebody who drinks vodka martinis, no vegetables, before lunch.

"Precisely." She smiled.

"Colonel?"

"Scotch, please," Mattingly said.

"Sir?" he asked Cronley.

"Jack Daniel's, please. On the rocks."

Their drinks were quickly served.

"I'd like to offer a toast," General Greene said. "To our happy little CIC community."

"Not to forget the ASA," Mrs. Schumann added, as she raised her glass.

"To our happy little CIC and ASA community," Mattingly toasted with no visible enthusiasm.

Yeah, the ASA, Cronley thought as they all sipped drinks.

Kloster Grünau and that station in Berlin are connected to the Vint Hill Farms ASA station in Virginia. Certainly the ASA here must also be connected. Does that mean then that the ASA here can read our encrypted traffic?

More important, why hasn't Mattingly told me whether or not they can?

Which leads me to wonder what else I should know he hasn't told me.

Mrs. Schumann's leg brushed against his, and he quickly moved his out of her way.

"Can I ask what this luncheon is about?"

Cronley asked.

"The CIC/ASA Officers' Ladies Club . . ." Mrs. Schumann began, turning to him on her swiveling bar stool. Cronley was standing, so when she swiveled toward him, her knee grazed his crotch.

"Of which Rachel, Mrs. Schumann, is the very capable president," General Greene furnished.

". . . has a 'Welcome Newly Arrived' luncheon every month . . ." she went on.

Cronley pulled back his crotch, which caused her knee to move off his crotch as far as the inside of his left knee, against which it now lightly pressed.

That has to be innocent.

The bartender saying "as before" may mean this is her second martini — or her fourth.

She's a little plastered — that would go along with those sad eyes — and doesn't realize what she's doing.

". . . to which all newly arrived CIC and ASA personnel," Mrs. Schumann continued, "and their dependents are invited. The idea is to welcome them, let them meet General Greene and Major McClung — he runs ASA EUCOM — and tell them what they can expect during their tour of duty in the Army of Occupation."

She took a sip of her martini, then turned

189

and set the glass on the bar. Her knee moved off his.

"You didn't come to yours, Cronley?" General Greene asked.

"No, sir. This is the first I've heard of it."

What actually happened, General, was that when I joined the happy little EUCOM CIC community, the XXIInd CIC Detachment in Marburg, the executive officer thereof, Major John Connell, welcomed me by inquiring of my qualifications to be a CIC agent, and then said, "Well, we'll find something for you to do where you can cause only minimal damage."

"Well, pay attention when we get in there. It's never too late to learn, wouldn't you agree?"

"Yes, sir."

General Greene's aide-de-camp appeared moments later to announce, "They're ready for you, Mrs. Schumann, and the colonel, sir. The captain?"

"Show Cronley where he's to sit at the head table."

"Yes, sir."

Cronley examined his drink, took another sip, then put the still-half-full glass on the bar. Mrs. Schumann put her martini glass on the bar, but only after drinking it dry. She then steadied herself to get off her bar stool by holding on to Cronley's arm.

[Four]

1210 30 October 1945

General Greene's aide installed Cronley in a chair near the center of the head table. He sat alone. Everybody else in the dining room was lining up across the room passing through the reception line. There were a dozen people in it, lined up apparently by rank. The first three people were Mrs. Schumann, General Greene, and Colonel Mattingly. Next was a large mustachioed major wearing the crossed semaphore flags insignia of the Signal Corps. Cronley decided he was probably Major McClung of the Army Security Agency.

A waiter in a crisp white jacket appeared and asked if the captain would like a drink.

"Jack Daniel's, *danke,*" Cronley answered, and then wondered if that had been smart.

I'm going to have to deal with Mattingly when this happy CIC/ASA community bullshit is over. And the way to do that is stone sober.

The drink was delivered as two officers made their way to their seats at the head table. They were both majors, and he saw from their lapel insignia — a silver cross and a golden six-pointed star — that they were both chaplains.

I knew the Army had them, but that's the first Jewish chaplain I've ever actually seen.

And why not a Jewish chaplain? There's a hell of a lot of Jews in our happy little CIC/ ASA community.

The Christian chaplain looked askance at Cronley's whisky glass.

Why do I suspect you're Baptist, Chaplain?

Even though he had very carefully nursed his Jack Daniel's, the glass was empty before all the handshaking was over and everybody came to take their seats at the head table.

Mrs. Schumann took her seat beside him, steadying herself as she did so by resting her hand high on his shoulder.

He smiled politely at her.

"Did anyone ever tell you that you have very sad eyes?" she asked.

"I wondered the same thing about you," he blurted.

And that's the last of the Jack Daniel's.

"Maybe we have something in common," she said.

He smiled politely at her.

"Major McClung," a voice boomed in his ear. He saw the mustachioed Signal Corps officer sitting next to him with his hand extended. "They call me 'Iron Lung.' "

"Jim Cronley, Major."

"Mattingly's man, right?" McClung boomed.

Cronley nodded.

He looked down the table and saw Mattingly sitting at the far side of General Greene.

He felt Mrs. Schumann's knee press against his.

The waiter appeared and placed drinks in front of the senior officers. And one in front of Cronley.

Well, I just won't drink it.

General Greene stood up, tapped his scotch glass with a knife, and announced, "Chaplain Stanton will give the invocation."

The Christian chaplain stood up, looked around impatiently, and then intoned, "Please rise!"

Everyone stood.

The invocation went on for some time. It dealt primarily with resisting temptation. Finally, he invoked the blessing of the Deity and sat down, and everyone did the same.

Mrs. Schumann leaned toward Cronley and whispered, "I thought he was never going to stop."

When she leaned away from him and shifted on her chair, her hand dropped into his lap. She found his male appendage and took a firm grip on it.

Holy Christ! Now what?

After a moment, and a final squeeze, she turned it loose.

He recalled the advice of a tactical officer at A&M. During a lecture on the conduct to be expected of an officer and a gentleman, he had cautioned the class about becoming involved with a senior officer's wife.

"It don't matter if she jumps on you and sticks her tongue down your throat. Keep your pecker in your pocket. It's like having a drunk guy on a motorcycle run into you when you're doing thirty-five in a fifty-five-mile-per-hour zone. Right and wrong don't matter. You're at fault."

He looked at Mrs. Schumann. She smiled and gave him a little wink.

He smiled back as well as he could manage.

He spent the rest of the meal with his legs crossed, sitting as close to Major Iron Lung McClung as he could, and not looking at Mrs. Schumann.

She made no further attempt to grope him until the affair was about to adjourn for farewell cocktails, and Mattingly came to stand behind him.

"I'm sorry I have to take you away from all this fun, Captain Cronley," Mattingly said. "But we still have our business to take care of."

"Yes, sir," Cronley said, and stood.

So did Mrs. Schumann.

"It was very nice to meet you, Captain Cronley," she said. "Perhaps we'll see one another again."

"Yes, ma'am."

She offered her right hand and quickly groped him with the left.

"My husband will be fascinated to hear I've met you."

[Five]

1310 30 October 1945

When the Army had requisitioned the Schlosshotel Kronberg to house OSS Forward, the German staff had come with it. Now, the hotel manager greeted the former commander of OSS Forward warmly.

Thus, Cronley was not surprised when, despite the inhospitable sign — THIS IS A FIELD GRADE OFFICERS' FACILITY — behind the marble reception desk, the smiling manager assured Mattingly that he would be happy to accommodate Captain Cronley and arrange for a staff car to take the captain to the Eschborn airstrip in the morning.

The room that the manager assigned Cronley was one of the better ones. A small suite, it was on the ground floor. French doors opened onto a flagstone patio overlooking the golf course.

In the sitting room, Mattingly waved Cronley into an armchair. He took the one opposite it, leaned forward, and waved his hand in the general direction of the main dining room.

"I'm sorry about all that. If I ever knew about that damned newly arrived luncheon, I forgot about it."

"Well, it gave General Greene a chance to stick it to you, didn't it?"

Mattingly's face tightened.

"You do have a flair for saying things you really shouldn't, don't you, Jim?"

"Sir, no disrespect was intended. But it was pretty obvious the general was sticking it to you. And liked it."

Mattingly considered that for a moment.

"Okay. That's as good a point to start as any. Did you wonder why General Greene was enjoying, to use your colorful phrase, sticking it to me?"

"Yes, sir. I did."

"I was assigned as his deputy commander over his objections. I didn't have the opportunity, the authority, to tell him why

196

until Admiral Souers gave me the authority when we were in Washington. I told Admiral Souers that I had to tell him, so that he could get Colonel Schumann off our backs. Greene has known about Operation Ost and what's going on at Kloster Grünau only since I told him the day we got back.

"Greene didn't like being kept in the dark. That's understandable. But now Schumann has been told to back off."

"He was told about Operation Ost?"

"Of course not. Greene just told him that Kloster Grünau is off-limits to him, and to forget about you, and you shooting up the engine in his car. With him in it."

"He apparently told Mrs. Schumann."

"They call that 'pillow talk.' It happens. I can only hope that Schumann told his wife not to spread it amongst the girls of the CIC/ASA Officers' Ladies Club."

"Do you think he did?"

"Probably. Tony Schumann is a good officer. But he's also Jewish, which means that he won't stop looking into the rumors that somebody is getting Nazis out of Germany to Argentina, and wondering if what's going on at Kloster Grünau has something to do with that."

"Jesus!"

"And General Greene knows what I'm

probably thinking about in that connection. So, yeah, he found it amusing that I showed up, with you in tow, at that CIC/ASA Officers' Ladies Club Welcome Newly Arriveds luncheon, to be met by Mrs. Schumann.

"In a way, it was amusing. But it could have turned out the other way. She could very easily have not been as charming to you as she was. Some wives might be offended that a young officer had shot out the engine of their husband's car and act accordingly. You follow me?"

"Yes, sir."

"She could have asked, 'I'm curious why, Colonel Mattingly, after Captain Cronley fired a machine gun at my husband, he's here and not in the EUCOM stockade awaiting court-martial?' "

I wonder why she didn't?

Maybe Colonel and Mrs. Schumann aren't the happy couple everyone thinks they are.

Happily married women don't usually drink four martinis before lunch and then grope officers under the table.

"As you suggested, sir, Colonel Schumann probably told her not to ask questions about what happened at Kloster Grünau."

"What I'm worried about, Jim, is that you don't fully understand (a) the absolute necessity of maintaining the security of

Operation Ost, and, more important, (b) that you're in a position where a careless act of yours can cause more trouble in that regard than you fully understand."

Here it comes.

"I must respectfully argue, sir, that I fully understand both."

"Then what the hell did you think you were doing when you interrogated the NKGB agent? I told Dunwiddie to deal with that situation."

When Cronley didn't immediately reply, Mattingly went on, "Cat got your tongue, Captain? I'm surprised. You usually have an answer for everything at the tip of your tongue."

"I have an answer, sir, but I suspect you're not going to like it."

"Let's find out."

"For one thing, sir, Major Orlovsky is my prisoner, not General Gehlen's."

"Your prisoner?"

"And I didn't like the way he was being treated by Gehlen's man, Bischoff."

"What do you mean *your* prisoner?"

"Sir, Orlovsky was arrested trying to sneak out of Kloster Grünau by one of my men. Doesn't that make him my prisoner?"

"I am beginning to see where you're coming from," Mattingly said after a moment.

"So tell me, Captain Cronley: What are your plans for your prisoner? What are you going to do with him?"

"I haven't quite figured that out, sir."

"Has it occurred to you that he may have to be disposed of?"

"If you mean shot, yes, sir."

"And, that being the case, it would be much better if he was disposed of by someone other than an American officer?"

"If Major Orlovsky has to be shot, sir, I'll do it. I'm not willing to turn that — or Major Orlovsky — over to Gehlen."

"It didn't take long for those new captain's bars to go to your head, did it?" Mattingly said furiously. "Just who the hell do you think you are?"

"I'm the officer you put in charge of security of Operation Ost, sir."

"Captain, I am the officer in charge of security for Operation Ost."

"Sir, that's not my understanding."

"What is your understanding, you impertinent sonofabitch?"

"That you, sir, are in charge of the European functions of Operation Ost, that Lieutenant Colonel Frade is in charge of the Argentine functions, that the whole thing is under Admiral Souers, and that, far down on the Table of Organization, I'm in charge of security for European functions under you."

"And would you say that gives me the authority to tell you what to do and how to do it?"

"So long as your orders are lawful, sir."

"Meaning what?"

"That I don't think you have the authority to grant authority to Gehlen to take prisoners, to interrogate prisoners, and certainly not to shoot them."

"Maybe you do belong in the EUCOM stockade. For disobedience to my orders to you to let Sergeant Dunwiddie deal with the NKGB problem."

"If you put me in the stockade, sir . . ." Cronley began, then hesitated.

"Finish what you started to say," Mattingly ordered coldly.

". . . or if I should drop out of contact for more than a day or two . . . or should something happen to me, Colonel Frade would want, would demand, an explanation."

"You've got it all figured out, haven't you? God damn you!"

Cronley didn't reply.

Mattingly tugged a silver cigarette case from his tunic pocket, took a cigarette from it, and then lit it with a Zippo lighter.

He exhaled the smoke.

"This has gone far enough," he announced.

He took another puff and exhaled it through pursed lips.

"My mistake was in taking you into the OSS in the first place," he said thoughtfully, almost as if talking to himself. "I should have known your relationship with Colonel Frade was going to cause me problems. And which I compounded by sending you to Argentina with those files."

He looked into Cronley's eyes.

"So, what do I do with you, Captain Cronley? I can't leave you at Kloster Grünau thinking you're not subject to my orders."

"Was that a question, sir?"

"Consider it one."

"You can let me deal with the problem of Major Orlovsky."

"What does that mean?"

"Let me see if I can get the names of Gehlen's people who gave him those rosters."

"And how are you going to do that?"

"I don't know. But I'd like to try. And, sir, I don't think that I'm not subject to your orders. I just think you're wrong for wanting to turn the problem over to Gehlen."

"Don't you mean 'General Gehlen,' Captain?"

"Herr Gehlen has been run through a De-Nazification Court and released from POW status to civilian life. He no longer has military rank, and I think it's a mistake to let him pretend he does."

"It makes it easier for him to control his people, wouldn't you say?"

"I don't care if they call him Der Führer. I am not going to treat him as a general in a position to give me orders. It has to be the other way around."

"Or what?"

"You have to go along with that, or relieve me."

"Whereupon you would tell Colonel Frade why I relieved you?"

"Yes, sir."

"And what makes you think Frade wouldn't think relieving a twenty-two-year-old captain who wouldn't take orders was something I had every right to do?"

"I'll have to take that chance, sir."

Mattingly looked at him a long moment. "My biggest mistake was in underestimating your ego," he said, almost sadly. "I should have known better. Why the hell couldn't you have stayed a nice young second lieutenant who only knew how to say 'Yes, sir' and wouldn't dream of questioning his orders?"

Cronley didn't reply.

"We seem to be back to: 'What the hell do I do with you?' "

"You can let me see how I do with Major Orlovsky."

"My question was rhetorical, Captain Cronley. I was not asking for a reply."

"Yes, sir."

"Prefacing the following by saying that this conversation is by no means over, I'll tell you what's going to happen now. In the morning, you will return to Kloster Grünau. I'll give you a week to see what you can learn from Major Orlovsky. One week. Seven days from now, you will come back here and report to me what, if anything, you think you have learned, and offer any suggestions you might have regarding the next step."

"Yes, sir. Thank you."

"Don't entertain any illusions that you have come out on top of our little tête-à-tête. Whatever happens, our relationship in the future will be considerably less cordial than it has been in the past."

"I understand, sir."

"Now, presuming you still take some orders, I don't want you to leave this room until you get in the staff car that takes you to the airfield in the morning. There is room service. You will eat your supper and breakfast in the room. Got it?"

"Yes, sir."

"I don't want you bumping into Mrs. Schumann. Your first encounter with her ended without anything untoward happening. I want to keep it that way."

"Yes, sir."

Mattingly got out of his chair and left the suite without saying another word.

Cronley looked at the closed door, and then wondered aloud, "Why the hell couldn't I have stayed a nice young second lieutenant who only knew how to say 'Yes, sir' and wouldn't dream of questioning my orders?"

Then he walked into the bathroom to meet the call of nature.

[Six]

When Cronley came back into the sitting room, he pushed the curtains on the French doors aside and looked out. It was drizzling, a precursor, he thought, of the bad weather moving in. Defying the drizzle, four golfers were walking down the fairway with their caddies trailing after them.

He let the curtain fall back, having remembered that there was room service.

A little celebratory Jack Daniel's is in order for the prisoner in Room 112.

After that confrontation with Mattingly, while things are certainly not ginger-peachy, Mattingly knows he can't let Gehlen's men shoot Orlovsky. At least right away.

He had just picked up the telephone when there was a knock at his door.

Shit! Mattingly's back with something devastating to say to me.

He swung open the door.

Mrs. Colonel Schumann was standing there.

"Yes, ma'am?"

"Aren't you going to ask me in?"

"Mrs. Schumann, I don't think that's a very good idea."

"Would you prefer that I cause a scene in the corridor?"

He backed away far enough for her to enter, leaving the door open.

She glanced at it. "If you leave the door open, someone's likely to see me in here."

"I don't think us being in here behind a closed door is a very good idea."

She moved quickly around him and slammed the door closed.

"I have no more interest in getting caught doing this than you do."

"Ma'am, I think you've had a little too much to drink."

"Just enough to find the courage to do this."

She advanced on him. He retreated until his back was against the door.

Jesus, she's going to grope me!

"Shut up and kiss me," she ordered. "And for God's sake, Jimmy, stop calling me 'ma'am.'"

She raised her face to his.

And then she groped him.

[Seven]

1405 30 October 1945

Why do I really not want to open my eyes?

Maybe I'm thinking that if I just lie here keeping them closed I won't have to face what I just did.

Cronley felt Mrs. Schumann's fingers on his face and opened his eyes.

She was beside him in the bed, supporting herself on an elbow, looking down at him.

"What did you do, doze off?" she asked.

She had a sheet and blanket over her shoulders, but they did not conceal her breasts, her stomach, or her large patch of black pubic hair.

"What we just did wasn't smart," he said.

"Probably not. But we did it, and we can't take it back."

He looked at her, and then away, and now he saw their clothing scattered between the bed and the door to the sitting room.

"So tell me about those sad eyes," she said.

He didn't reply.

"They're what attracted me to you. So tell me."

"You really want to know?"

"I really want to know."

"Okay. The day after we eloped, my wife was killed when a drunk hit her head-on with his sixteen-wheeler."

"Oh, Jimmy, I'm so sorry."

"Yeah."

"When did this happen?"

"Five days ago. No, four."

"I don't believe that. And if you think you're being amusing, you're not."

"Boy Scout's Honor, Mrs. Schumann. And if you don't believe that, try this on for size: That same afternoon, the President of the United States, the Honorable Harry S Truman, pinned the Distinguished Service Medal, and captain's bars, on me. And at nine o'clock — excuse me, let's keep this military — at *twenty-one hundred hours* that same night, Colonel Mattingly and I got on

208

the plane that brought us back here."

"My God, you're telling me the truth!"

"Yes, Mrs. Schumann, I'm telling you the truth."

"And now I did this to you. Jimmy, I'm so sorry. If I had known . . ."

"Mrs. Schumann, it takes two to tango, as they say in Buenos Aires, where, putting your credulity to the test once again, I was three days before I got married."

"You have every reason to be disgusted with me, but could you bring yourself to call me Rachel and not Mrs. Schumann?"

He looked at her and found himself looking into her sad eyes.

"Sure, Rachel, why not?"

"Jimmy, I am so very sorry."

"Rachel, if you're on a guilt trip, don't be. You may have noticed I was an enthusiastic participant in what just happened."

She smiled.

"I noticed. I feel a little guilty about . . . not knowing what happened to you. But not about what I did. Understand?"

"No."

"Are you interested?" she said, then before he could reply added: "I think I should tell you."

He still didn't reply.

"Despite what it looks like, I don't jump

into bed with every good-looking young officer I meet."

His face showed his disbelief.

"Or touch them under the table," she went on. "Testing your credulity, this is the first time I've ever been unfaithful to my husband."

"Is that so?"

"We grew up together. We got married when Tony graduated from college. I was nineteen. He went into the Signal Corps. His degree's in electrical engineering. We had our two children, Anton Junior, who's now fourteen, and Sarah, who's now twelve, when we were stationed at Fort Monmouth —"

"Rachel," he interrupted, "you don't have to do —"

She silenced him by putting her finger to her lips.

"It's important to me that you hear this. Tony was first a student and then an instructor at Monmouth. Then he went into the Army Security Agency, and we moved to Vint Hill Farms Station — do you know about Vint Hill, the ASA?"

Cronley nodded.

"And then the war came along, and somehow Tony moved into the inspector general business, first with ASA and then with the

210

CIC. I guess you know about Camp Hola-bird? In Baltimore?"

He nodded again.

"We went there, and we had just found an apartment when Tony was assigned to Eisenhower's Advance Party when Ike was sent to London. He made major, and then they sent him back to Washington, where he made lieutenant colonel. And then when the war was nearly over they sent him back here. He became involved in collecting evidence to be used against the Nazis when they were to be tried. I think his seeing what they did to the Jews was what did it."

"Did what?"

"Make him decide to assert his Jewish masculine superiority by . . . stupping it to every German shiksa he can."

"I don't know what that means. Stupped? Shiksa?"

"What it means is that when the kids and I got over here six weeks ago, I found out that Tony . . ."

She stopped, chuckled, then ran her fingers over his face tenderly. " 'Stupping,' my goy lover, is Yiddish for what you just did to me. *Goy* means 'gentile man.' And *shiksa* is Yiddish for 'gentile girl.' "

"How did you find out about your husband?"

"It doesn't matter. I found out."

"I'm sorry, Rachel."

She ran her fingers over his face again.

"So, what were my options? If I left him, the kids would have learned that not only is their father a sonofabitch stupping it to all the shiksas he can, but that he prefers them to me. And what would I do? I've been an officer's wife since I was a kid, I don't know how I would make a living."

She paused, then went on: "So, what did I do? I did what a lot of women here do — Tony's not the only officer who has found that fräuleins, or for that matter, *die Frauen,* are more interesting in bed than their wives. I started to drink, is what I did, Jimmy.

"And then I began to have this fantasy. I would pay the sonofabitch back. What's sauce for the goose, et cetera. I would find a lover, preferably a goy. That would show him."

"Christ, you're not going to tell him about us?"

She laughed and smiled.

"No, Jimmy, I'm not going to tell him about us. If I did, my children would learn that their mother's no better than their father. Or as bad as their father. It would be enough, I thought, that I would know I had paid him back.

"But the fantasy went nowhere. I didn't come across anyone that I wanted to take to bed. I began to understand that my fantasy was just that — fantasy.

"And then I ran into a young goy officer my husband really hates. More importantly, he had the saddest eyes I'd ever seen. Perfect, I thought. Except you showed no interest in me whatever. So I took another sip of my martini of liquid encouragement and . . . let you know I was interested. You still didn't show any interest, but — and this really came as a surprise — what I had done to you really excited me.

"I waited until Colonel Mattingly had driven away and then I came knocking at your door. And here we are."

When he didn't reply, she said, "No comment?"

He rolled on his side and looked at her.

"I'm glad you didn't give up, Rachel."

"I hope you're just not saying that."

He put his hand to her breast. She laid her fingers on top of his hand. He felt her nipple stiffen.

"Jimmy, are you feeling guilty about betraying the memory of your late wife?"

"She's dead, Rachel . . ."

"I feel so sorry for you."

". . . and I'm alive."

He took his hand from her breast, caught hers, and guided it to his member. She closed her fingers around it and it sprang almost instantly to life.

"Oh, God!" she said.

And then he rolled on top of her.

[Eight]

1430 30 October 1945

"You look lost in thought," Jimmy said to Rachel, who was standing before the mirror in the bath and combing her hair.

She turned from the mirror. She had showered and wrapped a towel around her waist, leaving her breasts uncovered.

"You're not supposed to be looking," she said, but didn't seem offended. She turned back to the mirror and resumed running the comb through her hair.

"I've got a lot to think about," Rachel said.

"Like what?"

"Like — not that it matters — I'm too old for you. Like I really have to keep Tony from finding out and, for different reasons, my kids from even suspecting."

"For different reasons?"

"Because Tony really hates you. My kids, thank God, don't even know you exist."

"Your husband hates me because of what

214

I did to his car?"

"Because he suspects you're involved in getting Nazis out of Germany to Argentina, and he can't do anything about it."

After a moment, Jimmy said, "And the different reasons for the kids?"

"No mother wants to have to come off the pedestal of virtue her kids have put her on."

"Then we'll just have to make sure your kids don't find out."

"The only way we could do that for sure would be for me to get dressed, walk out of here, and never see you again."

"Is that what you want to do?"

"No. But that's moot. Eventually, we're going to run into each other again. We're just going to have to be very careful."

"Can I interpret that to mean . . ."

"Do I want to be with you again? Of course I do. I know I should be overwhelmed with remorse right now, but the truth is I like standing here combing my hair while you stare hungrily at my breasts."

"Wow!"

"But we're going to have to be very careful and pray we don't get caught. And I mean that about praying. I don't want my kids to get hurt."

"Understood."

"Are you?"

"Am I what?"

"Involved in sneaking Nazis out of Germany to Argentina?"

"Jesus, Rachel!"

"I thought so. Tony is ordinarily very good at what he does, and so far as that business is concerned, he's passionate. I guess he feels that if he can stop it, that will be even better for his Jewish masculine ego than . . ."

"Stupping the shiksas?"

She laughed.

"If you suddenly start spouting Yiddish, people will wonder who's teaching you."

"Then I will spout it only to you, my shiksa."

She laughed and turned to him.

"I'm not your shiksa, *mein Trottel goy.* I'm your *khaverte.*"

"Is that what you think, Rachel, that I'm a fool of a Christian?"

"That's right, you do speak German, don't you? And Yiddish is really bastard German."

"My mother is a *Strasburgerin.* I got my German from her."

"I was just about to say, 'That was said lovingly,' but we have to be careful about using that word, don't we? Or even thinking about it?"

"Can you have a lover, be lovers, without love?"

"We're going to have to try to, aren't we? Or at least without saying it, or even thinking it?"

When he didn't reply, Rachel said, "Oh, my God, Jimmy. You're not thinking that what happened between us . . . That was lust, Jimmy. Lust. Not love."

He smiled.

"What's funny? This is not funny!"

"When I was in the eighth grade, thirteen, fourteen years old . . ."

"As old as Anton Junior. So?"

"Our teacher, Miss Schenck, introduced us to classical music. Started out easy. We were all ranch kids in West Texas. She set up her phonograph and said she was going to play a Viennese operetta for us. She said it was called *Die Lustige Witwe* and that meant 'The Merry Widow.' So I put up my hand and said, 'Excuse me, Miss Schenck, but *lustige* doesn't mean 'merry.' It means 'lusty.' And she said, 'What are you talking about?' So I told her, '*Lustige* means "horny." You know, like a bull is when you turn him loose in the pasture with the cows.' "

"Oh, Jimmy, you didn't!"

"Miss Schenk snapped, 'James Cronley,

you go straight to the principal's office! This instant!' "

Rachel laughed.

"So my mother was called in, heard what happened, and told me I was just going to have to learn (a) I should never correct my teachers, and (b) I should never try to explain what lust means to any female."

"And here you are discussing lust with me."

"Yeah."

"Can we leave . . . what we have . . . to that, Jimmy?"

"The only other alternative that comes to mind is chastity, and as I stand here 'staring hungrily' at your breasts, that doesn't have much appeal."

She smiled in the mirror. "To me either."

"If you really want to see lust in action, drop that towel."

"My God!" Rachel said, and shook her head in disbelief.

Then she put down the comb and dropped the towel.

[Nine]

1615 30 October 1945

"The kids get home from school about five," Rachel said. "I have to go."

She got out of bed and went to the arm-chair onto which she had put her clothing after gathering it up from where it had been on the floor.

"It was nice bumping into you, Mrs. Schumann. We'll have to try to get together again real soon."

"I'm going to do my best to see that doesn't happen for a long time. But when it does, you better remember to call me Mrs. Schumann."

"Yes, ma'am. Are you going to tell your husband about me?"

"Well, I'm not going to tell him everything, *mein Trottel*. It wouldn't surprise me that he's already heard that you were here with Colonel Mattingly."

"I should have thought of that."

"Yes, you should have," she said, turning her back to him to put on her brassiere.

"Rachel, about this unfounded rumor your husband has heard about some people smuggling Nazis out of Germany . . ."

"What about it?"

"For the sake of argument, let's say, hypothetically, that there's something to it."

"And?"

"You don't seem to be very upset about it."

"I don't like it. But I think General

Greene must know about it. And I'm sure Colonel Mattingly knows about it, and probably is involved with it. And I know you are —"

"You know nothing of the kind," he interrupted.

"If Tony strongly suspects you're involved, you're involved. And you as much as admitted to me you are. What did you expect I would think when you told me you had just been in Argentina? That you were on one of those ninety-nine-dollar all-expenses-paid Special Service tours, a little vacation from your exhausting duties in the Army of Occupation?"

She turned to face him as she stepped into her skirt.

"Rachel, you could cause a hell of a lot of damage to something very important if you dropped that little gem into any conversations you have with your husband."

"As I started to say, if General Greene and Colonel Mattingly know about it, and they do, then the fact that it's still going on tells me there has to be a good reason for it."

"There is."

"Hypothetically speaking, of course?"

"Hypothetically speaking."

She put her blouse on and buttoned it,

and then tucked it into her skirt, and then she reached for her jacket.

"Where do you live?"

"Hoechst. Not far. A little suburb not far from the Eschborn airstrip. It somehow didn't get leveled in the war."

She slipped into her shoes.

Jimmy got out of bed and went to her.

"Uh-oh," she said. "I don't think I'm going to like this."

"You won't like what?"

"Don't say anything foolish, Jimmy, please."

"Okay."

"And you don't have to tell me not to tell my husband about what you let slip."

"Thank you."

"And don't try to entice me back into bed. I really have to be at home when the kids get there."

"What gave you the idea I was going to try something like that?"

"This," she said, putting her hand on him. "You know what happens to me when it stands up and waves at me like that. I lose all control."

"What do I do now?"

"Kiss me quick, and then go back to bed. Alone."

He kissed her. It was quick.

She took her hand off him and walked out of the bedroom without looking back.

After a moment, he walked into the sitting room. Rachel was gone.

So, what do I do now?

I take a shower. Then I get dressed.

And, fuck Mattingly, I go to the dining room and get something to eat.

He looked at his watch.

Well, since the dining room doesn't open until five, and I can't drink as I'm flying in the morning, what do I do for the next thirty-five minutes?

I take a little nap is what I do for the next thirty-five minutes.

And then I take a shower and go get something to eat.

[Ten]

0800 31 October 1945

He first had trouble waking, and then he couldn't find the goddamned ringing telephone.

"Captain Cronley."

"Captain, your car is here to take you to the Eschborn airstrip."

"I'll be right there."

Jesus Christ, I never woke up!

V

[One]

U.S. Army Airfield H-7
Eschborn, Hesse
American Zone of Occupation, Germany

0825 31 October 1945

As the olive drab 1942 Ford staff car drove Cronley up to Base Operations, he saw that the Storch had been moved off the tarmac in front of Base Operations. It was now on the grass across from it — and the subject of attention of a group of officers, the senior of them a full bull colonel wearing Air Force insignia.

As Cronley got out of the car, he saw a lieutenant writing something in a notebook.

Probably the tail numbers and XXIIIrd CIC.

Colonel Wilson warned me the Air Force doesn't want the Army to have Storches. He wouldn't have given me his if there was any way he could have kept them. And he's much higher on the totem pole than I am.

So what the hell am I going to do if that colonel tries to grab my Storch?

The only thing I can try — hide behind the secrecy that covers the CIC.

And maybe be a little deceptive.

Cronley went into Base Operations and checked the weather map. The front had passed through the Munich area. Then he checked the local map, saw there was a small airstrip in Fulda, and filed a Visual Flight Rules flight plan giving that as his destination.

Then he walked out to the airplane and the officers examining it.

He did not salute, as he was wearing his civilian triangles, and civilians don't salute.

"Good morning," he said cheerfully.

"This your aircraft?" the Air Force colonel said.

"Well, actually it belongs to the Army," Cronley said, as he opened the rear window and tossed his overnight bag through it.

"It's my understanding," the colonel announced, "that all of these former German aircraft have been ordered taken out of service."

"I hadn't heard that."

"Well, that's my understanding. Who are you?"

"Why are you asking?"

"Because I'm the commanding officer of this airbase and want to know."

How come this Air Force colonel is commanding an Army airfield?

Because they're operating C-47s out of here

to train parachutists to guard the Farben Building, that's why.

Cronley produced his CIC credentials.

The colonel examined them, and then Cronley, carefully.

"See Eye See, eh?"

Cronley pointed to where XXIIIrd CIC was lettered on the vertical stabilizer.

"You're not very talkative, are you?"

"Colonel, we're trained not to be."

"And you're leaving now?"

"Right now."

"Have a nice flight."

"Thank you."

"Get him a fire guard," the colonel ordered, and then asked, "I presume you've filed your flight plan?"

Meaning you suspect if you ask me where I'm going, I'm liable to tell you that's none of your business, right in front of your men.

But clever fellow that you are, the minute I take off, you'll go into Weather/Flight Planning and look at my flight plan.

"Uh-huh."

Two Germans, under the supervision of a U.S. Army corporal, trundled up a large fire extinguisher on wheels.

Cronley climbed into the cockpit and strapped himself in. When the engine was running smoothly, he called the tower for taxi and takeoff permission, then signaled for the wheel chocks to be pulled. He gave the Air Force colonel a friendly wave and put his hand to the throttle.

When he was in takeoff position, he looked at Base Operations and saw the colonel and his men marching purposefully toward it.

What I hope happens now is he'll call the Fulda Air Strip, tell them a Storch is en route, and for them to find out what the Storch is doing there, and, if possible, keep it from leaving until he can find out why a Storch is flying when the Air Force doesn't want Storches to fly.

When he finally realizes that the Storch is not going to land at Fulda, he may decide to call the commanding officer of the XXIIIrd CIC and ask him what's going on. That will be difficult, as the XXIIIrd CIC is not listed in any EUCOM telephone directory.

He advanced the throttle.

"Eschborn, Army Seven-Oh-Seven rolling."

A minute or so later, he looked down at what he presumed was Hoechst.

There was an intact factory of some sort on the bank of what he presumed was the Main River. The factory for some reason he couldn't imagine had not been reduced to rubble by Air Force B-17s. Neither had a housing development near it.

Rachel is in one of those neat little houses down there, maybe having a cup of coffee after having fed Anton Jr. and Sarah their breakfast and loaded them on the school bus.

Jimmy boy, what the hell have you got yourself into?

He decided that there were two ways to attract the least attention to the Storch on the way to Kloster Grünau. One was to climb to, say, six thousand feet, and the other was to fly as low as he safely could. He reluctantly chose the former option, for, while "chasing cows" was always fun, he had to admit that he didn't have enough time in the Storch to play games with it.

As he made the ascent, he remembered that Colonel Mattingly had given him a week to get from Major Konstantin Orlovsky the names of which of Gehlen's people had been turned.

And Mattingly meant it.

What he sees as a satisfactory solution to the problem is that Gehlen and Company "without his knowledge" interrogate Orlovsky, such interrogation including anything up to and including pulling out his fingernails, or

227

hanging him upside down over a slow Apache fire, for no more than a day or two.

Why did he give me a week? What's that all about? Why not two days or two weeks?

He didn't pull that from thin air; he had that time period in his mind.

And if that interrogation produces the names, fine.

And if it doesn't, that's fine, too.

And if the names Orlovsky gives up — and he knows everybody's names; he had the rosters — are of innocent people, that's one of those unfortunate things that can't be helped.

They get shot and buried alongside Orlovsky in unmarked graves in the ancient cemetery of Kloster Grünau.

If nothing else, that will teach Gehlen's people — and whoever controls the disappeared NKGB officer Orlovsky — that the Americans can be as ruthless as anybody.

And we keep looking for the people who really have been turned so we can shoot them and plant them in the Kloster Grünau cemetery.

What Mattingly can't afford to have happen is for it to come out that we grabbed an NKGB officer. We are allies of the Soviet Union. We'd have to give him back, and the Russians could then, in righteous outrage, complain loudly that we are protecting two-hundred-odd Nazis from them.

So Orlovsky has to disappear. It doesn't really matter if he gives us the names of Gehlen's people who have been turned.

And Mattingly is right.

So why are you playing Sir Galahad?

The question now seems to be when did that week clock start ticking?

It's ticking for me, too. Maybe Mattingly has decided he needs that much time — but no more — to come up with some way to shut me up. He can't have me running to Clete — much less to Admiral Souers.

And if reason doesn't work . . .

"What a pity. Poor Cronley was just standing there when the truck went out of control. At least, thank God, it was quick. He didn't feel a thing."

No. Two deaths by an out-of-control truck would be too much of a coincidence.

"Poor Jimmy. He just couldn't handle the death of his bride. He was so young and he loved her so much. It was just too much for him. What did you expect? He put his .45 in his mouth."

That'd work.

Well, it won't.

Over my dead body, as the saying goes.

[Two]

Kloster Grünau
Schollbrunn, Bavaria
American Zone of Occupation, Germany

1305 31 October 1945

As Cronley made his approach, he saw Tiny
Dunwiddie leaning on the front fender of a
three-quarter-ton ambulance where the
road turned. The Red Cross panels had
been painted over, as the ambulance was no
longer used to transport the wounded or
injured.

*He either heard me coming or he's been
waiting for me, possibly with good news from
Mattingly.*

*"This is a direct order, Sergeant Dunwiddie.
When Captain Cronley gets there, sit on him.
By 'sit on him' I mean don't let him near the
man he's been talking to or near the radio. Or
leave. I'll explain when I get there. Say, 'Yes,
sir.' "*

When he taxied to the chapel to shut down
the Storch, he saw that while he was gone,
U.S. Army squad tents — six of them —
had been converted into what was a sort of
combination hangar and camouflage cover
large enough for both Storches.

He wondered whose idea that had been, and who had done it.

Then he saw Kurt Schröder and two of his mechanics working on the landing gear of the other Storch, Seven-One-Seven, which explained everything.

He shut down Seven-Oh-Seven, got out, gave Schröder a smile and a thumbs-up for the hangar, and then walked to where Dunwiddie was waiting. He got in the ambulance that was no longer an ambulance.

"The look on your face, Captain, sir," Dunwiddie greeted him, "suggests that things did not go well with Colonel Mattingly."

"No. They didn't. We need to talk, and I don't want anybody to hear what I have to say."

"Well, that's why I brought the ambulance."

He started the engine, drove out onto the runway, and stopped.

"Thanks to my genius," he said, "we can sit here in comfort while you share everything, and nobody can hear what you're saying."

Five minutes later, Cronley finished telling Tiny everything — with the exception of the intimate acts with Mrs. Colonel Schumann — he'd been thinking, even though halfway through the recitation he realized he sounded paranoid.

When Dunwiddie didn't say anything, Cronley said, "What are you thinking, Tiny? That my captain's bars have gone to my head? Or that I am paranoid? Or simply out of my mind? Or all of the above?"

Tiny shrugged his massive shoulders.

"What I was thinking was that I knew the first time I saw you that you were going to be trouble. To answer your questions, not in the order you asked them, Do I think you're paranoid about Mattingly? I really wish I could, but I can't."

"You don't?" Cronley asked in surprise.

"Did you ever wonder how he got to be commander of OSS Forward? And why Dulles, or whoever, gave him responsibility for Operation Ost?"

"He's good at what he does?"

Dunwiddie did not reply directly. He instead said, "Being a colonel and Number Two to David Bruce in London is not bad for someone who before the war was a weekend warrior lieutenant in the National Guard, and made his living as a professor of languages at a university run by the Episcopal Church. And he's a very young full colonel. You ever wonder about that?"

"The guy who gave us the Storches made light colonel at twenty-four."

"General White told me about Lieutenant Colonel Hotshot Billy Wilson. Different situation from Mattingly."

"How different?"

"Wilson got his silver leaf very early because even before Pearl Harbor, General White wanted small airplanes in the Army. Wilson almost single-handedly did that little chore for him. And then he did some spectacular things like flying Mark Clark into Rome the day it was declared an open city. And he's a West Pointer. That didn't hurt.

"Mattingly, on the other hand, got where he is by doing, ruthlessly, whatever had to be done in the OSS. And he'll do whatever he thinks has to be done here. I'm not sure that he'd go as far as getting you run over by a truck, or assisting your suicide, to keep it quiet. But only because he knows the OSS guy in Argentina would certainly ask questions. Mattingly didn't get where he is because he doesn't know how to cover his ass."

"You don't like him very much, do you?" Cronley asked, gently sarcastic.

Dunwiddie looked at Cronley as if making up his mind whether to say something. Finally, he said, "Just before General White left Germany for Fort Riley, I had a few minutes with him."

He saw the questioning look on Cronley's face, and explained, "He and my father are classmates at Norwich. 'Twenty. Old friends. General White knew my father would expect him to check up on me, so he had Colonel Wilson fly him into Eschborn. OSS Forward was still alive then, in the Schlosshotel. We had a cup of coffee in the snack bar.

"During that little conversation, the general asked, 'Chauncey, do I tell your father you still feel you made the right decision?' I asked, 'Sir, what decision is that?' And he said, 'To pass up your commission so that you could stay with the OSS Guard Company. Colonel Mattingly told me you said you saw that as the most important service you could render for the time being and getting your commission would just have to wait.' "

"I'll be a sonofabitch!"

"What I should have said was, 'Uncle Isaac, I hate to tell you this . . .' "

"Uncle Isaac?"

" '. . . but Colonel Mattingly is a lying sonofabitch. I never said anything like that. He told me not to worry about my commission, that he'd keep on you about it.' But I didn't. My thinking at the time was I knew

Uncle Isaac thinks Mattingly is a fine officer. So he was going to be surprised and disappointed if Little Chauncey suddenly came —"

"What's with this 'Little Chauncey' and 'Uncle Isaac'?" Cronley interrupted.

"I guess I never got around to mentioning that General White is my godfather. In private, he calls me Chauncey and I call him Uncle Isaac. His *I. D.* initials stand for 'Isaac Davis,' his great-grandfather. Or maybe his great-great-grandfather. Anyway, since I'm sure that Texas Cow College you went to taught you at least a little history, I'm sure you know who Isaac Davis is."

"Never heard of him."

"Isaac Davis on Easter Sunday, April sixteenth, 1775, fired, at Concord Green, Massachusetts, that famous shot heard 'round the world. That's who Isaac Davis is, you historically illiterate cowboy."

"No shit? He was General White's great-great-grandfather?"

"No shit. As I was saying before you so rudely interrupted me, Captain, sir, I thought that even if General White thought there had to be some reason for me to have suddenly come out of left field to call Mattingly a lying sonofabitch, he was leaving for the States the next day and he wouldn't have time to even ask Mattingly what the hell was going on or do anything about my commission. So I kept my mouth shut."

"You should have told him, Tiny."

"I thought about that when you mentioned Mattingly being worried about this OSS pal of yours . . ."

"Cletus Frade," Cronley furnished.

". . . in Argentina.

"But that's what they call water under the bridge, Captain, sir. To return to your questions: Do I agree with your assessment of how he wants to handle the problem of Orlovsky? Yeah, I do. I think what Mattingly wants to do is be looking the other way while Gehlen's people are interrogating Orlovsky and then shooting him in the back of the head."

"And you're okay with that?"

"No. For two reasons. One, it ain't right. And two, if that happens and it comes out, the entire Judge Advocate Corps of the U.S. Army is going to come after me."

He met Cronley's eyes, and then recited, " 'Article 118. Any person subject to this chapter who, without justification or excuse, unlawfully kills a human being, is guilty of murder, and shall suffer such death or such other punishment as a court-martial may direct.' That's not all of it, but you get the general idea."

"Actually, they'd come after me, Tiny. I'm in command here."

"That announcement answers your third question: Do I think your captain's bars have gone to your head? Yeah, I do. But in a good sense. You're thinking like a captain. You really grew up, Jimmy, doing whatever the hell you did in Argentina."

Cronley said what he was thinking: "I wish you were wearing these captain's bars, Tiny."

"Yeah. But I'm not. Which brings us to what do we do about Orlovsky? Bearing in mind that whatever we do is liable to bring the Judge Advocate General's Corps down on us, either for simple disobedience to a lawful order, or plotting mutiny — and plotting a mutiny is right up there beside Article 118 of the Uniform Code of Military Justice, 1928. 'Death or such other punishment as a court-martial may decide.' "

"Maybe we should just cave."

"That's not an option, Jim. What are you thinking?"

"I don't think that disorientation idea of Bischoff's is going to work. Orlovsky is either not going to give us the names, or he'll give us names of Germans who he hasn't turned."

"Agreed. Got a better idea?"

"Let's try something else."

"Like what?"

"It's going to sound pretty far off the wall," Cronley said, and then told him of his idea.

"You're right, that is off the wall. I wonder why Herr Bischoff, the Great Interrogator, didn't think of that really nasty approach. Or, for that matter, Mattingly. I would never have suspected that you're capable of being a bigger prick than either of them."

"Life is full of little surprises, isn't it? I take it you think it might work?"

"I don't know. However, in the absence of any other idea, let's give it a shot."

[Three]

Commanding Officer's Quarters
Kloster Grünau
Schollbrunn, Bavaria
American Zone of Occupation, Germany

1410 31 October 1945

Technical Sergeant Abraham L. Tedworth and Staff Sergeant Harold Lewis Jr. led Major Konstantin Orlovsky of the NKGB into the sitting room of Captain James D. Cronley Jr.'s quarters. Cronley and CIC Special Agent Chauncey Dunwiddie were seated at a table at which three places had been set.

Orlovsky was shuffling in his bare feet. His ankles were tied together with handcuffs and a short length of rope. A GI blanket had been tied around his shoulders. His hands were handcuffed behind his back. His head was inside a GI duffel bag, closed at his neck with a GI web belt.

"Take the bag off his head," Cronley ordered.

Tedworth did so.

"Good morning, Konstantin," Cronley said cordially, as the Russian blinked his eyes against the sudden exposure to light.

Orlovsky looked nervously around the room but did not reply.

"I'm sorry I had to have you trussed up like that," Cronley went on conversationally, "but I knew General Gehlen's people were going to see you walking over here, and we wouldn't want them to think we've become friends, would we? And then I had to consider the possibility that you would try to do something foolish, like trying to get away from the sergeants."

Again Orlovsky didn't reply.

"Chauncey and I" — Cronley nodded toward Dunwiddie — "you've met Chauncey, I think, if only briefly — we were talking and decided that after your stay in —

how shall I say this? — *das Gasthaus* — you'd probably like a shower and a shave and a change of linen. And afterward, that we could have a little chat over breakfast. So let's get to that."

He gestured to Tedworth and Lewis. Lewis dropped to his knees and started to free Orlovsky from the handcuffs around his ankles.

Cronley went on: "That long wooden pole, Konstantin, that Sergeant Tedworth is holding is a Louisville Slugger baseball bat. Normally used in our national sport. But in this case, I've told the sergeant that if you even look as if you have notions of declining our hospitality and leaving, he is to first smash your feet with it, and, if that doesn't have the desired effect, to start in on your knees."

Sergeant Lewis finished unshackling Orlovsky and then unlocked and removed his handcuffs.

"The sergeants will now assist you in your shower," Cronley said.

Lewis and Tedworth took Orlovsky's arms and marched him into Cronley's bedroom.

When the door was closed, Cronley said, "I hope that doesn't take long. I haven't had anything to eat since lunch yesterday."

"Feeding him breakfast was your idea,"

240

Dunwiddie replied, and then said, "You did a pretty good job on him. From the look on his face, he wouldn't have been surprised to find that he was being led into a Dachau gas chamber shower."

"Yeah. I saw that, too. And what worries me was that he didn't seem to give a damn. I think he's decided that he's as good as dead, so what the hell, get it over with."

Sergeants Tedworth and Lewis led Orlovsky back into the sitting room ten minutes later. He was still barefoot, but he was now dressed in an olive drab woolen shirt and OD trousers.

"Well, my stuff seems to fit, Konstantin," Cronley said. "I thought we were about the same size."

Orlovsky didn't reply.

"Sergeant Tedworth, why don't you give the Louisville Slugger to Dunwiddie? And then you and Sergeant Lewis can leave us alone while we have our breakfast. Tell Sergeant Whatsisname we want it now."

"Yes, sir."

"I didn't know what you like for breakfast, Konstantin," Cronley said, "so I told Sergeant Whatsisname . . ."

"Sergeant Warner, sir," Tedworth furnished as he handed Dunwiddie the baseball

241

bat. Dunwiddie rested it against the table.

". . . Right. *Sergeant Warner.* I don't know why I always forget his name. Unlike most mess sergeants, he's one hell of a cook. Anyway, Konstantin, I told Sergeant Warner to bring you what Chauncey and I are having. Orange juice, ham and eggs, and waffles. I hope that's all right with you."

"Why don't you sit down, Konstantin?" Dunwiddie asked. "Get your feet off the cold floor?"

Orlovsky took his seat, with his hands folded in his lap.

Dunwiddie offered Orlovsky his pack of Chesterfield cigarettes.

Orlovsky shook his head, and then said, "No, thank you."

It was the first he had spoken.

Nothing more was said by anyone until Sergeant Warner, who was wearing cook's whites, including an enormous floppy white hat, came into the room, carrying a large tray holding plates covered with upside-down plates. Sergeant Lewis followed him carrying a steaming coffeepot.

"Just put it on the table," Dunwiddie ordered. "We'll take it from there."

Dunwiddie picked up the coffeepot and poured from it.

"I take mine black," Dunwiddie said.

"How about you, Konstantin?"

"Black is fine, thank you."

Cronley removed the upside-down plate over his plate and looked appreciatively at what was to be his breakfast.

"Dig in, Konstantin," he suggested, "before it gets cold."

Orlovsky removed the plate over his breakfast and picked up a fork.

"Do they have waffles in Russia?" Cronley asked.

"We have something like what this appears to be."

"Your wife serves them like this, with maple syrup?"

"Excuse me?"

"Do you put maple syrup on them?"

"I don't know what maple syrup is."

Dunwiddie moved a small white pitcher across the table.

"Maple syrup," he said. "It's sweet. Spread butter on your waffle and then pour a little syrup on it."

Curiosity took over.

"What is it?"

"They drill holes in maple trees," Cronley explained. "They stick taps in the holes to collect the maple sap in buckets, then boil that down."

"And this is the real stuff, genuine Vermont maple syrup," Dunwiddie went on. "The best kind. My mother sends it to me."

"You're from Vermont?" Orlovsky asked.

Cronley's and Dunwiddie's eyes met for a moment.

We've got him talking!

More important, talking family!

"From Kansas," Dunwiddie said. "Manhattan, Kansas. Or Fort Riley. Same thing. We go to school in Vermont. Norwich."

"Konstantin has no idea what you're talking about, Chauncey," Cronley said.

"My family is Cavalry," Dunwiddie said. "Fort Riley has been a cavalry post for a long time, almost a hundred years. And we Dunwiddies have been there since they put up the first stockade. We're Buffalo Soldiers."

"Now you're really confusing him," Cronley said.

"When we were fighting the Indians, before our Civil War, 1861 to 1865, the Indians called us Buffalo Soldiers because of this," Dunwiddie said as he ran his fingers over his scalp. "They said we had hair like buffaloes."

"Cowboys and Indians," Orlovsky said.

"*Cavalry* and Indians," Dunwiddie said. "If it wasn't for the Cavalry, the Indians

244

would have run the cowboys out of the West."

"How interesting," Orlovsky said. "But you said you went to school in Vermont?"

"After the Spanish American War, 1898, especially after the Ninth Cavalry beat Teddy Roosevelt's Rough Riders up San Juan Hill in Cuba," Dunwiddie continued his lecture, "the Army finally got around to admitting that maybe black people could be officers. But they had to be college graduates. So my grandfather, Joshua H. Dunwiddie, who had been first sergeant of Troop B of the Ninth Cavalry, took his discharge and Teddy Roosevelt got him into Norwich . . ."

"Which is?"

". . . From which he was graduated in the Class of 1900 and commissioned a second lieutenant of Cavalry. My father is Norwich 'twenty, and I'm Norwich 'forty-five."

"It's a school, a military academy?"

Cronley offered: "We have a number of private military academies, Konstantin."

"Of which Norwich is the oldest," Dunwiddie said.

"I went to one of them, the Texas Agriculture and Military Academy," Cronley added. "And General George C. Marshall, who is our senior officer, went to another of them, the Virginia Military Institute. General Patton, come to think of it, went to VMI before he went to West Point."

"Anyway, we Dunwiddies go to Norwich. Where we learned to appreciate Vermont maple syrup, which is why, my mother having sent me a half dozen pints of it, you are now about to pour it on your waffles."

Orlovsky smiled and chuckled.

"You said you'd gone to Leningrad State University," Cronley said. "Is that where you got your commission?"

Orlovsky's face showed he was wondering if the question was innocent. And then Cronley saw disappointment on it when Orlovsky realized Cronley and Dunwiddie had an agenda.

Is he sorry he fell for our charm, and didn't immediately suspect an agenda?

Or maybe he's disappointed in me personally.

That disorientation of Bischoff's wasn't entirely ineffective. He had a lot of time to think in that cell with no lights and no company but the smell of his own feces.

And then I came along and was nice to him.

And was even nicer today.

He thought he had found a friend, and what he's disappointed about is that he knows he should have known better.

And then Cronley saw what he thought was resignation.

"No," Orlovsky said. "The Leningrad State University has no connection with the military or the NKGB. Actually, I was sent there by the NKGB. I took what you Americans would call a master's degree at Leningrad. Then I took what I suppose you could call my doctorate at the Felix Dzerzhinsky Federal Security Service Academy in Moscow. When I graduated, I was commissioned."

"As a second lieutenant?"

"As a captain."

He's telling the truth, which means (a) he suspects I already knew where NKGB officers come from, and (b) has decided that since he's a dead man, it doesn't matter what he tells me, unless it's the names of the Germans he's turned. And he's not going to give them to me.

"Who's Felix whatever you said?" Dunwiddie asked.

"Felix *Dzerzhinsky* founded the Cheka, which evolved over the years into the NKGB," Orlovsky replied. Then he laid his knife and fork neatly on his plate, and then pushed it several inches away from him.

"You can eat your breakfast, Konstantin," Cronley said. "You're not going to be shot.

At least not by us."

When Orlovsky looked at him but made no move, Cronley said, "Don't be a fool. After the starvation diet our pal Bischoff has had you on, you need the strength."

"I'm sure you've heard that we Americans always feed the condemned man a hearty meal," Dunwiddie said, and smiled.

Orlovsky considered both comments for a moment, then pulled the plate to him. He began to saw a piece off the ham steak, and finally said, "Thank you."

"Our pleasure," Dunwiddie said. "Think nothing of it."

Orlovsky smiled as he forked a ham chunk into his mouth. When he had finished chewing it appreciatively, he said, "Delicious. Thank you for . . . encouraging . . . me to eat it."

"We could do no less, Konstantin," Dunwiddie said.

"What did you really hope to gain from your hospitality?" Orlovsky asked. "You know I am not going to give what you're asking."

"I think you will," Cronley said, hoping his voice conveyed more confidence than he felt. "We have three or four days for you to consider the advantages of telling us."

"And after four days, I'll be shot?"

"Not by us," Cronley said.

"By Bischoff? Or another of Gehlen's people?"

Well, here goes.

This probably won't work, but since I can think of nothing else . . .

"If you are shot," Cronley said, "I'd say the odds are the shooter will be a fellow alumnus of the Felix Dzerzhinsky Federal Security Service Academy."

Orlovsky looked intently at him, but his face showed nothing.

"Your assets — the Germans you have turned, Konstantin, and are so nobly protecting — are going to be your downfall. Over the next few days, I'm going to make sure they see what great friends you and I have become. They're clever fellows, and I have every confidence that they will know how to pass that information along to whoever was out there waiting for you the night Sergeant Tedworth caught you."

He let that sink in for a moment, then went on: "There had to be someone waiting for you, Konstantin. You didn't miraculously appear at Kloster Grünau like the Christmas fairy does on Christmas Eve. As a matter of fact, I wouldn't be surprised if he — or they — are out there as we speak, peering at us through binoculars and wondering what the hell you're doing in here right now. As a matter of fact, I hope they are.

"Step Two, or Three or Four, presuming you remain uncooperative, will be your being trussed up like a Christmas turkey and loaded into my Storch. I will then fly you to Berlin, put you into the trunk of a staff car, and drive you into the Russian Zone, where I will leave you sitting on the curb."

Orlovsky looked as if he was going to say something, but Cronley put up his hand to stop him.

"I don't want to sound rude, but right now I want you to think things over very carefully before you say anything."

Cronley stood.

"Finish your breakfast, Konstantin," he said, then turned to Dunwiddie. "When he's finished, have him taken back to *das Gasthaus.*"

"Dressed like that?"

"Oh, no. Dressed as he was when we brought him here. For the time being, let's let everybody think we still don't like him."

"Yes, sir."

"I'll be in my office if you need me."

"Yes, sir."

"I'll see you soon, Konstantin, after you've had a little time to think things over," Cronley said, and then walked out of the sitting room.

[Four]

XXIIIrd CIC Detachment Officers' Open Mess
Kloster Grünau
Schollbrunn, Bavaria
American Zone of Occupation, Germany

1505 31 October 1945

Cronley was sitting alone at the bar with a bottle of Jack Daniel's when Dunwiddie walked in ten minutes later.

"It's a little early for that, isn't it, Captain, sir?" Dunwiddie greeted him.

"I've already had my breakfast, so why not?"

"Are you celebrating, drowning your sorrows, or just boozing it up?"

"I've been trying to make up my mind about that."

"Drinking just because it makes you feel good is decadent and depraved."

"I'll bet they taught you that at Maple Syrup U."

"Actually, my mother repeated that line to me no more than five million times."

Dunwiddie went behind the bar, took a bottle of Haig & Haig Pinch Scots whisky from the display, then sat on a stool next to

Cronley.

"However," he went on, as he poured a glass nearly full, "under the circumstances, I feel a little taste is in order."

He took a very healthy swallow of the whisky, and smacked his lips appreciatively.

If it's true, Cronley thought, *that the larger the corpus into which alcohol is introduced the less effect it has on said corpus, Tiny can do that all day without getting noticeably plastered.*

As far as normal-sized people like me are concerned, I better not have any more of this. Right now, getting even slightly plastered is something I can't afford to do.

"Speaking of your sainted mother, Tiny, I thought that story about her sending you maple syrup worked well with Konstantin. We've got to get him thinking about his mother, his wife, his family."

"Yeah."

"I wish I knew if his father is alive, if he has any kids."

"You're thinking that if we can get him thinking about his mommy and daddy, his loving wife, and their little ones, if any . . . ?"

"He might start to think that while a bullet in the back of his head might solve his problems, the NKGB might turn its kind attention to them. I'm pretty sure he's been trying very hard not to think of them, so we have to make sure he does."

"He looked very unhappy when Tedworth was leading him back to his cell."

"He looked very unhappy when Tedworth led him *in* from his cell. What we have to do is give him some hope for the future."

"And reminding him that he's got a family about to get sent to Siberia, or shot, because he got caught is going to give him hope for the future?"

Tiny, looking past Jim, then quickly covered his mouth with his hand and said, "Change the subject."

Cronley looked over his shoulder. Former Oberst Ludwig Mannberg had entered the room and was walking toward them.

"Ah, I'd hoped to find you here, Captain Cronley," Mannberg said, smiling and offering his hand.

Cronley smiled, remembering what Tiny had said about habitual handshaking Germans: *"They can't go to the can to take a leak unless they first shake hands with everybody in the room."*

I don't want to call him Herr Oberst, because he's not a colonel anymore and I don't want him to think I don't know that.

On the other hand, I don't want to piss him off, either. Unintentionally.

"Will you join us for a little taste, Herr Oberst?" Cronley said as they shook hands.

"It's a little early for me, thank you just the same," Mannberg said. "I'm hoping you can spare a few minutes for me."

"Anytime, Herr Oberst. You know that."

Mannberg gave his hand to Tiny, said, "Herr Dunwiddie," and then added, "I don't mean to be rude, but I was hoping to have a few minutes alone with Captain Cronley."

"Dunwiddie's my deputy, Herr Oberst. Anything you have to say to me —"

"Of course, of course," Mannberg said quickly. "No offense, Herr Dunwiddie."

"None taken," Tiny said. "What can we do for you?"

"It concerns the NKGB agent, Orlovsky."

"What about him?" Cronley asked.

"Well, what's happened is that Oberstleutnant Bischoff has gone to the general and said that somehow you and he got off on the wrong foot."

Cronley didn't reply.

"And the general asked me to see what I could do about straightening out the situation, the misunderstanding, between you."

"What misunderstanding is that?"

"Well," Mannberg said, "my understanding was that Herr Oberst Mattingly has told

Herr Dunwiddie to keep an eye on the situation for him while we deal with it."

"He did."

"Well, Bischoff said that you had issued orders that he was not to be allowed to further interrogate the Russian."

"I did."

"I don't understand, Herr Kapitän."

"I didn't like what Bischoff was doing to Orlovsky, and I saw that he wasn't getting anywhere with him, so I've taken over the interrogation."

"Oberstleutnant Bischoff is a highly trained, greatly experienced interrogator, our best."

"I can only repeat what I said, that I didn't like what he was doing to Orlovsky and I saw that he wasn't getting anywhere with him, so I took over the investigation. There's no misunderstanding."

"With all respect, Herr Kapitän Cronley, I must protest."

"Duly noted."

"And I must ask you to reconsider. The Russian must be broken."

"I intend to get the information we both want from him."

"And is Oberst Mattingly aware of what you have decided to do?"

"He didn't want to hear it, but I told him

anyway."

"And he approved?"

"You miss the point, Mannberg. Colonel Mattingly doesn't want to know anything about this situation. Since he didn't tell me to 'deal with the situation,' he can hardly tell me not to deal with it, can he?"

"But you have just said you have taken over the interrogation!"

"And I have. From Mr. Dunwiddie, who shouldn't have allowed Bischoff to interrogate my prisoner in the first place."

"Your prisoner?"

"I'm the commanding officer of the Twenty-third CIC. And of Kloster Grünau. Since my men arrested this fellow, whoever he is . . ."

"We know who he is!"

". . . then he's my prisoner. So far as I know, recently discharged from POW status former soldiers have no authority to arrest anyone, much less any authority to detain anyone, or interrogate anyone, do they?"

"This is not the reaction I expected from you," Mannberg said. "Would you be willing to discuss this with General Gehlen?"

"No."

"When he hears of our conversation, I feel sure he'll report it to Colonel Mattingly."

"When I told Colonel Mattingly about

what I had decided to do here, he didn't want to hear it. I don't think he'll be any more interested in hearing Herr Gehlen try to tell him what I've decided to do here."

"You understand, you must understand, how important it is we get the names of our traitors."

"I do. And when I have them, I'll tell you and then you and Herr Gehlen may offer your recommendations about what I should do with the people you have allowed to infiltrate the South German Industrial Development Organization and consequently put it under such an absolutely unacceptable risk of exposure."

"Frankly, Kapitän Cronley, I'm having trouble believing we're having this conversation. I don't like to think what General Gehlen's reaction to it will be."

"Well, I guess you'll know as soon as you tell him," Cronley replied. "Is there anything else on your mind?"

"No, thank you."

"And you're sure you won't change your mind about a drink?"

"That's very kind, but no thank you."

He offered his hand to Cronley, and then to Dunwiddie, and then walked out of the room.

When Mannberg was out of earshot, Tiny

said, "Absolutely fascinating. I've never seen anyone commit suicide before."

"You think that's what I did?"

"Gehlen will be on the phone to Mattingly thirty seconds after Mannberg tells him about this."

"I don't think so."

"Oh, come on!"

"We don't have a secure line. Gehlen's not going to get on an unsecure telephone and say, 'Colonel Mattingly, let me tell you what your crazy young captain's doing with the NKGB major we caught.' "

"Then he'll go to Frankfurt and tell him in person."

"Gehlen doesn't want to go to Mattingly with this unless he has to. So before he does, he'll try to reason with me. Or send Mannberg back to reason with me. I think it'll take him two days — three, if we're lucky — to realize I can't be reasoned with. So we have that much time to get those names from Orlovsky."

"And if he doesn't give them to us?"

"I don't know."

"If he does, Jim, then what are you going to do with him, send him to Argentina?"

After a moment, Cronley said, "Now there's a thought!"

"You didn't think of that?" Dunwiddie

asked incredulously.

Cronley's face showed that he hadn't.

"I'm so glad to hear that you've really thought this problem through," Dunwiddie said. "Answered all the little 'What if's' that came to mind."

"I don't think he'd believe me if I offered him Argentina," Cronley said thoughtfully. "Why should he?"

"You have an honest face?"

"There's only one way to find out," Cronley said, still thoughtfully. And then he ordered, "Get Tedworth on the phone. Tell him to bring Orlovsky back upstairs — at oh-five-hundred tomorrow. He should have had enough time to do some thinking by then. And at midnight, wake him up and feed him his lunch. Something nice, just so he thinks it's lunch. I want to keep him confused about what time it is."

[Five]

Commanding Officer's Quarters
Kloster Grünau
Schollbrunn, Bavaria
American Zone of Occupation, Germany

0505 1 November 1945

"Good afternoon, Major Orlovsky," Cronley said as Staff Sergeant Lewis pulled the

259

duffel bag from the Russian's head.

Orlovsky, who was again barefoot and covered with the blanket tied around his body, didn't reply.

"Captain, do you want me to take the cuffs off his ankles?" Lewis asked.

"Maybe that won't be necessary," Cronley said. "That will depend on the major's reply to what I'm going to ask him."

He waited until Orlovsky's eyes had time to adjust from the darkness of the duffel bag to the light in the sitting room.

"Have you had a little time to think about what's going to happen when they take you to NKGB headquarters in Berlin after they find you sitting tied up on the street by the Brandenburg Gate?"

"Of course I have," Orlovsky said.

"You think they're going to be just a little disappointed in you, allowing yourself to get caught here?"

Orlovsky didn't reply.

"And wonder what information you shared with us?"

Orlovsky's face remained expressionless.

"And I'm sure you've thought they are going to wonder if you really didn't tell us a thing. And the unlikelihood that they will believe you when you assure them that you lived up to your obligations as an NKGB officer. And what that will mean for you. And I don't just mean your being subjected to a lengthy interrogation."

"Maybe we could save a little time, Captain Cronley, if I told you I've given my situation a good deal of thought."

"Including what's very likely to happen to your family?"

Orlovsky exhaled audibly.

"There's not much I can do about that, is there?" Orlovsky asked.

"So, right now, you see the most likely scenario for your future is that after you fail to convince whoever runs the NKGB in Berlin that you lived up to your obligations as an NKGB officer, you will be shot in the back of your head, and your family will be sent to Siberia to remind other people like you of the price their families will pay for their failures."

"Or that you will . . . dispose . . . of me here."

"Which would have the same effect on your family. Consider this, Konstantin. If you don't show up, simply disappear, the NKGB won't really know that we've turned you, will they? They'll think we simply disposed of you. In that case, I submit there's a chance — a slight one, I admit — that they'll decide you died in the line of duty, and are a hero of the NKGB. That would work to encourage others, and if they treated your family well . . . you can see where I'm going with this . . ."

The telephone on the sideboard rang.

Sonofabitch! Why did that have to go off right now?

Cronley gestured for Dunwiddie to answer it and snapped, "I'm not available."

"No," Orlovsky said, "I don't see where you're 'going with this.' "

"Your other option is to let me arrange for you to disappear. And I don't mean into an unmarked grave here in the monastery cemetery."

"Twenty-third CIC, Dunwiddie."

"Disappear? How would I disappear? And you can't keep me in that cell forever."

"I can arrange for you to go somewhere safe."

"I doubt that. I'm a little surprised that you really thought you could offer me a refuge someplace in exchange for those names and I would turn them over to you."

"What about if I got you refuge somewhere, after which you would give me the names?"

"I'm sorry, Captain Cronley is not available."

"And once you had given me the names,

262

and I establish they are the names of the people you've turned, I put Gehlen to work getting your family out of Russia. You know he's got well-placed people in Moscow."

"You cannot expect me to take you seriously?"

"Sir, could I have Captain Cronley call you in ten minutes?"

"I'm perfectly serious, Konstantin. I'm offering you a new life in Argentina."

"Why would you expect me to believe something like that?"

"Aside from the fact that I'm telling you the truth, you mean? I'm not promising we can get your family out of Russia, but I'm promising I'll make Gehlen try. If you were a man, you'd take the chance to do whatever you could for your family."

"You sonofabitch!"

Dunwiddie carried the telephone to Cronley and extended it to him.

"I don't give a damn who it is. Tell him I'll call him back."

"Mattingly," Dunwiddie said.

Oh, shit!

Cronley took the telephone.

"Colonel, I can't talk to you right now. I'll call you —"

"Who the hell do you think you are, Cronley? You'll talk to me whenever I want to

263

talk to you."

"Yes, sir."

"What the hell is going on down there?"

"Sir, I'm interrogating . . . our guest."

"At five o'clock in the morning?"

"Yes, sir."

"The interrogation is over."

Cronley didn't reply.

"The answer I expect is, 'Yes, sir.' "

"Yes, sir."

"We'll discuss that situation when I see you."

"Yes, sir."

"How soon can you be at Eschborn?"

"Eschborn?"

"Goddamn you, Cronley, when I ask you a question, I expect an answer. How soon can you be at Eschborn?"

"Well, it's about a three-hour flight, give or take. And I don't know when daybreak is . . ."

"You can be there sometime around ten hundred hours," Dunwiddie furnished softly. "Daybreak here is about oh-six-thirty. Plus three hours. Around ten hundred, maybe a little before."

That means Tiny heard what Mattingly was saying. Which means Orlovsky heard what Mattingly was saying. Shit!

"Not until ten hundred hours?" Mattingly asked.

Which means he heard Tiny.

"Somewhere around ten hundred, yes, sir."

"Why can't you leave right now?"

"Colonel, I have to be able to see the runway to take off."

"Why can't you shine jeep or truck headlights on the runway?"

"Because I don't want to kill myself, sir. Substituting headlights for landing lights is an emergency procedure. Is this some kind of an emergency?"

"Spare me your smart-ass lip, Cronley."

"Yes, sir."

"On that subject, when you get here, you will speak only when spoken to. Got it?"

"Yes, sir."

"I don't want the subject of your interrogation to come up. Got it?"

"Yes, sir. Colonel, what's going on at Eschborn?"

"I just told you, goddamn it, that you are to speak only when spoken to. That means you don't ask questions. Got it?"

"Yes, sir."

"Get to Eschborn ASAP."

"Yes, sir."

A change in the buzz on the line told

Cronley that Mattingly had broken the connection.

Cronley handed the phone to Dunwiddie, then looked at Orlovsky.

"That was my colonel, Konstantin. He calls every so often to tell me how good a job I'm doing."

"I've had colonels like that," Orlovsky said. "I suppose this Argentina fantasy was his idea?"

"No. It's my idea. He doesn't know about it, and I'm not going to tell him."

"In other words, it wasn't a valid offer?"

"The offer is valid."

"Without your colonel's knowledge or permission?"

"Yeah. Without his knowledge or permission."

"Why should I believe that?"

"Because it's the only hope you have to do something for your family."

Cronley turned to Sergeant Lewis and ordered, "Lewis, uncuff the major. Get him something to eat, and when he's finished take him back to his cell."

[Six]

U.S. Army Airfield H-7
Eschborn, Hesse
American Zone of Occupation, Germany

0955 1 November 1945

Cronley parked the Storch on the grass across the tarmac from Base Operations and got out. He chocked the wheels and walked across the tarmac to see about getting the Storch fueled.

Aside from getting fuel, he didn't know what to do. Mattingly's Horch was nowhere in sight, and he didn't know if he was expected to go to the Schlosshotel on his own, or just wait for whatever was to happen in Base Ops.

The question was answered the moment he walked through the Base Ops door. There were half a dozen officers and noncoms in the foyer.

And a woman. She advanced on him.

"Captain Cronley, I'm Rachel Schumann, Colonel Schumann's wife. Do you remember me?"

"Yes, ma'am."

She gave him her hand and he shook it.

"General Greene asked me to pick you up and take you out to the Schlosshotel for the

267

meeting."

"That's very kind."

"My car is right outside," Rachel said, quickly reclaiming her hand.

"Mrs. Schumann, I have to see about getting my tanks topped off." He pointed to the Flight Planning/Weather room. "It'll take me just a minute."

"I'll wait in the car. It's a Chrysler Town and Country."

"It'll take me just a minute," Cronley repeated, and then watched her as she walked out of the building.

What the hell is going on?

Cronley slid onto the front seat of the wooden-sided station wagon, closed the door, and turned to Rachel. She had the engine running, and started off.

Well, I guess I don't get a welcoming kiss. Or a fond little grope.

What did you expect?

"We're going to have to stop meeting this way," Cronley said. "People will start to talk."

She chuckled.

"Rachel, what the hell is going on?"

"I don't know. Or I don't know much."

"Tell me what you do know."

She nodded. "Tony got in very late last

268

night from Kassel. This morning — he was going into work late, after lunch — we were having breakfast when General Greene called. He told Tony to come out to the Schlosshotel right then. Tony's driver had been told to pick him up for work at thirteen hundred, so with no staff car Tony asked me to run him to the hotel. When I was dropping him off, General Greene said he needed a favor. You were flying into Eschborn and needed a ride. So here I am."

"What's going on at the hotel?"

"All I know is that General Greene called the meeting. Putting you and Tony at the meeting . . ."

"And Mattingly?"

"I saw that enormous car of his in the parking lot . . ."

"His Horch?"

"Is that what it is? It suggests he's part of the meeting. Putting you and my husband and Colonel Mattingly at the meeting makes me think it has to do with what you're doing at wherever you are in Bavaria."

"Kloster Grünau."

"But that's just a guess."

"Good guess. Did anyone ever tell you you have very sexy knees?"

"Eyes off my knees and hands in your

lap," Rachel said, pulling down the hem of her skirt.

They were now on the rather narrow, curving two-lane road leading to the Schloss-hotel from the airstrip.

"You haven't told me what you know about this meeting," Rachel said.

"Mattingly called me at five this morning. He was more than a little pissed when he learned how long it was going to take me to get up here. That's all I know. Except that when I get here, I'm not to speak unless spoken to, and I am forbidden to ask questions."

There suddenly came from behind the sound of a siren.

Sirens, plural, Cronley thought as he turned to look behind the Chrysler.

He saw two M-8 armored cars — sort of light tanks, with wheels rather than tracks — coming up the road.

"What the hell is that?"

Rachel steered the car to the side of the road and stopped.

"I think it's golf time," she said.

"What?"

The M-8s were almost to them. Cronley saw they had chrome sirens and flashing red lights mounted on them. The men wore white Military Police accoutrements and chrome-plated steel helmets. He also saw they weren't going as fast as he had thought.

And there's nobody on the road ahead of them, so what's with the sirens?

The first M-8 rumbled past them. The MPs in it looked down at them.

Arrogantly, Cronley thought. *More than suspiciously, but that, too.*

Then the second M-8 rumbled past.

Cronley saw that its bulk had concealed what was behind it: an olive drab Packard Clipper. A small American flag was mounted on the right fender, and on the left was mounted a red flag with five stars in a circle.

It was impossible to look into the Packard as it passed. The windows were darkened.

"That has to be Eisenhower," Cronley said.

"God, you're clever," Rachel said, gently mocking him. Then she added, as a third M-8 passed them, bringing up the tail of the little convoy, "My love, even generals have to play golf."

"He's headed to the Schlosshotel to play golf?"

"Either that, or he's going to your meeting. I'd bet on the golf."

"And he needs that armored column to get to the golf course?"

"Ike didn't think he needed it either. He hates it. Actually, he said it was preposterous. But he finally deferred to the professional judgment of General Greene."

"I don't understand."

"Can you keep a secret?"

"Sometimes."

"Those MPs are really CIC agents."

"Really?" His surprise was evident.

"You didn't know that CIC is in charge of protecting Ike and Patton and people like that?"

"Not until just now."

"And running those security details is an additional duty for Tony. My husband."

"Fascinating. And you know what else is fascinating? There's nobody coming either way on the road."

"So?"

"So if I kissed you nobody would see."

She caught his hands and held them against the seat between them.

"Tony heard rumors that die-hard Nazis or Communists were going to try to assassinate Ike and General Patton. He didn't think they were all that credible, but you don't take chances. He went to General Greene, and General Greene went to Ike and Patton and told them he thought the threat was credible. Ike finally gave in and accepted. General Patton said he could protect himself, thank you just the same. So, now you know."

"Did you hear what I just said?"

"I'm surprised you're not riding around in one of those M-8s. You're CIC and an Armor second lieutenant."

"Actually, I'm Cavalry and a captain . . ."

"Only since last week," she interrupted.

". . . and they pulled me out of the Basic Officer Course at Fort Knox when I wasn't quite halfway through it."

"Why'd they do that?"

"They needed someone to run the CIC. What do I have to do to get you to kiss me?"

"Put your hands behind your back and promise to keep them there."

"Deal."

She looked in his eyes. "Oh, Jimmy, what are we going to do?"

"Stop talking."

Approximately forty-five seconds later, Rachel pushed him away, said, "You better get that lipstick off," and then set about repairing her own.

When they were moving up the road again, Rachel said, "I'm really sorry we did that."

"Thanks a lot."

"I won't be able to think of anything else

for the next twenty-four hours."

And then she groped him.

VI

[One]

Schlosshotel Kronberg
Kronberg im Taunus, Hesse
American Zone of Occupation, Germany

1020 1 November 1945

A captain wearing the aiguillette and lapel insignia of an aide-de-camp to a brigadier general got out of an armchair in the lobby as Rachel and Jimmy entered. He walked up to them.

"Paul," Rachel said.

"Rachel, the general said if you don't have time to wait for the colonel in the tearoom, we can take him into Frankfurt when this is over."

"I'll wait," Rachel said. "Paul, this is Captain Cronley."

The captain smiled and put out his hand. "Who I will now take off your hands. If you'll come with me, Captain?"

"Thank you for everything, Mrs. Schumann," Cronley said.

"My pleasure, Captain. Perhaps we'll see one another again."

The captain led Cronley across the lobby to a corridor, and then down the corridor to a door. There were two men standing by the door. They were wearing blue triangle insignia; Cronley guessed they were CIC agents. One of them opened the door and the other waved Cronley through it.

He found himself in what he decided was a private dining room. Three tables had been put together end-to-end at the far side of the room. There were more than a dozen officers at them. One of them, in the center, was Rear Admiral Souers. There were two brigadier generals — one of whom was General Greene. And Colonel Mattingly with three other full colonels. And a Marine Corps lieutenant colonel —

Jesus, that's Clete! What the hell is he doing here?

— then several other lieutenant colonels, including Lieutenant Colonel Schumann, whom Cronley had not seen since the incident at Kloster Grünau, and then several majors.

Some were wearing SHAEF shoulder insignia and a few had the new EUCOM shoulder insignia, a variation of the Supreme

Headquarters, Allied Expeditionary Force flaming sword insignia, made necessary when SHAEF had become European Command. The rest had what looked like a striped ball on their shoulders. This was the insignia of Army Ground Forces, which adorned the shoulders of many warriors assigned to the Pentagon.

"I'm glad you could finally find time for us, Cronley," Admiral Souers said. His tone was amused, not sarcastic. Several of the officers at the tables chuckled. "Take a seat, son."

Souers indicated a row of a dozen straight-backed chairs against the wall behind Cronley. He had just settled into one when Souers stood and barked, "Attention on deck!"

Three men entered the room.

"Keep your seats, please, gentlemen," the tallest among them said, and then, smiling at Cronley, took the straight-backed chair next to him.

He took a pack of Chesterfields from the pocket of a linen golf jacket. By the time he got a cigarette to his lips, one of the officers with him, a full colonel wearing the aiguillette and lapel insignia of an aide-de-camp to a general of the Army, had a flaming Zippo waiting.

"Good morning, sir," Souers said.

"Admiral. It's good to see you," General of the Army Dwight David Eisenhower said.

"With your permission, sir?" Souers asked.

Ike gave permission with a wave of the cigarette in his hand.

Jimmy saw the general's fingers were deeply yellow tobacco-stained.

"I think, with a couple of exceptions," Souers said, "we all know one another. The exceptions are my Marine aide-de-camp. While Lieutenant Colonel Frade is a Marine — a distinguished one, he has the Navy Cross — he's not really my aide. That's to keep people from asking questions. Colonel Frade has been running OSS operations in the Southern Cone of South America.

"The other officer who needs introduction is sitting next to General Eisenhower. Not one of the colonels, the captain. Captain Cronley is the officer charged with protecting Gehlen and Company."

Cronley saw Cletus Frade looking at him. Frade's face was expressionless.

What did I expect? That he'd wave at me, or wink, with General Eisenhower sitting next to me?

Frade nodded his head, just perceptibly. Cronley, deciding Eisenhower couldn't see him, winked.

"I sort of thought that's who you probably were," General Eisenhower said, turning to Cronley. "The President told me what you did in South America. Well done, son. I'm glad I've had this chance to meet you."

He gave Cronley his hand.

Cronley said, "Yes, sir. Thank you, sir."

"How do I get this started?" Souers asked rhetorically. "First things first is usually a good idea.

"Everyone knows that the OSS is now history. When that happened, as you all know, the Research and Analysis Branch of the OSS was transferred to the State Department and everything else to the War Department, with orders to shut everything down as quickly as possible.

"There was an exception to this otherwise blanket order. The President ordered the War Department to continue certain OSS operations which he considered necessary in the national interest.

"The Strategic Services Unit under Brigadier General John Magruder" — Souers pointed to one of the one-stars at the table — "was established under the assistant chief of staff, Intelligence, and assumed responsibility for certain of these operations, the ones that could not be turned off like a lightbulb.

"About the most important, and most secret, of these operations has been variously known as Operation Gehlen, Operation Ost, and is now, or will shortly be, the South German Industrial Development Organization.

"Most of you know something about General Gehlen turning over to the OSS, specifically to Colonel Mattingly of OSS Forward" — he turned and pointed to Mattingly — "all the files and assets of Abwehr Ost, said assets including agents in place in the Kremlin and the names of NKGB agents who had infiltrated the Manhattan Project.

"What only a few of you know — and I really hope only a few — is the price General Gehlen asked, and we paid and are paying, for General Gehlen's cooperation."

He stopped and looked at Eisenhower.

"You're on a spot, aren't you, Admiral Souers?" Eisenhower asked.

He took a drag on his cigarette and then slowly exhaled the smoke through thoughtfully pursed lips.

"Okay," Ike finally said. "And I offer this with the caveat that I'm prepared to deny it under oath, with both hands on a Bible. When Allen Dulles came to me and told me what Gehlen wanted, I knew I didn't have the authority to give him what he wanted. So I went to the one man who had that authority, he heard me out, and then said, 'Go ahead.' "

Cronley's eyes slowly scanned the room.

Everybody knew he meant President Truman.

I wonder why he didn't just say it?

"Thank you, sir," Souers said, and then continued: "The price Gehlen demanded was the protection of his men, and their families — including those of his men who were Nazis — from the Soviets. We met that price, and are continuing to meet it.

"We hid — are hiding — some of Gehlen's people in a former monastery in Bavaria and have moved some of them to Argentina." He turned and looked at Colonel Schumann. "That's the secret within the secret of Operation Ost. Some people, including the secretary of the Treasury, the Soviets themselves, the FBI, and Colonel Schumann, got wind of it somehow, and started looking into the operation. Schumann almost got shot when he got too close.

"That's why you're here today, Colonel. The rumor is true, Colonel. But from today your mission is to protect that secret, not make it known to all those people who with very good reason are furious that we're protecting some very despicable people.

"It has been debated at the highest level whether the intelligence we have already received and will receive in the future is worth the price we have to pay for it. The commander in chief has concluded it is.

"Now, what are we doing here? What's the purpose of this meeting?

"On January first, 1946, or shortly thereafter — in other words, two months from now — President Truman will establish by Presidential Finding an organization to be called the Central Intelligence Group. Congressional authority for the CIG will follow as quickly as that can be accomplished. It is the President's intention to send my name to the Senate for confirmation as director of the CIG.

"In the interim, the President has given me responsibility for running what's left of the OSS, and what has been transferred to the War Department until CIG is up and running.

"The CIG will be a peacetime version of the OSS. It will take over such things, including covert operations, such as Operation Ost.

"When the President told me of his plans, he said that one of his greatest concerns was the security of Operation Ost in the next two months. During, in other words, the final shutting down of the OSS and the transfer of General Magruder's Strategic Services Unit in the Pentagon to the CIG.

"The very next day, the President asked me to represent him at the funeral services of a young woman killed in a tragic automobile accident. Her husband, whom the President knows and admires, is an officer serving overseas who could not return for the interment."

"The President told me about your wife, Captain Cronley," General Eisenhower said. "I'm very sorry, son."

"Thank you, sir."

I wonder if you'd feel so kindly toward me if you knew that when you flashed by that Town and Country station wagon on your way here, I was in it, not remembering my dead bride, but wondering how I could get into Mrs. Colonel Schumann's pants.

"When I got to Texas," Souers went on, "I found Colonel Frade there. The . . . deceased . . . young woman, I learned, was his cousin and he had flown up from Buenos Aires for the funeral. General Donovan had told me specifically that I should not be surprised at anything Colonel Frade did.

"So I called President Truman and told him Frade was in Texas and did the President want to see him about the next sixty-day problem before Frade returned to Argentina?

"The President replied that while he would be happy to meet with Colonel Frade, he thought it would be best to have a meeting with all the concerned parties, that he didn't have to participate, and that, because most of the concerned parties were in Germany, the meeting should be held there — *here* — and as soon as possible.

"I said, 'Yes, sir.' And here we all are."

He paused, visibly made up his mind, and then continued: "I said a moment ago that Colonel Frade had flown up from Buenos Aires for the interment of his cousin. I think it germane to tell you that he did so at the controls of a Lockheed Constellation of South American Airways.

"South American Airways, an Argentine corporation, is an OSS asset. Colonel Frade is the airline's managing director — what we would call the president or chairman of the board. SAA has proved very useful in the discreet movement of people and certain files from Europe to Argentina.

"So I was not surprised when Colonel Frade suggested we use the SAA Constellation he'd flown to Midland to fly from there to Washington, pick up General Magruder and his people, and then fly to here.

"We did so. En route, Colonel Frade informed me that while he would have been happy to provide the aircraft free of charge, he could not do so because of Colonel Juan D. Perón.

"Currently Argentina's secretary of Labor and Welfare, secretary of War, and vice president, Perón, in Frade's judgment, is soon to become president of the Argentine Republic.

"He also sits on the board of directors of SAA, where, Frade tells me, he has been 'making noises' to the effect that SAA should be an Argentine government entity and not a 'private capitalistic enterprise,' especially one he strongly suspects is owned and run by American intelligence by whatever name.

"Frade has so far been able to keep Perón's hands off SAA, but feels that Perón learning that SAA has been making *pro bono,* so to speak, flights for the U.S. government would likely permit him to seize SAA now, rather than waiting until he becomes president.

"The OSS funds remaining are just about exhausted, so one of the problems we are going to have to deal with here today is funding SAA so that we can keep it as long as possible. And then decide what to do when, inevitably, and most likely sooner than later, Perón takes it over.

"General Eisenhower, I think I have said everything I have to say right now. Is there anything you wish to add, sir?"

Eisenhower stood. He put a Chesterfield to his lips and his aide-de-camp produced the Zippo. Ike took a deep drag.

"Gentlemen," he said, "I think I can sum this up in a few words. The exigencies of the current political situation vis-à-vis the Soviets have laid on your shoulders one hell of a burden. I have every confidence that you will successfully deal with it, because I have, as the President does, absolute confidence in Admiral Souers and every officer in this room." He paused. "Right down to the young captain beside me." That earned him the chuckles he expected. "And now I hear the summons of the links. Thank you for coming."

Eisenhower touched Cronley's shoulder, smiled at him, and then walked out of the room. His aides followed.

The only reason he was here was to make sure everybody knows that what we're doing has his and Truman's approval.

Souers waited until the door had closed after Eisenhower, and then said: "A break is in order. There's coffee and doughnuts in the tearoom, out the door, down the corridor, and turn right. And while you're drinking your coffee, if you happened to introduce one another, that'd kill two birds with one stone. We'll reconvene back here in half an hour." He looked at his watch. "Say at eleven-thirty."

Cronley saw that both Mattingly and Frade were walking toward him.

Jimmy thought that Frade looked just about as impressive in his uniform as Mattingly did in his.

Jesus, he really is a lieutenant colonel. I don't think I took that in until just now, when I saw him in his Marine Corps uniform.

On the other hand, I really am a captain, and who would have believed that?

I have a hard time believing it, even looking in a mirror.

But Eisenhower called me "captain" and who am I to argue with a five-star?

Mattingly got to him first.

"Be very careful, Captain Cronley, about what you say, and remember the less you say about anything, the better."

Clete arrived as Jimmy was saying, "Yes, sir."

Mattingly left, but Clete had either heard

what he said or seen the looks on their faces.

"What was that all about?"

"I'm fine, Clete. How about you?"

"Are you? How are you doing?"

Cronley shrugged.

"We've got a lot to talk about, but it will have to wait until this is over. Let's go find the tearoom."

Fine. That'll give me a chance to introduce you to my new girlfriend. She's waiting for her husband in there.

[Two]

1105 1 November 1945

In the tearoom, Cronley headed straight for the doughnut table. He wolfed down two of the enormous white sugar-coated cakes, and reached for a third.

"They don't feed you at your monastery?" Frade asked.

"I didn't have any breakfast. I had to get up in the middle of the night . . . and then had to take off as soon as I could see the far end of the runway."

"You flew here? I mean *you* flew here?"

Jimmy nodded.

"In a Piper Cub? What does the Army call them? L-4s?"

"In a Storch."

"Whose Storch?"

"I guess you could say mine. I have two of them."

"Mattingly didn't say anything about you having a Storch. Or Storches. Or about you flying."

"He was probably hoping that on my way here I would fly into one of the many rock-filled clouds we have in scenic Germany and he wouldn't have to talk about me at all."

"Why do I suspect that everything is not peachy-keen between you and Mattingly? What's that all about?"

"I'm sure he'll tell you in detail just as soon as he has the chance."

"I'm shocked. The way you talked about him in Argentina, I thought you were convinced he could walk on water and make the blind see with a gentle touch of his hand."

Cronley was about to reply when three officers — a full colonel, a lieutenant colonel, and a major — walked up to them. All three had Army Ground Forces shoulder insignia.

"Colonel Frade, I'm Jack Mullaney," the colonel said. "From General Magruder's shop? We met, very briefly, earlier."

Shop? What the hell does "shop" mean?

"How are you, Colonel?" Frade asked as

288

he shook Mullaney's hand.

"And this is Lieutenant Colonel Parsons and Major Ashley."

Frade shook their hands.

"This is Captain Cronley," Frade said.

Everybody shook hands.

"Actually, Colonel Frade, we were hoping Captain Cronley could point us toward the officer who will be running Mattingly's shop in Munich. Parsons and Ashley will be joining it, and would like to make their manners."

What the hell is he talking about?

Mattingly's shop in Munich?

"Make their manners"? What the hell does that mean?

"Sir, I don't understand," Cronley confessed politely.

"Perhaps the captain hasn't been brought into the Pullach operation," Lieutenant Colonel Parsons said.

"Is Pullach what you're talking about, sir?" Cronley asked. "You said Munich."

"Is that where the permanent compound will be, Jimmy?" Frade asked.

Cronley nodded.

"Well, now that we're all talking about the same thing," Colonel Mullaney said, "can you point out the officer in charge of the Pullach operation for us, Captain?"

"I'm in charge of Pullach, sir," Cronley said.

The three Pentagon intelligence officers were visibly surprised.

"Well, I will be when we get it open," Cronley clarified. "It's not quite finished."

Major Ashley blurted what all three of them were obviously thinking: "But you're only a captain!"

Frade chuckled and then took a bite of his doughnut.

"And a very junior captain at that," he said, with a smile, when he had finished chewing and swallowing.

"I see we're *not* all talking about the same thing," Colonel Mullaney said. "Let me rephrase: Captain, who will be *in command* of the Pullach operation when it's up and running? That's to whom we wish to pay our respects. Would you point him out, please?"

Frade pointed to Cronley.

"Colonel, can I try to clear this up?" he asked.

"Please do, Colonel," Mullaney said coldly.

"First, as to who will command Pullach. On the way over here, Admiral Souers said that Colonel Mattingly had told him that General Gehlen — who can be very difficult

290

— and Oberst Mannberg — Gehlen's Number Two — and Captain Cronley got along very well, and for that reason he had decided to give command of Pullach to Cronley. The admiral told me Mattingly thought that was a great idea."

"How can the captain command the Pullach operation if he will be outranked by Colonel Parsons and Major Ashley, whom General Magruder has assigned to Pullach?"

"I was about to get to that, Colonel," Frade said. "What I was going to say is that this new organization, the Central Intelligence Group, or whatever the hell it will be called, will inherit from the OSS its somewhat unorthodox philosophy of who does what. That is, the best qualified man gets the job, and his rank has nothing to do with it."

"I'm afraid I can't accept that," Colonel Mullaney said. "I'll discuss this with General Magruder and Admiral Souers."

"Well, I see we're off to a great start," Frade said. "I should have known something like this would have to be dealt with."

"Exactly what do you mean by that, Colonel?" Mullaney challenged more than a little nastily.

Frade looked around the tearoom.

"Admiral!" he called.

Cronley saw that Souers was talking to General Greene, Greene's aide-de-camp, and Lieutenant Colonel and Mrs. Schumann.

"Admiral!" Frade called again, and this time he got Souers's attention.

"Have you got a minute, Admiral?" Frade called.

Souers walked over to them, bringing everybody with him.

"Getting to know one another, are you?" the admiral smilingly inquired, and then asked, "Do we all know one another?" He looked around, decided that everyone did not know everyone, and began the introductions.

"This is General Greene, the Chief of EUCOM CIC," he said. "Captain Hall, his aide, Colonel Schumann, his IG, and the charming Mrs. Schumann. This is Colonel Mullaney, through whom we'll channel the analyses that Colonel Parsons and Major Ashley will develop at Pullach once Captain Cronley gets that up and running."

There was an exchange of handshakes and courtesies.

Frade waited until it had concluded, then announced: "Small problem, Admiral. Colonel Mullaney just announced that he cannot accept Captain Cronley as commander of Pullach."

"Oh?"

"Inasmuch as Cronley is junior to Colonel Parsons and Major Ashley," Frade went on.

"Well, I'm glad the question came up," Souers said. "Let's get it out of the way right now."

"It's not that I have anything against Captain Cronley, Admiral," Colonel Mullaney offered, "as far as I know he may be an extraordinary young —"

"Colonel," Souers interrupted him, "it doesn't matter what you think of Captain Cronley. What matters is your conception of your role in the South German Industrial Development Organization. Let me tell you how I see that. You are to facilitate, in the Pentagon, the transfer of intelligence produced at Pullach, when it's up and running, to your superiors in G-2 and Naval Intelligence. Even to the State Department. Without getting into where that intelligence came from. Any questions so far?"

"No, sir. Admiral —"

"You will also funnel requests for intelligence vis-à-vis our Soviet friends from ONI and G-2 to Pullach, without, it should go without saying, telling them to whom you are going for answers to their questions. Do you have any questions about that?"

"No, sir."

"As you can well imagine, it is in our interests to keep General Gehlen and his people happy. You understand that, of course?"

"Yes, sir, of course."

"General Gehlen has developed a rapport with Captain Cronley. They seem each to respect the other's role in the arrangement . . ."

Jesus, Cronley suddenly thought, *what's going to happen when he finds out this kissy-kissy relationship he thinks there is between me and Gehlen went out the window when I took the Orlovsky interrogation away from his interrogator? And then threw gas on the fire when, in a manner of speaking, I told Mannberg that he and Gehlen could take a flying fuck at a rolling doughnut if they didn't like it?*

". . . and for that reason, Colonel Mattingly gave command of Kloster Grünau to Cronley and recommended to me that he be placed in command at Pullach when that opens. I accepted that recommendation. That's it. It is not open for debate.

"Now, so far as your people at Pullach are concerned, they will serve there at Cronley's pleasure. They should have no question in their minds that Cronley will be in command. Any questions about that, Colonel?"

"No, sir. No questions."

"Good. I'm glad that's all cleared up," Souers said.

"I've got one more question, Admiral, that at best may seem ill-mannered," Frade said. "What's this lovely lady doing in here with all of us ugly old men?"

"Ugly old men talking about material classified Top Secret–Lindbergh, you mean?"

"Yes, sir," Frade said.

"We'd planned to get into this later," Souers said. "But since you brought it up, now's as good a time as any. General Greene?"

"Admiral Souers, Colonel Mattingly, and I were talking about needing a cover for Pullach," Greene began. "People are going to wonder about it. What Mattingly and I came up with, and suggested to the admiral, was that we let people think it's an ASA installation hiding under the South German Industrial Development Organization sign. Everybody, including the Soviets, knows we have the ASA, and keep its installations secret and behind barbed wire and armed guards.

"Major Iron Lung McClung, who runs EUCOM ASA, says it'll be no problem at all to move an ASA listening post — with its antennae farm — he already has in the Munich area into the Pullach compound. And — this was a gift from Above — Mc-Clung says he can set up some wire recorders he liberated from the Germans to transmit gibberish all the time in case those clever Soviets are listening.

"All the Americans in the compound will start wearing Signal Corps insignia. There's plenty of housing for dependents . . ."

Dependents? Wives and children? What the hell?

". . . so with almost no effort — most good ideas are simple ones — we have what we think will be an effective cover."

"And where does this charming lady fit into this effective cover?" Frade asked dubiously.

Jimmy noticed that that earned Clete a forced smile from Colonel Mrs. Schumann.

"It's important, Mattingly and the admiral agreed," General Greene said, "that while I keep abreast of what's going on at Pullach, my going there, except rarely, would draw attention to it. We then considered who, on the other hand, could go there frequently, without it looking suspicious."

Greene looked around and then answered his own question. "My IG is also the IG for

ASA. And this charming lady is president of the CIC/ASA Officers' Ladies Club. And sponsor of the CIC/ASA NCOs' Wives Clubs. No one would find anything suspicious in Colonel Schumann visiting Pullach every other week or so. Or that he be accompanied by his wife when he did. Or Mrs. Schumann going to Pullach alone to meet with the ladies."

Cronley looked at Rachel. She met his eyes momentarily.

"Which, I submit, neatly solves the effective liaison problem," Greene said.

"Mrs. Schumann of course has a Top Secret–Lindbergh clearance?" Frade asked drily.

"Does Mrs. Frade?" Admiral Souers asked.

"No. And I have never told her anything about anything that was classified in any way. Cross my heart and hope to die."

Everyone chuckled.

"Boy Scout's Honor," Frade added, making the Scout sign.

That got laughs.

Souers looked at his watch.

"We had better get back in there. We've got a lot to cover."

[Three]

Cletus Frade said, "In that case, forget it," and hung up the telephone.

He turned to Jimmy.

"The management regrets that it will take a half hour for room service."

"I'll go to the bar and get us something. Jack Daniel's?"

Clete went to a soft-sided suitcase, opened the zipper, and came up with a bottle of Dewar's scotch whisky.

"I learned to drink this in Argentina. Okay with you?"

"Anything."

"We don't have to have this conversation now, Jimmy. You want to wait until after dinner?"

"I'd like to pass on both."

Clete found glasses, poured whisky into them, then handed one to Cronley.

"You don't have any option about Colonel and Mrs. Schumann's kind invitation to dinner," Clete said. "You will go and smile.

298

I think Schumann will be very useful to you. He obviously likes you . . ."

He wouldn't if he knew I'm screwing his wife.

". . . and your only option about our talking is when we do it."

"Let's get it over with."

Clete tapped his glass to Jimmy's.

"Okay. Bad news first. The Old Man's had a heart attack."

"Jesus!"

"That's the reason I went to Midland. It was what Souers suggested in there, that it was another example of my tendency to act impulsively. I went only after I put everything on the scale and decided, fuck the OSS, they've just buried the Squirt, the Old Man had a heart attack, my family needs me. Making that decision took me all of two seconds."

"How is he?"

"When your father called me . . . it was the usual lousy connection . . . he said that the Old Man had had a heart attack on his Connie on their way out there, and they diverted to Dallas and rushed him to Parkland Hospital. He said it didn't look good, and that he would keep me posted.

"Hansel was with me. I told him to get out to Jorge Frade and get one of our Connies ready while I found our wives and told them why we would be out of town for a few days.

"That of course didn't work. Argentine women are big on family. When we took off an hour later, my wife and kids and Hansel's wife and kid were aboard. And so were two nannies, two hundred pounds of kiddy supplies, and Gonzalo Delgano —"

"Who?"

"You met him. He's SAA's chief pilot."

Cronley shook his head indicating he didn't remember.

"And another pilot, a radio operator/navigator, and a steward. Gonzo was not about to have the boss go flying in the fragile mental condition he was already in caused by the death of his sister, and further aggravated by the grave illness of his grandfather.

"Actually, I was pretty touched even though I wanted to go alone.

"About twenty-one hours later, we touched down at Midland — Gonzo graciously gave me the left seat for the final leg — and I looked out the window and there's the Old Man leaning on the fender of his Town and Country — you know, that enormous station wagon?"

"I've seen one or two."

"He was waiting for us. With Souers."

"I thought you said he had a heart attack?"

"My grandfather, with a straight face, said he had a little too much to drink on the airplane. Dr. Neiberger, at the Squirt's wake, or viewing, or whatever the hell they call it, told me he had had a 'medium to severe' heart attack probably brought on by stress. Aside from a daily aspirin — honest to God, an aspirin, to thin the blood — and avoiding stress, there wasn't much else that could be done for him. Neiberger also said the only way to keep him in the hospital would have been by force, and that would cause precisely the kind of stress he should avoid."

He paused, then said admiringly, "That Old Man is one tough sonofabitch."

"Yes, he is."

"I suppose you want to hear about the viewing and the interment."

"No, I don't."

Clete did not miss a beat: "The Squirt had a lot of friends and they all showed up, including a delegation of her sorority sisters from Rice. You, surprisingly, have more friends than I would have guessed and they all showed up, including a delegation from A&M who served as Marjie's pallbearers."

Jimmy suddenly felt his chest heave in an

enormous sob. His eyes began to water.

"All in all," Clete said — and then his voice broke. After a moment, and with great difficulty, he was able to finish, "It was quite an event."

He picked up the bottle of Dewar's and added to both their glasses.

"She was buried at Big Foot, of course. On your side."

"What does that mean, my side?"

"Really? I thought you knew. The cemetery, although it's on Big Foot, is jointly owned by the Howells and the Cronleys. The Howells get buried on one side and the Cronleys on the other. They buried the late Mrs. Cronley with her husband's family."

Jimmy looked at him with tears running down his cheeks.

"Actually, as it turns out, Marjie's about ten feet from her father," Clete said. "I don't know if Mom, or your mother, or your dad, set it up that way, but that's where the Squirt'll be from now on. Next to my Uncle Jim."

Jimmy thought that he hadn't really understood the convoluted family relations of Cletus Frade until he'd gone to Argentina, although he had wondered about them from the time he wore short pants. Starting with, he thought now, wondering why Jim and Martha Howell's "son" was named Frade instead of Howell.

Gradually, he had been able to put some of the pieces together.

Clete's "mom" wasn't his mother but his aunt. Beth and Marjorie — the Squirt — were his cousins, not his sisters. Their father, James Howell, was Clete's uncle. James was one of Cletus Marcus Howell's — the Old Man's — two children, the other being Clete's mother. She had died when Clete was an infant.

Jimmy seldom had heard her name, but the Old Man made it clear that the reason she died was that she had married "a despicable Argentinian sonofabitch." He knew this because that's how Cletus Marcus Howell referred to him on those rare occasions when the subject came up in Jimmy's hearing.

Jimmy had grown up thinking that Clete's father was some sleazy Mexican-type greaseball Casanova who had somehow managed to seduce a wholesome Midland girl, gotten her with child, watched her die — probably of the drugs and alcohol to which he had introduced her — and then abandoned her and their infant offspring. The baby — Clete — had then been taken in by James Howell, his mother's brother, and reared by him and his wife, Martha, as their own.

When Second Lieutenant Cronley had ordered one of Tiny's Troopers to put a couple of rounds from the pedestal-mounted .50 caliber Browning machine gun on his jeep into the engine of Lieutenant Colonel Schumann's staff car to convince the colonel that, IG or not, he was not going to be allowed into Kloster Grünau, he had been entirely within his rights to so.

Cronley had been authorized by Colonel Mattingly to take whatever action was necessary, including the taking of human life, to protect what was going on at Kloster Grünau from becoming known.

But there were ramifications to the shattered engine block. Colonel Schumann had gone to General Greene to report not only the assault upon his staff car, but to tell Greene that he was convinced the activity at the secluded monastery had a great deal to do with the rumor he had been chasing for some time — that renegade Americans were sneaking Nazis out of Germany to South America.

With great difficulty — as Mattingly had not been then authorized to tell Greene anything about Operation Ost — he had managed to dissuade Greene from sending the 18th Infantry Regiment to seize Kloster Grünau from whoever held it. But Mattingly knew that was a temporary solution at best, and that a very credible scenario was that Greene, after thinking it over, would send the 18th Infantry and tell him about it later.

If that happened, about seventy pounds, literally, of incriminating documents at Kloster Grünau would be seized. That simply could not be allowed to happen. Mattingly immediately collected the documents and Second Lieutenant Cronley from Kloster Grünau and took them to Rhine-Main airfield in Frankfurt.

There, after ordering Cronley to guard the documents with his life until he could place them in the hands of Lieutenant Colonel Frade and no one else, he put both on an SAA Constellation bound for Buenos Aires. Then he put himself on a Military Air Transport Service C-54, which departed Rhine-Main for Washington.

He had to convince Admiral Souers, who was presiding over the burial of the OSS, that General Greene and others had to be told of Operation Ost and ordered to support it. Otherwise Operation Ost was going to blow up in everybody's face, and those faces included President Harry S Truman's and General of the Army Dwight David Eisenhower's.

Mattingly's orders to Cronley were that once the documents were safely in Frade's hands, he was to catch the next Germany-bound SAA flight and return to Kloster Grünau, where he was to keep his mouth shut, and, if the 18th Infantry showed up, to stall them as long as possible before surrendering.

Cronley had not been able to comply with his orders.

Cletus Frade had met Jimmy Cronley's SAA aircraft at Aeropuerto Coronel Jorge G. Frade. He was driving a Horch automobile — very much like Colonel Mattingly's — and had with him his wife, a long-legged blond with a flawless complexion who spoke English like the King.

What Jimmy hoped was discreet questioning produced the information that the airport was named "Frade" because Clete had dedicated it to his father — *that despicable Argentinian sonofabitch?* — and that the Horch — "Nice car. Where'd you get it?" — had been his father's.

They drove into Buenos Aires, a city that didn't look like anything Mexican, and stopped at a mansion overlooking a horse racetrack. Clete had told him the mansion, built by his Grand-uncle Guillermo, was where Clete and his wife and kids lived because Dorotea thought the "big house" was about as comfortable as a museum.

When they went inside, things immediately became even more complicated.

The Old Man was there. And Martha and Beth and Marjie Howell.

All the Howell women kissed Cronley, which he sort of expected. What he didn't expect was the way the Squirt kissed him. Clete's baby sister wasn't supposed to kiss him that way, and he absolutely wasn't supposed to have the instant physical reaction to it that he did. All he could do was hope that no one happened to be glancing six inches below his belt buckle.

But even that went into the background when Cronley, almost casually, mentioned to Clete that he had been talking with some of Gehlen's people at Kloster Grünau about where a missing submarine, U-234, might have made landfall in Argentina, and they had come up with a very likely answer.

"Jesus Christ, didn't Mattingly tell you?" Clete said.

"What?"

"Apropos of nothing whatever, my last orders from General Donovan were to keep two things going at all costs — Operation Ost and the search for U-234. So tell me, what did you and the boys in the monastery come up with?"

Jimmy's reply had immediately triggered a good deal of frenzied activity adding to the frenzied activity already in progress, which included the attempted assassination of Colonel Juan D. Perón, whom Clete referred to as his Uncle Juan.

Jimmy still had trouble remembering exactly what had happened and when, but in about the middle of it he had been in Mendoza —

That was right after Clete flew there with a wounded Colonel Perón in the back of the machine-gun-riddled SAA Lodestar.

And before the Squirt told me she'd loved me all her life — and I took her virginity. The next and last time we Did It was in the Lord Baltimore Hotel.

That was after I got checked out in the Lodestar, then headed to the Straits of Magellan. And after I came back from down there with the uranium oxide from the U-234.

And we loaded it on the Old Man's Connie and flew it to Washington.

And the next thing I knew I was a captain.

And I was a widower — no — first I was a married man.

The next day I was a widower, and that afternoon I was a captain.

— on top of a mountain, in sort of a fort and prison run by Clete's deputy, Major Maxwell Ashton III, and for the first time Jimmy and Clete were alone for a few minutes and Jimmy had just blurted out, "What the hell's going on?"

"You mean here at Casa Montagna — aka Fort Leavenworth South?"

"Start with that."

"Well, it also was built by my Great-uncle Guillermo," Clete said, "which is why it's called Estancia Don Guillermo. I never met him, but I understand he was not crippled by modesty and self-effacement. I inherited it from my father, and placed it in the service of the Office of Strategic Services. Next question?"

"How'd you go from being a hotshot fighter pilot to the OSS, Clete? I still remember your mom showing me the picture of you being awarded the Distinguished Flying Cross for service there."

Clete turned his head slightly and nodded. "That's right. I never told you. As you know, I made Ace — that takes five kills and I got seven — with VFM-226 on Guadalcanal. For living to tell about it, there was a prize: The Corps sent me home to go on a

War Bond tour. You can imagine how much fun that was. And following the tour, the Corps was sending me to Pensacola to teach fledging birdmen.

"I was in my room in the Hollywood Roosevelt Hotel trying to decide who I was going to have to kill to get out of both the tour and flight school when a full bull Marine colonel showed up. He handed me a picture of a man wearing what looked like a German uniform. 'That's your father.'

"I said, 'Really?' and he said, 'We think he's going to be the next president of Argentina.'

"And I probably said, 'Really?' again, and he said, 'Lieutenant, we want you to go to Argentina and do two things. Blow up an ostensibly neutral ship which is supplying German submarines in the River Plate, and see what you can do to tilt your father to our side. Right now he's favoring Hitler, Mussolini, and Tojo.'"

"This is for real?"

Clete nodded again. "It was mind-blowing. I said, very respectfully, 'Sir, I have never laid eyes on my father. That's the first picture I ever saw of him. And I have no idea how to blow ships up. I'm a Marine fighter pilot.'"

"And?"

"He said, 'You *were* a Marine fighter pilot. What you are now is a Basic Flight Instructor on temporary War Bond Tour Duty en route to Pensacola. We'll teach you how to blow up ships, and I'm sure you'll figure out some way to cozy up to your daddy once you get to Buenos Aires.' "

"Jesus!"

"Three weeks later, I got off the Panagra Clipper in the River Plate. My cover was that I had been medically discharged from the Corps and was now going to make my contribution to the War Effort by making sure none of the crude or refined product that the Old Man shipped there from Howell Petroleum Venezuela wound up in German, Italian, or Japanese hands.

"The Old Man arranged for me to stay with his major customer, who is a real pain in the ass. All Señor Enrico Mallin knew about me was that I was the Old Man's grandson — not that my father was an Argentine.

"Two nights after I get to Buenos Aires, I'm having dinner with the Mallin family, trying to keep my eyes off his daughter —"

"His daughter?"

"Good-looking blond. You've met her. Her last name is now Frade."

"*That's* where you met her?"

311

"You want to hear this story or not?"

"Go!"

"The phone rings. The butler tells my future father-in-law it's for him. Señor Mallin snaps, 'You know I don't take calls at dinner,' and the butler replies, 'Señor, it is el Coronel Frade.'

"Mallin turns white. He takes the phone and oozes charm as he tells el Coronel Frade how pleased he is to hear his voice, and asks how might he be of service.

"A very loud voice that can be heard all over the dining room announces, 'It has come to my attention that my son is under your roof. I would like to talk to him.'

" 'Your son, *mi Coronel*?'

" 'For Christ's sake, Mallin! I know he's there. Get him on the goddamned phone!' "

Cronley laughed.

"How'd he know you were there?"

"You met General Martín. The guy who runs the Bureau of Internal Security. He was a light colonel then, Number Three at BIS. It was brought to his attention that an American named Cletus Howell Frade, whose passport said he was born in Argentina, had just gotten off the Panagra Clipper. He checked and — lo and behold! — there it was, el Coronel Frade had a son named Cletus Howell Frade. He asked my

312

father if there was anything el Coronel thought he should know about his son who had just arrived in Buenos Aires."

"Why'd he do that?"

"My father was about to stage a coup d'état, following which he would become president of the Argentine Republic . . ."

"He was what?"

". . . which Martín thought was a good thing, and didn't want anything screwing it up. Are you going to stop interrupting me?"

"Sorry."

"So I took the phone from Mallin. And a deep voice formally announced, 'This is your father. Would it be convenient for you to take lunch with me tomorrow?' I said, 'Yes, sir,' and he replied, 'The bar at the Alvear Palace. Half past twelve.' And he hung up.

"At twelve-forty the next day, ten minutes late — there are two bars at the Alvear, and I'd gone to the wrong one — I walked into the bar looking for a guy in a German uniform. No luck. But a guy wearing a tweed jacket and silk scarf looked hard at me. I walked over and in my best Texican Spanish asked if he was Colonel Frade.

" 'You're late,' he announced. 'I hate to be kept waiting. That said, may I say I'm delighted to see you've returned safely from

Guadalcanal.' "

"He knew you'd been on Guadalcanal?"

"Yeah. I found out later he knew just about everything else I'd ever done in my life, like when I was promoted from Tenderfoot in Troop 36, BSA, in Midland.

"Then he said, 'With your approval, I suggest we have a drink, or two, here and then go to the Círculo Militar for lunch. That's the officers' club.'

"In the next thirty minutes, over three Jack Daniel's — doubles — he politely inquired into the health of the Howells, including the Old Man, then announced I had arrived conveniently in time for the funeral next week of my cousin."

"You had a cousin down here?"

"Cousin Jorge, the son of my father's sister, Beatrice. Pay close attention, Jimmy, it gets complicated from this point.

"My father said Aunt Beatrice, who'd always been a little odd, poor woman, had just about gone completely bonkers when Cousin Jorge died in the crash of a Storch at Stalingrad. He was afraid she wasn't going to make it through the funeral, which was going to include the posthumous presentation of the Knight's Cross of the Iron Cross."

"You had a cousin who was a German

314

pilot at Stalingrad?" Jimmy said incredulously.

"He was an Argentine captain, at Stalingrad as an observer."

"Jesus Christ!"

"And sometime during this exchange of family gossip, I told him the bullshit cover story about me being medically discharged from the Corps, and how I was in Argentina to check on what happened to Howell Venezuela crude and refined product.

"To which he replied, 'Teniente Coronel Martín — who's seldom wrong — thinks the OSS sent you down here.' So I asked him who Martín was, and he told me, and I said he's wrong, to which he replied, (a) 'Please do not insult me by lying to me,' and (b) 'Don't worry about Martín. I can handle him until we get you safely out of the country.'

"Then he said it was time for lunch. I tried to be a gentleman and pay for the drinks, but my father waved at the barman. 'My son's money is no good in the Alvear. Make sure everyone knows that.'

"We walked out of the hotel. The Horch was parked there next to an Absolutely No Parking Or Stopping At Any Time sign. Enrico — you know Enrico . . ."

Jimmy nodded.

". . . was standing there holding the driver's door open. My father said, 'Cletus, this is Suboficial Mayor Rodríguez. We soldiered together for twenty-five years. Enrico, this is my son Cletus.'

"Enrico popped to attention. 'An honor, *mi teniente. El coronel* has told me what a fine officer of the Corps de Marines you are.' "

"I thought your father was a Nazi. Or a Nazi sympathizer."

"At the time, so did I. So then my father said, 'Get in the back, Enrico. Teniente Frade will drive.' I got behind the wheel and drove to the Círculo Militar, a couple of blocks away.

"I later found out I was the first person except Enrico my father ever let within ten feet of that steering wheel. He really loved his Horch. He died in it."

"What?"

"Assassinated. Two barrels of twelve-gauge double-aught buckshot to the face."

"Jesus Christ, Clete!"

"I'll return to that later. So we went to the Círculo Militar, where we had several more double Jack Daniel's while waiting for our lunch, during which time he introduced me to maybe half of the senior brass of the Ejército Argentino as 'my son, *Teniente* Cletus,

316

hero of Guadalcanal, where he shot down seven Japanese aircraft and earned the Distinguished Flying Cross.'

"During lunch, which was an enormous filet mignon served with two bottles of Don Guillermo Cabernet Sauvignon — from here, Jimmy, my father said it came from a 'little vineyard the family owns' . . . Okay, where was I? Oh. The important part. Over lunch, I heard my father's version of his marriage and why I was raised by Mom and Uncle Jim. It differed substantially from the Old Man's version."

"What was your father's version?"

"That he and my mother were married in New Orleans, in the Saint Louis Cathedral, with the Old Man's blessing. His poker-playing pal the Cardinal Archbishop did the honors. No one had ever told me that.

"My father's best man was his Army buddy, then Major Juan Domingo Perón. A year later, I was born — upstairs in this house, the attending physician was Mother Superior — and Tío Juan became my god-father."

"That old nun who just sewed up Perón?"

"One and the same. She runs the Little Sisters of Saint Pilar hospital. She also delivered both of my kids."

"So what the hell happened?"

"My mother, when she converted to Roman Catholicism, jumped in with both feet. The Old Man thought her conversion was no more than a formality to get the cardinal to marry them in the cathedral. But she became deeply devout."

"So what? I don't understand."

"She'd had trouble when I was born. Mother Superior warned her that future pregnancies would be dangerous. This was confirmed by other doctors."

"And your father didn't care, he just —"

"What my father told me, with tears running down his cheeks, was that he would cheerfully have started to worship the devil if that's what it would have taken to get my mother to get her tubes tied or let him use what he called 'french letters.' But my mother declared them mortal sins. She said it was in the hands of God."

"And she became pregnant?"

"And died, together with the child she was carrying, in childbirth."

"Here?"

"In New Orleans. My father said she didn't want to go there. But Mother Superior told her that it was her Christian duty to get the best medical attention possible. They left here — taking me with them — and flew to Miami and then New Orleans.

Where she died. And the Old Man went ballistic, blaming it all on —"

"That despicable Argentinean sonofabitch?"

Clete grunted. "Yeah. So when my father said that he intended to have my mother buried in the family mausoleum in the Recoleta Cemetery in Buenos Aires, the Old Man talked him into leaving the baby — me — with Mom and Uncle Jim in New Orleans until after the funeral.

"When my father came back to the States to get me, they stopped him at the border. The Old Man had arranged to have him declared a 'person of low moral character.' And when my father sneaked into the States from Mexico, he was arrested and did ninety days on a Texas road gang, after which he was deported and told if he tried to get into the States again, he'd do five years."

"Jesus . . ."

"Yeah. My father told me he had to give up, and decided that Mom and my Uncle Jim would do a better job of raising me than his sister Beatrice, who already showed signs of lunacy."

"And you believed your father's version?"

"Yeah. I did. Right from the start. I knew what a sonofabitch the Old Man can be. I love him, you know that, Jimmy. But he can be, and you know it, a three-star sonofa-bitch. And what my father told me the Old Man had done sounded just like what the Old Man would do.

"Anyway, I heard this while putting down all that booze, and then my father said, 'The family has a guesthouse in town. Across from the racetrack on Avenida Libertador. It's yours for as long as you're here.'

"He wouldn't take no for an answer. And since I knew Mallin didn't want me in his house — he'd seen the way I looked at his Virgin Princess, and I'd seen his reaction to learning who my father was — I agreed to take a look at the house. He introduced me to the housekeeper, who was Enrico's sister, and showed me around the place.

"In the master bedroom, he sat down and passed out. Enrico threw him over his shoulder and carried him home. Then I passed out.

"Three days later, after the guy running the OSS here — an absolute moron of a lieutenant commander — sent me on an idiot mission to Uruguay . . . But that's another story."

"Tell it."

"Okay. Why not? This clown sent Tony Pelosi, my demolition guy — you met him, too, the assistant military attaché from the embassy?"

"Yeah. The major from Chicago."

"Right. Well, Commander Jack Armstrong the All-American Asshole sent me and Tony — he was then a second lieutenant — to Uruguay. We went up near the Brazilian border and waited around in the middle of the night in a field until an airplane dropped us a package. The package had what looked like wooden boxes. The OSS in the States had cleverly molded explosives to look like wooden slats, then made the slats into boxes, and flew the boxes to the U.S. Air Force base at Puerto Allegre. After the exchange of many classified messages between the Air Force and Commander Asshole, who was the naval attaché at the embassy in Buenos Aires, an Air Force guy climbed into his plane. He then violated Uruguayan sovereignty and neutrality by flying into Uruguay and dropping the boxes to the OSS agents who were to use the explosives to blow up a Spanish freighter in Argentina. It was right out of an Errol Flynn–Alan Ladd movie."

"You and Pelosi used the explosives on the ship?"

Clete shook his head. "On the boat on the way back from Montevideo to Buenos Aires that night, Tony told me there wasn't enough explosive in the wooden slats to blow a hole in a medium-sized rowboat, but not to worry, he'd bought all the TNT we would need in a hardware store in downtown Buenos Aires."

"Incredible!"

"It gets worse. The OSS geniuses who had come up with their blow-up-the-Spanish-ship plan hadn't considered that the ship might have floodlights and machine guns in place to keep people from paddling up to her and attaching an explosive charge to her hull. When Tony and I finally found the ship, we knew we couldn't get closer to her than five hundred yards."

"So the ship didn't get sunk?"

"Oh, it got sunk all right, but by a U.S. Navy submarine. Tony and I flew over it in my father's Staggerwing Beechcraft, lit it up with flares, and the sub put two torpedoes in her. Which is, come to think of it, how come you were able to fly up here in my red Lodestar."

"Why red? This I have to hear."

"We heroes love nothing more than being able to tell of our exploits to appreciative and impressionable young men, so I'll tell you." He paused. "I'll start with the night I came back from Uruguay . . .

"When I walked into Grand-uncle Guillermo's house, I saw lights in the library and heard music — Beethoven — playing on the phonograph. I thought that it was probably my father, so I walked in. A young blond guy was sitting in an armchair, staring thoughtfully into a brandy snifter and waving his hand to the music.

"In my best Texican Spanish, I courteously asked who the hell he was.

"He jumped to his feet, bobbed his head, clicked his heels, and formally replied, 'Major Hans-Peter Ritter von Wachtstein of the Luftwaffe.'

"To which I naturally replied, 'First Lieutenant Cletus H. Frade of the United States Marine Corps at your service, sir.' "

"The enemy was in the library? You're pulling my leg . . ."

"Absolutely not. Hansel said, in Spanish, 'It would seem we are enemy officers who've met on neutral territory.'

"So I cleverly replied, 'That's sure what it looks like.'

"Hansel said, 'I have no idea what we should do.'

"To which I replied, 'Why don't you start by telling me what you're doing sitting in my father's chair, drinking his cognac?'

"That got his attention. He said, '*Herr*

Leutnant, please permit me to extend my condolences on the loss of your loved one, the late *Hauptman* Jorge Frade Duarte, whose remains I had the honor of escorting from Germany.'

"I suavely replied, 'Before we get into that, Major, is there any more of that cognac? I've had a trying day.' "

"So that's how you met Hansel!" Jimmy said, laughing.

Clete nodded. "An hour and a bottle and a half of cognac later, we were pals. What had happened was that my loony tune Aunt Beatrice, either not knowing or not caring that I was in the family guesthouse, sent Hansel there after he delivered Cousin Jorge's lead-lined casket."

"What was that all about? Sending the body home to Argentina?"

"Hansel told me the idea came from Josef Goebbels himself. Pure propaganda. The son of a prominent — very prominent — Argentine family gets killed in the holy war against the godless Communists. Germany and Argentina fight the holy war together."

"And how did Hansel get involved?"

"He's a legitimate German hero. He got the Knight's Cross of the Iron Cross from Hitler himself. And — an important 'and' — his father, one of the German generals in

324

from the beginning of the plot to assassinate Adolf, wanted to get the last of the von Wachtstein line out of Germany alive. Hansel's two brothers had already died in the war."

"And he told you all this the night you met him?"

"No, of course not. It came out later. That first night we just got smashed and agreed on a couple of things. For example, that fighter pilots are superior human beings and, unkindly, that Cousin Jorge not only didn't deserve the Knight's Cross of the Iron Cross Hansel was going to pin on his casket but was a goddamned fool for going to a war he didn't have to go to.

"The next morning, they sent people from the German embassy to get Hansel out of the house. We had decided we wouldn't mention to anyone that we'd met.

"The next time I saw him was the day of the funeral. He came to me at the Alvear hotel and told me to watch my back — the SS guy in the embassy had told him they were going to whack me."

"What?"

Clete nodded and went on, "And sure enough the next night, three Paraguayan hit men showed up at Uncle Guillermo's house and tried to do just that."

"Tried to assassinate you?"

"Obviously they failed. But they slit the throat of Enrico's sister before they came upstairs after me. Miserable bastards. She was a really good woman. She had known my mother — and me, too, when I was an infant — and told me a hell of a lot about my mother that nobody had ever told me before."

" 'They failed'?"

"I was waiting for them," Clete said simply. "I shot them."

"I never heard any of this."

"What was I supposed to do, Jimmy, write home? 'Dear Mom: Well, the news from the Paris of Latin America is that Nazis sent some Paraguayan assassins to my house last night. I had to kill all three. There's blood and brains all over my bedroom. PS — Tell Jimmy'?"

"Jesus!"

"They do a lot of that, assassinations or attempted assassinations, down here. Just before they shot at Tío Juan, somebody showed up at Martín's house to take him out. He had to kill three, too — and they were Argentine officers."

Cronley was silent for a moment, then asked, "You didn't get hurt? What did you do with the bodies? Did the cops come?"

"There was a water pitcher by my bedside. It got hit, exploded, and I had fifty or so crystal fragments in my face and neck. It wasn't serious but at the time I thought I was going to bleed to death right there.

"Yeah, the cops came. But so did Bernardo Martín. He got rid of the cops, then put me in an ambulance and hid me in the military hospital. A dozen BIS agents stood watch as they patched me up.

"The next day, Enrico showed up at the hospital with that shotgun you've seen him with. The newspapers reported a robbery in the Frade mansion and the police had been forced to shoot the robbers.

"Then my father showed up. Thoroughly pissed. Enrico would stay with me, he announced, until I could be loaded on the Panagra Clipper to Miami. I told him thanks but no thanks. I had been sent to Argentina to blow up a ship, and that's what I intended to do — it was my duty as an officer.

"He gave me a funny look, then he wrapped his arms around me. 'I should have known better. The blood of Pueyrredón flows in your veins as it flows in mine! You must do your duty! And it is clearly my duty to help you.'

"Whose blood?"

"Juan Martín de Pueyrredón's. It seems

he's my great-great-grandfather. He ran the English out of Buenos Aires in 1806 using gauchos from his estancia as cavalry. Big hero down here. Think Nathan Bedford Forrest.

"I didn't know that then. All I knew was that my father was emotional about our bloodline and trying to be a nice guy. I said something like, 'Thanks but unless you know where I can borrow an airplane to look for this Spanish ship . . .'

"To which he replied, 'There's half a dozen Piper Cubs and a Staggerwing Beechcraft at Estancia San Pedro y San Pablo. Or I can come up with something else.'

"He then told me the estancia was one of the family's little ranches, eighty-four thousand two hundred and five hectares. A hectare is two point five acres."

Jimmy whistled.

"He said the Cubs were useful to keep track of the cattle. The Staggerwing Beechcraft he'd bought to fly back and forth between Santo Tomé and Buenos Aires when he was commanding the Húsares de Pueyrredón Cavalry Regiment. He had a pilot, Gonzalo Delgano —"

"The SAA pilot?"

"The SAA *chief* pilot. My father told me I could use the Staggerwing to find the *Reine de la Mer,* the Spanish ship supplying German subs, if I gave my word of honor as an officer and gentleman that I'd leave Argentina immediately after I blew it up. I didn't think the Argentines were going to like a Yankee blowing up a ship in their waters and would put me in jail if they didn't shoot me. I agreed to his terms.

"So that's what happened. Tony and I found the *Reine de la Mer.* An American sub sneaked into the River Plate. Tony and I lit up the *Reine de la Mer* with flares from the Staggerwing and the sub put two torpedoes into her. A spectacular sight that Tony and I watched swimming around in the water into which I had dumped the Staggerwing after the machine guns on the *Reine de la Mer* had knocked out the engine."

"You got shot down?"

Frade nodded.

"Enrico picked us up in a speedboat. We hid in Buenos Aires for two days, then took the Panagra Flying Clipper to Miami. My father saw us off. He said" — Frade's voice started to break — "that he loved me and was proud of me and that we would see each other after the war."

"And?"

"And that was the last time I ever saw him."

Clete met Jimmy's eyes, cleared his throat, and went on: "Then my education in this business really began. You may find this hard to believe, but at that point in my life, I was as innocent and naïve as you are now."

"What the hell is that supposed to mean?"

"In Miami, I called Colonel Graham —"

"Who?"

"Colonel A. J. Graham, USMCR, OSS deputy director for Western Hemisphere Operations. The guy who I met in Hollywood and sent me to Buenos Aires. I was going to tell him Tony and I were in Miami and why. He said he already knew. Then he told me to go to New Orleans, to the Old Man's house, and take Tony with me. We were not only not to go home, we weren't even allowed to call home.

"Two days later, he showed up at the Old Man's house and announced the President was very pleased —"

"Roosevelt?"

Frade nodded.

"As proof thereof, I was now a captain, and Tony a first lieutenant. As soon as the paperwork caught up, I would get the Navy Cross and Tony the Silver Star.

"For a few wonderful seconds I saw a bright future. I'd go to Pensacola for the rest of the war and very, very carefully teach young men to fly. After the war, I'd get out of the Corps, fly to BA, marry Dorotea, and we'd spend the rest of our lives in a vine-covered cottage by the side of a road somewhere.

"Graham said, 'We now need to talk about you going back to Buenos Aires.'

"I replied, 'If I go back, two things will happen. Right after I shoot Commander Asshole, the Argentines will put me in jail or in front of a firing squad or both.'

"He said, 'You're replacing Commander Asshole as the naval attaché. You will have diplomatic immunity and can't be arrested for anything. Ditto for Pelosi — he's now an assistant military attaché.'

" 'You don't understand, Colonel, sir,' I said. 'The Argentines know I used my father's Staggerwing to light up the *Reine de la Mer*. They won't accept me as naval attaché.'

"Graham shook his head. 'The only way they could turn you down would be by accusing you of being involved in that. How could you possibly light up a ship the Argentine Foreign Ministry insists has never been in neutral Argentine waters?'

"He let me figure that out, then said, 'So far as your father's Staggerwing is concerned, the President decided it would be a nice gesture on his part, a token of the admiration of the American people for the man we think will be the next president of the Argentine Republic, to send him another. He's issued the necessary orders to see that's done immediately. You can tell him that when you get back down there, which will be as soon as the State Department gets off its bureaucratic ass and delivers your diplomatic passports and you get on a Clipper.' "

"And?"

"And . . . next day came the news that my father had been assassinated. The word Graham got was that the people involved with my father in Outline Blue, the coup d'état, were convinced the Germans were behind it, and were furious. Graham suggested I go back as an Argentine — since I was born here — and cozy up to whoever was the new president."

"Wasn't that risky?"

"Graham knew damned well how risky. But he saw how angry I was. It didn't occur to me that he was thinking, *What the hell, Frade's expendable.*"

"You're bitter?"

"I was for a while. But when I grew up, I realized that not being told you're considered expendable is one of the rules in this game we're playing. You should write that down."

"Would you believe I've already figured that out? That I'm considered expendable and nobody told me?"

"I think you're referring to Mattingly," Clete said. "I want to talk about that, but let me finish this first."

Cronley gestured *Go on.*

"Tony and I came back here on the next Clipper — Tony on a diplomatic passport, me as an Argentine citizen coming home to bury his father. The funeral was spectacular."

"Spectacular?"

"A delegation of Argentine Army brass met the Clipper. After stopping at the military hospital to pick up Enrico —"

"What was Enrico doing in the hospital?"

"Still bleeding from the multiple double-aught buckshot when they murdered my father. The only reason he was alive was that the guys with the shotguns apparently decided that anybody bleeding from so many holes wasn't worth shooting a third time.

"So we pushed Enrico's wheelchair out of the hospital and loaded him into an open Army Mercedes . . . I should mention he was wearing his dress uniform over nine miles of bloody bandages . . . and then drove to the Edificio Liberator, Argentina's Pentagon, where my father had been lying in state. In a closed coffin. There wasn't much left of his head.

"That afternoon they moved him to the family mausoleum in the Recoleta Cemetery. In a parade through downtown Buenos Aires. He was escorted by the entire Húsares de Pueyrredón regiment in their dress uniforms. I had never seen some twenty-two hundred men on horses in one place. The Argentine Army band marched along, playing appropriate music. Like I said, spectacular.

"Sometime during the funeral, Martín approached me and without coming right out and saying it — they call that obfuscation, and he's good at it — let me know that he was going to be the liaison officer between me and the Argentine brass — Army and Navy — and that as my father's son I was welcome in the land of my birth. I was not going to be stood against a wall for being a spy — as long as I didn't do anything stupid, like blow up neutral ships or shoot the SS officer at the German embassy who I suspected of having ordered the murder of my father.

"My Uncle Humberto, who is a good guy,

came to me right after the funeral. He said we had to talk about my inheritance and thought it best done at Estancia San Pedro y San Pablo. So we went out there, primarily because it was the only way I could get Enrico if not back in bed then at least off his feet."

"Explain that?"

Clete nodded. "Enrico told me that God had spared him so that he could protect me, and that he would be with me from that moment on. He wasn't kidding. I figured if I went to the estancia, Enrico could sit in an armchair and not bleed while I watched the grass grow, heard about my inheritance, and figured out how I could cozy up to whoever was going to be the new president.

"At the estancia was Gonzo Delgano. My father had told me that he knew — and Gonzo knew he knew, but both pretended they didn't — that his Staggerwing pilot was really a BIS agent keeping an eye on my father. I figured Martín was keeping him there to watch me, so I pretended I thought he was an airplane pilot, period.

"About the time Enrico stopped bleeding all over the carpets while following me around, maybe a week later, Tony showed up in his Army attaché's uniform to deliver a message. The U.S. Air Force base at

Puerto Alegre had an aircraft they were ordered to deliver to el Coronel Jorge Frade as a gift from the President of the United States. They had learned that he had passed, so who got the airplane?

"That was a no-brainer for me. I did. Uncle Humberto had explained that I had inherited everything my father owned. So I told Gonzo that we were about to get a Staggerwing to replace the one I had landed in the water and did he want to go to Brazil with me and check it out before I flew it back?

"He told me he would have to check with his wife.

"I knew, and he knew I knew, that he meant *Teniente* Coronel Martín. But what the hell?

"So we stopped in Buenos Aires long enough to pick up an impressive document saying that I was the sole heir of the late Colonel Frade, and flew to Puerto Alegre in a Brazilian Ford trimotor."

"And they gave you a replacement Staggerwing?"

"No. They gave me a Lockheed Lodestar painted Staggerwing red."

"What the hell?"

"Much later, I found out that what had happened was that when the order had come down from the commander in chief to instantly send a Staggerwing painted Staggerwing red to Brazil, for further shipment to a Colonel Frade, there was a little problem. There were no Staggerwings in the Air Force inventory, and Beech had stopped making them in 1939. There was, however, a Lodestar fresh from the factory, with an interior designed for the comfort of some Air Force general. So they painted it Staggerwing red and flew it to Brazil.

"Gonzo was less than thrilled. He had permission 'from his wife' to bring a Staggerwing into Argentina, not a sixteen-passenger twin-engine transport. I told him he could watch from the ground as I took off for Buenos Aires in the Lodestar."

"Where'd you learn to fly a Lodestar? In the Marines?"

"Well, I had some time in your dad's Twin Beech, of course, and I had some time in the right seats of Gooney Birds, C-47s, on Guadalcanal. I lied about how much time I had doing that, then talked the Air Force guy who'd flown the Lodestar to Brazil into giving me a quick transition — I shot a couple of touch-and-goes.

"At the last minute, Gonzo says he'll come with me if I agree to fly to Santo Tomé, in Corrientes, instead of Buenos Aires. I asked why, but he wouldn't tell me. Turned out my father had built an airstrip at Santo Tomé for the Staggerwing when he commanded the Húsares de Pueyrredón. I found out later he and Martín wanted me to take the Staggerwing there from the git-go."

"I don't understand."

"Telling me would've meant they'd have had to also tell me that General Rawson had decided he was going to have to take over for my father in Operation Blue, the coup d'état, and that was about to happen. If it fell apart, Rawson and the other senior officers would be jailed, or more likely shot. Unless they could get out of the country. To Uruguay."

"In the Staggerwing," Jimmy said, connecting the dots. "That nobody knew you had."

"Right. You can cram eight people into a Staggerwing if you have to. So we flew to Santo Tomé. Gonzo called Martín, and Martín told me to fly the Lodestar to Estancia San Pedro y San Pablo, without being seen, and keep it under cover until I heard from him.

"By then I had pretty much figured out what was going on. I asked, and he told me.

"A week later I got a call, and flew the

Lodestar to Campo de Mayo, the big army base, from where General Rawson was running the revolution."

Jimmy smiled. "And because the revolution succeeded, the Lodestar wasn't needed to get the brass out of Dodge City. But you still got to be a good guy by making it available."

"Ahem," Clete said theatrically. "Let me tell you how I got to be a good guy. *The* good guy. A hero of the revolution. Rawson had two columns headed for the Casa Rosada — the Argentine White House. Once they got there, the war would be over. But it didn't look like they were going to get there anytime soon, if at all. Both column commanders had decided the other guys were the bad guys — and they were shooting at each other.

"Everybody in the Officers' Casino, which was revolution headquarters, was running around like headless chickens. Rawson was in contact — by telephone, no radios worked — with one of the columns. He orders them to stop shooting at the other column.

" 'Not until they stop shooting at us!'

"Rawson could not reach the other column. 'What am I supposed to do? I cannot go there personally and tell them to stop. It would take an hour and a half to get there — and everybody will have shot everybody else.'

"I politely volunteered: 'General, if I may make a suggestion. There's a soccer field at the Naval Engineering School. I can land one of your Piper Cubs there and you can personally tell them to stop shooting at the other good guys and resume shooting at the bad guys.'

"Rawson was desperate. He let me load him in the back of a Cub. He was terrified. It was his third flight in a Cub. Worse, knowing both columns had machine guns, I flew there on the deck. Around and in between the apartment and office buildings, instead of over them.

"All of which convinced Rawson, who became president, that not only was I the world's best pilot, but at least as brave and willing to risk his life for Argentina as had been my great-great-grandfather Juan Martín de Pueyrredón.

"That paid off when we were starting up SAA and some bureaucrat discovered that I didn't have an Argentine pilot's license."

"Tell me about that . . ." Jimmy said.

But somebody at Casa Montagna had come looking for Clete, and he never had the chance to tell that story.

". . . that's where the Squirt'll be from now on. Next to my Uncle Jim," Clete now said.

And then he drained his half-full glass of Dewar's.

Jimmy held his glass out to be filled.

"You sure? You don't want to be shit-faced when we dine with the Schumanns."

"I'm sure."

And then he changed his mind.

"No. You're right. I want to be very careful around Colonel and Mrs. Schumann."

VII

[One]

Schlosshotel Kronberg
Kronberg im Taunus, Hesse
American Zone of Occupation, Germany

1805 1 November 1945

The huge dining room looked just about full. Officers in their pinks and greens and a surprising number in the rather spectacular Mess Dress uniform, and their ladies, filled just about every table.

"In my professional judgment," Lieutenant Colonel Cletus Frade, USMCR, said to Captain James D. Cronley Jr., AUS, as they stood in the doorway waiting for the attention of the maître d'hotel, "there are enough light and full bull colonels in this place to form a reinforced company of infantry. And they all seem to have brought two wives with them."

"And you've noticed, I suppose, that you and I are the only ones not wearing the prescribed uniform. You think they'll let us in?"

Frade was wearing his forest green Marine uniform and Cronley his olive drab — OD — Ike jacket and trousers. Both were "service" uniforms.

"We're about to find out," Frade said as the maître d' walked up to them.

"We are the guests of Colonel Schumann," Frade told him.

The maître d' consulted his clipboard, then led them to a table in a large alcove on the far side of the dining room.

Colonel Robert Mattingly was sitting alone at a table with place settings for ten people. He was wearing Dress Mess — an Army dinner jacket — with lots of gold braid stripes and loops and lapels showing the wearer's rank and branch of service, which in Mattingly's case was the yellow of Cavalry.

Mattingly stood as Frade and Cronley approached. He put out his hand to Frade.

"The Schumanns and General Greene and his wife should be here any moment." He looked at Cronley. "I really wish you had brought pinks and greens."

"Sir, you didn't tell me to." Then he added, "Sir, I'm obviously out of place here. Maybe it would be better if I left."

"Actually, Cronley, maybe that would be . . ."

Cronley saw that Clete had picked up Mattingly's quick acceptance of his offer to leave and didn't seem to like it.

"Just sit down and try to use the right fork," Frade said to Cronley, then looked at Mattingly. "Do these people always get dressed up like this, or is it some kind of holiday I'm missing?"

"I'd say what they're doing, Colonel — half of them, anyway — is making up for the good times they missed."

"I don't understand," Frade said.

"Well, Colonel . . ."

That's the second time Mattingly's called Clete "Colonel."

With emphasis. What's that all about?

Ah, he's reminding Clete he's a light bird talking to a full bull colonel and should have said "sir."

I wonder why Clete didn't?

". . . two months ago many of the officers here tonight — even some of the wives — were behind barbed wire in Japanese POW camps."

"Really?"

"The story I heard was that General George C. Marshall asked himself, 'What do I do with officers who've been behind barbed wire since 1942 when they're finally freed?' And then came up with the answer. He sent many of the ones from the Philippines and Japan here, and many of the ones from German POW camps to Japan.

"They get a command appropriate to their rank — nothing too stressful, of course — in Military Government or Graves Registration — there will be permanent military cemeteries all over Europe — or on staff somewhere. If they need medical attention, and a lot of them do, there are good Army hospitals here and in Japan. They get requisitioned quarters much nicer than what they'd get at Fort Bragg or Fort Knox. With cheap servants, not that cheap matters, as most of them got three years of back pay as soon as they got off the planes that flew them to the States. And nice clubs, with very low, tax-free prices. Getting the picture?"

"Fascinating," Frade said. "I never

thought about what would happen to them after the 'welcome home' parade."

"General Greene told me the story when I was ordered to give up this place — it was headquarters for OSS Forward — so they could turn it into a club for senior officers."

Cronley looked around the room. He couldn't tell, of course, which of the officers in their dress uniforms had been prisoners. But no one in the room looked anything like the hollow-eyed walking skeletons in rags he'd seen in the newsreels of prisoners being liberated.

Or even like Elsa.

He had first seen Elsa von Wachtstein not a month earlier, carrying a battered suitcase in a refugee line approaching a checkpoint three kilometers north of Marburg an der Lahn. She was emaciated, her face gray, her hair unkempt — a thirty-two-year-old who looked fifty. But she was the daughter of Generalmajor Ludwig Holz and daughter-in-law of Generalleutnant Graf Karl-Friedrich von Wachtstein — both brutally killed for their roles in the attempted assassination of Adolf Hitler in July 1944. Jimmy had last seen her in Buenos Aires, when she'd reunited with her brother-in-law — and now one of Clete Frade's closest friends — Major Hans-Peter von Wachtstein.

"And speak of the devil," Mattingly said as he got to his feet.

General Greene and a formidable-looking woman were walking up to the table.

Frade and Cronley stood.

"Good evening, General, Mrs. Greene," Mattingly said.

General Greene shook his hand. Mrs. Greene nodded.

"Mrs. Greene, may I introduce Colonel Cletus Frade, USMC, and Captain Cronley?" Mattingly said.

She nodded, and then asked, "How is it you're in olive drab, Captain?"

"Captain Cronley didn't expect to be here tonight, Grace," General Greene said.

"The dress code — it's posted as you come in — says 'Pinks and Greens, or more formal, after Seventeen Hundred.'"

"Grace, for God's sake, ease up," General Greene said.

I wondered before, Cronley thought, *why Rachel, and not the general's wife, was president of the Officers' Wives Club. Now I know. If this pain-in-the-ass was, there'd be nobody else in it.*

"Rules are rules and decorum is decorum," Mrs. Greene said.

"You're absolutely right," Frade then said. "I'd have him taken outside and shot but

I'm as guilty as he is. I'm not wearing a pink uniform either. I don't even own a pink uniform."

Both Mrs. Greene and Mattingly glared at him, she because she obviously was not used to being challenged, much less mocked.

Clete put away all that scotch! He's plastered!

And Mattingly sees it.

This is going to be fun. Or a disaster.

"Actually, Colonel Frade," Mattingly said, "the term is 'pinks *and greens.*' "

Frade ignored him. He wasn't through.

"Does this Army dress code prescribe female attire?" he asked.

"What do you mean by that?" she snapped.

"Just curious. In the Naval Service, officers don't tell our ladies what to wear. And of course vice versa."

Mrs. Greene's mouth opened in shock, but she didn't get to say whatever she had intended. General Greene, with relief evident in his voice, quickly announced, "Ah, here come the Schumanns and the Mc-Clungs."

Colonel Schumann was wearing Mess Dress; Major McClung pinks and greens.

When everyone was in the now-crowded alcove, waiters closed doors, ones that

Cronley hadn't seen before, shutting off the alcove from the main dining room.

When all the male handshaking and female cheek-kissing was over, and they took their seats, Rachel was sitting across, but not directly across, from Jimmy. He just had time to decide he wasn't going to get groped when he felt her foot pressing against his.

Momentarily, but long enough so there was no question of it not being by accident.

When a waiter appeared for their drink orders, Cronley tried to do the right thing. He really wanted a Jack Daniel's, but knew he shouldn't. On the other hand, he didn't like scotch, so if he ordered a scotch, not liking scotch, he would drink it slowly.

"I'll have a Dewar's please."

"Colonel Frade," General Greene began the dinner conversation, "I'd recommend the New York strip steak. Very good. They bring it in from Denmark."

"Why do they do that?" Frade asked.

"The club — clubs, plural — don't want to be accused of diverting the best beef from the Quartermaster refrigerators to the brass, taking it out of the mouths of the enlisted men, so to speak, so they go outside the system and buy it in Denmark."

"You look as if you don't approve, Colonel Frade," Mrs. Greene said. "Don't they do things like that in the Naval Service?"

"In the Marine Corps, I was taught that officers can have anything in the warehouse after the enlisted men get first shot at it."

Before his wife could reply to that, General Greene quickly said, "That strikes me as a very good rule."

"General," Frade asked, "did you ever notice that there's loops on the top of Marine officers' covers — the brimmed uniform caps?"

"As a matter of fact, I have."

"When I was a second lieutenant, I was told that was to identify officers who might have had their hands in the enlisted men's rations and make it easier for Marine marksmen in the ship's rigging to shoot them."

Greene, Colonel Schumann, and Major McClung laughed. Rachel Schumann and Mrs. McClung chuckled. Mrs. Greene's eyebrows rose. Mattingly managed a wan smile.

"I'd be interested to hear, Colonel," Greene said, "how you think the meeting went this afternoon?"

"Paul," Mrs. Greene said, "I didn't get all gussied up to come out to listen to you talk shop."

Her husband ignored her. "Your thoughts, Colonel?"

"General, in the Marine Corps, we have another odd custom. We ask questions like that of the junior officer present. That way, since they don't know what their seniors are hoping to hear, they have to say what they actually think."

"We do the same thing, Colonel," General Greene said, and his eyes went to Cronley. "Well, Captain, what impression did you take away from that long, long session this afternoon?"

Thanks a lot, Clete!

No matter what I say, it's going to be wrong.

What the hell! In the absence of all other options, tell the truth.

"Sir, from the bottom of the totem pole, it looked to me like those people from the Pentagon are very unhappy that there's going to be a new OSS. And/or that the Pentagon is not going to be running it."

Greene nodded and then made a *Keep going* gesture with his hand. Cronley saw that Mattingly was looking at him, obviously worried about what he was going to say next.

"Sir, I had the feeling that they were really upset to hear that I have the monastery and will be in charge of Pullach."

"I don't understand," Mrs. Greene said. "What monastery? What's Pullach?"

350

"If the general answers those questions, Mrs. Greene, I'll have to shoot both of you," Frade said.

Iron Lung McClung laughed loudly.

"Jim!" his wife said warningly.

"Grace," General Greene offered, "Captain Cronley is going to run a little operation in Pullach, which is a little dorf near Munich."

These people tell their wives about what we're doing?

How much do they tell them?

Probably everything.

Rachel seems to know everything that's going on.

And Clete mockingly gave Boy Scout's Honor that he had never told his wife anything.

So much for the sacred Need to Know.

"Why are the people from the Pentagon not pleased? Because he's only a captain?" Mrs. Greene asked. "And if they're not pleased, why is he going to be allowed to run it?"

"The simple answer, Mrs. Greene," Frade said, "is because Admiral Souers says he will. And quickly changing the subject, where is our leader tonight?"

"Having dinner with Ike, Beetle, and Magruder," Greene said.

"And here's our dinner," McClung said

351

as a line of waiters approached the table.

Cronley felt Rachel's bare foot on his ankle.

"And this admiral," Mrs. Greene relentlessly pursued. "He can just give orders to the Army like that? An admiral?"

"Yes, ma'am, he can," Frade said. Using his hands to demonstrate as he spoke, he went on, "This is the totem pole to which Captain Cronley referred, Mrs. Greene. We're all on it. Cronley is at the bottom" — he pointed to the bottom of his figurative totem pole — "and Admiral Souers is here" — he pointed again — "at the tip-top. The rest of us are somewhere here in the middle."

"Perfect description," General Greene said. His wife glared at both him and Frade.

"I'll tell you about it later, dear," Greene said. "Now let's have our dinner."

"I think you're right, Cronley," Major Iron Lung McClung said several minutes later. "Magruder, Mullaney, Parsons, and Ashley — the Pentagon delegation — are all probably outraged that they won't be taking over Pullach. But I wouldn't worry about it too much."

"Sir?"

"Magruder's not going to get anywhere at

dinner tonight complaining to Ike or Beetle. Not with Souers there. And when Magruder and Mullaney get back to Washington, who can they complain to? Not Souers. And so far as Parsons and Ashley, when they're at Pullach, the only one they can complain to about getting ordered around by you is Colonel Mattingly, and he's not going to be sympathetic."

"My only problem with that," Mattingly said, "is that being in charge may well go to Cronley's head. I'm going to have to counsel him to make sure that doesn't happen. He's more than a little weak in that area. He tends to assume authority he doesn't have and to act first and ask permission, or even counsel, later."

"You're kidding, right?" Frade said.

"No, Colonel Frade, I am not kidding," Mattingly said coldly. "He has a dangerous loose-cannon tendency."

"Jimmy," Frade said, "don't let your being given command of the monastery or Pullach go to your head. Or turn you into a loose cannon. Say, 'Yes, sir.' "

"Yes, sir."

"Consider yourself so counseled," Frade said, and then turned to look at Mattingly. "Jesus Christ, Mattingly!"

Rachel's bare foot, which had been caressing Cronley's ankle, suddenly stopped moving as Mattingly stood.

"I would remind you, Colonel Frade, that you are speaking to a superior officer," Mattingly said furiously.

"Senior, certainly," Frade said. "Superior, I don't think so."

"Ouch!" Iron Lung McClung said softly but audibly.

"What the hell set this off?" General Greene asked.

When there was no reply to what might have been a rhetorical question, Greene went on, "Junior officer first, Colonel Frade."

"I found Colonel Mattingly's gratuitous insult of Cronley offensive, General," Frade said.

"Frankly, so did I. But it didn't give you carte blanche to talk to Colonel Mattingly so disrespectfully."

"No, sir, it didn't. I spoke in the heat of the moment and therefore offer my apology."

"Colonel Mattingly?" Greene asked.

"Sir?"

"I think you should accept Colonel Frade's apology and then offer yours to Captain Cronley."

With a visible effort, Mattingly said,

"Apology accepted." After a pause, he went on: "Captain Cronley, it was not my intention to gratuitously insult you. If you drew that inference, I apologize."

Great.

But the minute Clete leaves Germany, I'm really fucked.

Rachel's foot on his ankle began to move.

General Greene looked at Cronley impatiently, and finally Cronley understood.

He stood up, came to attention, and said, "Sir, no apology is necessary."

He sat down.

"Sit down, please, Colonel Mattingly," Greene said. "Whereupon, we will all promptly forget the last three minutes or however long that little theatrical lasted."

There were chuckles.

"Can we get them to do it again?" Major McClung asked innocently. "Sort of a curtain call? I liked it."

"Jim, for God's sake!" Mrs. McClung said.

General Greene gave McClung a look that would have frozen Mount Vesuvius.

McClung seemed unrepentant.

Rachel's foot found Jimmy's ankle and instep again.

"Colonel Frade," General Greene said as he cut into his Danish New York strip steak,

"I'd like to ask you — you and Colonel Mattingly, but you first — what you consider the greatest threat to your operation between now and the time it comes under the new organization Admiral Souers mentioned."

Is he tactfully reminding Clete that Mattingly outranks him?

What is that saying? "There are nice generals, and there are generals who are not nice, but there is no such thing as a stupid general."

Clete didn't hesitate before replying.

"So far as I'm concerned, and I'm not saying this to agree with Admiral Souers . . ."

Clete picked up on that "who's junior?" implication.

He's good at this.

". . . the greatest threat to our nameless operation is that our Soviet friends are going to expose it. I say expose it because we would be fools to think they don't know about it. It is just a matter of time before they penetrate Kloster . . ." He paused, looking for the name by looking at Cronley.

"Kloster Grünau," Jimmy furnished.

". . . Kloster Grünau. And the Pullach installation, which, because it's not only not on a Bavarian mountaintop but close to Munich, will be an even easier target for penetration. I'm frankly surprised there hasn't been a penetration of the monastery already."

Cronley felt Mattingly's eyes on him.

What's he want?

Am I supposed to say, "Actually, now that you mention Russian penetration of my little monastery, I do have NKGB Major Konstantin Orlovsky locked up in a cell in what used to be the monastery chapel"?

Or keep my mouth shut?

"What about that, Captain Cronley?" Colonel Schumann asked. "Am I the only nefarious character you've caught trying to force his way into your monastery?"

Christ, now what do I say?

"Sir, you're the only one I've had to discourage with a machine gun."

My God, where did that come from?

General Greene laughed. Frade looked curious.

"Colonel Frade," Schumann said, "I wouldn't worry about anybody penetrating Cronley's monastery. I know from painful personal experience that Cronley's got it guarded by some of the toughest, meanest-looking Negro soldiers I have ever seen — they're all at least six feet tall, and weigh at least two hundred pounds — who are perfectly willing — willing, hell, *anxious* — to turn their machine guns on anyone trying to get in."

"Painful personal experience?" Frade replied. "I'd like to hear about that. And I guess I'll see Cronley's mean-looking troops when I go down there —"

"Excuse me?" Mattingly interrupted. "Colonel, did I understand you to say you're going to Kloster Grünau?"

"Yes, you did."

"May I ask why?"

"Yes, sir. Of course you may. Sooner or later, the Soviets are going to penetrate the monastery and/or the Pullach camp, no matter how many two-hundred-pound six-foot-tall soldiers with machine guns Cronley has guarding it."

"Colonel, are you going to answer my question?" Mattingly demanded curtly.

"That's what I'm trying to do, Colonel," Frade replied, and then went on: "If all they find is that we are employing a number of former German officers and non-coms to assist General Greene in his counterintelligence efforts, so what? Where we would be in trouble would be if they discovered — or actually tried to arrest under their Army of Occupation authority — former members of the SS whose names they know and whose arrests they have already requested. Or if they got their hands on any paperwork that could incriminate us."

He glanced at General Greene, and said: "Colonel Mattingly sent a great deal of the latter to me — Cronley carried it to Argentina — but I want to be absolutely sure he didn't miss anything."

He looked back at Mattingly: "So, to answer your question, Colonel Mattingly, what I plan to do at the monastery is get with General Gehlen and come up with a list of the ex-SS and everyone else with a Nazi connection that we have to get out of the monastery and Pullach and to Argentina as soon as possible. In other words, a list of those people we really can't afford to have the Soviets catch us with, prioritized on the basis of which of them, so to speak, are the most despicable bastards. They go first. Oberst Otto Niedermeyer and I have been thinking about this for some time —"

"Who?" General Greene asked.

"He was Gehlen's Number Two —"

"It's my understanding that Colonel Mannberg is Gehlen's Number Two," Mattingly said.

"Niedermeyer tells me he was," Frade replied. "And he's the officer Gehlen sent to Argentina" — Frade paused and chuckled — "doubly disguised as a Franciscan monk and *then* as a *Hauptscharführer.*"

"I don't understand," General Greene said.

"When they got to Argentina and took off their monk's robes," Frade explained, "they identified themselves as Obersturmbann-führer Alois Strübel and his faithful *Haupts-charführer* —"

"His faithful what?" Mrs. Greene asked.

Frade looked first at General Greene and then at Mrs. Greene before replying, "Sergeant major, Mrs. Greene."

"Go on, please, Colonel," General Greene said.

"Brilliant detective work by myself quickly discovered that Hauptscharführer Otto Niedermeyer was actually Colonel Niedermeyer. Gehlen apparently decided a sergeant major could nose around easier than a colonel."

"So he lied to us," Mattingly said.

"And I was shocked as you are that anyone in our business could possibly practice deception," Frade said. "But, as I was saying, Gehlen sent Niedermeyer to Argentina very early on in this process to make sure we were going to live up to our end of the bargain. He tells me he was Gehlen's Number Two, and I believe him. And I'm also convinced Niedermeyer was not a Nazi —"

"Why?" Mattingly interrupted.

"Could you just take my word for that, Colonel, and let me finish?"

"Go on," Mattingly said.

"So I believe the list of the Nazi and SS scum Niedermeyer gave me, again prioritized according to what kind of bastards they are, is the real thing. I'd be willing to go with it as-is. But as some — including Otto Niedermeyer — have pointed out, Gehlen can be very difficult, so I am going to politely ask him to go over Niedermeyer's roster."

"I got the impression this afternoon," Mattingly said, "that Admiral Souers wants to return to Washington as soon as possible."

"He does," Frade said.

"Then wouldn't it make sense for you to give me this list of yours and have me deal with General Gehlen? There's no reason for you to have to go all the way down there. It's a four-, five-hour drive."

When Frade didn't immediately reply, Mattingly went on: "And, really, the monastery and the people there are my responsibility, aren't they?"

Frade exhaled audibly.

"Admiral Souers planned to get into all of this with you tomorrow, but it looks like I'm going to have to get into it now."

"Please do," Mattingly said, rather unpleasantly.

Frade felt everyone's eyes around the table on him.

"The reason I have to go to the monastery," Frade began, "and to have a look at the Pullach installation is because Admiral Souers has ordered me to do so. And the reason he's done that is because, for reasons of plausible deniability, he has transferred command of Operation Ost — just Ost, not the South German Industrial Development Organization — to the Special Projects Section of the Office of the Naval Attaché at the U.S. embassy in Buenos Aires."

"To what, where?" Colonel Schumann asked.

"When the OSS shut down, its assets — including me — in the Southern Cone of South America were absorbed by the Special Projects Section of the Office of the Naval Attaché at the U.S. embassy in Buenos Aires. In other words, for the next sixty days, Operation Ost will be hidden there.

"That will allow General Greene and you, Colonel Mattingly, if — I actually should say 'when, inevitably' — the Soviets breach the security of the monastery or Pullach, to credibly deny you know anything about Operation Ost. All you're doing there is running a counterintelligence operation in which some former German officers and non-coms are employed."

"That makes sense," General Greene said thoughtfully. Then he chuckled. "Have a nice ride down the autobahn tomorrow, Colonel Frade. Maybe, now that you and Mattingly have kissed and made up, he'll loan you his Horch for the trip."

Frade smiled. "That would be very kind of him, but Cronley's going to fly me in his Storch."

That Mattingly was not amused was evident in his voice: "And how does Captain Cronley fit into this credible-deniability scenario?"

"In an operational sense, he will be the liaison between the monastery/Pullach, the Farben Building, and Buenos Aires."

"Who'll operate the link to Vint Hill Farms?" Major McClung asked.

"Cronley," Frade said.

Well, Cronley thought, *that answers the question "Does McClung know about the Collins and the SIGABA?"*

Then, without thinking about what he was doing, Cronley leaned back in his chair and put his hands behind his neck. When he saw that Frade, Mattingly, and Mrs. Greene were looking askance at him, he quickly lowered his arms, shifted in his chair, and moved it closer to the table. Rachel's toes moved immediately to his crotch. After a moment, she withdrew, and then put her foot back on his instep.

"And I'm sure you have considered the possibility," Mattingly said sarcastically, "that when the Soviets inevitably breach the security of Kloster Grünau or Pullach, they might wish to ask Captain Cronley what he knows about Operation Ost."

"All Cronley has to do is say, 'I'm the commanding officer of the guard company. Colonel Mattingly told me I don't have the Need to Know what's going on in the compound and am not to ask.' And, as Mrs. Greene and others have pointed out, he's only a captain. Captains are unimportant."

"And you think he could handle pressure like that?" Mattingly asked. His tone made it clear that he didn't think so.

"I do. But what matters is that Admiral Souers does."

"I'm really getting tired of all this shop talk," Mrs. Greene announced. "I want to dance."

"Colonel Frade," Colonel Schumann said, "do you think it would be useful if I took a look at your security arrangements for the Pullach operation? I know McClung is going down there in the near future, and I could go with him."

"I think that's a great idea," Frade said. "And — I don't know how this fits into your schedule, Colonel Mattingly — but how about us all meeting in Munich after I deal with Gehlen?"

Before Mattingly could answer, Rachel said, "Grace, if you and I went down there with them, we could see what will have to be done for the dependent quarters before people start moving in."

"That's not a bad idea," General Greene said. "I'd like to see the Pullach compound myself."

"We could take the Blue Danube," Grace Greene said, smiling. "It has a marvelous dining car. And then we can stay at the Vier Jahreszeiten. I like the Vier Jahreszeiten. There's nothing as nice in Frankfurt."

Cronley thought both that it was the first time the general's lady had smiled since she'd walked into the dining room and also that Frade's face showed that he had no idea what the Blue Danube was.

Cronley did: Tiny Dunwiddie had told him what had happened to the private trains used by Nazi bigwigs. The Army Transportation Corps had gathered them up and assigned Hitler's and Goering's to Eisenhower and U.S. High Commissioner for Germany John J. McCoy.

The other super-luxury private trains had been given to General George S. Patton and other very senior American officers. Except for one. While other deserving three-star generals had been scrambling for trains for themselves, that one, Tiny had told him delightedly, had been "lost" by an old 2nd Armored "Hell on Wheels" officer in Bad Nauheim. When Major General I. D. White returned to Germany to assume command of the U.S. Constabulary, it would be "found" with Constabulary insignia painted all over it.

What was left of the first-class cars and the best dining cars had been formed into trains and put into Army service between the six hubs of American forces in Europe — Paris, France; Berlin, Frankfurt, and Munich in Occupied Germany; and Salzburg and Vienna in "liberated" Austria.

The Paris–Frankfurt luxury train was dubbed the Main-Siener, making reference to the rivers that flowed through those cities, and the Berlin-Frankfurt-Munich-Vienna train the Blue Danube.

"Then it's settled," Frade said. "We'll all meet in Munich the day after tomorrow."

I'll be damned, he did know what the Blue

Danube was!

No. He just decided that if Mrs. Greene wanted to "take the Blue Danube," whatever it is, she was unstoppable.

"And now," Frade announced, "because Captain Cronley and I are going flying as the rooster crows tomorrow morning, I must beg that we be excused from this charming company."

Before Cronley could stand, Rachel's foot gave his instep a final caress, and when he shook her hand to say good night, she said, "Well, I guess we'll see each other soon."

[Two]

As they entered the lobby, Clete said, "Don't even look at the bar. We have more to talk about."

"Oh, boy, do we."

"What's that mean?"

"Wait until we're someplace no one can hear us."

When they were in Clete's room, he pointed to an armchair and then the bottle of Dewar's.

"Sit," he ordered. "And go easy on that."

"Yes, sir, Colonel, sir."

Clete smiled tolerantly.

"You ever notice, Jimmy, that when you

really need a drink you can't have one? God knows, after that goddamned dinner we're both entitled to drain the bottle."

Clete went to his luggage and pulled out a zippered leather envelope. He took from it an inch-thick sheath of papers, walked to Jimmy, and handed it to him.

"Sign where indicated."

"What the hell is this, Clete?"

"On top is what they call a Limited Power of Attorney. It gives former Kapitän zur See Karl Boltitz of the Kriegsmarine the necessary authority to do all that he has to do to manage certain property of yours in Midland County, Texas."

"What the hell are you talking about? My father has my power of attorney to run all the property I own."

"I know. But as soon as the probate judge of Midland County, Texas, is satisfied that you were in fact married to the former Marjorie Ann Howell, you'll own a lot more."

Jimmy looked at him for a long time before replying, his voice on the edge of breaking, "I don't think I ever knew it was 'Marjorie Ann.' "

"It was. And under the laws of the Sovereign State of Texas, upon the demise of the said Marjorie Ann Howell Cronley, all of her property passed to her lawful husband, one James Davenport Cronley Junior."

"Oh, shit!"

"Said property — the details are in those papers — includes two sections of land, including the mineral rights thereto, in Midland County, plus some cash in the First National Bank of Midland, including about two hundred and sixteen thousand dollars, representing her most recent quarterly dividend from the Howell Petroleum Corporation. And of course her Howell Petroleum stock. And some more. It's all in there."

"I don't want any of it," Jimmy said.

"You don't have any choice."

"Oh, God!"

"When the Old Man handed this to me, he said to tell you two things."

"Really?"

"He said to tell you that everyone who matters knows you'd much rather have the Squirt and two dollars than this inheritance, but that's the way the ball has bounced. And he said to tell you never to forget that for every dollar a rich man has, there are at least three dishonest sonsofbitches plotting to steal it from him."

Jimmy wiped a tear from his cheek with a knuckle.

"That sounds like the Old Man," he said, his voice breaking. Then he said, "Where does Boltitz fit in all this?"

"Very neatly. For one thing, he's about to be your brother-in-law."

"He's going to marry Beth?"

Frade nodded.

"Yeah. You saw them. We can't keep throwing cold water on them."

Jimmy laughed.

"The Old Man told Beth they should take a page from you and the Squirt and elope. I thought Mom was going to kill him. What they'll probably do is have a quiet wedding in Midland, and fuck what people say. Or a big one in Argentina — that's what Dorotea was trying to sell when I left. Anyway, he's going to be family, and since he's out of a job, there being no demand for U-boat skippers, he's going to need one. The Old Man is impressed with him and he told me — privately — that he's thinking of putting him in charge of his tanker operations.

"In the meantime, Karl can learn about the family business under the watchful eyes of Mom, Beth, and your dad. Understand?"

"Makes sense."

"The Old Man wants me to take over Howell Petroleum. The problem with that is I'm going to have to learn how to do that.

And I can't learn how to do that as long as I have Operation Ost to worry about. I promised Souers I'd stick around until the new Central Intelligence Directorate, or whatever the hell they're going to call it, is up and running. And then there's El Coronel, Incorporated, I have to worry about."

"What the hell is that?"

"Everything I inherited from my father. And I have already learned that what the Old Man told me to tell you is true. For every peso a rich gringo like myself has, there are at least three dishonest Argentine sonsofbitches trying to steal it."

Jimmy chuckled.

"So are you going to sign that power of attorney or not?"

Jimmy didn't reply. He instead poured Dewar's into two glasses, gave one to Clete, and then signed the paper. Then he wordlessly touched his glass to Clete's, and they took a healthy sip.

Jimmy gestured to the power of attorney: "When I signed the one for my dad, it had to be notarized. What are you going to do about that?"

"The Old Man's lawyers thought of that, too. They found out that a commissioned officer, such as myself, can witness the signature of someone junior to them, such

371

as yourself. I'm surprised you didn't know that, Captain Cronley."

"I'll be damned," Jimmy said, as Frade scrawled *Witnessed by C.H. Frade, LtCol, USMCR* and then his signature below Cronley's signature on the power of attorney.

Clete put the document in his luggage and then took the leather envelope and handed it to Jimmy.

"You get to keep that stuff. When you're all alone in your monastery, feeling sorry for yourself, you can take it out and read it and tell yourself, 'What the hell, at least I'm rich.' "

"Very funny. You through?"

"Yeah."

Jimmy drained his glass and pushed it away. "Okay. Speaking of the monastery, Clete: Despite what everyone seems to think, all is not sweetness and light between General Gehlen and me."

Clete's eyebrows rose.

"I don't think I'm going to like this," he said.

"Tiny's Number Two, Sergeant Tedworth, caught an NKGB officer sneaking out of the monastery —"

Clete silenced him with a raised hand.

"Let's get all the details in from the beginning," he said. "Tiny is who?"

"First Sergeant Chauncey Dunwiddie . . ."

"Well, Jimmy, I can understand why General Gehlen might be a little miffed that a twenty-two-year-old American captain who never saw a Russian a month ago decided he knows more about interrogating NKGB officers than Abwehr Ost experts. How do you even communicate with this guy? Sign language? You don't know three words of Russian. What the hell were you thinking?"

"Konstantin speaks English. And German."

"Konstantin? Sounds like you're buddies."

"I like him. Okay?"

"My God!"

"That — liking him — came after I decided that I wasn't going to — couldn't — stand around with my thumb up my ass watching while some Kraut kept him in a dark cell stinking from his own crap, following which he would be blown away. And knowing if anything came out about that, I'd be on the hook for it, not the Germans and not Mattingly."

"Oh, so that's it? You were covering your ass?"

"Fuck you, Clete!"

"What?" Clete said angrily. "Let's not forget, Little Brother, that your big brother is a lieutenant colonel and you're a captain. A brand-new captain."

"Sorry. Make that, 'Fuck you, Colonel.' "

Clete, white-faced, glared at him but said nothing.

"When Mattingly told Tiny to 'deal with' the Russian, all I had to do to cover my ass was look the other way and keep my mouth shut. He didn't tell me to deal with it. He told Tiny. You think I wanted to take on Gehlen and Mattingly? And now you?"

"Then why the hell did you? Are you?"

"Write this down, Colonel: *Because I saw it as my duty.*"

"You can justify that, right?" Clete said coldly.

"First, it was my duty to Tiny. An officer takes care of his men, right? A good officer doesn't let other officers cover their asses by hanging his men out to dry, does he?"

"That's it?"

"Two, I decided that what ex-Major Konrad Bischoff — Gehlen's hotshot interrogator — was doing to Major Orlovsky — the clever business of having him sit in a dark cell with a canvas bucket full of shit — wasn't going to get what we wanted from him. Actually, I decided Bischoff's approach was the wrong one."

"Based on your extensive experience interrogating NKGB officers?" Clete said sarcastically.

"Based on what you said at dinner, you're now the honcho of Operation Ost, so I'll tell you what I told Mattingly when I thought he was the honcho. As long as I'm in charge of Kloster Grünau, I'm going to act like it. If you don't like what I do, relieve me."

Clete didn't reply immediately, and when he did, he didn't do so directly.

"Why, in your wise and expert opinion, Captain Cronley, is Major Bix . . . Bisch . . ."

"Bischoff. Ex-Major Konrad Bischoff."

"Why do ex-Major Konrad Bischoff's interrogation techniques fail to meet with your approval?"

"Because they haven't let him see either that Orlovsky is smarter than he is — I don't know why, maybe he believes that Nazi nonsense that all Russians are the *Untermenschen* —"

"*Untermensch* is a pretty big word. You sure you know what it means?"

Cronley ignored the question.

"Or that my good buddy Konstantin Orlovsky has decided that, except for a bullet in the back of his head, it's all over for him. And in that circumstance he's not going to come up with the names of Gehlen's people

375

that he turned. Names, maybe, if that's what it will take to get out of his cell and shot and get it over with, but not the actual ones."

"But you have a solution for all these problems, right?"

"Would I be wasting my breath telling you, Clete?"

"We'll have to wait and see, won't we?"

"Look. When Mattingly called and told me to come here as soon as I could, I was talking to Orlovsky. I had just proposed to him that I arrange for him to disappear from the monastery —"

"Disappear to where?"

"Argentina. Where else?"

"My God!"

"And that, once he was there and gave me the names of Gehlen's bad apples, and we found out they were in fact the bad apples, I would pressure Gehlen to get Orlovsky's family out of Russia."

"If I thought you were into Mary Jane cigarettes, I'd think you just went through two packs of them. Listen to yourself, Jimmy! You're talking fantasy!"

"Maybe. But, on the other hand, if I turn Orlovsky back over to Bischoff, and we go down that road, what we're going to have is no names of the real turned Gehlenites, and a body in the monastery cemetery that just might come to light if the Bad Gehlenites let the Soviets know about it. Which brings us back to me not willing to let Tiny Dunwiddie or myself hang for that."

Clete thought that over for a long moment.

"What was the Russian's reaction?"

"What he's doing right now is thinking it over."

"He didn't say anything?"

"What he said was, 'Why would you expect me to believe something like that?' And I said because I was telling him the truth, that I wasn't promising to get his family out of Russia, just that I would make Gehlen try. I also told him if he was a man, he'd do anything he could to help his family. Then he called me a sonofabitch, and that was the end of the conversation."

Clete shook his head.

"But he's thinking about it, Clete. I know that in my gut. He doesn't give a damn what happens to him. But his family is different. He doesn't want them shot or sent to Siberia. What I did was . . . sow the seed, I guess . . . to start him thinking."

"And you really thought Mattingly would put Operation Ost at risk by trying to sneak an NKGB officer out of Germany? And that

Gehlen would risk his agents-in-place by trying to get an NKGB officer's family out of Russia? My God!"

"I thought I could sell both of them on the idea that if we turned Orlovsky — the NKGB didn't send a guy who graduated from spy school two months ago to penetrate Operation Ost — we'd all be ahead."

"That's pretty sophisticated thinking for a guy who — if memory serves — was about to graduate from spy school about that long ago. But didn't finish spy school because they needed his expert services here to run a roadblock."

"Yeah, and I probably didn't know much more about running that roadblock — or Kloster Grünau when they gave that to me — than you did about blowing up ships when you went to Argentina."

"Well, some things haven't changed. Your mouth still runs away with you, you're not troubled with modesty, and you have a hard time even admitting the possibility that you can be mistaken."

Jimmy didn't reply.

"I'll try to get you out of this, but don't get your hopes up," Clete went on. "I think you are probably going to spend the rest of your military career — how long are you in for?"

"Four years."

"The next three years and some months counting toilet paper rolls at Camp Holabird. Or some other place where they send stupid young intelligence officers so they can't do any more damage."

"If you're waiting for me to say I'm sorry, don't hold your breath."

"What time does the sun come up?"

"What?" Jimmy said, and then understood. "Half past six."

"And it takes how long to get to the airfield?"

"Fifteen minutes."

"Be waiting for me in the lobby at six. Good night, Jimmy."

[Three]

Cronley went to his room, took a shower, packed his bag, and went to bed.

There was a chance, he thought, that Rachel would somehow ditch her husband and come to see him. He had just decided that would be really stupid on her part and wasn't going to happen when there was a knock at his door.

And there she was.

"This is not smart," he greeted her.

"I know," she said, and pushed past him into the room.

"General Magruder came back from dinner with General Eisenhower," she said, "and asked Colonel Mattingly and my husband to join him for a drink in the bar. I passed. I said I was going to walk off all the food I'd had. We have no more than thirty minutes. That give you any ideas?"

She tugged off her shoes as she headed for the bed.

"Where were you?" Rachel asked, perhaps ten minutes later. "If you'd been here the first time I knocked, we'd have had an hour."

"Talking to Colonel Frade."

"About what?"

"Rachel, you don't have the Need to Know."

"Oh, sorry. I thought maybe you were talking about the Russian you caught at your monastery."

"What Russian? I don't know what you're talking about."

"No," she said, chuckling, "of course you don't. Need to Know and all that."

She looked at his face and then changed the subject.

"Maybe Tony will be called away somewhere and we can have a little time together in Munich."

"That would be nice. Rachel, what if your husband starts looking for you and can't find you?"

"That would be a disaster, wouldn't it?"

She put her clothes back on as quickly as she — they — had taken them off, and left.

VIII

[One]

Kloster Grünau
Schollbrunn, Bavaria
American Zone of Occupation, Germany

1005 2 November 1945

First Sergeant Chauncey Dunwiddie and Technical Sergeant Abraham L. Tedworth had heard the Storch approaching and were waiting next to the former monastery chapel when Cronley taxied up to it.

They spotted Frade and curiosity was all over their faces.

Frade and Cronley climbed down from the airplane.

Dunwiddie softly ordered, "Ten-hut!" Both non-coms popped to attention and crisply raised their hands to their eyebrows.

"Good morning, Colonel," Dunwiddie barked. "Good morning, Captain. Welcome home."

Frade and Cronley returned the salute. Dunwiddie and Tedworth crisply lowered their arms and popped to parade rest.

"As you were," Frade said. "Good morning."

"Colonel," Cronley said. "This is First Sergeant Dunwiddie and his field first sergeant, Technical Sergeant Tedworth."

Frade offered them his hand.

"My name is Frade."

"Yes, sir," the two non-coms said in unison.

"Command of Operation Ost has been given to me," Frade said. "So you now work for me."

"Yes, sir," they again said in unison.

"For the moment, Captain Cronley remains in command of the monastery. How long he will retain command depends in large measure on how much damage to our relations with General Gehlen has been caused by his taking over the interrogation of the NKGB agent.

"As you may have surmised from this odd uniform I'm wearing, I'm a Marine. In the Marine Corps, when you want the real story behind what looks like a FUBAR situation — you do know what FUBAR means, right?"

"Yes, sir," Dunwiddie said.

"Fucked Up Beyond All Repair, sir," Tedworth helpfully furnished.

"Correct," Frade said. "What you do is rustle up a couple of senior non-coms and ask them what the hell's going on, what went wrong, and what they think should be done about it. If you're lucky, you'll get the truth as opposed to them telling you what they think you want to hear."

Frade pointed at Tedworth.

"You first, Sergeant. Be advised I will tolerate no bullshit."

Tedworth, visibly uncomfortable, looked as if he was carefully considering his reply. Finally, just perceptibly, he gave a *fuck it!* shrug.

"Colonel, maybe Captain Cronley should have talked it over first with Colonel Mattingly and he probably should have been more tactful with Bischoff when he told him to butt out, but other than that, he was right."

"Captain Cronley isn't famous for his tact, is he?" Frade said, and then pointed at Dunwiddie.

"Sir, I agree with Sergeant Tedworth," Tiny said.

"Why doesn't that surprise me?" Frade asked. "What is your assessment, Sergeant, of the damage Captain Cronley's actions

383

have had on his — which are of course our — relations with General Gehlen?"

"Sir, I don't know."

"What is your assessment of General Gehlen?"

"Sir, do you mean do I like him?"

"Try that."

"Yes, sir, I do."

"But?"

"He's a general, sir. And a German. Generals, and maybe especially German generals, don't like having their decisions, their orders, questioned. Particularly by junior officers."

"But?"

"That's it, Colonel."

"Where is the Russian?"

"In his cell, sir."

"And General Gehlen?"

"He's in his office, sir."

Frade pointed at Tedworth.

"You will take me to the Russian."

"Yes, sir."

He pointed to Dunwiddie.

"You will present my compliments to General Gehlen. You will ask him if it will be convenient for him to meet with me in Captain Cronley's office after I've spoken to the Russian."

"Yes, sir."

Frade pointed to Cronley.

"You will go to your quarters and await my pleasure."

"Yes, sir."

[Two]

Office of the Commanding Officer
XXIIIrd CIC Detachment
Kloster Grünau
Schollbrunn, Bavaria
American Zone of Occupation, Germany

1025 2 November 1945

The office was furnished with a desk, on which sat two telephones — an ornate German instrument and a U.S. Army EE-8 field telephone — a typewriter, an ashtray made from a bent Planters peanuts can, a White Owl cigar box, and a box of large wooden matches.

There was a wooden office chair on wheels behind the desk. Two similar chairs without wheels were in front of it.

Former Generalmajor Reinhard Gehlen, who had on an ill-fitting, well-worn gray tweed suit, sat in one of the latter. He rose to his feet as Frade walked through the door that Sergeant Tedworth held open for him.

"General Gehlen?" Frade asked.

"I am Gehlen."

"My name is Frade, General," he said, offering the slight man his hand. "Sorry to have kept you waiting."

"I am pleased to finally meet you, Colonel Frade."

"Sergeant, please rustle up some coffee and maybe a couple of doughnuts for myself and the general, and then leave us alone."

"Coming right up, sir," Tedworth said.

Frade went behind the desk and sat down.

"We have a problem, General. But I think before we get into that, I should tell you why I said 'we.' For a number of reasons, including credible deniability, it has been decided to transfer command of Operation Ost to me. That's effective this morning."

Gehlen nodded but didn't speak.

An inner door opened. Cronley was standing in it.

"Colonel, I thought I should tell you that when I'm in my quarters I can hear whatever is said in here."

Frade considered his options for a moment and then said, "Take a seat."

"Yes, sir," Cronley said, and then sat in the chair across from Gehlen.

"*Guten Morgen,* Herr General."

"*Guten Morgen,* Jim."

"One might get the idea from that cordial, informal exchange, General," Frade said, "that you and Captain Cronley have developed a personal as well as a professional relationship."

"I think we have," Gehlen said. "Wouldn't you agree, Jim?"

Before Cronley could reply, Frade went on: "And that hasn't changed in the last couple of days?"

"Because of Major Bischoff, you mean?"

"That's your interrogation expert?"

"Yes."

"Then because of what happened between Captain Cronley and your major."

"I think, Colonel, that when I hear Captain Cronley's version of the dispute, and weigh it against Bischoff's, Bischoff's far greater experience in these matters will be evident. But that certainly won't cause me to dislike Jim."

"You haven't heard Cronley's version?"

"I was going to ask him about it today."

"Tell the general what you have been thinking, Captain Cronley," Frade ordered.

"I offered Major Orlovsky a deal, General," Cronley began.

"Based on his extensive experience in these matters, of course," Frade said sarcastically. "And his very fertile imagination."

The appearance of Sergeant Tedworth, carrying two coffee mugs and a plate of doughnuts, caused Cronley, at the last possible split second, not to say what had leapt to his lips.

Thank God!

Telling Clete to go fuck himself would have been really stupid. He couldn't let me get away with it in front of Gehlen, and Gehlen wouldn't like it either.

It would be one more proof for both of them that while Little Jimmy Cronley might be a nice boy, even a bright nice boy, that's all he is, and thus any ideas he has are beneath the consideration of Frade, Gehlen, Bischoff and Company, the Wise Old Men of Kloster Grünau.

"We're waiting, Captain Cronley," Frade said.

Try to sound like a fellow intelligence professional. Use big words.

"When I realized that Major Bischoff's deprivation of senses and humiliation tactics of interrogation were not working on Major Orlovsky, and actually were counterproductive — Orlovsky has resigned himself to being shot — I decided something else had to be done.

" 'What does this skilled NKGB officer want? What can I give him to get those names?'

"The answer was hope."

"I don't understand," Gehlen said.

"I told him, General, that if he turned, I would move him to Argentina, and once he was there, if he gave us the names of your people that he has turned, I would get you to get his family out of Russia."

The eyebrows on Gehlen's normally expressionless face rose.

"I see what you mean about a fertile imagination," he said.

"I went to see Major Orlovsky just now, General," Frade said. "I walked into his cell, gave him a moment to wonder who I might be, and then said, 'Well, Major, have you decided whether or not you want to go to Argentina?' "

"And?" Gehlen asked.

"What would you have expected his reaction to be, General?" Frade asked.

Gehlen considered the question for a moment before replying.

"I would guess that he wouldn't reply at all," Gehlen said. "Or that he would appear to play along, to see what he might learn."

"What he did, General, was lose control. And if he was acting, he's a better actor than John Barrymore."

"He lost control?"

"Only for a moment, but in that moment,

his chest heaved, he sobbed, and his eyes teared."

"Interesting," Gehlen said, softly and thoughtfully.

"He quickly regained control, but for a moment he had lost it."

"And what did he say?"

"When he thought he had his voice — and himself — under control, he said, 'Until you walked in here, Colonel, I really thought your young captain was desperately reaching for straws.' "

"Go on, please," Gehlen said.

"I suppose," Frade said, "I should've walked in there at least considering the possibility that my young captain had actually cracked Orlovsky — but I didn't. So, I said the only thing I could think of: 'Answer my question, Major Orlovsky.' "

"And?" Gehlen said softly.

"He said, 'It is possible, unlikely but possible, that we might be able to work something out.' To which I cleverly replied, 'We'll talk more about working something out,' and left."

Gehlen shook his head in disbelief, smiled, and said, "Jim, I underestimated you."

"It would appear we both did," Frade said.

"When I tell Konrad Bischoff this — if I tell him — he'll be devastated," Gehlen said, smiling. "I'm afraid he was looking happily forward to Jim getting his comeuppance from Colonel Mattingly."

"You're saying you think we can strike a deal with Orlovsky?" Frade asked.

"I think we would be foolish not to look very carefully at that possibility, no matter how remote it sounds."

"General, I happily defer to your greater expertise," Frade said. "Would you do that for us, sir? Lay it out?"

"Very well," Gehlen said. "Simply, what we have is a skilled NKGB agent now in possession of information regarding Operation Ost that we cannot permit him to pass on to his superiors. What we want from him are the names of those of my people he's turned. Now, what are we willing to pay for that information?"

Cronley began, "Sir —"

"Just sit there," Frade snapped.

"Colonel, may I suggest that Cronley has earned the right to comment?" Gehlen said.

"Make it quick, Jimmy."

"I was about to suggest that if we can turn him, he's got more to tell us than the names of the Germans he's turned."

"True. But I suggest we're getting a bit ahead of where we should be," Gehlen said.

"Go ahead, General, please," Frade said.

"Cronley will hold any further comments he might wish to offer until you're through."

Gehlen nodded. "Colonel, can you make good on the promise to take him to Argentina?"

"Qualified answer, General: Yes, but there are problems with that."

"Let's proceed with your ability to get him there, and deal with the problems later. The next question is: 'Would it be worth the risk to my agents in place for them to try to get his family out of Russia?' The answer to that, too, has to be qualified.

"Simple answer, yes. If we don't get the names of the people Orlovsky — or perhaps someone else in the NKGB — has turned, they can cause enormous damage. So, if you agree, Colonel Frade, what I suggest we do is accept that the information Orlovsky has is worth his price. You will establish a new life for him in Argentina and I will attempt to get his family out of Russia. What are the problems you see?"

"I hardly know where to begin," Frade said. "There's a number of them. Perhaps the greatest of them is that if I went to Admiral Souers with this — you know he's the ultimate authority?"

Gehlen nodded.

"I don't think he'd give me permission to

do it. So far, he doesn't even know we have Orlovsky. It almost came out at dinner last night, but the conversation went off at a tangent when Colonel Schumann regaled everyone with his descriptions of Sergeant Dunwiddie and his ferocious fellows, and the subject of NKGB penetration of Kloster Grünau got lost. Fortunately."

"I'm surprised Colonel Mattingly didn't bring Orlovsky to everyone's attention," Gehlen said. It was a question as well as a statement.

"So was I," Frade said. "I'm guessing he wanted to dump the problem in my lap. He would have preferred to hang Jimmy out to dry, but right now Admiral Souers — and for that matter, the President — think Cronley can walk on water. So that would be risky."

"Do you think you could go to Admiral Souers and argue the merits of taking Orlovsky to Argentina?"

"No, I don't," Frade said simply. "He would decide the risk to what I've got going in Argentina would be too great. And he'd probably be right. Which means that we're going to have to keep both Mattingly and the admiral in the dark about this operation."

"One, you're willing to do that? Two, can

you do that? And, three, if you can do it, for how long?"

"I'm willing to do whatever is necessary to protect Operation Ost. As far as keeping how I do that from the admiral and Mattingly, all I can do is hope that when they finally find out — and they will — it will be a done deal.

"Now, for obvious reasons, we can't just add Orlovsky to our family of refugees in Argentina . . ."

"Obvious reasons?" Gehlen asked.

"Before this interesting development came up, General, I was going to come see you with this" — he took an envelope from his tunic and handed it to Gehlen — "with the compliments of Oberst Otto Niedermeyer."

"I've been expecting this," Gehlen said.

"What is it?" Cronley asked.

"Why do I suspect, General Gehlen," Frade asked, smiling, "that you and Oberst Niedermeyer have a communications link I'm not supposed to know about?"

Gehlen smiled back. "Because you have a naturally suspicious mind. Which is very useful in our line of endeavor."

"What is that?" Cronley asked again.

And was ignored again.

"And," Gehlen went on, "possibly because Otto tells me that, for an Anglican, you have an unusually close relationship with a certain Jesuit priest and he told you."

Frade laughed. "No comment."

"You're wondering why Otto sent this with you, rather than using this communications link you suspect us of having?"

"Yeah."

"Because if he used — what should I say? — *the Vatican channel,* not only that Jesuit but others would have read it. There are some things we prefer not to share with Holy Mother Church."

"Shame on you," Frade said.

Gehlen and Frade were smiling at each other.

Gehlen has smiled more in this room in the last twenty minutes than in all the time I've known him.

And cracked jokes.

They just met and they're already buddies.

Even if Niedermeyer got word to Gehlen that he thinks Clete is a good guy, that wouldn't have made them pals.

They're kindred souls . . . what else could it be?

"What the hell is that?" Cronley asked for the third time.

Gehlen looked at Frade, who nodded his permission.

"Jim, it's a list of the Nazis who SS-Oberst

Niedermeyer thinks would cause us the greatest embarrassment if the Russians could prove they're here at Kloster Grünau. And a list of my people, some of them here, some in Argentina, who Niedermeyer suspects have already been turned or, in his judgment, are likely to turn if properly approached."

"What are you going to do about them? The people who have been turned?" Cronley asked.

Gehlen acted as if he had not heard the question.

"I think we're in agreement that we're going to have to move all of the people who can embarrass us out of Kloster Grünau as quickly as that can be done," Gehlen said.

"Mattingly suggested there may be a passport problem," Frade said. But it was a question.

"Our friends in Rome are very cautious," Gehlen said. "Perhaps that's why they have been so successful for so long. In this connection, they dole out passports very sparingly, never more than a dozen at a time."

"Mattingly told me that. But you have a dozen blanks?"

Gehlen nodded. "But they won't give us any more until our Jesuit friend in Buenos Aires reports to them that the travelers have passed through Argentine immigration and disappeared. After handing him their Vatican passports, which he has destroyed. I understand their concern, of course — this way no more than a dozen passports are ever at risk of coming to light at one time — but it causes problems."

"There will be an SAA Constellation here on Saturday," Frade said. "It will refuel in Frankfurt before flying to Berlin, and will refuel again in Frankfurt on the return trip. That will be on Sunday or Monday. Can you select the dozen people who pose the greatest embarrassment and have their passports ready in that timeframe, so we can load them on the Connie when it refuels in Frankfurt?"

"Two hours after I give the names to Oberst Mannberg, the passports will be ready."

"Mattingly has done all this before, and his system seems to work," Frade said. "When I see him in Munich tonight I'll tell him there are no problems about this."

"Does he know about Otto's list?"

"I'll tell him about it tonight — there was no opportunity at that Schlosshotel."

"Can I ask what you want me to do," Cronley said, "or what you're going to do about the people Colonel Niedermeyer thinks may have been turned?"

When he saw the looks on both men's faces he knew he had asked a question that he should not have asked. Confirmation came immediately.

"Did you say something, Captain Cronley?" Frade asked.

"It wasn't important, sir."

The moment Gehlen has proof that any of his people have been turned, that's the end of them. I should have known that.

Cletus knows that, and has decided it's Gehlen's problem, and Gehlen should deal with it.

But he seems to agree that Orlovsky is our problem, and that our solution should not be turning him over to Gehlen to be shot.

Why? Because he's a Russian?

And we captured him?

And what would have happened if Orlovsky hadn't broken down when Clete saw him?

Would Clete have then told me what Mattingly did — "Mind your own fucking business"?

A minute ago, Clete said, "I'm willing to do whatever is necessary to protect Operation Ost." That would obviously include killing Orlovsky.

Those who suggest I'm naïve or stupid or both are right on the money.

"As I was saying before we got into our theological discussion . . ." Frade began.

Gehlen smiled and chuckled.

". . . we can't move Orlovsky in with the other immigrants. We're going to have to get him to a safe house, provide him with bodyguards, et cetera, plus give him a large amount of cash to convince him that once he has given us the names, we won't betray him. That's going to be a lot of money."

"And getting his family out of Russia will cost a great deal of money," Gehlen said. "U.S. dollars open many doors in Moscow. Fifty thousand comes to mind. Is that going to pose a problem?"

Frade nodded. "For several reasons. The accounts of the former OSS are just about empty. Even if they weren't, I doubt I could ask for two hundred thousand dollars without offering a good reason. And while I have access to money in Argentina . . ."

"You mean your own money, right?" Cronley said.

". . . and have been using my own money to fund operations there — placing a child-like faith in Admiral Souers's promise I'll get it back when the Central Intelligence Directorate is up and running — I couldn't take another two hundred thousand out of the Anglo-Argentine Bank for unspecified purposes without the wrong people asking the wrong questions. Yes, General, money is going to be a problem. We're going to have to really think about that."

"What about documentation for Orlovsky?" Gehlen said. "To get him into Argentina, and then for him to become as invisible as possible once he is?"

"I'm sure our mutual friend the Jesuit can arrange a Vatican passport and a *libreta de enrolamiento,* the national identity document, for him," Frade said. "But that means he would have to be told what's going on."

"Is that a problem?"

"Not for me," Frade said, chuckling. "The wily Father Welner already knows all my secrets — well, almost all. But there are two things. The fewer people who know a secret, the longer it can be kept secret. Aside from Welner, I am only going to tell Major Ashton — my deputy, Major Maxwell Ashton the Third — and Master Sergeant Siggie Stein about any of this."

"Niedermeyer speaks highly of both," Gehlen said.

"And the only reason I'm going to tell them is that I think I may have to send Ashton over to deal with some people from the Pentagon who will be in Pullach and are very much aware they all outrank Cronley. If that becomes necessary, Stein will have to hold the fort in Argentina."

"Niedermeyer will have to be told, wouldn't you say?"

"Yeah, he will. I didn't think about it, but sure. Otto will have to be brought in on this."

Cronely put in, "You sound as if you think —"

"Not now, for God's sake, Jimmy," Frade shut him off, and then said, "I was wondering how the Vatican would react — maybe will react — when they find out they've issued a passport to an NKGB officer. Is that going to cause problems for you, sir?"

"Not if by the time they find out Orlovsky has seen the light and has put godless Communism behind him. But if he goes to Argentina, escapes his bodyguards, and heads for the nearest Russian embassy . . ."

"General, there's no Russian embassy in Argentina. Just an NKGB outpost pretending to be a trade mission. General Martín . . . ?"

"The chief of the Argentine Bureau of Internal Security?" Gehlen asked.

Frade nodded.

"Martín keeps a close eye on the tradesmen. But I don't want him to know about Orlovsky. He'd want to take him over. But that's not a big problem. I can make sure that Orlovsky doesn't get within a hundred miles of either him or the trade mission. The problem is the money."

"Let me get this straight," Jimmy said. "You sound — the both of you sound — as if you think I had a great idea and the only thing that's standing in the way of doing it is a couple hundred thousand dollars."

"So?" Frade asked. "You figured that out, did you, you clever fellow?"

"Yes, you can have it," Cronley said.

"I can have what?" Frade said, and then, understanding, added, "Oh."

"What you just figured out, you clever fellow."

Frade was silent for a long moment, then snapped, "Your automatic mouth is about to get you in more goddamned trouble than you can handle. Do you even realize that?"

"Sorry," Jimmy said. A moment later, he went on: "I'm really sorry. I just can't handle being treated like I'm part of this one second, then I'm an idiot second lieutenant the next."

"Well, you goddamned well better learn," Frade said icily. And then he chuckled. "You better remember, too, that you're an 'idiot *captain*,' Captain Cronley."

Their eyes met for a long moment. "You

402

sure you want to do this, Jimmy?"

Cronley nodded.

"Boltitz will have my power of attorney. You can tell him to give you the money, so that you can take it to Argentina to invest it for me. Nobody would question that. And he wouldn't have to be told what we're going to do with it."

"I don't understand," Gehlen said.

Frade ignored him. He said, "I really don't like taking your money, Jimmy . . ."

"Would you take it — I prefer 'borrow' to 'take,' let's say 'borrow' from now on — would you borrow it from the Squirt if she was still around?"

Frade ignored that question, too.

". . . but *borrowing* it would solve more than one problem," Frade went on. "I have to go to Midland anyway to pick up my wife and kids. If Karl took the money out of your bank in cash, that would solve the problem of getting it to Argentina. And then here to General Gehlen. No cashier's checks, no transfer wires, just all the cash we need, within a matter of days, and nobody asking questions."

"Do I understand that Jim is going to provide the funds we're talking about?" Gehlen asked.

Cronley nodded. "Yes, sir. And all I'm going to ask Colonel Frade to do is unscrew his left arm at the elbow and leave it with me in lieu of collateral."

Gehlen laughed out loud.

"The only thing missing is Orlovsky actually agreeing to turn," Frade said.

"If I may make a suggestion?" Gehlen asked.

"You don't have to ask, General," Frade said.

"I would suggest it might be a good idea not to seem too eager, to — now that you believe he's willing — have him worry that we don't trust him to carry out his end of the bargain. I know Jim doesn't think that Major Bischoff's disorientation theories are effective —"

"They weren't working, General," Cronley interrupted.

"Let me rephrase that: We know Bischoff's disorientation tactics did not work. But keeping Orlovsky disoriented until the moment we load him on an airplane might be a good idea."

"You want to bring Bischoff back into this?" Cronley asked suspiciously.

"I was thinking of doing this myself," Gehlen said. "If you're going to Munich, while you're gone I could chat with Major Orlovsky. We could talk, for example, about mutual acquaintances we have on the faculty of the Felix Dzerzhinsky Federal Security Service Academy and among the members of the People's Commissariat for Internal Affairs. That should get him wondering how many of them I've managed to turn."

"I didn't want to go to Munich in the first place," Frade said. "Now I really don't want to go. I'd love to watch a master of our trade at work."

"I'm flattered," Gehlen said.

"But I have to go, and I don't think I'll be coming back here. The sooner I can get to the States, the better."

"I understand," Gehlen said. "But speaking of my chat with Major Orlovsky: I have found it useful to have someone with me when I'm having chats of that nature."

"Major Bischoff?" Frade asked.

"Actually, I was thinking of First Sergeant Dunwiddie," Gehlen said. "Of course, he would have to be made privy to what we're doing."

"Jimmy, your call," Frade said.

"I don't have any problems with that at all."

"You can have the sergeant," Frade said. "But may I ask why?"

"Well, he's obviously extraordinarily

bright. Though another reason I'd like him in the room with me is that Major Orlovsky has had very little contact in Holy Mother Russia with men that size or with skin the color of coal. He finds them disconcerting."

Frade and Cronley chuckled.

"If that's the case, General," Cronley said, "you can have Sergeant Tedworth, too."

"That might even be better," Gehlen said. "One final thing. May I bring Colonel Mannberg into this?"

"Of course," Frade said. He paused, then went on: "That about winds it up for me here. Unless you have something else, General?"

Gehlen shook his head.

"In that case, sir, what I would like to do — if it makes sense to you — is go see Orlovsky, taking Cronley with me. I will tell him we have to leave — hell, I'll tell him the truth: I'll tell him I have to get back to the States, and then to Argentina, and that he will be dealing with you and Cronley."

Gehlen nodded. "I think it important that Jim remain involved."

"And this time, Captain Cronley, you will heed the sage advice of this expert interrogator no matter what he suggests."

Cronley nodded. "Yes, sir."

"And, Jimmy, you and I should get back

in the Storch and go to Munich. The sooner I can get a look at Pullach and get to Frankfurt, the better."

"Taking the Storch may not be a good idea. We better drive."

"Why?"

"The Air Force doesn't like Storches."

Cronley explained the trouble he had had at Eschborn and the trouble he thought they would encounter at the Army airfield outside Munich.

"I don't want to lose the Storch, Clete. Either of them. I think I'm really going to need them. And losing them's a real possibility."

"You are a lucky man, Captain Cronley," Frade said. "When you fly back here in your Storch after dropping me off at Rhine-Main tomorrow morning, you will be privileged to witness a genuine expert outwit a Russian NKGB agent. Few people have an opportunity to see something like that. And when we land at this airfield where you think they will try to take away your airplane, you will be privileged to watch a genuine Marine expert outwit difficult Army — or Air Force, as the case may be — bureaucrats in uniform. Few people are privileged to see something like that, either."

Cronley shook his head.

"Say, 'yes, sir,' " Frade said.

"Yes, sir."

General Gehlen laughed and smiled warmly.

Clete offered his hand. Gehlen took it, but what began as a formality turned personal. They wound up hugging each other.

[Three]

Schleissheim Army Airfield
Munich, American Zone of Occupation,
  Germany

1710 2 November 1945

"Schleissheim, Army Seven-Oh-Seven understands Number One to land on Two-four," Cronley said into his microphone, then moved the switch to INTERCOM and went on, "This is certainly going to be interesting."

"What?" Frade asked.

"Well, Schleissheim means 'Home of Strip,' so I'm hoping we'll be greeted by two fräuleins in their underwear. But I'm afraid what we're going to get is some of those officers I told you about, the ones who'll want to take my plane away from me."

"Just do what I told you to do. Say, 'yes, sir.' "

"Yes, sir."

Jimmy moved the switch back to TRANS-MIT and announced, "Seven-Oh-Seven on final."

A major, two lieutenants, and a sergeant walked up to the Storch as Cronley parked it in front of a building that combined Base Operations with a control tower, a double-door fire station, and what looked like a PX coffee shop.

The sergeant went to the tail and started writing on a clipboard.

"He's righteously writing down our tail numbers," Cronley announced.

"Go," Frade ordered.

Cronley climbed out of the airplane, took his CIC credentials from his pocket, and opened the folder so the major could get a quick look.

"Good afternoon," Cronley said cheerfully. "We're going to have to top off my tanks and then put the airplane in a hangar where as few people as possible will see it. Any problems with that?"

Clete was now out of the airplane.

The major saluted.

"Good afternoon," Clete said, crisply returning it, then addressed Jimmy: "We're running late. Where's the car?"

"I don't know, Colonel," Cronley said.

"Well, Major?" Frade demanded. "Where is it?"

"Sir, I don't know anything about a car," the major said.

"You did know we were coming, correct?"

"No, sir."

"My God, Mr. MacNamara!" Clete snapped to Jimmy. "Can't the Army do anything right? Does General Tedworth expect me to walk to the Vier Jahreszeiten? Find a phone somewhere and get General Tedworth on the line. If he's not available, I'll talk to General Dunwiddie."

"Yes, sir," Cronley said.

The major looked up from his clipboard and quickly said, "Colonel, we can get you a car. No problem."

"Please do so," Frade said. "And quickly. You heard me say we're running late. And when I come back here very early tomorrow morning, I expect my aircraft to be ready to go. Understood?"

"Yes, sir. No problem, Colonel."

The major's face showed that he was not going to ask any questions about the Storch. Colonel Frade turned his back to the major and winked at Captain Cronley.

"Take not counsel of your fears," he announced. "I believe General Patton said that, so you might wish to write it down."

[Four]

Hotel Vier Jahreszeiten
Maximilianstrasse 178
Munich, American Zone of Occupation,
  Germany

1745 2 November 1945

Sergeant Friedrich Hessinger, wearing pinks and greens, intercepted Cronley and Frade as they headed for the elevators in the lobby of the hotel.

Elegant as usual, Cronley thought. *The only thing missing is the blond — or two blonds — he usually has hanging on to his arms.*

"Colonel Mattingly and the others are waiting for you in the bar, Captain Cronley," he announced.

"Colonel, this is Special Agent Hessinger," Cronley said. "Freddy, this is Colonel Frade."

"It is my pleasure, Colonel," Hessinger said.

His accent was so thick that Frade, without thinking about it, replied in German.

"And mine. Who are the others?"

Hessinger recited: "General and Mrs. Greene, Colonel and Mrs. Schumann,

411

Major and Mrs. McClung, Captain and Mrs. Hall, and Major Wallace, sir."

"Wonderful!" Frade said sarcastically. "This should be lots of fun!"

Hessinger gave him a strange look.

"Lead on, Herr Hessinger," Frade ordered.

"Well, everybody's here," General Greene greeted them cordially.

"And about time, too," Mrs. Greene interrupted. "Mr. Hessinger and I want to get to the English Garden before everything is gone." She smiled at Hessinger. "Don't we, Mr. Hessinger?"

Hessinger had told Cronley about the English Garden. It was in the famous Munich park that Germans swapped silverware, crystal, paintings, et cetera, with the Americans for cartons of Chesterfields, Hershey bars, and Nescafé. It was officially illegal, but no one seemed to care.

Hessinger, who had apparently been drafted as interpreter for the general's lady, smiled wanly back.

"Yes, ma'am."

"Everybody knows everybody else, right?" General Greene asked.

Frade did not know Major Wallace. That introduction was made.

Chairs were produced for Frade and Cronley. They sat down.

"We were beginning to worry," General Greene went on, when they had taken their seats. "I gather you drove from the monastery?"

"No, sir," Frade said. "We flew. I'm going to have to fly to Frankfurt first thing in the morning, so we came by Storch."

"Mattingly and I were just discussing those German airplanes, the Storches, clearing up the mystery, so to speak," Greene said, smiling broadly.

"What mystery is that, sir?" Frade asked.

"It was something right out of an Abbott and Costello routine. You know, 'Who's on first?' " Greene said. "I got a call from an Air Force colonel several days ago demanding to know why a stork with Twenty-third CIC painted on its tail had just taken off from Eschborn. I thought maybe he was drunk, so I said if this was one of those 'Why does a chicken cross the road?' jokes, I didn't have the time for it.

"That pissed him off, so he said I would be hearing from someone else in the Air Force. Sure enough, fifteen minutes later an Air Force two-star is on the phone. This one I knew. Tommy Wilkins. Good guy. We were at the War College together.

" 'Paul,' he says, 'what's your version of the encounter you just had with my guy?'

"So I told him, ending that with 'Tommy, I didn't even know what the hell he was talking about. A stork with Twenty-third CIC painted on its tail?'

"Whereupon Tommy grows very serious. 'Hypothetical question. If I asked you why the CIC is flying Storch aircraft around after we've grounded them, you couldn't answer because it's classified and I'm not cleared for that, right?'

"That was the first I realized his colonel had been talking about an airplane, not that big bird that brings babies . . ."

Frade and McClung laughed out loud.

". . . and the first time I realized he had said Twenty-third CIC had been painted on the tail of the big bird which had just delivered a baby to Eschborn . . ."

Everyone at the table but Mrs. Greene was now either laughing or giggling.

". . . and that suggested our own Colonel Robert Mattingly was involved, so I rose to the occasion and said, 'Tom, that about sums it up.'

"To which he replied, 'I thought it had to be something like that. Sorry he bothered you. I'll turn him off. Your storks are free to fly.' "

414

"General," Frade said, "thank you very much. Cronley says he needs the Storches. What they are, sir, is sort of super Piper Cubs. Among other advantages, you can get — actually, stuff — three people in them. You can get only two in a Cub."

"When can I go to the English Garden?" Mrs. Greene inquired.

"Well, now that Colonel Frade has flown in in his stork," General Greene said, "we can sort things out. What I suggest, dear, is that Mr. Hessinger drop Major Wallace at the *bahnhof*, then take you to the English Garden. What's departure time of the Blue Danube, Wallace?"

"Twenty-twenty, sir."

"I figured someone should be holding down the shop in the Farben Building, since we're all here, and Wallace volunteered," General Greene explained.

"I'm tempted to get on the train with him," Frade said. "But I really should have a look at Pullach, even in the dark."

"Not a problem, Colonel," Major Wallace said. "The engineers are working around the clock. The site is covered with flood-lights."

"How many of you ladies are going with Grace?" Greene asked.

"I'll pass," Rachel said. "I'm too tired to

do all that walking. Can I go to Pullach?"

"Certainly."

"And I'll go with Rachel," Mrs. McClung announced. "You can find some wonderful things in the English Garden but I want to see Pullach."

"You can see Pullach in the morning," Mrs. Greene proclaimed. "Come with me."

So you, Mrs. McClung, Cronley thought unkindly, *can carry whatever she swaps her Chesterfields and Hershey bars for that exceeds Freddy's carrying capacity.*

"What would you like Mary-Beth and me to do, General?" Captain Hall asked.

Mrs. Greene answered for her husband: "You two can come with me. There is safety in numbers."

"To further complicate things," Frade said, "I'd hoped to have a private word with you, General, and Colonel Mattingly. When can you fit that into our schedule?"

"Okay," General Greene said. "Munich Military Post gave me a staff car . . ."

"Only because I insisted that Captain Hall call down here and get you one," Mrs. Greene interrupted.

". . . a requisitioned old Packard limousine," Greene went on. "It has a window between the front and back seats. You, Mattingly, and I can have that private chat on our way to Pullach. And back. And there's a car here, right?"

"Two, sir," Major Wallace said. "We have a Kapitän and an Admiral."

"Captain Cronley's in special agent mode," Greene said, pointing to the blue U.S. triangles on Cronley's lapels, "so he can drive the Schumanns in one of them. The Schumanns and Major McClung." He paused. "Okay? The only question seems to be where are all these cars?"

"Yours is outside, General," Major Wallace said. "The others are in the basement garage."

"Let's get this show on the road," Greene said. "Otherwise it'll be midnight before we get to eat. Go get the cars. We'll meet in front."

[Five]

Cronley pulled up the Opel Kapitän behind the Packard in front of the hotel as a natty sergeant took the cover off a red plate with a silver star in its center mounted on the rear bumper. The sergeant then scurried to the side of the car and opened the door for General Greene, Mattingly, and Frade.

Cronley found the limousine fascinating. He couldn't identify the year, but guessed it was at least ten years old. It looked like something a movie star would own, and he wondered who it had belonged to, and how it had survived the war looking as if it had just come off the showroom floor.

It was only when the passenger door started to open that he wondered if he was supposed to have jumped out and opened the door as the sergeant had on the Packard. He looked to see who was getting in.

"I'll ride in front with Jim," Rachel announced to her husband and Major McClung, "and leave the backseat for you two."

The Packard moved off. Jimmy followed it.

Rachel's left hand slid from her lap and into Jimmy's.

When she didn't find what she was looking for, she shifted on the seat, looked into the backseat, and innocently asked, "How far is this place?"

"About twenty miles," Iron Lung McClung boomed.

Rachel's right hand, searching for what she wanted, found it, arranged it so that she could find it again with her left hand when she had turned back on the seat, and then did so.

Two minutes later, his crotch becoming uncomfortably tight, Jimmy pushed her hand away. She caught his hand and moved it to her knee, then put her hand back on his crotch.

What the hell? Her husband's three feet away!

If she keeps this up . . .

As if she had read his mind, she took her hand off him, then pushed his hand away from her knee, and finally folded her hands together in her lap. And then she chuckled.

About a half hour later, the Packard braked so suddenly that Cronley almost ran into it.

"What the hell?" Iron Lung McClung boomed from the backseat.

"We've been stopped," Jimmy reported.

He could see there was a barrier — two-by-fours laced with concertina barbed wire — across the road. Four men armed with U.S. Army .30 caliber carbines had approached the Packard. They appeared to be wearing U.S. Army fatigue uniforms that had been dyed black.

This won't take long, Cronley decided.

Generals generally get to go wherever they want to go.

Four minutes later — it seemed longer than that — Major McClung boomed again from the backseat: "Cronley, go up there and see what the hell's going on."

"Yes, sir."

When Cronley walked to the nose of the Packard, there were now six men in black-dyed fatigues and a U.S. Army Corps of Engineers lieutenant in woolen ODs standing in front of the barrier. Plus General Greene, Colonel Mattingly, and Lieutenant Colonel Frade.

"Absolutely no one, Captain Cronley," Frade said with amusement in his voice, "gets into the Pullach compound without the specific permission of the Engineer major in charge of this project. He is at supper and has been sent for."

"On one hand," Mattingly said, "I have to say I'm impressed with the security but —"

"On the other hand," General Greene interrupted him, "I'm getting more than a little annoyed standing here in the god-damned road waiting for this goddamned major."

"You understand, Lieutenant," Cronley asked, "that this is a highly classified project being built for the Counterintelligence Corps?"

"We have been instructed not to get into that, sir," the lieutenant said.

Cronley produced his CIC credentials.

The Engineer officer, who looked to be about as old as Cronley, was clearly dazzled.

"I can vouch for these officers," Cronley

said. "Move the roadblock out of the way."

"Yes, sir," the lieutenant said, and signaled for the men in the dyed-black uniforms to do so.

"I'm starting to like you, Cronley," General Greene said.

"When the major comes, sir, what do I tell him?" the lieutenant asked.

"Tell him to find us and be prepared to explain to me why this project is not yet finished," General Greene said.

"Yes, sir."

"Let's get this show on the road," General Greene ordered.

Everyone got back into the cars and they drove past the roadblock.

[Six]

Two hundred yards down the road they were stopped at another roadblock manned by carbine-armed men wearing dyed-black U.S. Army fatigues.

"Go see," Major Iron Lung McClung bellowed from the backseat.

As Cronley walked to the old Packard limousine he sensed that McClung had also gotten out of the Kapitän and was walking behind him.

And as they reached the Packard, a jeep came racing toward the barrier.

421

A lieutenant colonel and a major, both in fatigues, jumped out of the jeep and approached the Packard as General Greene, Colonel Mattingly, and Lieutenant Colonel Frade emerged.

The lieutenant colonel saluted.

"Lieutenant Colonel Bristol, General. There was no heads-up that you were coming, sir."

"They call that 'conducting an unscheduled inspection,' Colonel," General Greene said. "It has been my experience that you often learn a great deal during unscheduled inspections."

"Yes, sir. General, if you'd like to come with me to the headquarters building, there's a plat, a map, of the compound. I could explain what we're up to."

"Let's have a look at it. Lead the way, Colonel."

They got back in their cars and followed the Engineers' jeep past another roadblock and to a large two-story, freshly painted villa in the center of the village.

A large, also freshly painted, sign was mounted on the impressive building that was the General Offices of the South German Industrial Development Organization. It read:

GENERAL-BÜROS SÜD-DEUTSCHE INDUSTRIELLE ENTWICKLUNGSORGANISATION

What Cronley was seeing now was so distinctly different from what he remembered of "the Pullach compound" that he actually wondered if they were in the same place.

When he had first gone to Kloster Grünau, Dunwiddie had taken him on a fifteen-minute tour of what was to be, he said, "our new home away from home." Then they had seen no more than a dozen Engineer troops under a sergeant erecting a crude basic fence — barbed wire nailed to two-by-fours — around a block in the center of the village.

Now, that simple fence was gone. In its place were three far more substantial barriers. One was where the simple fence had been, around the center of the village. A second encircled the entire village, and a third was two hundred yards outside that. They had all been constructed of chain-link fencing suspended between ten-foot-tall concrete poles. Concertina barbed wire had been strung both along its top and on the ground.

All of the fences had signs mounted at ten-yard intervals that were stenciled with

SÜD-DEUTSCHE INDUSTRIELLE ENTWICK-
LUNGSORGANISATION and, under that, in
large red lettering, *ZUTRITT VERBOTEN!*

When everyone went into the building,
they found that an eight-by-four-foot sheet
of plywood on a tripod had been erected in
the foyer. On it was a map of the compound.

"This is not what I expected," General
Greene said after taking a quick look.
"There's more here than I thought there
would be."

Mattingly spoke up: "There's something,
General, that I guess I should have told you
about sooner."

"Which is?" Greene said not very pleasantly.

"General Clay sent for me just before I
went back to Washington," Mattingly explained. "When I reported to him, he told
me, in confidence, that as of January first,
1946, he was going to be relieved as Eisenhower's deputy and appointed military
governor of the American Zone of Occupied
Germany.

"Then he said he was sure that I would
understand that as military governor he
didn't want the Russians — he said 'our
esteemed allies the Soviets' — coming to
him with some wild accusation that we were
hiding Nazis in a monastery in Bavaria. He

424

said that I would also understand that as military governor he would be very interested in German industrial development.

"General Clay then asked me why I still had a reinforced company of Second Armored Division soldiers guarding 'God only knew what' in my monastery and why the compound at Pullach, which was being built for the South German Industrial Development Organization, wasn't finished.

"At this point I decided that someone had made General Clay privy to Operation Ost. I told him the reason the South German Industrial Development Organization was not up and running in Pullach was because the Engineer battalion assigned to Munich Military Post had other projects that were apparently more important than the Pullach compound. I told General Clay I had been reluctant to press the issue because, if I did, Munich Military Post would ask questions about the South German Industrial Development Organization I would not want to answer.

"General Clay then reached for his telephone and asked to be connected with the commanding officer of Munich Military Post. When he came on the line, General Clay said it had come to his attention that the Pullach project was running a little behind schedule and he had been wondering why.

"The post commander apparently replied to the effect that the Pullach compound project was lower on his list of priorities than a gymnasium and a Special Services library that the Engineers were building.

"General Clay replied — and this is just about verbatim — 'Screw your goddamned gymnasium and your goddamned library. Get a goddamned Engineer battalion over to Pullach today and get that goddamned compound built yesterday.' "

"Ouch," General Greene said.

"General Clay then concluded the conversation by saying something to the effect that 'the next time the deputy commander of European Command tells you he wants something built, it would behoove you to build it immediately, rather than when you can conveniently fit it into your schedule.' "

"Ouch, again," General Greene said.

Mattingly turned to Bristol. "Colonel, can you pick up this narrative?"

"Yes, sir. I was at the gymnasium site when the post commander showed up and relayed General Clay's orders to me. I said, 'Yes, sir. I'll go out there first thing in the morning.'

"He said, 'You will go out there now,

426

Colonel. And I suggest you take a cot and a sleeping bag with you, because you're not going to leave that site until the project is completed.' I called my wife, told her I would be out of town for a few days, went by my office and picked up the plans — your plans, I believe, Colonel . . . ?"

Mattingly nodded.

". . . and came out here with a handful of my people. By the time we got here, it was too dark to do much of anything but set up the cots, although I did call my headquarters and told them to start moving equipment out here. Then I went to bed.

"I got up at first light and walked around the area, making up my mind what had to be done and when. Then a puddle jumper flew over, twice, and landed on that road out there." He pointed. "I went out to ask the pilot what the hell he thought he was doing.

"General Clay got out of the L-4, greeted me cheerfully, and said he hoped I had coffee and a couple of doughnuts, as he hadn't had any breakfast. As we walked here, he said, 'One of the first things you're going to have to do is extend that runway. My pilot wasn't sure he could land on it.'

"I said, 'Sir, that isn't a runway.'

" 'It will be,' he said. 'And I have a few

other little changes to make to Colonel Mattingly's plans for this place.' It took him about an hour. I'd forgotten, if I ever knew, that he was Corps of Engineers — you don't think of general officers as having a branch of service — but he quickly showed he was one hell of an engineer. Anyway, he said, 'Get me a sheet of plywood. We'll use it as a plat.'

"And then he sketched the village, freehand, on this" — he pointed to the sheet of plywood — "with a grease pencil, and showed me where he wanted the fences to be, the barracks for the American guards, and the tent city for the Poles . . . the *Polish*."

"Those men in the dyed fatigues?" General Greene asked.

"Yes, sir. They're former Polish soldiers. They'd been German POWs. He said they didn't want to go home because the Russians were now running Poland, so Ike had decided he wasn't going to make them go home. He said they'd make good guards around our installations and to put them to work. General Clay said if you wanted to keep them on, after the compound is open, we could start building barracks for them."

"Start building, Colonel," Mattingly said. He turned to Cronley. "What do you think,

Cronley?"

"I'm like you, Colonel. I didn't expect anything like this."

"Well, I suggest you'd better get used to it. It looks to me as if this place is just about ready for you to move into it, and that's what you're going to do, the minute it's ready."

"I'd estimate a week, sir, to complete everything," Colonel Bristol said.

"Colonel," Major McClung said, "have you been told we're going to put an ASA listening station in here?"

"No," Bristol said simply.

"Well, we are," General Greene said. "Is that going to be a problem?"

"I don't know what that will entail, sir."

McClung said, "A building . . ."

"That should be no problem."

". . . and an antenna farm near the building."

"I'm back, Major, to I don't know what that will entail."

"Why don't you come back and show him in the morning, McClung?" General Greene ordered. "My stomach is growling and I've already seen what I came to see."

[Seven]

The Main Dining Room
Hotel Vier Jahreszeiten
Maximilianstrasse 178
Munich, American Zone of Occupation,
  Germany

2215 2 November 1945

Rachel had teased him to erection on the drive back to Munich, but had then withdrawn her hand.

When they reached the hotel, Cronley decided that was the last he would see of her tonight — and for a while. It already was late and after dinner everyone would retire, the Schumanns together. And after he flew Clete to Frankfurt first thing in the morning, he would fly back to Kloster Grünau, not to Munich.

She was now sitting across from him in the alcove off the main dining room, but her foot was out of range of his ankle.

She's lucky her husband doesn't show any signs of even suspecting what she was doing to me in the front seat. Correction. I'm lucky . . . we're both damned lucky.

"I want to say this while everyone's here," Frade announced as they were having their

430

dessert. "I've decided to send my deputy, Major Max Ashton, over here to assume command of this end of Operation Ost . . ."

Shit, Cronley thought. *So I am being relieved.*

And I had just about decided my half turning of Orlovsky had kept me my job.

". . . Not only is the Pullach compound too much for one man to handle, but those Pentagon types — Lieutenant Colonel Parsons and Major Ashley — who are going to be at Pullach for General Magruder worry me.

"As most of us saw, they are very much aware they outrank Captain Cronley. What I'm going to do as we're flying back to Washington is try to convince General Magruder that Colonel Parsons would be much more valuable sitting at his Pentagon desk than he would be here. If he doesn't agree — and I don't think he will, as it's pretty clear to me that they are very much interested in having Army G-2 take over Operation Ost — then I'm going to go to Admiral Souers and tell him what I'm thinking. I'll probably lose that battle as the admiral doesn't need one more fight with the Pentagon. In other words, over my objections, Parsons will probably show up at Pullach.

"If that happens, Colonel Mattingly, I would appreciate it if you would whisper in Parson's ear that while he might outrank Major Ashton, he doesn't outrank you."

"Consider it done," Mattingly said, smiling.

"Now, as far as who runs Pullach: Cronley dealt with a serious problem out there in the last few days to the complete satisfaction of Colonel Mattingly, General Gehlen, and me."

To Mattingly's complete satisfaction? That's hard to believe.

"What sort of a problem? May I ask?" Colonel Schumann asked.

"You may ask, Colonel, but Colonel Mattingly and I have decided the fewer people who know about it, the better. I'm sure you'll understand. The point is Cronley has established a close rapport with General Gehlen that I found at first hard to believe. But it's real, and I am not going to endanger it by telling Gehlen that Major Ashton will now be running things.

"So Cronley will run General Gehlen, so to speak, answering only to me. And Major Ashton will run everything else, answering to both Colonel Mattingly and me.

"I'm well aware this command structure would look very odd on a Table of Organization, but that's the way it's going to be." He paused and smiled. "As they told me on my very first day in the Marine Corps, 'If you don't like the way things are run around here, learn to.'"

When that got the chuckles Frade expected, he stood up.

"Say 'good night' to the nice people, Captain Cronley. We have to get up with the birds to go flying."

Cronley showed Frade to his room, two doors down from his, and asked, "What did you tell Mattingly about Orlovsky?"

"I told him that I had made it perfectly clear to you that you were going to let General Gehlen handle it."

"You're devious, Colonel."

"Thank you," Clete said.

Then he punched Jimmy affectionately on the shoulder and went into his room.

Ten minutes later, as Cronley came out of the shower, there was a knock at the door.

That has to be Rachel. Is she out of her mind?

A moment later, she pushed past him into the room.

"What about your husband?"

"He, the general, and Iron Lung are having a nightcap. We have thirty minutes, maybe a little more."

"And if we don't and he goes to your room and you're not there?"

"I'll tell him I took a walk."

By then she was sitting on the bed, removing her shoes.

Their mating didn't take long, which Cronley decided was probably because of what she had done to him going to Pullach and back.

As she dressed, she asked, "What was that serious problem you dealt with to everybody's satisfaction, and Colonel Frade didn't want to talk about?"

"If he doesn't want to talk about it, that means I can't."

She didn't press the question, and three minutes later she was gone.

But something about her asking it bothered him.

He couldn't define what bothered him, and decided it was just feminine curiosity.

He took another shower and fell into bed.

IX

Schleissheim U.S. Army Airfield
Munich, American Zone of Occupation,
  Germany

0645 3 November 1945

Cletus Frade followed Jim Cronley into the
Weather/Flight Planning room at Base
Operations and watched as a sergeant gave
Cronley a weather briefing.

Then he followed Cronley to a row of
what looked like lecterns, or headwaiter's
tables, where pilots, standing up, prepared
their flight plans.

"What do you think of the weather,
Jimmy?"

"It's a little dicey. And since I will be
transporting a senior officer, I thought I'd
file IFR."

"Could you make it to Kloster Grünau
VFR?"

"In this kind of weather, the only way to
get into Kloster Grünau International is by
following CC Flight Rules. But, yeah, I
could. I will, after I drop you off in Frankfurt, if that's what you're asking. Not a
problem."

"CC for Chasing Cows?" Clete asked, smiling.

Jimmy smiled back and nodded.

"What would happen if you took off from here on a Local VFR, closed it out in the air, and then went CC to Kloster Grünau?"

"You want to go to Kloster Grünau? What about Frankfurt?"

"Answer the question."

"Why are we going to sneak into Kloster Grünau?"

"Because General Gehlen called last night and said he would really like a word with me before I go to Argentina. And I don't want Mattingly to know I had a final word with General Gehlen before I went to Argentina. Which means that after I have a final word with General Gehlen, before you fly me to Frankfurt so that I can go to Argentina you should avoid telling Colonel Mattingly —"

"That you had a final word with General Gehlen before you went to Argentina?"

"My, you are clever for a young Army officer."

They were smiling at each other.

"Don't let this go to your head, Colonel, sir, but after you go to Argentina, I will miss you."

"Yeah. Me, too, Jimmy."

Jimmy folded the aerial chart on which he had been about to prepare his flight plan and stuffed it in his jacket.

Then the two of them walked out of the Weather/Flight Planning room and the Base Operations building and started looking for the Storch.

[Two]

Kloster Grünau
Schollbrunn, Bavaria
American Zone of Occupation, Germany

0740 3 November 1945

As the Storch made the final approach to Kloster Grünau, Clete saw an ambulance parked just off the end of the runway and of course felt compelled to comment: "Oh, an ambulance is on station. I guess they've seen you try to land here before."

Jimmy didn't reply.

When he touched down, the ambulance followed the Storch down the runway to the tarpaulins beside what had been the chapel. Frade could now see that First Sergeant Dunwiddie was behind the wheel of the ambulance and General Reinhard Gehlen in the passenger seat beside him.

Frade and Cronley got out of the Storch,

and General Gehlen got out of the ambulance.

"Thank you for coming," he said. "I thought it was important."

"Not a problem," Frade said.

Gehlen indicated that Frade should get in the seat he had just left.

"No, sir," Cronley said. "The colonel will ride in the back, where he can apologize to me for making yet another hasty judgment."

Frade looked at him expectantly.

"If the colonel looks closely he will notice that while this vehicle began life as a Truck, a three-quarter-ton four-by-four Ambulance, it is no longer used in that capacity. The colonel will notice there are no red crosses on the sides or the roof. Additionally, if the colonel looks at the door, he will see the legend INDIGENOUS PERSONNEL TRANSPORT VEHICLE #5, and if he looks at the bumpers he will see that the markings indicate it is in the service of the 711TH QM MKRC. That stands for 'Quartermaster Mess Kit Repair Company.' "

"Okay, okay," Frade said. "Can I get in it now? It's as cold as a witch's teat out here."

"Not until I'm finished," Cronley said.

Frade was about to snap, "Finish later," but he saw the amused smile on Gehlen's face and held his tongue.

"The other four indigenous personnel transport vehicles of the 711th QM MKRC are, in fact, used to transport indigenous personnel. But those indigenous personnel are not mess kit repairers, but, in fact, associates of General Gehlen. The 711th Quartermaster is a figment of Dunwiddie's imagination. That keeps curious people from asking the wrong questions."

"Got it," Frade said. "How much longer is this lecture going to go on?"

"Not much longer, bear with me. Now, Indigenous Transport Vehicle #5, this one, is a deception within a deception, thanks again to the genius of First Sergeant Dunwiddie. This vehicle, as you will soon see, has two armchairs mounted inside where they used to put stretchers. When the senior staff of Kloster Grünau has something to talk about we don't wish to share with anyone else, we get in what is now our Truck, a three-quarter-ton four-by-four Mobile Secure Room and drive out on the runway."

"Clever," Frade said.

"Which is what I suspect the general had in mind today. Do you have any questions, Colonel, sir, or is everything clear in your mind?"

"How do I open the back door?"

"I will accept that as an apology for your cruel remarks about my reputation as a pilot."

"Shut up, Jimmy," Frade said, smiling, "and get in the goddamned truck. Or whatever the hell it is."

Frade settled himself in one of the armchairs, looked around, saw a table with a coffee thermos and mugs on it, and said, "Nice. And clever."

Gehlen turned from the front seat. "Yes, it is. And Dunwiddie does get the credit. Shortly after Sergeant Tedworth arrested Major Orlovsky and we had to deal with the unpleasant fact that the NKGB is among us, I mentioned idly that I was a bit concerned that our conversations in Jim's office might be overheard. He told me he'd been working on a solution, then took me for a ride in this."

"Is that what you wanted to talk about?" Frade said. "Are the people the NKGB turned — I suppose I mean Orlovsky turned — becoming a greater problem?"

"They are, but that's not what I wanted to talk to you about, what I thought you should hear."

"Okay. Shoot. Anything you have to say I'll listen to."

"How about anything First Sergeant Dunwiddie has to say?"

The question took Frade by surprise.

"Excuse me?" he asked.

"Your hesitation — indeed, your not answering that question at all — proves that Sergeant Dunwiddie was right again."

"I don't know what you're talking about, General."

"As I told you I was going to, I took Dunwiddie with me when I talked to Major Orlovsky. After our first chat — we've had three with him, the last at midnight, just before I called you — Dunwiddie said that he thought he had detected in Orlovsky something I hadn't."

"Which was?" Frade asked.

Gehlen didn't reply directly. Instead, he said, "I thought he was wrong, or perhaps reaching, as you Americans say, for a straw. But in the second meeting, I approached the subject at its fringes, and began to see what Dunwiddie suspected."

"Which was?"

Again Gehlen ignored the question.

"What Dunwiddie suspected was not only possible but likely. Improbable, I had thought at first. Now I thought it was likely. So after the second chat with our friend Konstantin, I asked Chauncey . . ."

"Chauncey?" Frade interrupted.

". . . how he would suggest I attempt to exploit the window he had opened. He suggested that I permit him to try exploiting what he saw. After some thought, and frankly without a great deal of enthusiasm, I told him to go ahead. So we had our third chat with Friend Konstantin. Two minutes into Chauncey's interrogation, it was clear that he was right in his assessment of the chink in Orlovsky's armor — and well on the way to cracking the chink wide open."

"What chink?" Frade said.

And was again ignored.

"At that point, we stopped. Or I told Chauncey to stop. When we were alone, I told him that what we had to do now was get you to come back. Obviously, we couldn't discuss this on the telephone. Whoever my traitors are, they are capable of tapping our telephone lines and probably are doing so.

"Chauncey said that the call would have to come from me. That you would not be inclined to either believe him or trust his skill. Or his judgment. So I called. Before he tells you what he has done, and what he believes we should do, I want to say that I called you because I think he's absolutely right."

Frade looked at Dunwiddie in the driver's seat.

"Okay, Dunwiddie, let's hear it."

"Major Orlovsky is a Christian, Colonel," he began.

"We don't ordinarily think of NKGB officers as being Christians, do we?" Frade asked thoughtfully.

"No, sir. I am presuming his superiors are unaware of it."

"I presume you're telling me he takes it seriously?"

"Yes, sir. That's my take."

"So what?"

"Two things, sir. He might already be questioning the moral superiority of the Communists."

"And you believe, I gather, that the Soviet Union is governed by acolytes of Marx and Lenin? Heathen acolytes, so to speak?"

"I know better than that, Colonel," Dunwiddie said. "What I'm suggesting is that if Orlovsky is a — what? — sincere Christian, then he can't be comfortable with state atheism and what the Communists have done to the Russian Orthodox Church."

"I've always felt that suppression of the Russian Church was one of the worst mistakes Stalin made," Gehlen said. "And the proof of that is that he has not been able to stamp out Christianity. After Chauncey brought this up, I remembered that at least half of the people we've turned have been Christians."

"I thought we were listening to what Sergeant Dunwiddie has to say," Frade said not very pleasantly.

"And if he is a Christian," Dunwiddie continued, "then he is very much aware of his Christian duty to protect his wife and children. We've already seen suggestions of that."

"We're back to 'so what?' " Frade said.

"When the Germans attacked what they believe is Holy Mother Russia — and, tangentially, I've always been curious about why an atheist state uses the term 'Holy Mother Russia' so often — it was his patriotic duty to defend it."

"And, at the risk of repeating myself, so what?"

"We've done nothing to the Soviet Union, actually the reverse. So why are they attacking the United States? If we can get him to ask himself that, and then prove we're the good guys by making a bona fide effort to get his family out of Russia . . ."

Frade looked at him a long moment, then said, "Dunwiddie, if you were in Orlovsky's shoes, remembering you didn't get to be an

NKGB major by being stupid, would you believe General Gehlen or Captain Cronley or me when one of us said, 'Trust me . . .' What the hell's his name? *Konstantin.* 'Trust me, *Konstantin,* if you change sides, we'll get your family out of Russia and set you up with a new life in Argentina'?"

"I might if a priest told me that," Dunwiddie said.

"You have two options there, Sergeant, if you think it through. You either dress up some guy as a priest — who your pal Konstantin would see through in about ten seconds — or you find some priest willing to go along with you. How easy do you think that will be?"

"You already have a priest," Dunwiddie said evenly.

"What priest? Wait . . . you mean Father Welner? You're suggesting I bring Welner here from Argentina to deal with Orlovsky?"

"Yes, sir."

"Jesus, Clete!" Jimmy blurted. "That would work."

"Oh, for Christ's sake!" Frade said. "That's preposterous." He stopped. "On the other hand, it just might work."

"That's what Sergeant Dunwiddie and I concluded, Colonel," Gehlen said. "The question then becomes: Will Father Welner be willing to participate?"

"General, the question our wily Jesuit friend will ask himself is: 'What's in this for me?' 'Me' being defined as the Society of Jesus. And from what I've seen of them — and Welner — he will regard this as a heaven-sent opportunity. They get no-cost-to-them access to a senior NKGB officer and they get an 'I owe you' from both me and you. And probably from General Martín as well. That's the only downside I see, Martín being brought into this."

"What I was asking was: Isn't Father Welner likely to consider the moral implications of him being used to turn Major Orlovsky? The first thing we want from Orlovsky is the names of my people he — the NKGB — has turned. And Father Welner knows what will happen to them when we know who they are."

"When Father Welner was explaining to me how things were in Argentina, and God knows I needed an explanation —"

"Otto Niedermeyer told me that you were very close to Father Welner, but never offered an explanation of how that came to happen," Gehlen interrupted.

Frade correctly interpreted it to be more of a question than a statement.

"He was my father's confessor and best

friend," Frade said. "Because my father was about as religious as I am, and had good reason to hate the Church —"

" 'Hate the Church'?" Gehlen parroted in surprise.

Frade paused before deciding to answer the question.

"My mother was a convert to Roman Catholicism," he said finally. "After having been warned that a second pregnancy would be very dangerous, she dutifully obeyed the Catholic rules forbidding contraception and died in childbirth. After her funeral, the next time he entered a church was at his own funeral. You heard he was assassinated?"

"At the orders of the SS," Gehlen said. "Otto told me. I'm very sorry."

"On the day of my father's funeral, Welner came to me. He said that whether or not I liked it, he considered himself my priest, my confessor, and hoped that he and I could become as close as he and my father had been.

"I didn't know what his motives were, whether he was trying to put me in his pocket for the good of the Church or whether it really was because of the personal relationship he said he had with my father. I suppressed the urge to tell him to get lost. Over time, I have come to believe that it was probably a little of both. He and my father had been very close. And now I was sitting on the throne of my father's kingdom. Jesuits like to get close to the guy on the throne. Anyway, truth being stranger than fiction, the wily Jesuit and I became, we are, good friends.

"When he was explaining to me how Argentina worked, he said the primary reason Argentina tilted heavily toward the Axis had less to do with their admiration for Adolf Hitler and National Socialism than it did with what they had seen in the Spanish Civil War. That had been a war, they believed, between the Christian forces of Franco and the godless Republicans, read Communists. The Germans made sure the Argentines knew the Republicans had murdered four thousand–odd priests —"

"And thirteen bishops," Gehlen said.

"So you think that's true, that the Republicans murdered priests and nuns out of hand?" Frade asked.

"And bishops. I saw evidence of one such sacrilege one beautiful spring day in 1937."

"You saw it?" Cronley blurted.

Gehlen nodded.

"I think I missed the actual sacrilege by an hour. Maybe two. My team — I was then a brand-new major — and I were driving down a road near Seville. As we approached a picturesque little village, there was a priest hanging from every other telephone pole. And then when we got to the center of the little village, we found, lying in a massive pool of blood in front of the burned-out church, a dozen nuns who had obviously been violated before they were murdered. And a bishop tied to a chair. He had been shot in the back of the head. Our sergeant theorized that he had been forced to watch the raping of the nuns, but there is of course no way we could know that for sure."

"Jesus Christ!" Cronley exclaimed.

"Captain Cronley gets the prize for today's most inappropriate blasphemy," Frade said darkly.

"I think that was an expression of disgust, rather than blasphemy," Gehlen said.

"Possibly," Frade said. "I'll give him the benefit of the doubt. Before we got off the subject, I was about to say that I don't think Father Welner will have any moral problems helping us turn an NKGB officer. I suspect he feels — for that matter, the Catholic Church feels — much the same way about Communists as General Philip Sheridan felt about the Indians on our Western plains."

"Excuse me?"

"General Sheridan was quoted as saying

that the only good Indian was a dead one," Frade said.

"That's a bit brutal," Gehlen said. "But Communism poses the greatest threat to Roman Catholicism there has ever been, and I'm sure the Vatican is fully aware of that."

"My grandfather," Frade said, "who is the exact opposite of an admirer of the Catholic Church, says that to understand the Catholic Church you have to understand that its primary mission is its preservation."

Gehlen didn't reply to that. He said, instead, "Dunwiddie has recognized another problem: Unless we can get Orlovsky out of here and to Argentina without the wrong people learning about it . . ."

He left the sentence unfinished, but Frade took his meaning.

"Yeah," Frade agreed. His face showed that he had both not considered that problem and was, without much success, trying to find a solution.

"Shoot him," Cronley said. "And then bury him in the dark of night and in great secrecy, in an unmarked grave in the Kloster cemetery."

Frade understood that immediately, too.

"That'd work. I presume, General, that despite Captain Cronley's determination to conduct Orlovsky's burial in the greatest secrecy it would not go unnoticed?"

"I think we could count on that, Colonel," Gehlen said.

"And then," Frade said, "you're going to have to figure a way to get the corpse from its unmarked grave and get it onto a Connie in Frankfurt without anybody —"

"Without anybody," Gehlen said, laughing, "dropping to their knees in awe at a second resurrection."

"I'll leave the solution to that problem in your capable hands," Frade said. "Not that I think, with Sergeant Dunwiddie's exception, that you're all that capable, but because I really have to get to Rhine-Main now."

"Thank you very much," Gehlen said. "Your confidence in us inspires me."

Frade chuckled, then said, "When I spoke with Admiral Souers last night, I told him we'd go wheels-up at noon. The admiral does not like to be kept waiting."

"Do you want to see Major Orlovsky before you go?" Gehlen asked.

"Your call, General."

"Chauncey?" Gehlen said.

"Sir, I think a brief visit. Shake his hand, tell him you're off to Argentina and look forward to seeing him there. That's it."

"I agree," Gehlen said.

"Then that's what I'll do. Jimmy, after you drop me at Rhine-Main, I want you to go back to Munich. You are authorized to tell Sergeant Hessinger that we're going to take Orlovsky to Argentina. Only, repeat only, Sergeant Hessinger. Not Major Wallace. Make sure Hessinger knows he's not to tell Wallace or Mattingly anything about this. I'm telling you this, giving you this order, before witnesses. My stated reason for this is that if this thing blows up in our faces, Mattingly and Wallace will be off the hook. Understand?"

"Yes, sir."

"And if they don't know about it, they can't get in the way," Frade added.

"You consider that a problem?" Gehlen asked.

"Colonel Mattingly," Frade said, "is very skilled in the fine art of covering his ass. I'm just helping him do that."

Gehlen shook his head and smiled.

"Let's go see Major Orlovsky," Frade said. "And while I'm doing that, Jimmy, you can top off the tanks in the Storch."

"How about some breakfast first, and then top off the tanks?"

"Have the mess make us some bacon-and-egg sandwiches," Frade ordered. "We can eat them on the way to Rhine-Main. We can't make Admiral Souers wait for us."

[Three]

Rhine-Main USAF Base
Frankfurt am Main, Hesse
American Zone of Occupation, Germany

1100 3 November 1945

"Rhine-Main Ground Control, Army Seven-Oh-Seven," Cronley said into his microphone. "Request taxi instruction to parking location of South American Airways Lockheed Constellation tail number Double-Zero-Five. If you can't see me, I am a Storch aircraft on taxiway sixteen left."

There was no reply, just sixty seconds of hiss. Finally, Cronley called again. "Rhine-Main, Army Seven-Oh-Seven. Do you read me?"

"Army Seven-Zero-Seven, hold one," Ground Control replied.

"They seem to have lost your airplane," Cronley said to Frade.

"What the hell?" Frade replied.

"Army Seven-Zero-Seven, Rhine-Main Ground. Be advised South American Airways Double-Zero-Five is parked in a secure area and you are not, repeat not, authorized to enter secure area."

"Rhine-Main Ground, Army Seven-Oh-Seven. Be advised I have the captain of South American Double-Zero-Five aboard. What do I tell him?"

"What the hell?" Frade asked again.

There was another sixty seconds of nothing but hiss before Rhine-Main replied: "Army Seven-Zero-Seven, Rhine-Main Ground. Hold in present position. A *Follow me* will meet you."

"Seven-Oh-Seven understands hold for *Follow me.*"

The *Follow me* — a jeep painted in a yellow-and-black checkerboard pattern, with a large sign reading FOLLOW ME mounted on its rear — came racing onto the taxiway ninety seconds later. It was accompanied by two Military Police jeeps, each holding four military policemen. The *Follow me* turned and backed up to the nose of the Storch. The MP jeeps began to take up positions on either side of the Storch. When they had done so, the *Follow me* started to move.

"What the hell's going on, Clete?"

"Whatever it is, Jimmy, I don't like it."

The *Follow me* led them away from the terminal, and finally to a remote airfield compass rose. Three staff cars were parked on the grass beside the rose.

An MP captain carrying an electric bull-horn walked onto the compass rose.

"Pilot, shut down your engine and exit the aircraft!" he ordered.

"Why do I think we're under arrest?" Jimmy said.

When he had shut down the Storch and was starting to climb down from the aircraft, three men in civilian suits and snap-brim hats and an Air Force major got out of the staff cars.

When both Frade and Cronley were out of the airplane, the three men and the major walked closer. One of them produced credentials and announced, "Federal Bureau of Investigation. Let's see some identification."

"Major, I am Lieutenant Colonel Cletus Frade, U.S. Marine Corps —"

"I told you I wanted to see your identification," the FBI agent snapped, interrupting him.

". . . And I am on a mission classified Top Secret–Lindbergh," Frade finished.

"God damn you," the FBI agent said, "I said I want to see your identification."

"Major, if this civilian swears at me again, I'm going to punch him into next week," Frade said.

"On the ground. Get on your knees and then lay on your stomach!" the FBI agent ordered furiously.

Frade turned to the Air Force major. "I will show you my identification, Major."

"On the goddamned ground, goddamn it!" the FBI agent barked.

The Air Force major, looking very uncomfortable, quickly walked past the FBI agents and saluted. Frade returned it.

"Sir, I'm Major Johansen, the assistant base provost marshal. May I see your identification?"

Frade produced it. The major examined it, and Frade, very carefully.

"The colonel is who he says he is," Johansen said. "Lieutenant Colonel Frade, U.S. Marine Corps."

"And the other one? Who is he?"

"Major Johansen," Frade said, "what I want you to do right now is call General Walter Bedell Smith — Frankfurt Military 1113 — in the Farben Building —"

"I asked who this other man is," the FBI agent snapped. "It is a federal crime, a felony, to interfere with an agent of the FBI in the execution of his office. I am asking for the last time for the identity of this young man. Specifically, are you James D. Cronley Junior?"

Jimmy snapped back: "What did this Cronley guy do, rob a bank?"

"Get on the phone now, Major," Frade said. "That is a direct order."

The major looked at him for a long moment, then said, "Yes, sir."

He signaled for one of the jeeps to come to them. When it had, he gestured for the driver to hand him the microphone of the shortwave radio behind the rear seat.

"This is Major Johansen," he said into it. "Get on the telephone and call Frankfurt Military . . ." He looked at Frade.

"One-one-one-three," Frade furnished.

"Tell them Colonel Frade, USMC, is calling for General Smith. Then stand by to relay both parts of the conversation if we can't hear him," the major ordered. He turned to Frade. "This shouldn't take long, sir."

Everyone heard whoever was on the other end of the shortwave net reply to Johansen, "Frankfurt Military 1113. Yes, sir."

"Thank you," Frade said.

"Office of the deputy commander, Sergeant Major King speaking, sir."

"Colonel Frade calling for General Smith," Major Johansen said.

"Hold one, please, Colonel," the sergeant major said.

The major handed Frade the microphone.

"Colonel," a new voice said. "This is General Porter. General Smith is en route with Admiral Souers to meet you at Rhine-Main. He may already be there. But is there something I can do for you?"

"Hold one, please, General," Frade said. He turned to the FBI agent. "Are you going to fold your tent and get the hell out of here, or would you like me to tell General Porter what he can do for me?"

The FBI agent glared at Frade for a moment.

"You haven't heard the last of this, Colonel." He then gestured to the others to follow him.

"No, thank you, sir," Frade said. "Just checking. I'm at Rhine-Main."

"Have a nice flight, Colonel," General Porter said.

"Thank you, sir. Frade out."

The FBI agents got in one of the staff cars and it drove off.

Frade handed the microphone to the Air Force major.

"Thank you, Major."

"May I ask, sir, what that was all about?"

"You can ask, but I can't tell you," Frade said, smiling. "If I did, I'd have to kill you."

The major chuckled.

"On the other hand, you can tell me what the FBI told you about us. And that's not in the order of a suggestion."

"Sir, he said that they were investigating the exfiltration of Nazis from Germany into Argentina."

"He told you we were suspected of exfiltrating Nazis out of Germany? Into Argentina?"

"He implied that, Colonel."

"Cronley, show the major your credentials," Frade ordered.

Cronley did so.

"When I saw Twenty-three CIC on your vertical stabilizer," the major said, as he handed them back, "I cleverly deduced the CIC might somehow be involved in this. You're sure you can't tell me how?"

"I can tell you this much: What I am going to do is exfiltrate Admiral Sidney Souers, who is senior counselor to President Truman, out of Germany into Washington, D.C. He's been here conferring with General Eisenhower."

"Yes, sir, I know. We've had your airplane under heavy security since it arrived."

"I'd love to know how the FBI came up with that me-smuggling-Nazis-out-of-Germany theory."

"No telling, Colonel. But it does make

you wonder if the FBI is as perfect as they would have us all believe, doesn't it?" He paused. "I'm sorry about all this, Colonel."

"Forget it. You were just doing your job."

"Is there anything I can do for you, sir?"

"Two things. You can take me to my airplane and arrange for Cronley to top off the tanks in the Storch."

"Why don't I send for a fuel truck and then take you to your airplane in my car?"

"How about having the *Follow me* lead Cronley and his Storch to the Connie?" Frade asked. "That way I will have to take my suitcase out of the airplane just once instead of unloading it into your car, et cetera?"

"Done," the major said. "I'll have the fuel truck meet us at your Constellation."

"I will go in the Storch," Frade said. "Even with a *Follow me* to lead him, Cronley — he learned to fly last week — would probably get lost between here and there in your great big airport."

The major laughed out loud.

"Colonel, thanks for not being sore about this. The FBI came into my office, waving their credentials. And, frankly, I've heard the rumors about Nazis escaping to South America. I just . . ."

"I probably would have reacted the same way."

"That's very good of you, sir."

"I will mention what happened to General Smith," Frade said. He turned to Cronley. "All right, Special Agent Cronley. Into the airplane, and please remember to engage your brain before starting the engine."

The major laughed out loud again.

"I'll follow you over there," he said.

"What was that comedy routine all about?" Cronley asked, as he taxied the Storch across the airfield. "You sounded like a combination of Jack Benny and Will Rogers."

"Pay attention, Jimmy," Frade snapped, his tone making clear that he was deadly serious. "The damned FBI showing up here poses a greater threat to what we're doing — on several fronts — than the people the NKGB has turned. High on this list is the distinct possibility that when Mattingly hears about it — and we have to assume he will — he will immediately shift into Cover His Ass mode and decide to throw you to the wolves. And I won't be here to protect you."

"You think he may already have done that?

How come the FBI was here in the first place?"

"I don't know. They may have just put the SAA Connie under surveillance to see if I was going to sneak Nazis onto it. That doesn't make a hell of a lot of sense, because I'd be a fool to do that with Admiral Souers aboard. But on the other hand, the FBI does a lot of things that don't make sense."

"They asked, specifically, if I was James D. Cronley Junior."

"Well, they've been looking for you since you were in Washington. Maybe they spotted you at the Schlosshotel Kronberg or the Vier Jahreszeiten. Anyway, they know you're here. They regard you as the weakest link in the fence we've built around Operation Ost. And they really want to know about that. J. Edgar Hoover would really like to have that on Truman. And it would be almost as good — maybe better — for them to find out this renegade operation of the President is holding an NKGB officer they haven't told Army G-2 they have. And are taking him, or have taken him, to Argentina."

"Understood."

"Yeah, I think you do."

"Practically, what can happen? Say I can't manage to dodge them? Say they show up at Kloster Grünau? I kept Colonel Schumann out of there, and he had, arguably, a right to know what's going on in there. They don't. What are they going to do? Complain to whom? Mattingly would have to tell them that what's going on there is none of their business. Otherwise, he would be the guy who blew Operation Ost and that would be the same thing as betraying the President."

"Okay. But they don't know that, Jimmy. What they *know* is that there is a twenty-two-year-old junior Army officer who they think knows all about Operation Ost. With reason, they feel all they have to do is wave their FBI credentials in his face, he'll piss his pants, then tell them anything they want to know."

"You don't think what happened just now might make them wonder about that?"

"You mean your wiseass crack? 'What did this Cronley guy do, rob a bank?' "

"Yeah."

"That was clever, but all it really did was make that FBI guy decide, 'Okay, I can't deal with this wiseass now. I'll have to wait until Frade is gone. No problem. All things come to he who waits.' "

"I'm not going to blow Operation Ost, Clete."

"Don't underestimate the FBI. They're not stupid, and right now they're under a lot of pressure — if not from Hoover himself, then from Clyde Whatsisname, his deputy — to find out whatever they can about Operation Ost. You're going to have to be very careful."

"Clyde Whatsisname?"

"Hoover's deputy director. Admiral Souers told me he's the guy in charge of the private files — usually detailed reports of sexual escapades — Hoover uses to hold over people, especially politicians." He paused and chuckled. "Jimmy, please tell me you're not fucking somebody you shouldn't be fucking. That would be all we need right now. The Federal Blackmail Institution would love to have something like that on you."

Jimmy laughed, because he knew that was the reaction Clete expected.

But I am fucking somebody I shouldn't be fucking.

And I can't afford to have — what did Clete call it? — the Federal Blackmail Institution catch me doing it.

Okay. Auf Wiedersehen, Rachel! Affair over!

You go back to the colonel and the kiddies.

And I try to start thinking with my head instead of my dick.

It never should have started. What the hell was I thinking?

Then he repeated: "I'm not going to blow Operation Ost."

"I wish I was as confident about that as you are."

"What do you want me to do, say it again? Okay. I'm not going to blow Operation Ost."

"When was the last time you saw a grown man pout?"

"What?"

"Pout. You know, stick your lip out and look sad so everybody feels sorry for you."

"What the hell are you talking about now?"

"Enrico," Clete said. He pointed.

They were approaching the Constellation. Sergeant Major Enrico Rodríguez, Cavalry, Argentine Army, Retired, was sitting on the stairway leading up the open rear door of the aircraft. His Remington Model 11 riot shotgun was in his lap.

And he was indeed pouting.

"I didn't want to take him to the meeting at the Schlosshotel Kronberg. It would have been awkward all around. So I made him stay with Gonzo Delgano. 'For just overnight.' And then you and I went to Munich the next morning . . ."

"And he's really pissed."

"Yup. And he's really pissed."

"He loves you, Clete."

"Yeah, I know."

Cronley and Frade got out of the Storch.

Enrico pretended not to see them.

"Enrico, you want to help me with my bag?" Frade called.

Rodríguez walked to the Storch, said, *"Teniente,"* to Cronley, and took Frade's bag.

He ignored Frade.

"Actually, Enrico, that's *Capitán*," Frade said.

"Capitán," Enrico said, and marched with Frade's bag to the ladder and carried it up and into the airplane.

"How long are you going to be invisible?" Jimmy asked.

"God only knows. Enrico can stay pissed — pout — longer than my wife."

"Here comes my gas truck."

"As soon as you're topped off, get out of here and down to Munich. Try to confuse the FBI about where you're going. You probably won't be able to, but try."

"At the risk of repeating myself, Colonel, sir, I'm not going to blow Operation Ost."

"So you said."

"And here comes the admiral," Frade said, pointing.

A convoy was approaching the Constellation. First an M-8 Armored Car, then a Packard Clipper with a four-star license plate, then a Buick Roadmaster with a one-star plate, and then another M-8.

"Major Johansen is dazzled by all those stars," Frade said. "Good."

"What?"

"We will now make our manners to the deputy commander in chief, U.S. Forces, European Theatre. With a little luck, he will be cordial, and the Air Force major will see that you have friends in high places and decide it's highly unlikely that people like you and me would be sneaking Nazis — or anyone else — out of Germany. That may very well come in handy when you are trying to sneak your buddy Konstantin through his airport."

The convoy stopped. Drivers jumped out and opened doors. General Walter Bedell Smith, Rear Admiral Sidney W. Souers, and a full colonel wearing the insignia of an aide-de-camp to a four-star general got out of the Packard Clipper.

Frade saluted crisply.

"Good morning, sir!" he barked.

Smith, Souers, and the aide-de-camp returned the salute.

"Ready to go, are we, Frade?" Souers said.

"We just got here ourselves, sir. But we should be."

"I don't think you have met Colonel

Frade, have you, Beetle?" Souers said. "And I know you haven't met Captain Cronley."

Brigadier General John Magruder and Colonel Jack Mullaney got out of the Buick and walked quickly up to them, obviously determined not to miss anything.

They arrived in time to hear General Smith ask, "The officer who found the U-234?"

"Yes, sir," Frade said. "That's him."

"Well done, son," General Smith said, pumping Jimmy's hand.

"Thank you, sir," Cronley said.

Gonzalo Delgano came down the stairs. He was wearing his SAA uniform.

"Don Cletus, we're ready to go anytime you are."

"Gentlemen, this is Captain Delgano," Frade said. "South American Airways chief pilot."

Hands were shaken.

The drivers of the staff cars carried luggage aboard.

"Have a nice flight," General Smith said.

"Thank you for all your courtesies and hospitality," Admiral Souers said.

He shook Cronley's hand and then waved for Frade to precede him up the stairs.

Clete put his hand out to Jimmy and said, "We'll be in touch."

"Yes, sir."

"Aw, hell," Frade said. "In Argentina, men can kiss their friends."

He hugged Jimmy and wetly kissed his cheek.

"Be careful, Little Brother," Frade said, then quickly climbed the stairs. Admiral Souers followed him.

"Only a Marine would dare to do that," General Smith said, chuckling.

"Captain Cronley," Major Johansen said, "if you refuel your aircraft here, the Constellation will have to wait until you're finished."

"Then let me get out of here," Cronley said.

"Why don't we all get out of the way?" General Smith said, and motioned for his aide-de-camp to get into the Packard.

Major Johansen and Cronley saluted as the convoy drove off the compass star.

Cronley got back in the Storch and fired it up as ground crews moved fire extinguishers into place for the starting of the Constellation's engines. The *Follow me* jeep flashed its lights as a signal it was ready for Cronley to follow him.

The fuel truck and Major Johansen's staff car followed the Storch to the threshold of a runway.

The Constellation, running on two engines, came down the taxiway and lined up with the runway.

As Cronley got out of the Storch, the Constellation started the other engines and ran them up.

And then started to roll.

Jimmy watched it take off.

And suddenly felt very much alone.

He showed the fuel truck crew where the tanks were. Topping them off took no more than a few minutes, but by the time they were finished, the Constellation was out of sight.

That reinforced Jimmy's feeling of being very much alone.

He turned to Major Johansen.

"Thanks for everything, Major," he said, and saluted.

"Have a nice flight," Johansen said. "And come back. The next time, I promise not to meet you like you've just robbed a bank."

"I just may take you up on that, sir."

Ninety seconds later, he reported, "Rhine-Main Departure Control. Army Seven-Zero-Seven rolling."

As he broke ground and pointed the nose of the Storch south, he thought that he could easily make Munich in less than two hours. It was about 300 kilometers from Frankfurt am Main to Munich, and the Storch cruised at about 170 kilometers per hour.

Then he remembered that Frade had ordered him to try to confuse the FBI about his destination.

He said, "Shit!" and reached for the microphone.

"Rhine-Main Area Control, Army Seven-Oh-Seven. Change of flight plan. Close out Direct Rhine-Main Schleissheim. Open Direct Rhine-Main Eschborn for passenger pickup."

It was a flight of only a few minutes, and it took him over Hoechst.

Right down there is where Lieutenant Colonel and Mrs. Schumann and their children have their quarters.

What the hell was I doing, screwing a colonel's wife? A married woman with children?

Well, it may have had something to do with the fact that in a twenty-four-hour period, I had been married, my wife was killed, and the President of the United States pinned captain's bars on me.

Not to mention what happened at the mouth of the Magellan Straits.

I was understandably under an emotional

strain. That just might have had something to do with my stupidity.

On the other hand, I do have a tendency to do amazingly stupid things, don't I? As well as an extraordinary ability to justify whatever dumb fucking thing I may have done — such as fucking somebody I shouldn't be fucking, as Clete so aptly put it.

Well, at least Rachel's down there and I'll be in Munich or at Kloster Grünau.

And ne'er the twain shall meet, as they say.

"Eschborn, Army Seven-Oh-Seven, at fifteen hundred feet, three miles south. I am a Storch aircraft, I say again, Storch aircraft. Request straight-in approach to Runway Thirty-five. I have it in sight.

"Eschborn, Army Seven-Oh-Seven at the threshold of Three-five. VFR to Hersfeld. Request takeoff permission.

"Hersfeld, Army Seven-Oh-Seven, request approach and landing. I am a Storch aircraft, I say again, Storch aircraft, at fifteen hundred four miles south of your station.

"Hersfeld, Army Seven-Oh-Seven understands Number Two to land on Three-three after an L-4.

"Hersfeld, Army Seven-Oh-Seven . . . *Oops!* I came in a little long. I'd better go around. I should be able to get it on the ground the next try. Please close out my

472

VFR flight plan at ten past the hour. Thank you."

When I am absolutely sure that I'm out of sight of the Hersfeld tower, in the interest of pilot safety I will climb to say five hundred feet and go to Munich.

[Four]

Hotel Vier Jahreszeiten
Maximilianstrasse 178
Munich, American Zone of Occupation,
  Germany

1655 3 November 1945

And what am I going to do, Cronley wondered, as he reached for the doorknob of Suite 507, *if Sergeant Freddy Hessinger has taken off for the day? Go look for him in that whorehouse? Or if Major Harold Wallace is here?*

Sergeant Hessinger was at his ornate desk in his usual pinks-and-greens officer's uniform. The door to Wallace's office was closed; there was no way to tell if he was in it or not.

"I was wondering where you were," Hessinger greeted him.

It came out, "I vus vondering vair you vur."

Cronley managed not to smile.

473

"Your girlfriend has been looking for you," Hessinger added.

Jesus Christ! Does Freddy know?

Cronley sat down in one of the two upholstered chairs facing Hessinger's desk before asking what he hoped would sound like an innocent question.

"What girlfriend would that be?"

"Mrs. Colonel Schumann, that one."

"What the hell are you talking about?"

Cronley hoped that question also sounded innocent.

"She telephoned twice and came in once. I think she wants you to buy her dinner."

"Why would I want to do that?"

"Because she is a colonel's wife and he went to Vienna and left her here and you are a captain and she thinks she's entitled."

"Screw her."

"I don't know how nice that would be, but I do know it would be very dangerous. Colonel Schumann is not a nice man."

"Speaking of nice men, where is Major Wallace?"

"He is at the bar of the officers' club."

"Here in the hotel?"

"No. At the Signal Battalion."

"Freddy, we have to talk, and Major Wallace can't know we did, or what we talked about. Either him or Colonel Mattingly."

"Why do I think I'm not going to like this? Does this have something to do with the NKGB-er Sergeant Tedworth caught at Kloster Grünau?"

"How'd you hear about that?"

"Tedworth told me."

"He has a big mouth. He should have known better."

"We trust each other. What about the NKGB-er?"

"We think we turned him."

"I doubt that. He's NKGB. They are not known for turning. Being smarter than their captors, yes. Turning, no."

"I think we have, Freddy."

"We? Who is we? You and Dunwiddie?"

"And General Gehlen."

"Gehlen thinks you have turned the NKGB-er?"

"He thinks we have him well on the road to turning, and that when we get him talking to the priest Frade is sending from Argentina, he will turn."

"What priest? From Argentina?"

"He's a Jesuit who's been involved with getting people to Argentina for the Vatican. We're going to take Orlovsky to Argentina."

"What I think you should do is start from

the beginning," Hessinger said. "The beginning is when you were in trouble with Mattingly because you stuck your nose into Gehlen's interrogation of the Russian."

"A lot's happened since then."

"That's why you should start from the beginning," Hessinger said reasonably.

"Okay. I guess the most important thing is that Mattingly is no longer in charge of Operation Ost. Frade is . . ."

". . . and so," Cronley concluded, "as soon as Frade took off for the States, I came here. After, of course, trying to confuse the FBI about my destination. Further deponent sayeth not."

Hessinger grunted thoughtfully.

"Freddy . . ." Cronley began.

"The one maybe big problem I see," Hessinger interrupted him, "is getting the NKGB-er through the airport in Frankfurt. If we get caught loading him on an Argentine airliner . . ." He stopped, then asked, "Why are you looking at me funny?"

"I was about to ask, 'Now that you know what's going on, will you help?' You sound as if you're already enlisted."

"I think of it more as being drafted one more time. I didn't enlist in the Army, I was drafted. And I have no more choice here

476

than when I got that *Your friends and neighbors have selected you* postcard from my draft board."

Cronley chuckled.

"You want to explain that?"

"Is necessary?"

"Yeah, I think so, Freddy."

"Okay. When I got my draft notice, I started researching the Army."

"You did what?"

"I wanted to learn what I could expect. So I went to the library —"

"And got a book?" Cronley said, chuckling. *"What to Expect When You're Drafted?"*

"Not a book. Books plural. About military ethics."

"There ain't no such animal."

"Yes, there is. A good officer has dual loyalty."

"What the hell does that mean?"

"Up and down. A good officer is loyal to his superiors and his subordinates. They taught you about this when you went to that Texas military school, right?"

"It was mentioned once or twice. So what?"

"It didn't take me long to figure out Mattingly. His is only up."

"Excuse me?"

"His loyalty is upward only. People under

him are expendable."

"That's true, but so what?"

"So I knew it was only a matter of time until he expended me."

"Okay."

"Then you showed up. And I saw that yours is both ways."

"How do you know?"

"If yours was only upward, to Mattingly, you would have kept your nose to yourself and let him get away with what he was trying to do to Dunwiddie. Get Dunwiddie to shoot the NKGB-er and him know nothing about it. You didn't. You were loyal downwards. If you're at the bottom, like I am here, loyalty downwards is very important."

"Well, then, welcome to our little conspiracy, Freddy."

"Like I said, I see only one maybe big problem. Getting the NKGB-er onto the Argentine airplane. We'll have to think about that."

"Why don't we find a quiet corner of the dining room and think about it there? While I'm eating. The only thing I've had to eat all day is a bacon-and-egg sandwich."

"Because you are going to call Mrs. Colonel Schumann and ask her what you can do for her. Probably dinner."

"I'd rather not."

"I'd rather not be here. I would rather be back at Harvard chasing Wellesley girls and working on my doctorate. But I am here."

"Then you take her to dinner."

"She doesn't want to have dinner with me. I'm an enlisted man. Besides, what we are trying to do is important. And you know you can't afford to have Mrs. Colonel Schumann pissed at you."

He picked up the elaborate old-fashioned telephone on his desk.

"Kindly connect me with Mrs. Lieutenant Colonel Schumann," he ordered.

"Maybe she's not there," Cronley said after a moment. "Maybe she got tired of waiting for me."

"Good afternoon, Mrs. Schumann. This is Special Agent Hessinger. I have found Captain Cronley for you. One moment, please."

He put his hand over the microphone, said, "Be charming," then extended the receiver to Cronley.

"Good afternoon, Mrs. Schumann. This is Captain Cronley. How are you? Special Agent Hessinger tells me you're all alone in Munich."

"The colonel had to go to Vienna," Rachel said.

"So Hessinger told me. I was wondering

if you're free for dinner."

"As a matter of fact, yes, Captain Cronley, I am."

"When would you like me to call for you?"

"Actually, I'd be open to an invitation for cocktails, too."

"You mean right now?"

"Could you fit me into your busy schedule?"

"With pleasure. The thing is, I've been flying just about all day . . ."

"Flying? Where?"

". . . and I need a shower and a fresh uniform. Could you meet me in the bar in, say, thirty minutes?"

"I'll be waiting. Thank you so much, Captain Cronley."

"Yes, ma'am."

Cronley stood and put the receiver back in its cradle.

"How'd I do?"

"You're no Cary Grant, more like Humphrey Bogart. Anyway, all you have to do is keep her happy."

"How do I do that?"

"By doing whatever she wants you to do."

"You going to be here when I've fed her?"

"No. I get off at five. It's now five-fifteen. How about I meet you in the dining room for breakfast at seven?"

"I'll be there."

[Five]

As he went into his room, after a moment's indecision, Cronley dropped a matchbook in the doorjamb so it wouldn't close.

He didn't know if Rachel would come to his room instead of waiting for him in the bar. He hoped she wouldn't. But she might. She seemed oblivious to the risks of their getting caught. And he didn't want her to be seen knocking at his door. By Freddy Hessinger, for example, who might be leaving his down-the-corridor office as she did so.

After thinking about this, too, he laid an Ike jacket with the insignia of captain of Cavalry on the bed before going in the shower. That would enable him to play the role of the nice captain entertaining the colonel's lady at dinner in the colonel's absence. Colonels' ladies do not fool around with young captains. They just might fool around with CIC special agents.

What stupid games am I playing?

He got as far as the bathroom door before returning to the bed. He put the captain's jacket back into the closet and tossed the Ike jacket with civilian triangles he had been wearing all day onto the bed.

481

He was standing naked in front of the sink several minutes later wiping shaving cream from his face when Rachel came in.

"Why do I think you knew I wasn't going to wait for you in the bar?"

"Because you know I know you take chances you shouldn't take?"

She walked up to him and put her hand on him and then pulled his face down to hers. She kissed him lewdly for a moment, then pulled away.

"That's what you're not going to get," she said, "because you were flying your damned Russian around all day and not paying attention to me."

Then she walked out of the bathroom.

He finished wiping the shaving cream off his face and put on his underwear before going back into the bedroom. She was sitting in an armchair, her legs crossed and showing — he was sure intentionally — a good deal of leg.

"Well, are you going to say you're sorry?" she asked.

"For what?"

"You know for what. I spent all day waiting to just hear from you."

"What was I supposed to do, Rachel, call your room?"

"Why not?"

" 'Colonel Schumann, this is Cronley. Can I speak with your wife?' Come on, Rachel."

"Tony went to Vienna. You knew that."

"I didn't."

"On the phone just now you knew."

"Hessinger had just told me."

She considered that.

"I spent all day waiting for you to call."

"I'm sorry. Frade wanted me to fly him to Frankfurt. I flew him to Frankfurt. I waited for him and the admiral to take off. He took off. I came back here. The defense rests."

"I believe you," she said after a moment. "I'm sorry."

"Not necessary."

"You want to know how sorry I am?"

"You're going to slash your wrists?"

"Come here."

He walked closer to her. She sat forward in the armchair.

"Closer," she ordered. "I'm sorry I thought you spent all day with that Russian."

She put her hand to his shorts, pushed them aside, and took him into her mouth.

Some time later, she tucked it back in.

"That's how sorry I am," she said. "Forgive me?"

"My God!"

483

"But that's all you get now. I spent two hours in the beauty salon making myself pretty for you, and I don't want to mess my hair. Right away. After dinner is another matter."

[Six]

"I can't believe you ate all that," Rachel said, as he put his knife and fork across the plate that had held a medium-rare porterhouse steak, baked potato, and buttered peas.

"I said all I had to eat all day was a bacon-and-egg sandwich," he said, then drained what was left of his double Jack Daniel's rocks.

"I hope you got your strength back, you poor starving boy."

"That was a very nice steak."

"And a large one. I had an idea when I was sitting under the dryer in the beauty shop," she said.

"Why do I think it was lewd?"

"I don't suppose you could put me in that German airplane of yours and fly me up to your monastery? Just the thought of doing it there feels delightfully lewd."

"I couldn't fly you there without a lot of people asking questions."

"But you can use that Opel Kapitän, right?"

Cronley nodded.

"So you could drive me to your monastery tomorrow?"

When he didn't reply immediately, she went on: "Everybody knows I stayed here when Tony went to Vienna so I could look into the enlisted men's welfare facilities. No one would ask questions if I went there. And while I was there, perhaps the commanding officer would show me his quarters. I'd really like to have the commanding officer show me his quarters."

"Great idea, except that I'm under orders to stay here until I hear from Colonel Frade."

"Hear from him about what?"

"He didn't choose to tell me that."

"Damn."

"I would be delighted to show you my commanding officer's quarters in Pullach tomorrow."

"I really would like to tell Tony that I got into the monastery after you shot up his car to keep him out. We couldn't make a quick trip early in the morning?"

"Maybe after I hear from Colonel Frade."

"I suppose that's better than a flat-out 'Hell no, Rachel, you can't go to my monastery.' "

"I'm being charming as I have designs on your body."

Cronley then had a fresh disturbing thought: *Now that I have decided — and really believe — Mrs. Colonel Schumann is really somebody I shouldn't be fucking, what's going to happen when we get upstairs? What if I can't get it up?*

X

[One]

The Dining Room
Hotel Vier Jahreszeiten
Maximilianstrasse 178
Munich, American Zone of Occupation,
  Germany

0655 4 November 1945

Special Agent Friedrich Hessinger was sitting at a small table in a far corner of the dining room when Cronley walked in.

A waiter followed Cronley to the table and took their order. When he had gone, Hessinger asked, "How did it go with Mrs. Colonel Schumann last night?"

"I bought her dinner and then we went to bed."

"You weren't listening when I told you

486

that would be dangerous?"

It took a moment for Cronley to take his meaning.

"Screw you, Freddy."

"A little joke," Hessinger said. "But you should watch what you say. You should have said, 'After dinner she went to her room. And then I went to mine.' "

"Fuck you."

"You shouldn't talk to me that way. Officers are not supposed to say unkind things to enlisted men. It hurts our feelings. And then we can go to the inspector general to complain. You know our IG, right? Colonel Schumann?"

Delighted with his own wit, Hessinger was smiling broadly.

"And today what are Mrs. Colonel Schumann's plans for you?"

"I'll call her after we eat and see how I can be of service."

"Do that. We can't afford to have her pissed at you."

Cronley didn't think Rachel was pissed at him, but he did suspect that the bloom had begun to come off their roses, so to speak.

After dinner, when they had gone to his room, there had been maybe ten minutes of athletic thrashing about on his bed, followed by maybe sixty seconds of breath-catching. Then Rachel had matter-of-factly announced that she'd better get back to her room, "Tony will probably call." She had then dressed as quickly as she had undressed and left.

That was probably, he decided, his punishment for his refusal to take her to Kloster Grünau. His reaction to her leaving had been one of relief. Although Ole Willie had answered the call of duty, the cold fact seemed to be that since he now accepted that he really shouldn't be fucking Rachel, he really didn't want to.

There were a number of reasons for this, high among them that the late Mrs. James D. Cronley Jr. had startled him by returning to his thoughts while he and Rachel were having dinner. While he didn't think the Squirt was really riding around on a cloud up there playing a mournful tune on her harp while looking down at him with tear-filled eyes as he wined, dined, and prepared to fuck a married woman who had two children — he wasn't completely sure she wasn't, either.

It had also occurred to him that maybe Rachel had also been thinking of her children, or more accurately, as herself as the mother of two children who should not be fucking a young captain. Maybe, he thought, she had for the first time really considered the consequences of their getting caught.

"She wanted me to take the Kapitän and drive her to Kloster Grünau," Cronley told Hessinger. "She said she would love to be able to tell her husband that she got into the monastery after he couldn't."

"Taking her to Kloster Grünau would be even more stupid than taking her to bed. What did you tell her?"

"That I had been ordered to stay in Munich until I heard from Colonel Frade."

"And she believed you?"

"She didn't like it, but she believed me."

"I asked you what do you think she'll want you to do for her today?"

"Probably take her to the Pullach compound. She wants to see how the Engineers are coming with the service club."

"A lieutenant and three sergeants from the ASA in Frankfurt were on the Blue Danube last night. Major McClung sent them to install a Collins radio and a SIGABA in the compound. The lieutenant wanted to know where you wanted him to put it. I told him you would let him know."

"Where did McClung get a SIGABA and a Collins?"

"I guess Colonel Frade brought them with him from Washington."

"He didn't say anything to me."

"Maybe he had other things on his mind. I don't think you should let Mrs. Colonel Schumann know about the radios when you're in Pullach."

"You don't trust her?"

"She's a woman. Women like to talk. She gets together with the girls at the CIC/ASA Officers' Ladies Club. 'You won't believe the fancy radio I saw when I was checking on the club in the Pullach compound.' "

"Okay. Point taken, Freddy."

"I wish she wasn't going to the Pullach compound at all. But when I asked Major Wallace, he said we don't want to make Colonel Schumann unhappy, which he would be if Mrs. Colonel Schumann was unhappy because she couldn't go to the compound."

"Well, I agree with you. I'll see what I can do with Mattingly."

"I don't think he'll want to make Colonel Schumann unhappy, either. Where do you want the radio?"

"Where would you recommend?"

"Your quarters. In a closet in your room where nobody can see it."

"You going to tell McClung's lieutenant,

or should I?"

"You go out there and tell him. Officers don't like enlisted men telling them what to do."

"I never heard that."

"I am constantly amazed at all the things you have never heard."

"Officers don't like smart-ass sergeants reminding them how dumb they are, either."

"I can't help being a smart-ass sergeant. I went to Harvard."

"Did I ever tell you I wanted to go to Harvard?"

"No."

"They wouldn't let me in."

"Why not?"

"My parents are married."

"That's funny. I like that. But enough of this camaraderie — since they wouldn't let you into Harvard, I will tell you that means no more friendly good-fellowship . . ."

"I never heard that."

"I am not surprised. Let's get back to business. How do you plan to get the NKGB-er from where he is now onto the Argentine airplane?"

"Before or after we bury him — maybe before we execute him — we load him onto a Storch. And then, obviously, I fly him to Frankfurt."

"We come back to Frankfurt in a minute, Jimmy. Let's talk about the burying of him."

"Okay. I don't have much experience in this sort of thing, and happily defer to your expertise."

"Fortunately for you, we have an expert in this sort of thing — his name is Gehlen — at Kloster Grünau. What I propose to do is work this plan out between you and me. And then, when we agree on what we think should be done, we bring General Gehlen in on it. That okay with you, Jimmy?"

Cronley thought that it was strange — even funny — that Hessinger, whom he thought of as an overeducated clerk, had even come up with a plan. But he liked him, and didn't want to hurt his feelings.

"Fine," Cronley said. "Go ahead."

"The problem is that we have to do something that will look like the real thing to different groups of people. We have to fool not only the Germans who the NKGB has turned — and since we don't know who they are, that means all the Germans — and just about all of Dunwiddie's men."

"Why do we have to fool Tiny's people?"

"Because if they know what's really going on they will talk about it, and there goes the secret."

"Point taken."

"We can't do this with just Dunwiddie and Technical Sergeant Tedworth, so the first thing we have to do —"

"Why can't we do it with just Tiny and Tedworth?"

"Who's going to dig the grave and carry the body to it? And then fill it up again?"

"Okay."

"We're going to have to get five more of Tiny's people involved."

"Five? Just to dig the grave and —"

"Three to dig the grave and two to drive the ambulance."

"What ambulance?"

"The one we're going to send to that airfield near Frankfurt, the one by the senior officers' club."

"Eschborn? Why are we going to send an ambulance . . . Oh, you mean one of the transport vehicles?"

"Of course. Why would we send an ambulance to Eschborn?"

"Freddy, why are we going to send anything to Eschborn?"

"Because that's the way we're going to get the NKGB-er onto Rhine-Main airfield. Nobody's going to look for a Russian agent in the back of an ex-ambulance with 711TH QM MKRC painted on its bumpers. But I am getting ahead of myself. We start with H hour, like they started D-day at Normandy."

"What the hell does that mean?"

"Let me explain. We have things over which we have no control. One is when the Argentine airplane will leave Frankfurt. Another is when we shoot the NKGB-er. There we have a problem, as that has to happen in the dark, after we have the grave dug. So that is one piece of information we have to have. Three pieces. One, how long it will take to dig the grave. Two, how long it will take to carry the body from the chapel to the grave. And three, how long it will take to fill in the grave.

"So we start with H hour. That will be when we shoot him. In that connection, I suggest that there be three shots. With a .45 pistol. They're very noisy. One shot to wake everybody up and, thirty seconds later, two more shots so everybody knows what they heard was shooting.

"Now, as I started to say, the next number we need, what we have to find out, is how long it is going to take to dig the grave. When you get back up there, and I suggest you do this in the dark, take the gravediggers out in the country someplace and have them dig a grave. In the dark. Simulating as much as possible what they will do when they actually dig the grave. Say that takes an hour. Add a half hour. That means the shooting would take place at H hour minus one-point-five. You understand all this?"

Cronley nodded.

"There are a lot of other blanks to fill in," Hessinger went on. "For example, how long does it take to fly from Kloster Grünau to Eschborn?"

"We better figure on three hours."

"Then, presuming you would take off from Eschborn as soon as you could, when you had enough light to see the runway . . . You understand where I'm going with this?"

"Yeah, I do. And I'm impressed, Freddy."

"I think of it as sort of a chess game. Now, another time we need is how long it will take to drive the ambulance from Eschborn to Rhine-Main."

"Depending on the time of day, an hour to an hour and a half."

"And what time of day would the airplane take off?"

"That we could control," Cronley said. "To a degree."

"How big a degree?"

"After the airplane is refueled and the passengers loaded, we could arrange for the takeoff to be delayed, say, two hours. But we couldn't arrange for it to take off before it was ready."

"What about this? Could we arrange for the airplane to be ready to take off at . . . I don't know what I'm asking here."

"You mean, could we arrange for the airplane to take off at, say, ten o'clock in the morning? Make that eleven — three hours after I took off from here at, say, seven? Plus an hour to get to Rhine-Main from Eschborn. Yeah. We would just have to delay it from taking off the night before. That could be done."

"How?"

"By getting on the Collins and talking to the SAA Constellation."

"I didn't know the Argentine airplanes have Collins radios. Our kind of Collins radios."

"I'll make sure the one that's coming here for Orlovsky does."

"You can see where we have a lot of work to do."

"I think that's what's known as an understatement."

"Well, we have until nine o'clock to work on it."

"Until nine? What happens at nine?"

"You call Mrs. Colonel Schumann and say, 'Good morning, Mrs. Schumann, what can I do for you this morning?' That's what happens at nine." Hessinger stood. "Let's

496

go to the office and get this started."

"What about Major Wallace? We can't let him see what we're doing."

"If he went to the Signal Battalion officers' club last night, he won't come into work until ten, if then." He paused. "Leave money for the waiter. I read an Army Regulation that officers aren't supposed to take gifts from enlisted men."

[Two]

0905 4 November 1945

"Hello?"

"Good morning. How did you sleep?"

"You heard from Colonel Frade? We can go to the monastery?"

"No word from him yet. Would you like to meet in the dining room before we go to Pullach?"

"You mean for lunch?"

"I meant now, for breakfast."

"Meet me in the dining room at twelve-thirty."

Click.

Apparently, the bloom is even further off the rose than I originally thought.

"What I would suggest," Sergeant Hessinger said, "is that I stay here and think about what we are going to do with the

497

NKGB-er, and you take the Kapitän and drive out to Pullach and see the ASA lieutenant. And while you're driving out there, and while you are driving back, you think what you can do to make Mrs. Colonel Schumann happy. Right now I have the feeling she doesn't like you very much."

[Three]

The South German Industrial Development Organization Compound
Pullach, Bavaria
The American Zone of Occupied Germany

0935 4 November 1945

Cronley's Opel Kapitän stopped at the outer roadblock to the compound. It was guarded by three Polish guards armed with carbines and dressed in black-dyed U.S. Army fatigues.

One of them walked up to the staff car, took a good look at Cronley, then signaled to the others to move the barrier — concertina barbed wire nailed to a crude wooden framework — out of the way. When they had done so, he signaled that Cronley could enter.

That won't do, Cronley decided as he drove slowly to the second roadblock.

That guy saw a staff car and a man in uniform and just passed me in. He should — at least — have asked me for my identification.

And that concertina wire has to go, too. If we're going to pretend that what's going on in here is an industrial development organization, the entrance can't look like a POW enclosure.

And maybe get those Poles some different uniforms. So they look like cops, not soldiers.

And, obviously, the sooner I get some of Tiny's people down here the better.

Two hundred yards down the road, there was another checkpoint. More Poles in dyed fatigues, but also an American soldier, a stocky technical sergeant armed with a .45 as well as a carbine.

He walked up to the Kapitän and waited for Cronley to roll down the window.

"You from the CIC?" the sergeant asked.

"That's what's painted on the bumpers, Twenty-three CIC," Cronley replied.

"Where's Captain Cronley?" the sergeant asked.

Obviously, the sergeant does not think I could be a captain.

Well, there are very few twenty-two-year-old captains.

"My name is Cronley." He produced his CIC credentials.

The sergeant saluted. Cronley returned it.

"Sorry, Captain."

"I look so young because I don't drink, smoke, fornicate, or have impure thoughts," Cronley said. "I'm actually thirty-six."

The sergeant laughed.

"Yeah, you are. Sir, there's a Signal Corps lieutenant looking for you."

"Where is he?"

"At your quarters."

"My quarters?"

"You're going to be the CO of whatever this is, right?"

Cronley nodded.

"Then your quarters are right next door to the general offices. You know where that is?"

Cronley nodded again.

"There's a sign on it. Says 'Military Government Liaison Officer.' In English. And in German."

"I think I can find it. Thanks."

Three minutes later, having passed through the third, inner checkpoint — this one manned by three Polish guards and two American soldiers — he found a Signal Corps lieutenant he thought was the one looking for him. He and three soldiers were sitting in a three-quarter-ton truck parked in front of a small house. It was next to the larger building on which was a sign identifying it as the GENERALBÜROS SÜD-DEUTSCHE INDUSTRIELLE ENTWICKLUNGS-ORGANISATION.

If these guys came on the Blue Danube train from Frankfurt, where did they get the truck?

The sign on the smaller building was only slightly smaller.

UNITED STATES MILITARY GOVERNMENT LIAISON OFFICER US-MILITÄR REGIERUNG LIAISON OFFIZIER

Clever intelligence officer that I am, I guess that's what Mattingly decided they should call the commanding officer. You really wouldn't want to hang a sign that read OFFICE OF THE CIC OFFICER IN COMMAND OF THIS OPERATION WE DON'T WANT ANYBODY TO KNOW ABOUT.

Cronley pulled the Kapitän in beside the truck and got out. The lieutenant got out of the truck and walked over to the staff car. So did the men with him. They were all sergeants, he saw, a sergeant, a staff sergeant, and a technical sergeant.

"You're from the Twenty-third?" the

lieutenant asked.

Cronley nodded.

"Where's Captain Cronley?"

"You're looking at him."

The lieutenant's eyebrows rose.

That's two people in a row who can't believe that sweet-faced Little Jimmy Cronley could possibly be a captain.

No. Not two. Five. Two of the sergeants look incredulous. The older one, the tech sergeant, looks disgusted.

And I really can't get indignant, because they're right; I shouldn't be a captain.

More important, I really have no business being put in charge of this place.

When did Frade say Major — what's Polo's name? — Major Maxwell Ashton III is going to get here?

"Sir, I'm not trying to be difficult," the lieutenant said, "but have you got some identification?"

Cronley produced his CIC credentials.

"I look younger than I am," Jimmy volunteered, "because I don't drink, smoke, fornicate, or have impure thoughts."

I didn't even think before that came out of my mouth.

Maybe what I really should be is a Special Services comedian, entertaining the troops.

The lieutenant and the tech sergeant

laughed.

"Maybe I should try that," the lieutenant said. He put out his hand. "Sir, my name is Stratford" — he pointed at the sergeants one at a time — "and this is Tech Sergeant Mitchell, Staff Sergeant Kramer, and Sergeant Fortin."

Cronley shook their hands. None of them said a word.

"Sir, we've got a system for you," Stratford said. "I guess you know that?"

Cronley nodded.

"I think you also know what kind of a system," the lieutenant said. "The one classified Top Secret."

"I've been wondering where you got it," Cronley said.

"Major McClung . . ." He paused, asking with his eyes if Cronley knew who he meant.

"Iron Lung. Also known as 'the Whisperer.'"

That got smiles from the two junior sergeants, a look of displeasure from the tech sergeant, and an uncomfortable smile from Lieutenant Stratford.

"Major McClung," Stratford went on, "had one system in the vault with the crypto machines. There was a sign on it, 'Not to Be Issued Without Specific Authorization from CO, ASA Europe.' I guess we now have that authorization. You have the access code, right? Otherwise we're just spinning our wheels."

"I have the access code for the SIGABA at Kloster Grünau, if that's what you mean," Cronley said.

"Major McClung told us we're not supposed to say out loud either of the two things you just said out loud," Technical Sergeant Mitchell said.

"Thank you, Sergeant Mitchell, I'll keep that in mind," Cronley said, then turned to Stratford. "What do you mean, without the code we'll be spinning our wheels?"

"Well, we can install those unnamed devices, but they won't work without the access code. Major McClung didn't give it to us."

"Probably because he didn't have it," Cronley replied. "How long is it going to take you to get these nameless devices up and running?"

"Not long. The ASA guys here in Munich — the ones who are going to move in here — put up the antennas with the antenna farm they're going to use. They were not told what they were for and know better than to ask. They ran a buried cable over there."

He pointed between the headquarters and

liaison officer buildings. Cronley saw a coil of heavily insulated cable.

"So all we have to do is run that into wherever you want these installed in your building."

"Let's do it."

"Before we do: Major McClung said he thinks you know how to operate these things, but not how to maintain them. True?"

"True."

"All of us have Top Secret clearances . . ."

"What about Lindbergh?"

"Lindbergh?"

"Top Secret–Lindbergh."

"Never heard of it."

"Major McClung has. He's got one. That's the clearance we work under here."

"So where does that leave us, sir?"

"I don't know. You were saying?"

"The major said you can have us — one of us, several of us, or all of us — for as long as you need us."

"To keep these nameless devices running, as well as install them?"

Lieutenant Stratford nodded.

"The system here," Stratford said, "and at that other place we're not supposed to say out loud. I thought you might want to make up your mind about what you're going to need before we install these things."

"Well, that's very nice of Major Mc-Clung," Cronley said. "Let me think about it."

And he did so out loud: "So, if I said just one of you would be enough to set up the system here, and at the other place, the rest of you could wait in the truck and would not know what actually happened to those things we're not supposed to talk about?"

"That's the idea. I could probably offer a helpful suggestion if I knew what was going on here and at the other place we're not supposed to say out loud. But you can't tell me, right?"

"No, I can't," Cronley said. "Or . . . Two things. There is actually another place with a system. And I'm making up my mind just how much I can tell you."

"I understand."

"Decision made. I'll keep everybody. If it turns out I don't need everybody, I can . . ." He stopped. "If it turns out I don't need everybody, I'll still have to keep everybody."

"Because everybody would know all about these things we can't say out loud?" Lieutenant Stratford asked, smiling.

Cronley nodded.

"Your call," the lieutenant said.

"How is the Whisperer going to feel if I

keep all of you?"

"I got the impression it's really your call, that you get whatever you think you need, including all of us."

"All of you, then. They call that redundancy. It's important that these things work over the next ten days."

"Okay, let's get them up and running. You show us where you want them."

"I really wish I could tell you more," Cronley said as they walked to the door of what was going to be his quarters.

Before he actually reached the door, he realized that he was going to have to do exactly that.

[Four]

When Cronley pushed open the door and walked into the building, he saw desks, tables, chairs, and filing cabinets fresh from a Quartermaster Depot. Corrugated paper was still wrapped around the legs of the metal furniture.

When he opened a door on the right side of the room, he found a stairway going up. He took the steps two at a time, and the lieutenant and the sergeants followed him.

They found themselves in a large room. There was more furniture, including a bed and bedside table, also obviously fresh from a QM warehouse. There were three doors leading out of the room. One door led to a bathroom, and the others onto closets, one of which was a small room.

Lieutenant Stratford and his sergeants looked at him expectantly.

Well, I might as well get this over with.

"Let me have your attention," Cronley began. "Before we get started, a couple of questions and then a little speech. You know that Major McClung, who knows what's going on here, has volunteered your services for indefinite TDY. I can't tell you for how long that will be, but figure on ninety days. Anyone have a problem with that? And before you ask, no, you can't bring your *Schatzi*s down here from Frankfurt."

That earned some chuckles.

"Anyone want to go back to Frankfurt?"

No one responded.

"Next question: You first," he said, pointing to the junior ASA man, Sergeant Fortin. "How do you feel about black people?"

"Sir?" the sergeant said. The question was obviously confusing.

"Simple question, Sergeant Fortin. How do you feel about black people? More specifically, how would you like to have a black first sergeant?"

"A black first sergeant?"

508

"The Pullach compound will be guarded by a reinforced company of soldiers from an anti-tank battalion of Second Armored. They're all black, including their first sergeant, who is six feet four and weighs maybe two-eighty. When provoked, he can be one mean sonofabitch. Since I have no intention of setting up a separate white guy/black guy operation, now that you're going to be here, this big black guy will be your first sergeant. Do you have any problems with that?"

"Sir, I don't know."

Cronley did not hesitate: "Okay. Go wait in the truck. If you tell anyone what you saw here, or think you saw here, you're going to find yourself on a slow boat to the Aleutian Islands, where you can count on counting snowballs for the next couple of years. Go."

Fortin started for the stairwell.

"What about you, Sergeant Kramer?" Cronley asked the younger of the staff sergeants. "You have problems with working under a black top kick?"

Fortin, almost to the stairwell, turned.

"Sir?"

"What?"

"How does this black first sergeant feel about white guys?"

"Valid question," Cronley replied. "I look at him as my best friend. As far as I know, the feeling is mutual."

"He's a pretty good soldier?"

"He made first sergeant at twenty-one when all the other non-coms in his company were killed or wounded. He comes from an Army family. His great-grandfathers were Cavalry soldiers who fought Apaches and Comanches in the West, and two of his grandfathers riding with the Ninth Cavalry beat Teddy Roosevelt's Rough Riders up San Juan Hill in Cuba during the Spanish-American War. That answer your question?"

"I'll stay, sir."

"Because of what I said?"

"Sir, Major McClung said what you're doing here is important. That, and what you said about this black guy being your best friend. And what the hell, we're all in the same Army, right, sir?"

"Yes, we are." Cronley turned to Kramer and Mitchell. "Either of you have any problems about First Sergeant Dunwiddie?"

Both said, "No, sir."

"Okay. Welcome to the *General-Büros Süd-Deutsche Industrielle Entwicklungsorganisation.* In English, that's the General Offices of the South German Industrial Development Organization. Now — and really pay attention to this — what follows is classified Top Secret–Lindbergh. The use of deadly force has been authorized to preserve the secrecy of anything connected with this operation.

"This organization formerly was known as Abwehr Ost. I will now tell you what Abwehr Ost was and what it's doing now. Shortly before the war was over . . .

". . . Any questions?"

Staff Sergeant Kramer chuckled.

"Did I say something amusing, Sergeant?" Cronley snapped.

"No, sir. I was just thinking, now I know how you people got away with shooting up the IG's car."

"How'd you hear about that?"

"I was in the CIC/ASA motor pool, sir, when they dragged it in. Colonel Schumann's driver was still in shock."

"And?"

"So I asked him what had happened, and he said they were in the Bavarian Alps on some back road Schumann insisted they take and they came across a CIC detachment — in a monastery — that Colonel Schumann had never heard of. So he decided to have a look. A lieutenant told him that he couldn't come in —"

"That was me," Cronley said.

"And the colonel said, 'Don't be absurd. Go around him.' And then three of the . . ."

"Of the what?"

"He said 'three of the largest, meanest-looking . . . Negroes' — that's not *exactly* what he said, sir, if you take my meaning — he'd ever seen let loose with a pedestal-mounted .50 cal Browning."

"This story is all over the ASA, is it?"

"Yes and no, Captain Cronley," Lieutenant Stratford said. "Has everybody heard it? Yes. Is anybody going to talk about it, except within the ASA? No. The same afternoon they dragged Colonel Schumann's staff car into the motor pool, Major McClung went down there and told everybody that nobody had seen a shot-up staff car. The ASA is in the business of keeping secrets."

"I didn't mean to interrupt this, sir," Staff Sergeant Kramer said.

"I'm glad you did," Cronley said. "It reminded me of something else I need to say. I don't know how this idiocy got started, but the Army pretends that cryptographers and radio operators — hell, clerk typists — don't read or understand what they're typing, encrypting, decrypting, or transmitting or receiving.

"I don't go along with that. So long as you're here, I not only expect you to read whatever we send or receive over these devices, but to understand what's being said. If you don't understand something you've handled, ask. Everybody got that?"

There was a chorus of "Yes, sir."

"Okay. Get a desk and chair from downstairs. We'll set these things up in the larger of these two closets."

The three non-coms went to the stairwell, then down it.

"Permission to speak, sir?" Stratford said when they were out of earshot.

"I went to Texas A&M, Stratford. Not West Point. You don't have to ask my permission to say anything."

"Yes, sir. I wanted to say that was very impressive. You handled that very well."

Cronley didn't reply.

Stratford said: "Tell me. Did this enormous first sergeant of yours go to college?"

"As a matter of fact, he did."

"Norwich?"

Cronley nodded.

"Me, too. When I heard that line about the Buffalo Soldiers beating Teddy Roosevelt up San Juan Hill, I knew it had to be Dunwiddie. He was a rook — a freshman — when I was in my senior year. But you pay attention to rooks who are as big and black as Dunwiddie."

"I'm really glad to hear you know Tiny, Stratford."

"How come he's not an officer?"

"Because he got screwed out of his commission by a white officer."

[Five]

The ASA technicians had the Collins and the SIGABA set up far more quickly than Cronley expected they would.

Sergeant Kramer, who had changed his mind about staying, looked up from the desk.

"All we need now, sir, is the access code and the name you want to call this station."

"Let me sit down there, please," Cronley said.

"I'm a pretty good typist, sir."

"As the result of a month's detention when I was in the sixth grade, so am I. I often think that typing is the most valuable skill I brought into the Army."

The sergeant laughed and stood. Cronley took his chair.

There was a telephone dial on the front of the SIGABA. Cronley dialed in the access code. Green indicator lights illuminated. A message appeared on the screen: ENTER STATION ID.

"What shall we call our little station?"

Cronley wondered aloud. "Where are we? Munich. What comes to mind when you hear Munich? Hitler's beer garden. Beergarden? Better, *Beermug.*"

He began typing.

A strip of paper began to snake out of the SIGABA, as simultaneously the message was typed on a roll of paper by the teletype typewriter that was part of the SIGABA/Collins system.

When he had finished typing, and the teletype typewriter stopped clattering, Cronley tore the paper tape free and fed it back into the SIGABA. Then he tore what the teletypewriter had printed from the machine, read it, and then handed it to Sergeant Kramer.

"Pass it around when you're finished," he ordered.

"Yes, sir."

PRIORITY

TOP SECRET LINDBERGH

DUPLICATION FORBIDDEN

FROM BEERMUG

MSG NO 00001 1100 GREENWICH 4

NOVEMBER 1945

TO VINT HILL SPECIAL

WISH TO JOIN TANGO NET

ACKNOWLEDGE

END

ALTARBOY

TOP SECRET LINDBERGH

"Sergeant Mitchell, right? Cronley asked the technical sergeant.

"Yes, sir."

"You're senior, so you get the dirty job. You are hereby appointed Classified Documents NCO. I don't suppose you have a weapon?"

"A .45. In the truck, sir."

"Not doing you much good there, is it? Go get it. When you have it, I will give you this, which you will keep on your person until I can get my safe moved here from Kloster Grünau. I will then give you the combination to the safe. Got it?"

"Yes, sir."

The SIGABA began to whir.

"Hold off on getting your pistol until we hear what Vint Hill has to say," Cronley ordered.

The teletypewriter began to clatter. When it fell silent, Cronley tore off the message, read it, and handed it to Mitchell.

"After you've read that, go get your pistol," he ordered.

"Yes, sir."

PRIORITY

TOP SECRET LINDBERGH

DUPLICATION FORBIDDEN

FROM VINT HILL TANGO NET

1103 GREENWICH 4 NOVEMBER 1945

TO BEERMUG ATTENTION ALTARBOY

REF YOUR MSG NO 00001 1100 GREENWICH 4 NOVEMBER 1945

   1-WELCOME TO TANGO NET

   2-ACKNOWLEDGE ENCRYPTED TEXT FOLLOWING BY DECRYPTION

FDHSG ASDPW QLPDH GSHII PXCBD
GOPWN ABDKD HHSDF

END

TOP SECRET LINDBERGH

"We will now see if the decrypt function works," Cronley said.

He took the tape, found the encrypted message, tore it off, pushed a key that caused another green light — this one indicating EN/DECRYPTION FUNCTION ACTIVATED — to come on, and then fed the tape into the machine.

The teletypewriter began to clatter:

MARY HAD A LITTLE LAMB ITS
FLEECE WAS WHITE AS SNOW

"Now let's see if it works the other way," Cronley said, and began typing again.

The newly appointed Classified Documents NCO came back into the room — now armed with a Model 1911A1 .45 ACP in a leather holster dangling from a web belt — in time to see the end of the tape swallowed by the machine.

He leaned over and watched the teletypewriter chatter out a copy of Cronley's reply:

PRIORITY

TOP SECRET LINDBERGH

DUPLICATION FORBIDDEN

FROM BEERMUG

TO VINT HILL TANGO NET

REF YOUR REPLY TO MY NO 00001
1100 GREENWICH 4 NOVEMBER 1945

   1-MARY HAD A LITTLE LAMB ITS
     FLEECE WAS WHITE AS SNOW

   2-ACKNOWLEDGE ENCRYPTED TEST
     FOLLOWING BY DECRIPTION

SLEST YEWHA DEKLS WKLDK ZSHGF
HSGSG

END

ALTARBOY

TOP SECRET LINDBERGH

Vint Hill's reply came almost immediately:

PRIORITY

TOP SECRET LINDBERGH

DUPLICATION FORBIDDEN

FROM VINT HILL TANGO NET

1103 GREENWICH 4 NOVEMBER 1945

TO BEERMUG ATTENTION ALTARBOY

REF YOUR MSG NO 00001 1100
GREENWICH 4 NOVEMBER 1945

   1-ROSES ARE RED VIOLETS ARE
      BLUE AND I THINK I LOVE YOU

   2-ANYTHING ELSE?

END

TOP SECRET LINDBERGH

"Oh, yes, there is," Cronley said out loud.
"The important part."
He began to type again:

520

PRIORITY

TOP SECRET LINDBERGH

DUPLICATION FORBIDDEN

FROM BEERMUG

TO VINT HILL TANGO NET

REF YOUR REPLIES TO MY NO 00001
1100 GREENWICH 4 NOVEMBER 1945

REQUEST TANGO NET BACKUP IF
NECESSARY FOR MY DIRECT CONNECT
WITH

   1-VATICAN

   2-TEX

   3-POLO

   4-SAILOR

   5-RANGER

END

ALTARBOY

TOP SECRET LINDBERGH

"Who the hell are they?" the staff sergeant blurted, and then added: "Sorry, sir."

"I'll tell you in a minute," Cronley said. And again there was an almost immediate response:

PRIORITY

TOP SECRET LINDBERGH

DUPLICATION FORBIDDEN

FROM VINT HILL TANGO NET

1103 GREENWICH 4 NOVEMBER 1945

TO BEERMUG ATTENTION ALTARBOY

REF YOUR MSG NO 00001 1100 GREENWICH 4 NOVEMBER 1945

  1-TANGO NET WILL BACK UP AS NECESSARY YOUR DIRECT CONNECTION TO

  1-VATICAN

```
2-TEX

3-POLO

4-SAILOR

5-RANGER

2-ANYTHING ELSE?
```

END

TOP SECRET LINDBERGH

"Okay. Done. That's what we needed," Cronley said, and then began to type:

```
PRIORITY

TOP SECRET LINDBERGH

DUPLICATION FORBIDDEN

FROM BEERMUG

TO VINT HILL TANGO NET

THAT'S IT MANY THANKS
```

TOP SECRET LINDBERGH

Everybody in the room was looking at him, wondering what was to come next.

If you don't know what you're doing, plunge ahead.

He looked at his watch.

It's quarter to twelve.

Oh, shit!

"Okay. This will be quick, as I have a social engagement — taking a lady to lunch — that I can't get out of.

"First things first. From this moment, whenever I'm not here, there will be somebody in this room. Somebody with a pistol. No one is to get into this closet except you three, Special Agent Hessinger, First Sergeant Dunwiddie, Lieutenant Stratford, and me. Plus whoever Dunwiddie or the lieutenant thinks should be allowed in here. Understood?"

There was another chorus of "Yes, sir."

"Captain," Sergeant Mitchell asked, "you going to tell us who those other people on the net are?"

"Absolutely," Cronley said. "Vatican is the monastery. Tex is Colonel Cletus Frade, USMC, our commanding officer and the officer in charge of Operation Ost, and that station is in Buenos Aires. Polo is Major Maxwell Ashton the Third, Frade's deputy, and that station is in Mendoza, which is in the foothills of the Andes Mountains on the border between Argentina and Chile, where we operate the relocation program. Major Ashton will shortly — I hope within a matter of days — be coming here to take over command of the compound. Sailor is in Berlin, in what used to be Admiral Canaris's home until the Nazis found out we had turned him. You should know — everyone should, for that matter — that the Nazis sent Canaris to a concentration camp, tortured him, hung him dead, leaving his naked corpse to rot. They confiscated all his property. When Second Armored went into Berlin, the OSS took over his house. And, finally, Ranger is Frade when he has this system mounted in whatever airplane he's flying."

He looked around. "Any questions?"

"Sir, this Marine colonel has got a Collins/ SIGABA on his airplane?" Staff Sergeant Kramer asked dubiously. "It's not an aircraft system."

If I answer that question, there will be more, and I will be late for my lunch with Rachel and the bloom will really be off our rose.

On the other hand, if I don't answer it, or answer it less than fully, these guys — and they're all smart, they wouldn't be in ASA unless they were — will decide I'm handing them a line of bullshit. And I can't afford that.

So fuck Rachel. Figuratively speaking, of course.

"At Polo is a guy, Master Sergeant Siggie Stein, who is not only Major Ashton's deputy but our commo chief. He figured out a way to install the Collins/SIGABA system on aircraft."

"Sir, this sergeant is this major's deputy?"

"The way things work around here is the best man for a job gets it, regardless of his rank . . ."

Fifteen minutes later, he decided that for once he might have made the right decision.

What I had was a lieutenant and three sergeants — all good people; McClung sent me the best he had — who had suddenly been put on indefinite Temporary Duty doing they knew not what in the middle of nowhere.

They were understandably less than thrilled.

After telling them everything, I now have, I think, a lieutenant and three good non-coms who are looking forward to being part of Operation Ost.

And maybe, just maybe, they may have decided that the baby-faced captain isn't such a candy-ass after all.

XI

[One]

*The Dining Room
Hotel Vier Jahreszeiten
Maximilianstrasse 178
Munich, American Zone of Occupation,
   Germany*

1325 4 November 1945

There was a colonel and a formidable-looking woman almost certainly his wife sitting at the table next to where Rachel had been waiting for him for almost an hour.

When Rachel blows up — and why else would she still be waiting for me, if not to blow up? — the colonel and his lady are going to get an earful.

"Mrs. Schumann, I'm so sorry to be late —"

"Don't be silly, Special Agent Cronley," Rachel said. "Special Agent Hessinger was kind enough to come by and tell me you were unavoidably detained. And the colonel made it perfectly clear to me that your entertaining me until he gets here depended

527

on the press of your duties. Say no more. Please sit down."

That was obviously intended for the ears of the colonel and his formidable lady.

Rachel is, after all — maybe above all — a colonel's lady. Like Caesar's wife, colonels' ladies have to be above suspicion. They shouldn't be suspected of, for example, fucking young officers.

Maybe that's what's behind the bloom coming off the rose. Rachel has had time to think about what we've been up to. And wants to stop.

That's what it has to be. I got lucky again.

"Thank you," Cronley said, and sat down.

He had just adjusted his chair and reached for the napkin when he felt her foot searching his crotch.

[Two]

Suite 527
Hotel Vier Jahreszeiten
Maximilianstrasse 178
Munich, American Zone of Occupation, Germany

1415 4 November 1945

"Sweetheart," Mrs. Rachel Schumann said to Captain James D. Cronley Jr., "don't be offended, but you need a shower."

They had been in Suite 527 perhaps two minutes, just long enough for them to be partially disrobed. That was, Rachel had pulled her dress over her head, and then pulled Jimmy's trousers and shorts down to his ankles. She was now on her knees, with his member in her hand.

It was the smell, or perhaps the taste, of the latter that she apparently found offensive.

"Go on," Rachel went on. "I don't know what you were doing all morning with that Russian of yours, but you smell like him. Don't worry. I'll be here when you come out."

Obviously, his naïve hope of an hour before that he had gotten lucky again and was going to be able to get out of their relationship before it exploded in his face was just that, a naïve hope born of desperation.

Rachel got to her feet. Jimmy stepped out of the trousers and shorts gathered at his ankles. He walked to the bathroom, shedding his Ike jacket as he reached it. He went into the bathroom, took off the rest of his clothing, and got into the shower.

As the cold water poured down on him, the conclusion he was forced to draw was that Rachel was bonkers.

There were a number of facts to support this theory, starting of course with the simple fact that she had enticed him into the relationship. It was not his Errol Flynn–type woman-dazzling persona that had made him irresistible to her, which would have been nice to believe, but something else, and that something else was that she was not playing with all the cards normally found in a deck.

Now that he thought about it, he had known that something was wrong from the beginning. He had again thought of this — that Rachel was irresponsible, which is a polite way to say bonkers — at lunch.

Shortly after his lunch had been laid before him, the colonel and his formidable lady who had been at the adjacent table finished their lunch and left. With no others close to them, Rachel decided she could speak freely.

"I suppose it's too much to hope that when you were at the Pullach compound with your Russian friend, you found someplace we can go?"

"I was out there alone, Rachel. Major Mc-Clung sent an officer down with some communications equipment and I had to show him where it was to be installed."

"Then I guess we'll have to go to your

room here. Do you always eat so slowly?"

"Going to my room would be dangerous. Maybe we could go to yours."

"What are you talking about, dangerous?"

He had then explained, in great detail, why going to his room would be dangerous, and to her room, only slightly less so:

His room, Suite 527, was at the far end of the fifth-floor corridor, the interior end, so to speak. Away from the front of the hotel. The rooms at that end of the corridor, suites 501 and 502, the windows of which looked out upon Maximilianplatz, were permanently reserved for the use of Brigadier General H. Paul Greene, chief, Counterintelligence, European Command, and Colonel Robert Mattingly, his deputy. Neither officer was in Munich.

Suites 503 through 505 came next. Suite 503 was assigned to Major Harold Wallace, and 504 and 505 had been set aside for the use of senior officers of the ASA/CIC community visiting Munich. Such as Lieutenant Colonel and Mrs. Schumann, who had been placed in Suite 504.

The two-door elevator bank came next, replacing Suite 506. Next came Suite 507, which served both as the offices of the XX-VIIth CIC Detachment and quarters for Special Agent/Sergeant Friedrich Hessinger.

"So going to either my room or yours, Rachel, would be dangerous . . ."

"We have to go somewhere, sweetheart."

". . . my room more so because to get to it, when we got off the elevator, to get to my room, 527, we would have to walk past the door to 507, which is where Major Wallace and Special Agent Hessinger work. They often leave the door open, and they frequently leave the suite for one reason or another. Our chances of being seen going from the elevator to your room, 504, would be much less as we wouldn't have to walk past 507."

"Well, we can't go to my room, silly boy. What if Tony came back early and walked in on us?"

Since Cronley knew that the northbound Blue Danube, the only way he knew that Colonel Schumann could get to Munich from Vienna, didn't arrive until 1640, he didn't think this posed as much of a threat as Rachel did. But it was possible. And he didn't think arguing about it would be wise.

They had gone to his room, slipping undetected down the corridor past Suite 507's closed door. Getting back on the elevator — in other words, again passing Suite 507, without attracting Freddy Hessinger's attention — was something he had not wanted to think about.

Cronley stayed in the shower until he realized he was shivering and only then, reluctantly, added hot water to the stream to get rid of his chill.

So, what do I do now?

The first problem is getting Rachel out of here without getting caught.

No. That's the second problem. The first is getting back in bed with her and performing as she expects me to.

And what else?

As he warmed himself in the shower, and then as he dried himself, he considered all of his options, all of the potential disasters that could — and were likely to — happen.

And then he summed it up, in sort of an epiphany:

The worst thing that's going to happen is not that Tiny Dunwiddie and Freddy Hessinger will learn that I'm incredibly stupid and an asshole, or that Mattingly will know that he's been right all along about me being grossly incompetent, or that Clete will learn that I'm a three-star shit for fucking a married woman before, almost literally, the Squirt was cold in her grave. It will be that I've failed to follow the oath I took the day my father pinned my gold bar onto my epaulet at College Station.

I swore to defend the Constitution of the United States against all enemies, foreign and domestic, so help me God.

And if the Soviet Union isn't a foreign enemy of the United States, who is?

And speaking of God, how does that go in "The Book of Common Prayer"? I've said it enough. But for the first time in my life, I know what it means . . .

"Almighty and most merciful Father,

"We have erred and strayed from Thy ways like lost sheep.

"We have followed too much the devices and desires of our own hearts.

"We have offended against Thy holy laws.

"We have left undone those things which we ought to have done . . ."

Guilty on all counts. And there's nothing I can do about it.

Except for the last.

I am not going to leave undone those things I know have to be done.

I am going to protect Major Konstantin Orlovsky from getting shot and buried in an unmarked grave because that's a convenient solution to the problem for Colonel Mattingly.

I am going to convince that NKGB sonofabitch that it's his Christian duty to do what he can for his wife and children by turning.

I am going to get him on a plane to Argen-

tina, and then I am going to make sure that General Gehlen does whatever he has to do to get Orlovsky's family out of Russia.

And after that, what?

I don't really give a damn. It doesn't matter.

Back to the immediate problem: getting Rachel out of here without getting caught.

No. I got that wrong again.

First, getting Ole Willie to stand up and do his duty, which may be a hell of a problem, and then getting Rachel out of here without getting caught.

He wrapped a towel around himself and walked into the bedroom.

He looked for his Ike jacket, intending to hang it up, then saw it was hanging on the back of a chair, with his trousers and shorts folded neatly on top of it.

I guess Rachel did that to pass the time. Or just to be nice.

Rachel was in the bed, with a sheet drawn over her. Her clothing was neatly folded on a chaise longue.

"Did you ever play doctor when you were a little boy?" Rachel asked.

"Excuse me?"

" 'You show me yours and I'll show you mine'?"

She threw the sheet off her.

He walked to the bed and dropped the towel.

She reached for him.

A few seconds later, another philosophical truism from his days at College Station came to him: *A licked prick has no conscience.*

[Three]

Schleissheim U.S. Army Airfield
Munich, American Zone of Occupation,
  Germany

1605 4 November 1945

"Lieutenant, what would I have to do to get you to give me half a dozen jerry cans of avgas to take with me?" Cronley asked.

"Why would you want to do that?"

"This airplane seems to run better if I put avgas in it."

"In other words, it's a CIC secret?"

"My lips are sealed. Two elephants and a rhinoceros could not drag that secret from me."

"The avgas is no problem. The cans are."

"I can get them back to you in a couple of days."

"Why not? Let me have your ID, so I can write down to whom I am loaning six jerry cans and thus placing my military career in jeopardy."

Jimmy reached into his Ike jacket for his credentials, which he always carried in the left inside pocket. The folder wasn't there.

"What the hell?" he said.

A quick, somewhat frantic search found the credentials in the right inside pocket.

Thank God!

A CIC agent losing his credentials is a mortal sin.

Right up there, for example, with getting caught fucking a CIC colonel's wife.

Mattingly would be almost as delighted with the former as he would be with the latter.

They must have fallen out when Rachel hung my uniform up.

He handed them over.

Ten minutes later, he told the Schleissheim tower that Army Seven-Oh-Seven was rolling.

[Four]

Kloster Grünau
Schollbrunn, Bavaria
American Zone of Occupation, Germany

1650 4 November 1945

Army Seven-Oh-Seven taxied very slowly to the tent hangar beside the chapel and stopped. The pilot got out.

"I was getting worried you weren't going to be able to make it back," First Sergeant Chauncey L. Dunwiddie greeted Captain James D. Cronley Jr. "It's getting dark."

"I noticed. I could barely see some of the cows I chased in the fields between Munich and here. And the runway was just about invisible as I landed."

"Well, to coin a phrase, all's well that ends well." He handed him a SIGABA printout. "This came for you."

"I can't read it in this light."

"Then get in the ambulance. In the back. There's a dome light. Lights."

Cronley got in the back of the ambulance and found the dome light switch. Dunwiddie got behind the wheel.

Cronley looked at the printout:

PRIORITY

TOP SECRET LINDBERGH

DUPLICATION FORBIDDEN

FROM TEX

VIA VINT HILL TANGO NET

0710 GREENWICH 4 NOVEMBER 1945

TO POLO

INFO COPY TO VATICAN ATTENTION
ALTARBOY

   1-IN DC 0500 GMT

   2-DEPART FOR MIDLAND 0800 GMT

   3-ESTIMATED DEPARTURE FOR BUE-
     NOS AIRES 1600 GMT

   4-ESTIMATED ARRIVAL BUENOS
     AIRES 1200 GMT 5 NOVEMBER

   5-URGENT YOU BE THERE TO MEET
     ME WITH BAGS PACKED FOR
     MONTH AWAY

   6-URGENT YOU DO WHATEVER IS
     REQUIRED TO HAVE THE JESUIT
     AVAILABLE TO ME ON ARRIVAL

TEX

END

TOP SECRET LINDBERGH

Cronley folded the message and put it in

his pocket.

"I don't get that back?"

"I'm considering showing it to Major Orlovsky."

Cronley then handed Dunwiddie a large manila envelope.

"One good turn deserves another," he said. "This is for you."

"What is it?"

"Fat Freddy Hessinger's step-by-step instructions for the accomplishment of our noble mission."

Dunwiddie removed the sheath of paper the envelope contained, then announced, "I can't read this up here."

"I was about to suggest you come back here, where, as you pointed out, there are dome lights."

"But you decided that you would rather go to the bar and have a little something to cut the dust of the trail, and I can read it there?"

"You are a splendid NCO, First Sergeant Dunwiddie, always anticipating the desires of your commander."

Dunwiddie started the engine and drove down the road.

"Curiosity overwhelms me. How does Fat Freddy suggest we handle our noble mission?"

"He thinks we should, as Step One, determine how long it will take to dig and then fill in a grave. He says we should determine that by actually digging a grave and then filling it in."

"Jesus, I never thought about that. We have to know that, don't we?"

"Indeed we do. Fat Freddy also suggests that we use a .45, which is noisy, for the execution. Three shots. First shot to wake people up, then thirty seconds later two more shots, to provide confirmation that somebody's shooting something."

"Someone," Dunwiddie corrected him automatically as they bounced down the road. "Fat Freddy really thinks of everything, doesn't he?"

"Yes, he does. He regards our problem as sort of a chess game."

"You ever play chess with him?"

"The last time, Fat Freddy whipped my ass in seven moves."

"I don't even want to think about how often he's whipped mine."

"Wait till you read Fat Freddy's Operations Order. He solves problems I never even thought of."

"Do you think, maybe, that it's time we stopped making fun of Fat Freddy?"

"So ordered," Jimmy said.

[Five]

A number of problems that neither Captain Cronley nor First Sergeant Dunwiddie had suspected would arise vis-à-vis grave-digging arose when the test grave was actually dug.

The first step had been the recruitment of the gravediggers. There were three criteria for selection. First was that there be three diggers, two to dig and one to be a spare. The second was the character of the diggers. They had to be responsible senior non-commissioned officers who could be told what was going on, and who could be relied upon to keep their mouths shut about it now and in the future. Third, the diggers had to be physically up to the task. Digging a hole six feet deep by ten feet long and four feet wide in the shortest possible time was obviously going to require a good deal of physical exertion.

First Sergeant Dunwiddie marched three such men into the commanding officer's quarters. They were Technical Sergeant

James L. Martin, who was six feet three inches tall and weighed 235 pounds; Staff Sergeant Moses Abraham, who was six feet two inches tall and weighed 220 pounds; and Staff Sergeant Petronius J. Clark, who was six feet four inches tall and weighed 255 pounds.

"I'm sure First Sergeant Dunwiddie has explained something of what's going on here," Cronley began. "But let me go over it again. I'm sure you've heard that we caught a man trying to get out of here. You may not know that he's a Russian, a major . . ."

He stopped.

"Why do I think I'm telling you something you already know all about?" Captain Cronley asked. "Specifically, why do I think that Staff Sergeant Harold Lewis Junior has let his mouth run away with him?"

Everyone looked uncomfortable. No one replied.

"Before this goes any further, Tiny, get that sonofabitch in here!" Cronley ordered furiously.

When Dunwiddie hesitated, and looked as if he was about to say something, Cronley snapped, "That was a goddamned direct order, Sergeant Dunwiddie. Get that loose-mouthed little bastard in here. Now!"

Dunwiddie left the room.

Well, you really blew that, stupid!

Officers are supposed to maintain a cool and calm composure, and they absolutely should not refer to non-commissioned officers, no matter what they have done, as "sonsof-bitches" or "loose-mouthed little bastards."

He became aware that all three non-coms were standing at rigid attention.

"In case you're wondering what's going to happen next," Cronley said, still furious, "I am going to hand former Staff Sergeant, now Private, Lewis a shovel, with which he will dig graves all day until I can get the sonofabitch on a slow boat to the god-damned Aleutian Islands, where he will dig graves in the goddamned ice until hell freezes over."

There was no response for a full minute.

"Permission to speak, sir?" Technical Sergeant Martin barked.

After a moment, Cronley gestured and said, "Granted."

"Sir, with respect, the sergeant suggests that the captain is going to need four shovels."

"What in the name of Jesus H. Christ and all the saints of the Mormon Church from the Angel Moroni on down are you talking about?"

"Sir, the sergeant respectfully suggests

that whatever the captain intends to do to former Staff Sergeant, now Private, Lewis, the captain should do to us, too."

After a moment, Cronley said, "You're all in this together, right? That's your mind-boggling idiot fucking suggestion, Sergeant? That you're the Three Goddamned Musketeers of Goddamned Kloster Grünau? All for one and one for all?"

"Sir, with respect, yes, sir, something like that."

After another moment, Cronley said, "Okay, Sergeant. Now tell me what in your obviously warped mind it is that tells you I should do anything like that. It better be good."

"Yes, sir. Sir, the sergeant requests the captain consider that the three of us, plus Private Lewis, and First Sergeant Dunwiddie were the only non-coms left after the Krauts kicked the shit out of Company C, 203rd Tank Destroyer Battalion in the Ardennes Forest."

"You're talking about the Battle of the Bulge?" Cronley asked softly.

"Yes, sir. And after that, sir, we have been sort of like the Three Musketeers, as the captain suggests. Real close. No secrets between us. But, sir, that doesn't mean we share what we have with anyone else, just with each other. Harold — excuse me, sir — *Private Lewis* thought we should know about you running that Kraut sonofabitch off when he was tormenting the Russian and he told us. Sir, we wanted him to tell us. So we're in this deep shit as deep as he is."

Cronley looked at him a moment and then said, "Stand at ease."

The three moved from attention to parade rest, which was not at ease.

"If we are going to have an amicable relationship in the future, you're going to have to start obeying my orders," Cronley said. "Or don't you know what at ease means?"

They relaxed.

First Sergeant Dunwiddie and Staff Sergeant Lewis came into the room.

That was quick.

Dunwiddie had Lewis stashed somewhere close.

Why should that surprise me?

Staff Sergeant Lewis marched up to Cronley, came to attention, raised his hand quickly to his temple, and barked, "Sir, Staff Sergeant Lewis, Harold, Junior, reporting to the commanding officer as ordered, sir."

Cronley crisply returned the salute.

"Permission to speak, sir?" Dunwiddie asked.

"Denied. You just stand there with Sergeant Loudmouth, First Sergeant, while I have a word with the Three Musketeers of Kloster Grünau."

"Yes, sir."

"Some of you may have noticed a few moments ago that I said unkind things about Sergeant Lewis, including questioning the marital status of his parents. Not only was I rude to each of you but I used profane and obscene language. I also used blasphemous language to describe our home here in Kloster Grünau. You may consider this an apology."

There was silence for a long moment. It was broken by Staff Sergeant Petronius J. Clark, the largest of the Musketeers, whose deep voice would make most operatic basso profundo sound, in comparison, like canaries.

"Aw, shit, Captain," his voice rumbled, "Tiny told us you was Cavalry before you got stuck with this intelligence bullshit. We're Cavalry. We wouldn't respect an officer who didn't know how to really eat ass colorfully, like you just did."

Cronley turned to Lewis.

"Tell me, Sergeant, how skilled are you with a shovel?"

"Sir?"

"A counter-question is not a reply, Sergeant."

"Sir, I expect I'm about as skilled as anyone else."

"First Sergeant, load the Three Musketeers and Sergeant Loudmouth and four shovels into an ambulance. We are going off into the night to dig a grave. Make sure we have flashlights."

A number of things became apparent almost as soon as they reached a small pasture that was a five-minute drive from Kloster Grünau.

The first was that a pickax was going to be required. Cronley sent Staff Sergeant Abraham back to fetch two of them.

The second was that the Army expression "Flashlights go dead just when you need them" was right on the money.

As soon as Sergeant Abraham returned from Kloster Grünau, he was sent back for a supply of flashlight batteries and a tape measure.

While he was gone, Technical Sergeant Martin and Staff Sergeant Lewis labored hard, and rather ineffectively, at their digging in the light of the ambulance's headlights.

When Abraham returned, Martin and

Sergeant Lewis — now working in the faint light of the flashlights — took the tape measure and marked off the length and width of the hole to be dug, using rolls of medical adhesive tape conveniently found in the ambulance.

"Stand inside the adhesive tape," Captain Cronley ordered. "When you get down a little deeper, you're going to have to work inside the walls of the grave. You might as well get used to that."

When Sergeants Martin and Lewis complied, it became immediately apparent that two men could not simultaneously labor to deepen a grave while both were inside the dimensions of said grave. Testing proved this was especially true when one of the gravediggers required the use of a pickax in his labors.

"Well, we'll do it like a relay race," Captain Cronley announced. "First, the pickax man will dislodge the soil. He will then exit the grave and the shoveler will enter, remove the loose soil from the grave, then exit the grave to be replaced by a man with the pickax. *Und so weiter.*"

This modus operandi proved far less effective in practice than in theory. Too much time was lost changing laborers. There would be additional lost time as the grave deepened — six feet being one hell of a hole — and the pickax man had to crawl out before the shoveler could climb in.

A modification of the relay-race method was adopted. Working as fast as he could, one gravedigger would wield the pickax and then shovel the loosened dirt out of the hole. He would repeat this cycle three times. By then, the gravedigger was sweating and panting heavily and had to be replaced.

He would then be helped out of the grave and, now shivering in the near freezing temperature, be helped back into the field jacket and shirt he had removed to facilitate his pickax and shovel wielding. As he did so, a fresh gravedigger would quickly remove his field jacket and shirt, and then enter the grave to repeat the process. *Und so weiter.*

By 2100, it had been determined it was going to take two hours and thirty minutes to dig a grave — much longer than any of them had thought it would — and forty-five minutes to fill it up.

The burial party then got back in the ambulance and jeep and returned to Kloster Grünau.

[Six]

Commanding Officer's Quarters
Kloster Grünau
Schollbrunn, Bavaria
American Zone of Occupation, Germany

2145 4 November 1945

Captain Cronley, First Sergeant Dunwiddie, and Technical Sergeant Tedworth watched as the medic liberally daubed merbromin on the hands of the gravediggers. The topical antibiotic stained the wounds a bright red.

When Cronley first saw the blisters, he thought it was kind of funny. Enormous, muscular men with delicate hands. Then he got a better look at the blisters and had second thoughts.

These guys are not only in pain now, but have been in pain since probably after the first five minutes of furiously swinging the pickaxes and shovels.

And they hadn't said a word.

He had then sent for Doc, the medic sergeant, who had been in the NCO club having "a couple of beers," he'd said, when he arrived a hair's-breadth from being royally drunk.

"Doc," Cronley said, "I was about to suggest a bottle of Jack Daniel's to comfort our afflicted brethren. Would that be medically appropriate?"

"Sir, that's probably a very good idea. What the hell have they been doing?"

"Field sanitation. Digging latrines," First Sergeant Dunwiddie answered for him.

"First Sergeant, get a bottle of Jack Daniel's from the bar, then send our walking wounded to bed," Cronley ordered. "No. Change of plans. I'll want a word with them after you leave, Doc."

"Yes, sir."

When the medic had, none too steadily, left the room, Cronley asked, "Why do I think that when Doc gets back to the NCO club, he's going to say, 'I don't know what the captain had those guys doing. They claimed digging latrines, but I don't believe that. They had the biggest blisters I've seen since Christ was a corporal. They were digging something.'

"And then do you think it's possible that someone will guess 'Maybe they're digging a grave for that Russian that Sergeant Tedworth caught and they're going to shoot?' Everyone of course knows about the Russian because of Sergeant Loudmouth."

"Oh, God!" Dunwiddie said. "I should have thought about that!"

"Let me catch up with Doc Lushwell, Captain," Tedworth said. "I'll tell him to keep his yap shut."

"Thank you, but no thanks. If you think about it, what's wrong with somebody guessing we're going to shoot the Russian? If that word gets out — and I think it will — it will come to the attention of the Germans the NKGB has turned. Then they won't be so surprised when they hear the shots when we 'execute' him."

"Yeah," Staff Sergeant Petronius J. Clark boomed appreciatively. "That's how it would work all right."

Then he blew gently on his red merbromin-painted hands and winced at the stinging sensation.

"Let's carry that one step further," Cronley went on. "Sergeant Loudmouth, please present my compliments to Major Orlovsky and tell him I would be pleased to have him attend me in my quarters."

"Captain, you going to tell the Russian that we was digging graves?" Sergeant Clark asked dubiously.

"That's exactly what I'm going to tell him. What are you waiting for, Sergeant Loudmouth? Go get Major Orlovsky."

"With respect, sir," Dunwiddie said. "You sure you know what you're doing?"

"No, Sergeant Dunwiddie, I do not. Go get the Jack Daniel's and some glasses."

[Seven]

Staff Sergeant Harold Lewis Jr. and two soldiers from *das Gasthaus,* as Cronley had called the cell in the basement of the former chapel, led Major Konstantin Orlovsky of the NKGB into the room. Orlovsky's head was covered with a duffel bag. He had a blanket over his shoulders, held in place with straps. His hands were handcuffed behind him and his ankles shackled.

Cronley gestured for Lewis to take off the duffel bag.

"Good evening, Konstantin," Cronley greeted him cordially. "Some things have come up that we need to talk about. I thought you'd be more comfortable doing so here, over a little Tennessee whisky and some dinner, than in *das Gasthaus.*"

Orlovsky didn't reply.

"Sergeant Clark, would you be good enough to take the restraints off Major Orlovsky?" Cronley went on. "And then, after he's had a shower, get him into more comfortable clothing?"

Orlovsky came back into the room, now wearing the German civilian clothing he had been wearing when Sergeant Tedworth had captured him as he tried to sneak out of Kloster Grünau.

"First Sergeant Dunwiddie, Staff Sergeant Clark, and I are delighted that you could find time in your busy schedule to join us," Cronley said, waving him into a chair at the table. "Please sit down."

Orlovsky obediently sat.

"What'll it be, Konstantin?" Cronley asked. "Whisky? Vodka?"

"Nothing for me, thank you."

"Pour a little Jack Daniel's for the major, please, Sergeant Clark," Cronley said. "He may change his mind."

"I never change my mind," Orlovsky said.

"We say, 'Never say never,' " Cronley said. "Pour the Jack, Sergeant."

"Yes, sir."

"You know what's wrong with that disguise you were wearing?" Cronley said. "If you don't mind me saying?"

Orlovsky said nothing.

"You're too well nourished, too chubby, for a German. You should have figured out a way to make your skin look gray, for your cheekbones to be more evident. Forgive me, Konstantin, but what you look like is an American trying to look like a German."

Orlovsky shook his head in disbelief.

Sergeant Clark put a glass before the Russian and then poured two inches of Jack Daniel's into it.

"Ice and water, Major?" Clark boomed. "Or you take it straight?"

Cronley saw that Orlovsky had involuntarily drawn himself in when the enormous black man had come close to him, then recoiled just perceptibly when Clark had delicately poured the whisky with his massive, merbromin-painted hand.

Orlovsky was disconcerted to the point where he forgot that he never changed his mind.

He said, "Straight's fine. Thank you," then picked up the glass and took a healthy swallow.

"I saw you looking at poor Sergeant Clark's hands. Aren't you going to ask what he did to them?"

"No."

"Tell the major how your hands got that way, Sergeant," Cronley ordered.

"Digging that goddamned practice grave," Clark boomed.

There was no response.

"Aren't you curious about the phrase 'practice grave'?"

"No."

"We was digging a practice grave," Sergeant Clark volunteered. "To see how long it's going to take us to dig the real one for you."

"Quickly changing the subject," Cronley put in, "how does pork chops and applesauce and green beans sound for dinner?"

"That would be very nice," Orlovsky said.

"Would you tell the cook that, please, Sergeant Clark?"

"Yes, sir," Clark boomed, and marched out of the room.

"I suppose that happens in the Red Army, too," Cronley said.

"What?"

"That senior sergeants like Clark, who have held their rank for some time, develop soft hands. I mean, so that when they are called on to perform some manual labor of the type they were accustomed to perform when they were privates, they're not up to it. Those hands must really be painful."

"Obviously."

"Well, we've learned our lesson. The next time we dig your grave, we'll be good Boy Scouts."

"Excuse me?"

"The Boy Scouts is an American organization that one joins at age nine, as a Cub Scout, and remains in, generally, until the age of eighteen, or until the Scout discovers the female sex. Whichever comes first. Roasting marshmallows over an open fire is great fun, but for an eighteen-year-old it can't compare with exploration of the female anatomy."

Orlovsky shook his head in disbelief again.

"How did I get on that subject?" Cronley asked rhetorically. "Oh! I started out to say that the motto of the Boy Scouts is Be Prepared. That's what I meant when I said the next time we dig your grave, we'll be good Boy Scouts. By that I mean, we'll be prepared. The gravediggers will have gloves to protect their hands."

Orlovsky didn't reply.

"Do you remember the first time you went on a successful exploratory mission like that, Konstantin? Perhaps with the young lady who eventually became Mrs. Orlovsky and the mother of your children?"

"You do not actually expect me to answer a question like that!"

"I wasn't asking for the details, Konstantin. I'm an officer and a gentleman. That would be like asking a fellow officer and gentleman what exactly he did on his honeymoon, and how often he did it. Bad form. All I was asking was if you remembered."

Orlovsky failed in his attempt not to smile.

"Captain Cronley, you are very good. If I

did not know who you are, and what you are trying to accomplish, I would believe that you were an amiable lunatic."

"I remember my honeymoon well. Probably because it happened so recently and was so brief. Do you remember yours? Or was it so long ago that you've forgotten? Or maybe not all that pleasant?"

Orlovsky's face tightened. He looked at Cronley in cold anger.

"Dunwiddie, I seem to have offended the major, wouldn't you say?"

"From the look on his face, sir, I would say that you have. I don't think he likes being reminded of his honeymoon. Or, for that matter, his wife. Or his children."

Orlovsky turned his coldly angry face to Dunwiddie.

"Well, Konstantin," Cronley went on, "since I've offended you — unintentionally, of course, I just didn't think that anyone would want to forget his honeymoon — let's see if we can find something safe to talk about."

"Please do," Orlovsky said, meeting his eyes.

"But what? How about this? Do they have Boy Scouts in Russia? And presuming they do have Boy Scouts, were you one? Is that a safe enough subject for an amiable pre-dinner conversation between us?"

"At one time, there were Boy Scouts in Russia."

"I didn't know that," Dunwiddie said. "Really? Or do you mean there was a Communist version of the Boy Scouts?"

"Both," Orlovsky said. "Before the revolution there were Boy Scouts, on the British pattern. My father was one. So was the Czarevich Alexei, as a matter of fact."

"The who?" Tiny asked.

"I think he means the son of the last emperor, Czar Nicholas the Second," Cronley furnished. "If memory serves, Lenin considered him as much of a threat to Communism — the thirteen-year-old and his four sisters — as the czar, so he sent the Cheka to Yekaterinburg . . ."

"He sent the what?" Tiny interrupted.

". . . where they were being held and on July seventeenth, 1918, blew the whole family away," Cronley said, and then formed a pistol with his right hand and added, *"PowPowPowPow."*

"Why am I not surprised that your memory serves you so well on this point?" Orlovsky asked icily.

"Do that again for me," Tiny said.

"Lenin sent the Cheka, which is what they called the NKGB in those days, to Yekaterinburg, which is about a thousand miles east of Moscow, and where the Imperial family was being held, and then" — Cronley made a pistol again and pointed it at Orlovsky — "*PowPowPow*. Blew them all away and dumped the bodies in a well so they couldn't be found. Have I got that right, Konstantin? You're a proud member of the NKGB, right? You should know."

"Go to hell, Captain Cronley," Orlovsky said.

"I seem to have offended him again," Cronley said. "So let's get back to talking about the Boy Scouts. You say, Konstantin, that there is a sort of Boy Scouts in Russia?"

"The Young Pioneers," Orlovsky said.

"The Young Pioneers? And were you a Young Pioneer?"

"I was."

"And your son, is he a Young Pioneer?"

"He's not old eno— God damn you to hell!"

"Sorry. Believe me, I know how painful it is to talk about someone in your family, someone you love, who you will never see again."

"You sonofabitch!"

"Let's get back to the Boy Scouts, the Young Pioneers. Do they have an oath, Konstantin?"

Orlovsky stared at him a long moment, then finally said, "I don't know what you mean."

"An oath. 'On my honor, I will do my best to do my duty to God and my country, and to obey the Scout Law, to help other people at all times, to keep myself physically strong, mentally awake, and morally straight.' Like that. That's the Boy Scout oath. Do the Young Pioneers have an oath like that?"

"Yes, they do. We do. And a motto much like yours. We say 'Always Prepared,' not 'Be Prepared.' "

"That's not much difference. Tell me, how do you handle the God part?"

"The God part?"

" 'I will do my best to do my duty to God.' That part. How is that handled in the atheistic Soviet Union's Young Pioneers?"

"There is of course no reference to a superior being in the Young Pioneers."

"Oh, I get it. You say, 'I will do my best to do my duty to Josef Stalin and the Central Committee'?"

Dunwiddie laughed, earning him an icy look from Orlovsky.

"Isn't that a little hard on Christians like you?" Dunwiddie pursued. "Or, maybe, you and the wife are raising the kids as good

Communist atheists?"

Orlovsky didn't reply.

" 'Now I lay me down to sleep, I pray Comrade Stalin my soul to take,' " Dunwiddie went on. "That the sort of prayers you teach your kids, Konstantin?"

After a long pause, Cronley said, "I don't think Konstantin's going to answer you, Tiny."

"Doesn't look that way, does it?"

"I will have nothing further to say about anything," Orlovsky said. "I would request that I be returned to my cell, but I suspect that would be a waste of my breath."

"One, we haven't had our dinner yet, and two, you haven't seen this," Cronley said. He took Frade's message from his pocket and tossed it onto the table. "Read it, Konstantin."

For a moment, it looked as if Orlovsky was going to ignore the message. Then he unfolded it and glanced at it.

"You do not actually expect me to believe that you would show me a bona fide classified message?" Orlovsky asked.

"I thought he said he wasn't going to say anything about anything," Tiny said.

"NKGB officers, Sergeant Dunwiddie, like women, always have the option of changing their minds," Cronley said. "Isn't that so, Konstantin?"

Orlovsky shook his head in disgusted disbelief.

"Let me explain the message to you," Cronley said.

"Wouldn't that be a waste of time for both of us?"

"Well, chalk it up to professional enrichment," Cronley said. "Didn't they teach you in NKGB school that the more you know about your enemy, the better?"

"As I have no choice, I will listen in fascination to your explanation."

"Great! Thank you so much. At the top there, it says 'Priority.' That shows how fast the message is supposed to be transmitted. 'Priority' is ahead of everything but 'Urgent.' 'Urgent' doesn't get used very often. For example, so far as I know, the last time 'Urgent' was used was on the messages that told President Truman the atom bombs we dropped on Japan went off as they were supposed to. Got the idea?"

Orlovsky didn't reply.

"Next comes the security classification. I'm sure you know what 'Top Secret' means. 'Top Secret Lindbergh' is a special classification dealing with anything connected with a special project we're running. You may have heard that we've been sending members of Abwehr Ost to Argentina to keep them out of the hands of the NKGB . . ."

"I am a little surprised that you are admitting it," Orlovsky said.

"Why not? For one reason or another, you're not going to tell anybody I said that. That next line, 'Duplication Forbidden,' means you're not supposed to make copies of the message. Copies of messages tend to wind up in the hands of people who shouldn't have them. I'm sure you can understand that.

"Next is what we call the signature blocks, who the message is from, when it was sent, how, and to whom. Tex is Colonel Frade, who sent this message via Vint Hill, which is a communications complex in Virginia. I'm sure that you know what Greenwich Mean Time is."

Orlovsky nodded.

"Polo is Colonel Frade's deputy, Major Maxwell Ashton the Third. They call him Polo because he spends his off-time in Argentina playing polo. Do they play polo in the Soviet Union?"

"Not so far as I know."

"Hell of a game. The next line says Altarboy — that's me — gets a copy at Vatican. That's what we call Kloster Grünau. You know, because of the religious connection.

"Now, to the message itself. The first paragraph means that Colonel Frade arrived in Washington, D.C., at five in the morning Greenwich time. What it doesn't say — we're presumed to know this — is that he took off from Frankfurt, flew to Prestwick, Scotland, then across the Atlantic to Gander, Newfoundland, and from Gander to Washington. He was flying a Lockheed Constellation. You ever see a Constellation, Konstantin?"

"No."

"Magnificent airplane! Four engines. It can carry forty passengers in a pressurized cabin for four thousand three hundred miles at thirty-five thousand feet at better than three hundred knots. You know what a knot is, right?"

Orlovsky, in a Pavlovian response, nodded.

"Impressive, if true," he said.

"Well, you play your cards right, Konstantin, and maybe I can get you a ride in one."

"I think that is highly unlikely."

"The next paragraph, two, says he's leaving Washington for Midland at eight o'clock Greenwich time. Midland is in Texas. Colonel Frade and I grew up there. My wife was just buried there, beside her father, who raised Colonel Frade from the time he was an infant . . . Oops, sorry. I forgot that talking about wives, especially dead ones, upsets you —"

"You sonofabitch! If you think that this . . . this constant reference to wives and families is going to permit you to change my mind about my doing my duty —"

"I wouldn't even dream of trying," Cronley said. "You wouldn't believe anything I said about your duty to either God or your family."

"Correct. And I don't want to hear it."

"I give you my word of honor as an officer and a gentleman that after I explain the rest of this message I will never again bring up your family, or mine, or God, in an attempt to get you to do anything."

"Forgive me if I have trouble believing that."

"I understand. It's not like I'm a priest, right? I mean, a priest wouldn't lie, but you can't be sure that I wouldn't, right?"

"Get it over with, please."

"Now, the reason Colonel Frade is going to Midland is because he took his wife and their two kids to my wife's funeral. And come to think about it, Hans-Peter von Wachtstein's wife and their kid. Hans-Peter — we call him 'Hansel,' as in Hansel and

Gretel — is Colonel Frade's best friend. Before he started flying Constellations for South American Airways, he was a Luftwaffe fighter pilot. A very good one. Adolf Hitler personally hung the Knight's Cross of the Iron Cross around his neck. That was before, of course, Hansel decided it was his duty to his God, his country, and his family to turn."

"My God! You have absolutely no shame, no sense of decency!"

"Anyway, Hansel went with Colonel Frade to Midland for the funeral of my wife. As a friend. And what Colonel Frade's going to do in Midland is pick up his wife and their kids, and Hansel's wife and their kid, and fly them back home to Buenos Aires.

"Probably, they'll fly from Midland to Caracas, Venezuela, and then straight down across South America to Buenos Aires. Where they expect to arrive at noon tomorrow, Greenwich time. That's nine o'clock in the morning in Buenos Aires.

"Now, the last two paragraphs: Colonel Frade ordered Major Ashton to be prepared to go somewhere for a month. Somewhere is here. As soon as Colonel Frade explains to him what's going on here, he'll put him on the next South American Airways Constellation to Frankfurt. That could happen within hours, but within twenty-four hours, in any event.

"When he gets here, he'll take over from me. What that will mean, I can't tell you. Because I don't know.

"In the last paragraph, Colonel Frade orders Major Ashton to have Father Welner — 'the Jesuit' — available. That really means 'find out where he will be, so I can go to him.' Colonel Frade can't order the Jesuit around. He's a very important priest. He's Colonel Juan Perón's confessor. You know who Colonel Perón is, right?"

"I neither know nor care."

"Well, Argentina has a president . . . and now that I think of it, Father Welner is his confessor, too. But it's generally agreed that Colonel Perón — he's secretary of Labor and Welfare, secretary of War, and vice president — actually runs the country. Taking care of people like Colonel Perón keeps Father Welner pretty busy, and there's no way of knowing where he might be in Argentina at any particular time. But once Major Ashton finds him, and then Colonel Frade talks to him, he'll come on the next SAA flight. That will put him in here twenty-four hours — or forty-eight — after Ashton gets here. You understand?"

Orlovsky didn't reply.

"Captain," Tiny said, "you didn't tell him why Father Welner is coming here."

"I thought I did."

"No."

"Didn't I tell you Father Welner is coming to see you, Konstantin?"

Orlovsky again shook his head in disgust, or resignation, or both.

"No, you did not. You also did not offer a reason why this holy man, this powerful Jesuit, this confessor to these very important people, would be willing to do anything an American intelligence officer would ask him to do."

"Okay. Fair question. I said Welner is a powerful, important priest. I didn't say he was a saint. He'll understand that you are in possession of a lot of information the Vatican would like to have. And because the interests of the Vatican coincide with our interests here . . . Getting the picture?"

"So you are saying, admitting, that the holy man, this priest, is really nothing more than an intelligence officer for the Vatican?"

"Oh, no. First, he's absolutely a priest. He has a genuine interest in saving lives and souls. Like yours. And those of your wife and children."

"For God's sake, why do you think I would believe anything he would say?"

"One look in his eyes, Konstantin, and you'll see that the soul-saving comes first. Closely followed by his sincere interest in the souls of your wife and your kids. And, of course, keeping your wife and kids out of a cell in that building on Lubyanka Square. Or being sent to Siberia — like the family of Czar Nicholas the Second — and shot."

Orlovsky shook his head.

"I've been trying to tell you that your willingness to die — to have us kill you — is the same thing as committing suicide. Suicide, as you know, is a mortal sin. And that you're making this worse because your suicide will affect your family. And that we can change that whole scenario by getting you to Argentina, and then have General Gehlen try to get your family out of Russia. You don't believe me. What we're hoping is you will believe Father Welner."

"What you are hoping is that you can turn me. Which is a polite way of saying turn me into a traitor."

"And you'd rather be a hero? Maybe have a little plaque with your name on it hanging on the wall of that building on Lubyanka Square in Moscow? 'In Loving Memory of Major Konstantin Orlovsky, who loved Communism more than his wife and children and committed suicide to prove it.'

Maybe, if they don't shoot your wife and kids out of hand, and if they somehow manage to survive Siberia, she could someday take the kids — by then, they'd be adults — to Lubyanka and show them the plaque. 'That was your daddy, children. Whatever else he was, he was a good Communist.' "

Orlovsky didn't reply.

"Well, enough of this," Cronley said. "I'm hungry. Sergeant Dunwiddie, why don't you go find out what the hell is delaying our dinner?"

"Yes, sir."

Staff Sergeant Clark and First Sergeant Dunwiddie returned to the room several minutes later, carrying plates of food.

"That will be all for the moment, Sergeant Clark," Cronley said. "Except for the Tabasco. You forgot the Tabasco."

"Sorry, sir. I'll go get it."

"Please do. I really like a couple of shots of Tabasco on my pork chops."

Orlovsky looked at the plate of food before him and crossed his arms over his chest.

When Clark returned with the Tabasco, Cronley said, "Thank you. I'll call for you when I need you."

"Yes, sir," Clark said.

Cronley shook the red pepper sauce onto

his pork chops.

"I don't know if you know Tabasco, Konstantin. I really do. But some people find it a little too spicy."

Orlovsky didn't reply.

Neither Cronley nor Dunwiddie said another word during the next fifteen minutes, during which they just about cleaned their plates. Orlovsky did not uncross his arms.

"Clark!" Cronley called.

Clark came into the room.

"Major Orlovsky will be returning to *das Gasthaus* now. Will you assist him in getting dressed?"

"Yes, sir."

Five minutes later, Clark led Orlovsky back into the room. He was again shackled and handcuffed and had the duffel bag over his head.

"Good night, Konstantin," Cronley said. "Sleep well."

There was no reply.

Cronley gestured for Clark to lead him away, and Clark did so.

Two minutes later, as Dunwiddie poured coffee into Cronley's cup, he asked, "Well?"

"I was tempted just now to call him back and ask him if he didn't think not eating was cutting off his nose to spite his face, but I decided I'd already pushed him as far as I should."

"Maybe too far?"

"I don't know. I spent most of the time as we dined in stony silence wondering whether I was a very clever intelligence officer who knew how to break an NKGB officer or a very young, very stupid officer absolutely unqualified to mentally duel with a good NKGB officer. And, in either case, a candidate for the Despicable Prick of All Time Award." He paused, and then added: "I really wish I didn't like the sonofabitch."

"So, what happens now?"

"Only time will tell. It's now in the hands of the Lord. You may wish to write that down."

"Actually, I think we did pretty good," Dunwiddie said.

"Really?"

"You may wish to write this down. 'Then conquer we must, when our cause it is just. And this be our motto: In God is our trust.' It gets us off the hook, Despicable Prick–wise."

"What the hell is that?"

"It's from the last verse of 'The Star-Spangled Banner,' " Dunwiddie said. "They didn't sing that at Texas Cow College?"

XII

[One]

Commanding Officer's Quarters
Kloster Grünau
Schollbrunn, Bavaria
American Zone of Occupation, Germany

0705 5 November 1945

Captain Cronley was shaving when First Sergeant Dunwiddie came into his quarters.

"Gehlen and Mannberg walked into the mess as I walked out," Dunwiddie announced.

"Thank you for sharing that with me."

"I thought you should have it in mind when you read this," Dunwiddie said, holding up a SIGABA printout.

Cronley turned from the mirror and put his hand out for the sheet of paper. His eyes fell to it:

```
PRIORITY

TOP SECRET LINDBERGH

DUPLICATION FORBIDDEN

FROM VINT HILL TANGO NET
```

0850 GREENWICH 5 NOVEMBER 1945

TO VATICAN ATTENTION ALTARBOY

FOLLOWING BY TELEPHONE FROM TEX
0825 GMT 5 NOV 1945

BEGIN MESSAGE

NOW SOLVED BANKING PROBLEMS WILL
DELAY ESTIMATED DEPARTURE TIME
UNTIL 1000 MIDLAND TIME 6 NOVEM-
BER STOP TEX END

END MESSAGE

END

TOP SECRET LINDBERGH

When he had finished reading it, he returned to shaving.

" 'Now solved banking problems'?" Dunwiddie asked.

"I guess Clete had a little trouble getting
the money out of the bank."

"What money out of what bank?"

"I just remembered that the opportunity
never presented itself for me to share this
with you," Cronley said, as he examined his

576

chin in the mirror, then took another swipe at it with his razor.

"That would seem to be the case. What's it all about?"

Cronley picked up a towel and wiped what was left of the shaving cream from his face.

"Gehlen told Clete and me he needs fifty thousand dollars, and now, to send to Russia to grease palms to get Orlovsky's family out. And Clete needs money to hide Orlovsky in Argentina. The OSS account is empty. Clete can't use any of his money without the wrong people asking questions. So I'm loaning it to him. To us. To Operation Ost. I'm supposed to get it back when this new Central Intelligence Directorate, or whatever the hell they're going to call it, is up and running."

"I was about to say . . . I will say: I suppose that's a good example of putting your money where your mouth is. Next question: Where the hell did you get fifty grand? Are you that rich?"

"Actually, I'm loaning Operation Ost two hundred thousand."

"Jesus Christ! You had that much money in the bank?"

"The former Marjorie Ann Howell, who had been Mrs. James D. Cronley Junior for just over a day at the time of her untimely demise, had that much — and more — in her account. And under the laws of the Sovereign State of Texas, upon her demise all of her property passed to her lawful husband."

"Oh, shit."

"Gehlen doesn't know where the money is coming from, and I don't want him to know."

"Why the hell not?"

"I just don't, okay?"

Dunwiddie held his hands up in a gesture of surrender.

"What I've been trying to talk myself into," Cronley said, "is that the Squirt wouldn't mind — might even sort of like — that her money is being used to get somebody's wife and kids out of Russia and started on a new life in Argentina. Especially if she knew what the alternative scenario is."

"Jesus Christ, Jim!"

"I've also been thinking I'm glad the Squirt didn't see me in my despicable prick role. That I don't think she would understand."

"From what you've told me about her, I don't know if she would or not," Tiny said, paused, and then went on: "Yeah, I do. She would know you were doing that because it had to be done."

" 'Then conquer we must,' right?"

"That stuck in your mind, did it?"

"Do you think it's time to show Fat Fre— *Sergeant Hessinger's* OPPLAN to Gehlen?"

"Are you going to show him that message?"

"Don't we have to show both messages, the first one, too?"

"If you decide you do, then you might as well show him Hessinger's plan. You're going to have to eventually."

"I like it better when you say 'we' instead of 'you.' "

"Unfair, Jim. I'm marching right beside you down Suicide Row, and you know it."

"Yeah, I do." Cronley punched Dunwiddie affectionately on the shoulder. "And I appreciate it."

[Two]

Former General Reinhard Gehlen was sitting with former Colonel Ludwig Mannberg when Captain James D. Cronley Jr. and First Sergeant Chauncey L. Dunwiddie walked into the small — one table — room that served as the senior officers' mess.

Both Germans rose to their feet, and Cronley as quickly gestured for them to remain seated.

I did that with all the practiced élan of my fellow Cavalry officer Colonel Robert Mattingly, but we all know it's just a little theater.

The four of us know who's low man on the protocol totem pole. On the totem pole, period.

What is that line? "In the intelligence business, nothing is ever what it seems to be."

"Guten Morgen," Cronley said.

"I hope you're free to join us," Gehlen replied in German.

"Thank you," Cronley said, as he and Dunwiddie sat. "We haven't had our breakfast."

A German waiter in a starched white jacket appeared immediately. Cronley and Dunwiddie ordered.

When the waiter had left, Cronley told Dunwiddie to close the door, then handed both messages to Gehlen.

"I think you should have a look at these, sir."

After reading them, Gehlen said, "I have some questions, of course, but before I ask them, have I your permission to show the messages to Mannberg?"

Is he really asking that question, or is he playing me for the fool he thinks I am? The fool I probably am.

What am I supposed to say with Mannberg sitting at the table? "I'd rather you didn't."

Or am I being paranoid?

Was the question just courtesy?

Or even more than that, to courteously make the point to me and Mannberg that he recognizes that I'm in charge?

"I've assumed all along that Ludwig is in this as deep as we are," Cronley said. "Isn't he?"

Where the hell did that come from?

My mouth was on automatic. I heard what I said as it came out.

But I think I just drove the ball into the general's court. From the look on his face and Mannberg's, so do they.

Score one for the Boy Intelligence Officer?

"I appreciate your confidence, Captain Cronley," Mannberg said.

"Let's get the questions out of the way," Cronley said. "And then we'd like to get your opinions on something else."

"How much are you going to tell the Russian about these messages?" Mannberg asked after Cronley had, so to speak, translated the code in both messages and then answered the questions the messages raised for the Germans.

"The Russian," not "Major Orlovsky." You don't give up, Ludwig, do you?

In your mind he's a Russian and therefore a

member of the Untermenschen.

"Dunwiddie and I had Major Orlovsky to dinner last night. He didn't eat but he did read the first message."

"You didn't feed him?" Mannberg said. "I had the impression your theory of interrogation was Christian compassion."

Well, fuck you!

"No, we didn't feed him . . ." Cronley began, wondering how far he could go in telling Mannberg to go fuck himself without forcing Gehlen to come to Mannberg's aid.

Dunwiddie stepped up to the plate.

"Captain Cronley did a masterful job of introducing God and a Christian's duty to his wife and children into the conversation. That seemed to kill Major Orlovsky's appetite."

" 'Masterful'?" Mannberg parroted, a hair's-breadth from openly sarcastic.

"Absolutely masterful," Tiny confirmed. "The proof of that pudding being Major Orlovsky called Captain Cronley a sonofabitch at least four times and damned him to hell at least three."

Gehlen chuckled.

"That's progress," Gehlen said. "The only reaction you and Bischoff could get out of the major was a cold look of Communist disdain. Anything else come out of the dinner?"

"Well, sir," Tiny said, "we learned that his son is too young to be a Young Pioneer."

"And that the Czarevich Alexei was a Boy Scout before the Cheka shot him," Cronley said. "We got him talking, General. Not much, but talking."

"That's a step forward," Gehlen said.

"And you showed him these messages?" Mannberg asked, his tone suggesting he didn't think doing so was a very good idea.

"I showed him Message One, only," Cronley said. "I have a suggestion for Message Two, but first I want you to have a look at a proposed Operations Plan I had the chief of my General Staff draw up."

He motioned for Dunwiddie to produce Hessinger's plan.

Mannberg stood to look over Gehlen's shoulder as Gehlen opened the folder.

The waiter appeared. Gehlen quickly closed the folder. The waiter silently placed their breakfast before Cronley and Dunwiddie, then left. Dunwiddie again closed the door. Gehlen opened the folder and Mannberg again rose to read the document over Gehlen's shoulder.

Cronley and Dunwiddie turned to their breakfast.

"Rather thorough, isn't it?" Gehlen finally said. "I don't know who the chief of your General Staff is, but he certainly proves he has the every-detail-counts mentality of a good staff officer."

"Yes, sir. That was the conclusion First Sergeant Dunwiddie and I reached before we decided we would no longer refer to Sergeant Hessinger as 'Fat Freddy.' "

"Would you be surprised to hear I'm not surprised?"

"General, nothing you do will ever surprise me."

"I got into a conversation with the sergeant at the Vier Jahreszeiten one day while waiting for Colonel Mattingly. I was not surprised that he was familiar with Helmuth von Moltke the Elder's 'no plan survives contact with the enemy' theory."

"I think they even teach that at Captain Cronley's alma mater," Dunwiddie said.

Cronley gave him the finger.

"But I was surprised at Hessinger's argument that the seeds for it can be found in von Moltke's book *The Russo-Turkish Campaign in Europe, 1828–1829*. Are you familiar with that?"

"No, sir," Cronley and Dunwiddie said on top of each other.

"Ludwig?"

"I know of the book, sir."

"But you haven't read it?"

"No, sir."

"Not many have. Hessinger has. He can quote from it at length. And did so to prove his point. A very welcome addition to our little staff for this operation, I would say."

"Yes, sir. I fully agree," Cronley said. "You noticed in his plan that he said we should determine how long it will take to dig the grave?"

Gehlen nodded.

"Makes sense," he said.

"Well, we've done that. And we told Major Orlovsky we did," Cronley said.

"And showed him the proof," Dunwiddie said.

"You showed him a grave?" Mannberg asked, incredulously.

"We showed him Staff Sergeant Clark's painfully blistered hands, and then Sergeant Clark told him how he'd blistered them. I don't think Major Orlovsky thought we just made that up."

Gehlen chuckled.

"You said you had a suggestion about the second message?" he asked.

"Yes, sir," Cronley replied. "Before we get into what else I think we should do, I thought I would suggest that you take Message Two to *das Gasthaus* and show it to Major Orlovsky."

"And what would you advise the general to say to the Russian when he's showing him what you're calling Message Two?"

"Herr Mannberg," Cronley said coldly, "the way this system works is that I go to General Gehlen for advice, not the other way around."

"No," Gehlen said. "The way this works, the only way it can work in my judgment, is that we seek each other's advice. This has to be a cooperative effort, not a competitive one. What do you think I should say to Orlovsky when I show him Message Two?"

Mannberg, ole buddy, the general just handed you your balls.

Cronley said: "Sir, we have a saying, 'play it by ear.' I wouldn't know what to suggest you tell him. I just thought he should see Message Two, and I thought — not from logic, just a gut feeling — that it would be better if you showed it to him. Okay, one reason: I think the major has had about all of me and Dunwiddie that he can handle right now."

Gehlen nodded, then asked, quoting Cronley, "What else do you think we should do?"

"Some of it's on Hessinger's OPPLAN.

But he didn't get all of it, because he didn't have all the facts."

"For example?" Mannberg asked.

Cronley ignored him.

"The Pullach compound is just about ready," Cronley said. "A platoon of Dunwiddie's men are already on the road down there to both augment the Polish DPs —"

"The who?" Mannberg interrupted.

"The guards. They are former Polish POWs who didn't want to return to Poland because of the Russians. As I understand it, General Eisenhower was both sympathetic and thought they could be useful. So they've been declared Displaced Persons — DPs — formed into companies, issued U.S. Army uniforms dyed black, and lightly armed, mostly with carbines. Sufficiently armed to guard the Pullach compound. No one has told me this, but I suspect the idea is that once Tiny's people are in place, they'll be removed. I'd like to keep them. I'm suggesting that Colonel Mattingly and General Greene would pay more attention to that idea if it came from you, instead of me. And I further suggest your recommendation would carry more weight if you began it, 'When I inspected the Pullach compound . . .' "

"And when am I going to have the op-

portunity to inspect the Pullach compound?"

"I was thinking that right after you show
Major Orlovsky Message Two, that we fly
down there. You and me in one Storch, and
Dunwiddie in the other."

"Flown by Kurt Schröder?" Gehlen asked.

"Yes, sir."

"May I suggest," Mannberg said, "that
when you land at the Army airfield in Munich, a German flying a Storch is going to
draw unwanted attention? I don't believe
Germans are supposed to be flying American Army airplanes."

His tone suggested that he was trying to
explain something very simple to someone
who wasn't very bright.

"He has a point, Jim," Gehlen said.

"Nor am I supposed to be flying Army
airplanes. And we're not going into the Munich Army airfield. There's a strip of road
inside the compound that General Clay
used when he flew there in an L-4, a Piper
Cub. If he got a Cub in there, Schröder and
I can get Storches in. And while he's there,
Schröder can tell the Engineers what they
have to do to make the strip better. Maybe
find some building we can use as a hangar,
or at least to keep the Storches out of sight.

"So far as anyone asking questions about

Schröder flying, I don't think that's going to happen, and even if it did, Dunwiddie can use his CIC credentials to keep from answering questions. That's what I did. It worked."

Gehlen looked thoughtful for a moment, then said, "Well, if there is nothing else, I suggest that I show Major Orlovsky Message Two, and then that I go inspect the Pullach compound."

[Three]

The South German Industrial Development
  Organization Compound
Pullach, Bavaria
The American Zone of Occupied Germany

0945 5 November 1945

Cronley found without trouble the stretch of road he intended to use as a landing strip. But then he made a low pass over it to make sure there was nothing on it to impede his landing. There was.

An enormous Army truck was parked right in the middle. It had mounted on it what to Cronley, who had grown up in the Permian Basin oil fields, looked like an oil well work-over drill.

What the hell?

His passenger quickly assessed the situation and over the interphone calmly inquired, "What are you going to do now?"

"General, I'm going to make another pass over the strip. People will be looking at us. When they do, you and I are going to wave our hands at them, hoping they understand we want them to move that truck."

Cronley switched to AIR-TO-AIR and with some difficulty managed to relay that order to Kurt Schröder and Tiny Dunwiddie in their Storch.

It all proved to be unnecessary.

When Cronley began what was going to be his hand-and-arm-waving pass over the road, he saw the truck had already been moved off.

He landed. Schröder put his Storch down thirty seconds later.

A jeep rushed up to them. It was being driven by Lieutenant Colonel Bristol, the Engineer officer in charge of the Pullach compound building project. Lieutenant Stratford, the ASA officer sent by Major Iron Lung McClung to install the Collins/ SIGABA system, was with him.

Bristol and Stratford got out of their jeep and were standing beside Cronley's Storch when he climbed out.

"Oh, it's you," Bristol said.

"Sir, why do I think you're disappointed?"

Cronley asked.

"Absolutely the contrary," Bristol said. "When I saw two idiot pilots wanting to land on what is not a landing strip, I was afraid General Clay had come back."

"General Gehlen, this is Colonel Bristol, the Engineer officer in charge of setting up the compound."

Bristol, in a Pavlovian reflex to the term "general," popped to attention and saluted. After a just perceptible hesitation, Gehlen returned it.

"I've been hoping I'd get to meet you, sir," Bristol said.

"Very kind of you, Colonel. But I don't think we're supposed to exchange military courtesies."

"My fault," Cronley said. "I should have said 'Herr Gehlen.' But I have a lot of trouble remembering General Gehlen is no longer a general."

"Cronley," Bristol said, "general officers are like the Marines. Once a general, always a general. And especially in this case. When General Clay told me what's going on here, he referred to the general as General Gehlen, and went out of his way to make sure I understood the general is one of the good guys."

"Again, that's very kind of you," Gehlen

said. "And of General Clay."

"So welcome to your new home, Herr Gehlen. I hope you'll let me show you around. Perhaps you'll have a suggestion or two."

"Since you brought up the subject, Colonel . . ."

"Yes, sir. What's your pleasure?"

"Would it be possible to extend this runway a little? Actually, for some distance?"

"Well, that's on my list, sir. And just now it went to the top of the list."

"Would it be too much to ask that it be done before we leave? My friend Kurt Schröder" — he pointed at Kurt — "once told me you need more runway to take off than to land."

"Herr General, wir können hier gut raus," Schröder said.

Bristol's eyebrows went up as he looked at Schröder, who was wearing the Constabulary pilot's zipper jacket that Lieutenant Colonel William W. Wilson had given Cronley.

"I don't know why I'm surprised," he said. "I guess a lot of you CIC guys speak German. I guess you'd have to."

An explanation, or a clarification, proved to be unnecessary, as there was an interruption: Dunwiddie, who was wearing his rank-insignia-less CIC uniform, was looking intently at Lieutenant Stratford, and vice versa.

Then Stratford put his hands on his hips and barked, "Well, you miserable rook, don't just stand there slumped with your mouth open and your fat belly hanging out, come to attention and say, 'Good morning, sir.' "

Dunwiddie said, "I'll be goddamned — it is you!"

Stratford walked quickly to Dunwiddie, started to offer his hand, then changed his mind and hugged him. Dunwiddie hugged him back, which caused him to lift Stratford at least eighteen inches off the ground.

"These two, Colonel Bristol," Cronley said drily, "were once confined to the same reform school in Vermont. The large one is my Number Two."

Cronley thought: *They're pals. Great!*

Stratford is going to be very useful. And not only with the ambulances.

"Be advised, Cronley," Bristol said sternly, "that I find derogatory references to Norwich University, the nation's oldest and arguably finest military college, from which Lieutenant Stratford and I are privileged to claim graduation, totally unacceptable."

Oh, shit!

Bristol's cold glower turned into a smile.

"Relax," he said. "Stratford warned me that I should expect — and have to forgive — such behavior from a graduate of Texas Cow College."

He walked over to Stratford and Dunwiddie with his hand extended.

"Jack Bristol, Dunwiddie. Class of 1940. You're Alphonse's little brother, right? We were roommates."

Oh, am I on a roll!

During the next two hours, while he learned more about Norwich University, its sacred and sometimes odd customs, and its long roster of distinguished graduates, than he really cared to know, Cronley also had reason to believe that he was indeed on a roll.

It took him less than a half hour to conclude that the stories he'd heard that Norwich graduates could give lessons in ringknocking to graduates of West Point — and for that matter to graduates of Texas A&M, the Citadel, and VMI — were all true. They really took care of each other.

That first came up when Tiny asked Colonel Bristol about the Polish DP guard force. Colonel Bristol told Dunwiddie they had been assigned to him for as long as he thought they'd be necessary. And he immediately asked Dunwiddie if he wished to dispense with their services when the rest of his men arrived.

"No, sir. I'd like to keep them as long as possible," Tiny replied.

"That shouldn't be a problem," Bristol said without hesitation. "What I'll do is leave a squad, or maybe a platoon, here to keep the place up. I think General Clay would expect me to do that. And they'll need the DPs to guard them, of course. That'll give you a couple of months to figure out a justification to keep them permanently."

After that, Cronley, who had already decided that the situation required that he bend the Need to Know rules out of shape insofar as Lieutenant Stratford was concerned, decided they were also going to have to be bent almost as far for Colonel Bristol.

The first step there was to explain to Bristol exactly what was going to take place in the South German Industrial Development Organization compound, who was going to be inside it, and then to ask his recommendations about providing the necessary security.

Bristol was happy to sketch out on the plywood map what he thought should be done. His plan essentially required the installation of more chain-link fences. The outer line of fences would surround the whole village. It would be guarded by the Polish DPs. They would be housed in buildings between the outer fence line and the second line of fences.

Anyone driving past the Pullach compound would see only them and the SÜD-DEUTSCHE INDUSTRIELLE ENTWICKLUNGS-ORGANISATION signs posted on the fence. But not the black American soldiers guarding it with heavy machine guns.

They would be there, of course, but out of sight from the road. They would control passage into the second security area. They would be housed in the area between the second fence and the third. And this area would contain not only the refurbished houses in which they would be housed, but their mess and their service club as well.

As this was being discussed, Cronley was reminded that Mrs. Anthony Schumann handled enlisted morale for the ASA/CIC community. He had quickly dismissed her from his mind. He would deal with her later. Right now, he was on a roll.

Like the first two fences, the third fence, two hundred yards in from Fence Line Two, had already been erected. It, too, would be guarded by Tiny's Troopers. Colonel Bristol sketched in, with a grease pencil, where he thought additional fences should go. There should be a new, inner compound, housing only the headquarters of the Süd-Deutsche Industrielle Entwicklungsorganisation and five refurbished houses.

One of these would be for General Gehlen and another for Ludwig Mannberg, and their families. A third would be for visiting VIPs — such as General Greene, Colonel Mattingly, and Lieutenant Colonel Schumann. The fourth would house Lieutenant Colonel Parsons and Major Ashley, the Pentagon's G-2 representatives, and the fifth the Military Government Liaison Officer. That meant Cronley now and, when Major Ashton arrived from Argentina, Polo and Altarboy.

The Vatican ASA listening station and quarters — all in one refurbished house — would have sort of a compound of its own in the area between Fence Line Two and Fence Line Three.

"Setting those few fences shouldn't take long," Colonel Bristol said. "Not with the White Auger."

"The what, sir?" Cronley asked.

"The White Auger. The truck that we had to move off the strip so you could land."

Cronley still seemed confused, so Colonel Bristol provided a further explanation.

"That White Model 44 truck. It has an auger mounted. Drills a hole five feet deep in a matter of seconds." He demonstrated, moving his index finger in a downward stabbing motion and making a *ZZZZZ, ZZZZZZ, ZZZZZ* sound.

"Yes, sir. The sooner you can get to this, the better."

"I'll get right on it. I'll have all the fences up in two days, tops."

Colonel Bristol was even more obliging when it came to extending the runway, putting up a shed large enough to get both Storches out of the weather, and doing something about getting them a means to refuel the airplanes.

"I think a jeep-towable regular gas truck would work just fine," he said. "And I've got a couple of them I can spare."

Things went even better when Bristol was showing Gehlen the house he would occupy. It gave Cronley the chance to take Tiny and Lieutenant Stratford next door to the house that would be occupied by the Military Government liaison officer "to show Dunwiddie where you installed the SIGABA system."

As soon as they walked into the room,

Sergeant Mitchell of the ASA handed Cronley a SIGABA printout.

"This came in not sixty seconds ago, sir," he said.

Cronley read it:

PRIORITY

TOP SECRET LINDBERGH

DUPLICATION FORBIDDEN

FROM VINT HILL TANGO NET

1250 GREENWICH 5 NOVEMBER 1945

TO VATICAN ATTENTION ALTARBOY

COPY TO BEERMUG ATTENTION AL-
TARBOY

POLO ATTENTION POLO

FOLLOWING BY TELEPHONE FROM TEX
1235 GMT 5 NOV 1945

BEGIN MESSAGE

THANKS TO OLD MAN BANKING PROB-
LEMS SOLVED EARLIER THAN EX-

PECTED STOP DEPARTING MIDLAND
CASH IN HAND 1300 GMT STOP TEX

END MESSAGE

END

TOP SECRET LINDBERGH

Cronley handed the message to Dunwiddie, then did some arithmetic aloud: "It's six thousand miles, give or take, from Midland to Buenos Aires. At three hundred knots, give or take, that's nineteen hours. Factor in two hours in Caracas for refuel and another two hours for maybe a bad headwind, that's twenty-three hours. That'll put them into Jorge Frade at twelve hundred Greenwich — fourteen hundred our time — tomorrow."

"Thank you for sharing that with us," Dunwiddie said.

"Which means that twenty-four hours after that, best possible scenario, forty-eight hours after that, worst scenario, or thirty-six hours after that, most likely scenario, Major Ashton will get off a South American Airways Constellation in Frankfurt. To which I say, Hooray!"

"You really want this guy to come, don't

you?" Tiny asked.

"This will probably shock you, Sergeant Dunwiddie, but I am really looking forward to having Major Ashton relieve the unbelievably heavy burden of this command from my weak and inadequate shoulders."

Cronley turned to Lieutenant Stratford.

"Now, when Major Ashton gets off that Constellation in Frankfurt, we have to get him here without anyone knowing we're doing so. The way we're going to do that is meet the airplane with a three-quarter-ton ex-ambulance. The bumpers of that vehicle identify it as having come from the motor pool of the 711th QM MKRC."

"The what?" Stratford asked.

"The 711th Quartermaster Mess Kit Repair Company."

"I have the strangest feeling you are not pulling my chain," Stratford said.

"We're not," Dunwiddie said.

Cronley went on: "Sequence of events. We hear, from the SIGABA aboard the Constellation, when it takes off from Lisbon, when it will arrive in Rhine-Main. I then get in one of our Storches and Kurt gets in the other one. We fly to the airfield at Eschborn . . ."

"I know where it is," Stratford said.

". . . where the ambulance, having been

stashed somewhere safe, has gone to meet us —"

" 'Stashed somewhere safe'?"

"That's where you come in," Dunwiddie said.

"I get in the ambulance," Cronley continued. "We drive to Rhine-Main. Major Ashton gets in the ambulance. We drive back to Eschborn. We get back in the Storches and take off. The ambulance then departs for where it had been stashed."

"You want me to stash your ambulance for how long?"

Cronley didn't answer.

"Phase two," he said. "Two to four days after that, the Storches fly into Eschborn again. This time they have a passenger. The passenger and I get in the ambulance, which has come from its stash place to meet me. We drive to Rhine-Main. The passenger — who may have a companion, we haven't decided about that yet — gets on an SAA airplane. The ambulance drives me back to Eschborn and the Storches take off. The ambulance drives off, destination Kloster Grünau."

"Who's the passenger?"

"If I told you, I'd have to kill you."

"He is not pulling your chain," Dunwiddie said.

"For how long am I supposed to stash your ambulance?"

"Maybe two ambulances?" Cronley asked. "I am a devout believer in redundancy."

"Two ambulances."

"Thank you," Cronley said. "When I get back to Kloster Grünau, we'll send them to Frankfurt. In other words, from tomorrow until this is over. At least a week. Maybe ten days."

"We've got a relay station outside Frankfurt, in an ex-German kaserne not far from the 97th General Hospital. I could stash your ambulances there in what used to be stables for horse-drawn artillery."

"Thank you," Cronley said again.

When they came out of the building, intending to join Colonel Bristol and General Gehlen, Technical Sergeant Abraham L. Tedworth rolled up in a jeep. He was heading a convoy. Behind him were three canvas-backed GMC 6×6 trucks — each towing a trailer — and three jeeps, also towing trailers and with their .50 caliber Browning machine guns now shrouded by canvas covers.

Sergeant Tedworth got out of his jeep. He put his hands on his hips and bellowed at the 6×6s, "Get your fat asses out of the trucks and fall in!"

Lieutenant Stratford was visibly impressed as forty black men, the smallest of whom was pushing six feet and two hundred pounds, all armed with Thompson submachine guns, poured out of the trucks and, without further orders, formed four ten-man ranks, came to attention, then performed the Dress Right Dress maneuver.

Sergeant Tedworth took up a position in front of them, did a crisp about-face, and then saluted Cronley, who was by then in position, with First Sergeant Dunwiddie standing the prescribed "one pace to the left, one pace behind" him.

"Sir," Tedworth barked, "First Platoon, Company C, 203rd Tank Destroyer Battalion, reporting for duty, sir."

Cronley returned the salute.

"Welcome, welcome," Cronley said. "At ease, men."

They looked at him curiously.

"I'm sure you all noticed the precision with which First Sergeant Dunwiddie marched up behind me," Cronley said. "This officer" — he pointed to Stratford — "Lieutenant Stratford is responsible. He taught First Sergeant Dunwiddie all he knows about Close Order Drill."

This produced looks of confusion.

"I shit you not," Cronley said solemnly.

This produced smiles.

"And after he did that, Lieutenant Stratford taught Rook Dunwiddie, as he was known in those days, how to tie, as well as shine, his boots and other matters of importance to a brand-new soldier."

This produced wide smiles and some laughter.

"He will, I am sure, be happy to explain all this to you as he shows you around your new home," Cronley said. "First Sergeant, take the formation."

Dunwiddie was unable to restrain a smile as he saluted and barked, "Yes, sir."

Well, that does it, Cronley thought as Dunwiddie started off on what was obviously going to be a familiarization tour of the Pullach compound.

Tiny's Troops are here. The SIGABA is up and running. Those two bastards from the Pentagon will shortly arrive. The compound is now open for business.

And Major Ashton will soon be here to take the heavy burden of command from my shoulders.

"Very impressive," Stratford said. "Where did you get them?"

"From General I. D. White," Cronley said.

"They were part of the Second Armored Division. And, yes, Lieutenant Stratford, I do know where General White got his commission."

A fresh idea came to his mind.

I'll take Colonel Bristol, General Gehlen, and Lieutenant Stratford to lunch at the Vier Jahreszeiten hotel.

I owe Bristol and Stratford a hell of a lot more than a meal, but it will if nothing else show them how grateful I am.

I also can introduce all of them to Major Wallace and Fat Freddy. Excuse me, Special Agent Hessinger. There are self-evident advantages to that for the future.

I will call Hessinger and tell him to come out here with the Opel Kapitän.

Hell, I'll call Hessinger and tell him to come out here in Major Wallace's Opel Admiral. After all, Bristol is a light bird and Gehlen a former general. Rank hath its privileges, like getting a ride in the biggest car.

The more he thought about it the more it seemed like a good idea, and that it was one more proof he was on a roll.

"I thought we were through in there," Stratford said when he saw Cronley start back into the Military Government Liaison Office building.

"I've got to make a telephone call. Wait

here, or come with me."

"How do these phones work?" Cronley asked Sergeant Mitchell. "Phrased another way, is Munich a long-distance call or can I dial a Munich number?"

"You can dial a Munich number," Mitchell said, and handed him a mimeographed telephone book.

Cronley found what he was looking for and dialed it.

"Twenty-Third CIC, Agent Hessinger speaking, sir."

"First let me say how happy I am to find you at your post, and not cavorting shamelessly with some naked blond Fräulein . . ."

"Don't tell me where you are," Hessinger said.

"What? Why not?"

"Because the FBI is here, and if they're listening to the telephone, and I think they are, they'll learn where you are and go there."

"The FBI is in your office?"

"No. Not anymore. They were here. They were here at eight o'clock this morning."

"Were there?"

"They left. But there's two of them in the lobby, another in the garage, and I would be surprised if they're not at Schleissheim Army Airfield. So I wouldn't go there, either, if I was you."

"What did they want?"

"You."

"Did they say why?"

"They told Major Wallace it concerned a matter of national security they were not authorized to share with him."

"Let me talk to him."

"He's not here. After he told them to get the fuck out of his office, and they did, he got in the Admiral and left."

"Where did he go?"

"If I told you that, the FBI would know, too. You can probably guess where he went."

One of two places, Cronley thought.

Either Kloster Grünau to warn me. Or the Farben Building to see Mattingly.

Cronley was silent a moment.

"Freddy, if they've tapped your phone," he said, finally, "the FBI will know you've told me all this."

"So what? They can't do anything about that. If they say anything, they're admitting they tapped this telephone line. They're not authorized to tap it, and I know that, and they know that I know that."

"Under those circumstances, I suppose I could safely say something myself, couldn't

I? Like, 'FBI agent eavesdropping on this private conversation, go fuck yourself!' "

"That wasn't very smart," Hessinger said.

"No. It was, however, satisfying. And on that cheerful note, I will say goodbye, Special Agent Hessinger."

"No. Not yet. There's more."

"What?"

"Mrs. Colonel Schumann wants her Leica camera back."

"What Leica?"

"The one she says she left in the Kapitän when you took her to the bahnhof to meet her husband the colonel."

"I know nothing about a Leica."

"She says you have to have it. She's so sure you have it that she didn't go to Frankfurt this morning with the colonel. She says she wants it back before she gets on the train to Frankfurt at four-forty."

"She's still at the hotel?"

"Waiting for you to give back her Leica."

That's not what she's waiting for.

"You call Mrs. Schumann, tell her I'm in Berlin, that I don't have her goddamned Leica, and that I will get in touch with her as soon as possible."

"I would rather not do that."

"That wasn't a suggestion."

"Would it bother you if I told you that

609

sometimes I like you less than I do at other times?"

"Not at all. Goodbye, Special Agent Hessinger."

What I have to do now, obviously, is get General Gehlen back to Kloster Grünau. The one thing I can't afford is the FBI asking him questions.

Tiny will want to get his people settled, and then Kurt Schröder can fly him home.

No. What I have to do first is let Clete know about the goddamned FBI. Then I can get the hell out of Dodge.

"Sergeant Mitchell, let me at the keyboard, please," Cronley said, and when Mitchell had, he sent:

```
PRIORITY

TOP SECRET LINDBERGH

DUPLICATION FORBIDDEN

FROM BEERMUG

VIA VINT HILL TANGO NET

1000 GREENWICH 5 NOVEMBER 1945
```

TO POLO

URGENT PASS FOLLOWING TO TEX IM-
MEDIATELY ON HIS ARRIVAL

1-AT LEAST SIX FBI APPEARED
VIER JAHRESZEITEN 0800 THIS
DATE LOOKING FOR ME. FAILED
TO DO SO.

2-BELIEVE WALLACE HEADED TO
TELL MATTINGLY.

3-DEPARTING NOW FOR VATICAN
WITH GEHLEN.

4-ELEMENTS 10TH CAV HAVE TAKEN
OVER SECURITY OF COMPOUND.

5-URGENTLY REQUEST QUICKEST
DISPATCH OF HELP.

ALTARBOY

END

TOP SECRET LINDBERGH

XIII

[One]

Staff Sergeant Harold Lewis Jr.'s jeep followed Cronley's Storch down the runway when it landed. Lewis was waiting for him when he climbed out of it.

The first question Cronley put to him was had Lewis seen or heard from Major Harold Wallace.

Lewis said he had not.

"How's our friend in *das Gasthaus*?"

"He's still not talking to us, sir. He did, though, really wolf down his breakfast."

"Well, he didn't eat much for dinner last night."

Jesus, was that only last night?

"And this just in, sir," Lewis said, handing him a SIGABA printout.

Cronley read as far as the first paragraph before deciding that Major Ashton was not good at following — or more likely didn't want to follow — the prescribed literary rules for messages, which called for the mes-

612

sages to say what had to be said formally and in as few words as possible.

PRIORITY

TOP SECRET LINDBERGH

DUPLICATION FORBIDDEN

FROM POLO

VIA VINT HILL TANGO NET

1000 GREENWICH 5 NOVEMBER 1945

TO VATICAN ATTENTION ALTARBOY

BEERMUG ATTENTION ALTARBOY

   1-FBI LOOKING FOR YOU HERE
      TOO. OUR FRIEND THE ARGEN-
      TINE J. EDGAR TOLD THEM
      NOTHING BUT ASKED ME IF YOU
      HAVE BEEN ROBBING BANKS.

   2-LEAVING MOUNTAINTOP VERY
      SHORTLY TO WELCOME TEX ON
      HIS ARRIVAL.

3-OUR JESUIT FRIEND WILL ALSO
BE IN THE WELCOMING CROWD.

POLO

END

TOP SECRET LINDBERGH

Cronley handed the printout to General
Gehlen.

"The Argentine J. Edgar?" Gehlen asked.

"J. Edgar Hoover heads the FBI. The
Argentine version of that is the BIS. He's
talking about General Martín, who heads
the BIS."

"I should have thought of that," Gehlen
said. "Mountaintop, I assume, is the establishment in the Andes?"

"The foothills of the Andes. Mendoza."

"And the Jesuit will be in Buenos Aires
when Colonel Frade arrives. I hope he'll do
what Frade asks."

"I think the problem was in finding him.
I'm sure he'll do what we want him to do,
it's in his interest as well as ours."

"And a final question. Why is the FBI so
interested in finding you?"

"I've thought about that," Cronley said.
"The best scenario I can come up with is

that J. Edgar himself, probably because someone told him there was a young second lieutenant on Clete's grandfather's airplane, said, 'Get to him.'

"That makes sense. If you're going to break someone, it makes more sense to go after a twenty-two-year-old second lieutenant than it does someone like Colonel Mattingly or Colonel Frade or Major Wallace. If he knew about Dunwiddie, Hoover would have sent his people after him, for the same reasons.

"So Hoover is waiting to hear what the young second lieutenant said after they broke him, and all that these guys can report is they haven't been able to break him because they can't even find him. They're embarrassed and under a hell of a lot of pressure."

"And, if somehow they do find you, can they break you?"

"No," Cronley said. "I've thought about that, too."

"You sound very confident."

"I'm not going to let them break me. What we're doing is important. I'm not going to let them hold Operation Ost over the President. I know I'm expendable, so what happens to me, *if* they catch me — *es wird sein Wille.*"

Gehlen laughed.

"I think that's *que será será* in Spanish, am I correct?"

"Yes, sir. At least that's what it is in Texican, which I speak."

"Do you plan to show this message to Major Orlovsky?"

"I will, if you agree it's the smart thing to do."

"He's liable to ask questions about the FBI."

"Which we will answer truthfully."

"He's liable to wonder that, if they find you, you might break, and he would be left hanging in the wind."

"But he will also know — I hope — that we're telling him the truth."

After a just perceptible pause, Gehlen nodded.

Cronley turned to Sergeant Lewis.

"Are you going to remember to keep your mouth shut, or should I continue to call you Sergeant Loudmouth?"

"My mouth is shut, sir."

"Okay. Sergeant Lewis, go to Major Orlovsky . . . No, first things first."

He reached in his pocket and handed him a slip of paper.

"Those are the names of the three men Dunwiddie has picked to drive two ambulances to the Pullach compound. They will first pack them with as much stuff from here as will fit. They will take with them enough clothing to last a week. I am telling you, but you are not to tell them, that they'll be in Frankfurt for about a week. Sergeant Dunwiddie will tell them the rest when he sees them. Get them on the road as soon as possible."

"Yes, sir."

"When you have done that, go to *das Gasthaus* and show Major Orlovsky this last message. Tell him if he has any questions, General Gehlen and I will be happy to answer them if he can find time in his busy schedule to take lunch with us."

"In other words, sir, go get the Russian?"

"No. Do exactly what I just told you to do."

"Yes, sir."

"And, Sergeant Lewis, round up Colonel Mannberg and tell him that General Gehlen and I request the pleasure of his presence at lunch."

"Yes, sir."

"Sergeant Lewis sounds better than Sergeant Loudmouth, wouldn't you agree, Sergeant Lewis?"

"Yes, sir."

"Christians, such as myself and General

Gehlen, Sergeant Lewis, believe to err is human, to forgive divine. You may wish to write that down."

"Yes, sir. Will that be all, sir?"

"Carry on, Sergeant Lewis."

[Two]

Commanding Officer's Quarters
Kloster Grünau, Schollbrunn, Bavaria
American Zone of Occupation, Germany

1235 5 November 1945

Preceded by Staff Sergeant Harold Lewis Jr., two of Tiny's Troopers led Major Konstantin Orlovsky into the room. The Russian was shackled, his arms strapped to his sides, his hands cuffed behind him, and he had a duffel bag over his head.

Cronley gestured for Lewis to take off the bag.

"Konstantin," Cronley said as Orlovsky squinted in the sudden light, "I asked Sergeant Lewis to tell you that General Gehlen, Colonel Mannberg, and myself would be pleased to have you join us for lunch, over which we will answer any questions you might have about the latest SIGABA message. And if you just came to ask questions about the latest SIGABA message, I will understand that is a matter of principle. But I hate to ask my men to go through the inconvenience of getting you out of what you're wearing and into something more appropriate for lunch if it is your intention to sit there with your arms folded self-righteously across your chest while you watch the three of us eat. Which is it to be?"

"I accept your kind invitation to lunch," Orlovsky said.

"Please assist the major in changing, Sergeant Lewis," Cronley ordered.

When they had gone into Cronley's bedroom and the door had been closed, General Gehlen very quietly said, "An unorthodox interrogation technique, but I'm starting to think an effective one. Wouldn't you agree, Ludwig?"

"Captain Cronley has the advantage of a *Strasburgerin* mother. Everyone knows Strasbourgers can charm wild beasts."

Does he mean that? Or does he realize I've won the interrogation technique argument with the general?

Orlovsky came back into the room, now dressed in olive drab trousers and a shirt from Cronley's closet.

"Can I have Sergeant Lewis get you a beer, Konstantin?" Cronley asked.

"That would be kind of you."

"Get the major a beer, please, Sergeant Lewis. And then ask them to serve our lunch."

"Yes, sir."

"Before we get into any questions you might have about the SIGABA message, Konstantin, Ludwig — Colonel Mannberg — is curious why you changed your mind about breaking bread with us."

"I gave the matter some thought after I passed on dinner last night," Orlovsky said. "I realized there was nothing I could do to get you to stop this . . . this childish theater of yours. And then it occurred to me that there was no reason I shouldn't eat while I was being forced to listen."

"That not eating was sort of cutting off your nose to spite your face?"

Orlovsky shook his head.

"If you like," he said.

"Good for you. And you're drinking beer, presumably, because of what Christ said according to Saint Timothy?"

"Excuse me?"

" 'Take a little beer for thy stomach's sake and thine other infirmities'?"

"Wine, Jim," Gehlen said, chuckling. "Take a little *wine* . . ."

"Is that what He really said?" Cronley

asked innocently.

"Actually, I think what He said was vodka," Orlovsky said.

"And, Ludwig, you didn't think that Konstantin had a sense of humor," Cronley said. "Sergeant Lewis, go to the bar and get a bottle of vodka. Major Orlovsky needs a little belt."

"That's going too far, Captain Cronley," Orlovsky said. "I will have one beer. One. But I'm not going to let you ply me with alcohol."

"Well, you can't blame me for trying. What was it Lenin said, 'All's fair in love and war'?"

"Lenin said nothing of the kind," Orlovsky said.

"If you say so," Cronley said. "So, what didn't you understand in the SIGABA message? Let's get that out of the way before the meat loaf arrives."

"You remember what I said about the last message? That you can't possibly believe I would believe you would show me a classified message?"

"Yes, I do. And I remember what I replied. 'Why not? You're never going to be in a position to tell anyone about it.' So tell me what aroused your curiosity."

"The FBI is looking for you?"

"I can see where you might find that interesting. The FBI is the Federal Bureau of Investigation. It's run by a man named J. Edgar Hoover. It's something like your organization, the NKGB, except they don't have cells in the basement of their headquarters building where they torture people, and they can't send people they don't like to an American version of Siberia. We don't even have an American Siberia.

"All the FBI can do is ask questions. What they want to ask me is what I know about the rumor that we're sending some of General Gehlen's people and their families to Argentina to keep them out of the hands of your former associates in the NKGB. As I don't want to be asked that question, I have been making myself scarce."

"You have succeeded in making me curious. Your FBI doesn't know what you've been doing?"

"We don't think they have the Need to Know, so we don't tell them."

"Well, what if they find you?"

"Then I will do one, or both, of the following: I will tell them I have no idea what they're talking about and claim the Fifth."

"What is 'the fifth'?"

Cronley held his right arm up as if swearing to an oath, and said, "I claim the protection provided by the Fifth Amendment of the Constitution of the United States and decline to answer the question on the grounds that any answer I might give might tend to incriminate me.' That's called 'claiming the Fifth.' "

"You're admitting that what you're doing is illegal?" Orlovsky asked.

"I didn't say that. Is Operation Ost illegal? No. It's been approved at the highest levels of our government. It's clandestine, because we don't want it all over the front page of the *Washington Star* newspaper. Got it?"

"Let's say I heard what you said."

"Good. I would hate to feel you weren't listening," Cronley replied. "Now, the Argentine J. Edgar to whom Major Ashton — I did tell you, didn't I, that Polo is Major Maxwell Ashton? That he's the officer coming here to take the heavy burden of command from my inadequate shoulders?"

"I heard that, too," Orlovsky said.

"Where was I? Oh. The Argentine J. Edgar to whom Polo Slash Major Ashton refers is General Bernardo Martín, who heads the Argentine Bureau of Internal Security. He and Colonel Frade work closely together and have become friends."

"You're suggesting that Colonel Frade turned the head of the Argentine security agency?"

"No. I didn't say that. Colonel Frade's father, also known as Colonel Frade, did that. He turned Martín. Or General Martín turned himself."

"Turned himself?"

"At one time, the president of Argentina, who was not a very nice man, suspected there was a coup d'état under way which would see him replaced as president by Colonel Frade the elder. He charged Martín, then a lieutenant colonel, with stopping it.

"Martín, realizing that Colonel Frade would be a much better president than the incumbent, decided that his duty as an officer whose primary allegiance should be to his country could not follow these orders. So he turned and allied himself with Colonel Frade. The coup d'état was successful."

"You don't really expect me to believe that Colonel Frade's father is the Argentine president?"

"I didn't say he was. The Nazis had Colonel Frade assassinated. They didn't want him to be the president. They are not nice people."

"And yet you are protecting Nazis from justice," Orlovsky said.

"That's true. That was the price General

624

Gehlen negotiated for his turning. He knew what the NKGB would do to his officers, and to their families, if they got their hands on them. And so do you, Konstantin. General Gehlen decided turning, and saving his officers and their families from the NKGB, was the honorable thing for him to do as an officer and a Christian. Even though he knew some of his officers were Nazis and deserved to be hung."

Orlovsky didn't reply as his eyes met Gehlen's, and Gehlen nodded once.

Cronley went on: "Saving innocent wives and children from unpleasantness, even death, is the honorable thing to do if one has the choice, wouldn't you agree, Major Orlovsky?"

"Treason is never honorable," Orlovsky said, looking at Cronley.

"Sometimes treason is the only alternative to doing something truly dishonorable," Gehlen said.

"Nothing is ever black or white," Cronley said. "Do they say that in Russia, Konstantin?"

"Would you be offended if I told you I'm more than tired of hearing your perverse philosophy? You sound like nineteen-year-olds in the first year of university."

"We used to say," Mannberg offered,

"when I was in the first year of university, that 'perversion, like beauty, is in the eye of the beholder.' "

"When I was in my first year at my university," Cronley said with a straight face, "I didn't know what perversion was. We don't have much of that sort of thing in Texas."

All three shook their heads in disbelief.

"Moving right along," Cronley said after a moment, "in the next two paragraphs Major Ashton tells us that he is leaving Mendoza — our operation there is literally on a mountaintop — to meet Colonel Frade when he arrives in Buenos Aires.

"The Jesuit priest is Father Welner. Although he didn't say so, I suspect that General Martín will also be at the airfield when Colonel Frade arrives. He'll have to be brought into this eventually, and sooner is usually better than later."

No one said anything.

"So, I think in the next forty-eight to seventy-two hours, the Good Jesuit should be here to offer his wise counsel. He and Major Ashton. I hope."

Again there was no response.

"So unless you have further questions, Konstantin?"

"None, thank you."

Cronley raised his voice. "Sergeant Lewis!

Have lunch served! And don't forget the vodka for Major Orlovsky."

Lunch was served. A bottle of beer and a bottle of vodka were placed before the Russian.

He ate his lunch.

He did not touch the vodka.

In the course of conversation, General Gehlen asked Orlovsky if he was familiar with the theory of Field Marshal Helmuth Karl Bernhard Graf von Moltke that no plan survives contact with the enemy.

Orlovsky said he was.

Gehlen said: "A friend of mine recently suggested that the roots of that theory can be found in von Moltke's *The Russo-Turkish Campaign in Europe, 1828–1829*. Are you familiar with that, Major Orlovsky?"

Orlovsky said he was.

"What do you think of my friend's theory that in that book was the first time von Moltke said what he said so often later."

Orlovsky told him he'd never considered that before, but now that he thought about it, the general's friend was obviously right.

The Russo-Turkish campaign of 1828–1829 was then discussed at some length by General Gehlen and Major Orlovsky. Captain Cronley and Colonel Mannberg, who knew next to nothing about the campaign, sat and listened and said nothing. Both were deeply impressed with the erudition of the general and the major, and both wondered privately if they should make an effort to get their hands on a copy.

When lunch was over, Orlovsky refused a brandy to top the meal off, but had two cups of coffee.

Then Captain Cronley summoned Staff Sergeant Harold Lewis Jr., and Orlovsky was taken into Cronley's bedroom, changed back into his prisoner's clothing, re-shackled and re-handcuffed, covered again with a blanket and a duffel bag, and returned to *das Gasthaus.*

After he had gone, Cronley asked, "How do you think that went?"

After a moment, Gehlen said, "I don't know. Either he's coming around, or he's smarter than both of us."

Cronley had a number of immediate thoughts.

The first was, *Is it possible that Orlovsky is smarter than Gehlen? God knows he's smarter than I am. Not to mention more experienced.*

The second was, *If Gehlen doesn't know how that went, how can I be expected to know?*

The third was, *He left Mannberg out of that.*

"Both of us" is not "we."

The fourth was, *I'm going to have to do something about Rachel before that blows up in my face.*

[Three]

Kloster Grünau
Schollbrunn, Bavaria
American Zone of Occupation, Germany

1505 5 November 1945

Cronley watched as the three GMC 6×6 trucks that had carried the First Platoon of Company C, 203rd Tank Destroyer Battalion to the Pullach compound approached Kloster Grünau. The jeeps that had been with them had apparently stayed at the compound. That meant the jeeps — more specifically their pedestal-mounted .50 caliber Browning machine guns — were already guarding the compound, and that in turn meant the compound was up and running. And, finally, that in turn meant that the sooner everybody going to the compound got there, the better.

As the first truck rolled slowly past Cronley, Technical Sergeant James L. Martin jumped nimbly to the ground with what Cronley considered amazing agility for someone of his bulk.

Martin saluted.

"How'd it go, Sergeant?" Cronley asked as he returned the salute.

"Dunwiddie said he'd give you a full report when he gets here, sir, but it went well. Clark and Abraham should be halfway to Frankfurt with the ambulances about now. That ASA lieutenant . . . ?"

"Stratford?"

"Yes, sir. Lieutenant *Stratford* sent one of his non-coms with them to make sure there's no problems stashing the vehicles. He, the sergeant, is going to get on his radio net and tell the lieutenant when they're there, and that info will be relayed here to you on the SIGABA."

"Good thinking."

"Tiny said he's going to stay as long as he can before he gets that Kraut to fly him home, so he should be here just before it gets dark."

"Good," Cronley said, and decided this was not the time to suggest, politely or otherwise, that Germans normally do not like to be called Krauts.

He had an off-the-wall thought: *I guess if you're as large as Martin, you get used to saying just about anything you please, because only someone larger than you can call you on it, and there aren't very many people larger than Martin.*

General Gehlen walked up to them.

Martin saluted.

He's not supposed to do that, either. But this isn't the time or place to get into that, either.

"How are you, Sergeant Martin?" Gehlen asked. He did not return the salute.

Martin picked up on it.

"Sorry, sir. Captain. It's just that I'm an old soldier and I know the general was a general . . ."

"Try a little harder, and all will be forgiven," Cronley said.

"Yes, sir."

"I was wondering when you planned to start moving my people," Gehlen said.

Martin looked at Cronley. "Tiny . . . First Sergeant Dunwiddie said to tell you, sir, Captain, that you can start sending them anytime."

"I was going to suggest, Captain Cronley, that we send Herr Mannberg to the Pullach compound early on," Gehlen said.

"You're going to go back as soon as you load up, right?" Cronley asked Martin.

"Yes, sir. Taking three more jeeps."

"General Gehlen, please tell Herr Mannberg to pack his bags and that he has a choice between riding in the cab of a truck

631

or in a jeep."

"Which will leave how soon, would you say?"

"Forty-five minutes," Martin furnished.

"And what are your plans to move the families?" Gehlen asked.

"We're down to two ambulances — personnel transport vehicles — now that we sent two to Frankfurt, right?" Cronley asked.

"Six," Martin corrected him. "Tiny had them paint over the red crosses and the bumpers on four more ambulances a couple of days ago."

Proving once again that First Sergeant Dunwiddie, who knows how to plan ahead, should be in command here, not me.

"I didn't know that," Cronley confessed. "Now that I do, what about setting up a convoy to leave in, say, an hour and a half, all the trucks, and all the ambulances and three jeeps? Can your people handle that, General?"

"They'll be ready," Gehlen said. "And I have one more suggestion to make, if I may?"

Cronley nodded.

"I don't think any of my people should leave the Pullach compound until further notice. Mannberg could ensure that they don't."

Gehlen saw the confusion on Cronley's face.

"Leaving the compound," Gehlen clarified, "would afford those of my people who have turned the opportunity to communicate with the NKGB."

"I should have thought about that," Cronley said.

"You've had a lot on your mind," Gehlen said.

That was kind of him.

He knows almost as well as I do, though, that Little Jimmy Cronley is way over his head in running this operation.

As darkness fell, Cronley thought he saw another proof of his incompetence — or at least his inability to think problems through — within minutes of Dunwiddie's return to Kloster Grünau in the other Storch.

Dunwiddie reported that they had heard from Lieutenant Stratford's sergeant that the two ambulances had arrived at the ASA's relay station outside Frankfurt.

"I told them to leave wherever they are at 0900 for Eschborn. One at 0900 and the other at 0930."

"Why are they going to do that?" Cronley asked.

"So (a) they know how to get to Eschborn, and (b) we know how long it's going to take them. We'll use the longest time as the standard."

"I should have thought of that, too," Cronley confessed.

Dunwiddie looked at him curiously. Cronley explained that he had also not thought about confining the Germans to the Pullach compound so that the turned Germans known to be among them could not communicate with the NKGB.

Dunwiddie's response was much like General Gehlen's.

"You've got a lot on your plate, Jim. Don't worry about it," he said. "Okay, I figure if you leave at first light for Eschborn, you should be back here at, say, half past two."

"Right."

Tiny has a good reason that I should fly to Eschborn. I will pretend I have thought of that good reason, because I don't want to look as incompetent as I am.

Oh. General principles. To be as sure as possible that a plan will work, perform a dry run.

Jesus, I didn't think of even that!

"How's Konstantin?" Dunwiddie asked.

"We — Gehlen, Mannberg, and I — matched wits again with him at lunch. General Gehlen and I are in agreement that we don't know who won. But he did eat his lunch and drink a beer."

"Well, I will examine the subject carefully at supper and then render my expert opinion. But Gehlen said he can't tell who's winning?"

"That's what he said."

Cronley had a sudden epiphany, and blurted it out.

"I can. I do. Orlovsky's winning. Or he thinks he's winning, which is just about the same thing. He thinks that he's got us figured out and that he's smarter than we are. Which is probably true."

"I have the feeling you decided that just now."

"I did. I don't know why I didn't — or Gehlen didn't — figure that out earlier, but that's it. I'm sure of it."

"What didn't you figure out?"

"He was too relaxed. There was no battle of wits, because he wasn't playing that game. Instead of us playing with him, he was playing with us. Now we're back to my examining the subject at dinner."

"Let's go talk to Gehlen."

■ ■ ■ ■

"Jim, I don't know," General Gehlen said as Dunwiddie freshened the Haig & Haig scotch whisky in his glass. "But I did have a thought about Konstantin that I didn't share with anyone."

"What kind of a thought?"

"What you and Tiny would probably call a wild hair."

"Let's hear it."

"I don't think Major Konstantin Orlovsky is quite who we think he is."

"I don't think I understand."

"I think he may be further up in the NKGB hierarchy than we think. I suspect he may be at least a colonel, and may even hold higher rank."

"Would the NKGB send a senior officer over a barbed-wire fence?" Dunwiddie asked.

"They wouldn't do so routinely, which is one of the reasons I never mentioned this to anyone."

"What does Mannberg think of your theory?" Cronley asked.

"I never mentioned this to anyone, Jim," Gehlen repeated. There was just the hint of reproof in his tone of voice.

Cronley picked up on it and said, "Sorry, sir."

Gehlen accepted the apology with a dismissive wave of his hand.

"Going down this street," Dunwiddie said, "why would the NKGB send a senior officer over a barbed-wire fence?"

"We don't know who gave him those rosters," Gehlen said. "I have been working on the assumption that it was one of my captains or majors. Now I have to consider the likelihood that it was one of my lieutenant colonels, there are fifteen, or colonels, of whom there are six."

"Including Mannberg?" Tiny asked.

"Including Ludwig Mannberg," Gehlen said. "There aren't many justifications for the NKGB to send a major — much less a lieutenant colonel or a colonel — 'over a barbed-wire fence,' as you put it, Tiny."

"What would they be?"

"Short answers: to establish contact with someone of equal rank, or to convince someone fairly senior that the agent who was controlling them was telling them the truth. In other words, that they were indeed dealing with a senior NKGB officer, not just an agent."

"I'm not sure I understand you, General," Dunwiddie said. "Do you think it is *likely*

Orlovsky is more important — a far more senior officer — than we have been thinking? Or that it is *possible but unlikely*?"

"I wouldn't have brought this up if I believed the latter."

"Supper, now that I know this, should be very interesting," Dunwiddie said.

"We are not going to have the sonofabitch to supper," Cronley said.

"We're not?" Gehlen asked.

"I don't want the bastard to know we're onto him," Cronley said. "You, General, might — you probably could — be able to hide what you think about him. Dunwiddie and I are amateurs at this and he'd probably sense something."

"Additionally," Gehlen said, "since the basic idea is to keep him off balance, if he's not invited he'll wonder why."

"You think I'm right, sir?" Dunwiddie said.

"I know you are." Gehlen looked at Cronley. "And I say that because I believe it, not because it means I can ask Tiny to pour a bit more of the Haig & Haig into my glass."

[Four]

Kloster Grünau
Schollbrunn, Bavaria
American Zone of Occupation, Germany

1605 6 November 1945

In the Storch, Cronley literally heaved a sigh of relief when he saw the floodlights on the perimeter of Kloster Grünau. "Dicey" had been too inadequate a term to describe his chances of getting home.

The weather had been deteriorating when he had taken off for Eschborn, and all the way to Eschborn he had been very much aware that the smart thing for him to have done would have been aborting the flight and trying later.

But he knew he was running out of time. He had to try.

Both ambulances had been waiting for him when he landed. He learned that it had taken them just about an hour to drive from the ASA Relay Station to the airfield. That meant he would have to allow three hours on "D-Day" for that part of the plan. Half an hour, after he had the ETA of the SAA Constellation at Rhine-Main, to contact the Pullach compound and tell them to radio the Relay Station and send the ambulances to Eschborn. Another hour for the ambulances to drive to Eschborn, and another hour for the ambulances to drive to Rhine-Main. And thirty minutes "just in case."

That sounds very neat and doable.

But what if the weather on D-Day is even worse, absolutely unflyable, than it is today?

Cronley put the Storch down safely on the runway, then taxied to the chapel, where he found the converted ambulance waiting for him.

He was not surprised that no one came out to push the Storch under the tent hangar, or that no one got out of the ambulance. Pounding all around was what the weather people termed "heavy precipitation."

He got out of the Storch, ran through the fat, cold raindrops to the ambulance, and got in the back.

General Gehlen turned from the front seat and handed him a towel.

"Your arrival cost Sergeant Dunwiddie a bottle of whisky," Gehlen said. "It was his belief that if you ever got here, you would be walking. I had more faith."

"I should have walked," Cronley said as he dried his head and face.

"Colonel Frade has been heard from," Gehlen said, and handed him a SIGABA printout. "Bad news."

"Jesus . . ." Cronley said as he looked at the sheet:

PRIORITY

TOP SECRET LINDBERGH

DUPLICATION FORBIDDEN

FROM TEX

VIA VINT HILL TANGO NET

1115 GREENWICH 6 NOVEMBER 1945

TO VATICAN ATTENTION ALTARBOY

INFO COPY TO BEERMUG

1-ON ARRIVAL OF UNDERSIGNED BUENOS AIRES 1005 GMT 6 NOVEMBER GENERAL MARTIN AND FATHER WELNER INFORMED UNDERSIGNED MAJOR ASHTON HAD BEEN STRUCK BY HIT-AND-RUN DRIVER AS HE EXITED TAXI OUTSIDE AVENIDA LIBERTADOR HOUSE 1605 GMT 5 NOVEMBER.

2-ASHTON CURRENTLY IN SERIOUS BUT STABLE CONDITION GERMAN HOSPITAL SUFFERING BROKEN RIGHT LEG, LEFT ARM, SEVERAL RIBS, CONCUSSION AND INTERNAL INJURIES. WHEN CONDITION PERMITS HE WILL BE FLOWN TO UNITED STATES.

3-GENERAL MARTIN THEORIZES, UNDERSIGNED CONCURS, MOST CREDIBLE SCENARIO IS THAT HIT-AND-RUN WAS ATTEMPTED ASSASSINATION BY PARTIES UNKNOWN WHO FOLLOWED ASHTON FROM JORGE FRADE ON HIS ARRIVAL FROM MENDOZA.

4-GENERAL MARTIN THEORIZES, UNDERSIGNED CONCURS, PARTIES UNKNOWN MOST LIKELY ARE NON-GEHLEN NAZIS, OR CONTRACT EMPLOYEES THEREOF, WHO WISHED TO USE ASHTON'S ASSASSINATION AS PROOF TO OTHER NON-GEHLEN GERMANS THAT SS IS STILL FUNCTIONING IN ARGENTINA.

5-THESE THEORIES DO NOT REPEAT

DO NOT EXCLUDE THE POSSIBIL-
ITY THAT ATTEMPTED ASSAS-
SINATION IS IN SOME WAY CON-
NECTED WITH OUR FRIEND
KONSTANTIN. MARTIN CONCURS.

6-CRITICALLY EXAMINE AND RE-
INFORCE AS NECESSARY ALL
SECURITY MEASURES IN PLACE
REGARDING KONSTANTIN, PAY-
ING PARTICULAR ATTENTION TO
ABSOLUTELY DENYING HIM OP-
PORTUNITY TO COMMUNICATE
WITH HIS SUPERIORS OR THOSE
GERMANS WHO HAVE OR MAY HAVE
REPEAT MAY HAVE BEEN TURNED.

7-WELNER DEPARTING BUENOS
AIRES ABOARD SAA FLIGHT 707
2000 GMT 6 NOVEMBER. ETA
RHINE-MAIN WILL BE SENT FROM
LISBON.

8-UNDERSIGNED HAS FULL CONFI-
DENCE IN YOUR ABILITY TO
HANDLE CHANGED SITUATION.

TEX

END

TOP SECRET LINDBERGH

"I wish I did," Cronley said.

"What?" Tiny asked.

"Have full confidence in my ability to handle the changed situation."

Tiny said, "I doubled the guard on *das Gasthaus* and barred all Germans but the general from getting anywhere near it or Orlovsky. It was all I could think of to do."

"That's good, but the downside is that we just told a bunch of Good Germans we don't trust them."

"The Good Germans, as you call them," Gehlen said, "they will understand. Those who have sold their comrades out will be frustrated."

"Let me throw some more ice water on our unhappy situation," Tiny said. "If the general is right, and of course he usually is, and Orlovsky is more important than we thought, and the NKGB is as good as we know they are, aren't they likely to try to get to Orlovsky through my guys? Money talks."

"You think that is likely?" Gehlen asked.

"Unlikely, but possible. So what I'm going to do is make snap judgments about who might be tempted, which will probably be wrong, and make sure the guys who can't be tempted — Martin, Abraham, Clark, Tedworth, and Loudmouth Lewis — keep an eye on them."

"You going to tell the guys why?" Cronley asked.

"I don't see how I can't tell them."

"Then do it," Cronley said.

"If Father Welner leaves Buenos Aires at . . ." Gehlen began.

"Twenty-hundred," Tiny furnished. "That's midnight here."

". . . midnight tonight, when will he get to Frankfurt?"

"At midnight tomorrow," Cronley said. "They'll fly Buenos Aires–Dakar–Lisbon–Frankfurt. With fuel stops, that adds up to almost exactly twenty-four hours. And fucks up my idea of flying Welner here in a Storch. I can't get in here in the dark. Which means I couldn't leave Eschborn until three hours before daybreak, or four in the morning. What would I do with a Jesuit priest for the time between when I pick him up at Rhine-Main and can take off from Eschborn?"

"Let him sleep in one of the ambulances," Tiny said.

"Or," General Gehlen said, "can we contact the plane en route?"

"Why?"

"To tell them not to arrive in Frankfurt before daylight the day after tomorrow."

"That would do it," Cronley said.

"Better yet, since the plane hasn't left Buenos Aires yet," Tiny said, "we can get on the SIGABA now and tell them not to arrive in Frankfurt until ten hundred the day after tomorrow."

"Driver," Cronley commanded regally, "take me to the SIGABA device."

"Your wish is my command, sir," Tiny replied.

[Five]

Room 506
Park Hotel
Wiesenhüttenplatz 28-38
Frankfurt am Main
American Zone, Occupied Germany

0955 8 November 1945

Captain James D. Cronley Jr. — who was not wearing the insignia of his rank, having decided the persona of a dashing agent of the Counterintelligence Corps was more appropriate for the situation — examined himself in the mirror on the wall.

What the hell. I'll try it again.

"It" was establishing contact with Mrs. Rachel Schumann by telephone. The ostensible purpose of the call would be to tell her he knew nothing of the Leica camera she had told Freddy Hessinger she had left in the Opel Kapitän.

The actual purpose of the call was two-fold. First, to keep their affair from blowing up in his face right now. And second, to gracefully ease his way completely out of the affair as soon as possible.

That he didn't have a clue how to accomplish either of these objectives was beside the point. He knew he had to try.

He had flown into Eschborn late the previous afternoon, with a more than reluctant — actually terrified, as it was his first flight ever — Staff Sergeant Harold Lewis Jr. Cronley brought Lewis in the belief that it would be useful for Father Welner, when he got off South American Airways Flight 707 from Buenos Aires, to have a little time with Lewis to discuss Major — or Colonel or whatever the hell he really was — Konstantin Orlovsky before he met him.

Lewis had not only spent more time with the Russian than anybody else, but had interesting insights about what made him tick. And Cronley suspected Lewis had been kind to Orlovsky behind Bischoff's back when the German had been tormenting him. That might be useful.

When the ambulances had met them at Eschborn, it had been Cronley's intention to spend the night at the ASA Relay Station. The ASA sergeant who had come with the ambulances said that his presence there as either a captain or a CIC agent would draw unwanted attention to the ambulances. He suggested Cronley get a room at the Park Hotel.

Cronley knew the Army-run hotel, which was very near to the Frankfurt Hauptbahnhof. It provided Army of Occupation officers and their families a waypoint to spend a night when they arrived from — or were going to depart from — the Rhine-Main Airfield.

Second Lieutenant Cronley had spent his first night in Germany there, en route from Camp Holabird to the XXIInd CIC Detachment in Marburg an der Lahn. It was in the lobby of the hotel the next morning that the commanding officer of the XXIInd — on hearing of Cronley's sole qualification to be a CIC officer, his fluent German — had told him he would find an assignment for him where he could cause the least amount of damage.

So Cronley went in one of the ambulances to the Park Hotel, and Sergeant Lewis went in the other to the ASA Relay Station with orders to pick him up at the hotel at ten o'clock in the morning.

Once Cronley had checked in, he went to the bar and had two drinks of Haig & Haig to give him the courage to call Rachel. That worked as far as his going to his room and dialing the number. But when, on the third ring, the phone was answered — "Colonel Schumann" — the liquid courage evaporated and he hastily hung up.

Cronley went to the telephone and dialed the number of the quarters of Lieutenant Colonel and Mrs. Schumann. This time, there was no answer at all, even after he let it ring ten times.

He hung up, picked up his overnight bag, and went down to stand in front of the hotel to wait for Sergeant Lewis.

[Six]

Incoming Passenger Terminal
Rhine-Main USAF Base
Frankfurt am Main
American Zone, Occupied Germany

1010 8 November 1945

Cronley saluted the Reverend Kurt Welner as the Jesuit priest came out of the building.

"Welcome to Germany, Father Welner," he said. "Sergeant Lewis will take your bag,

649

sir, and the ambulance is right over there in the parking lot."

"Thank you, Jim. How are you?"

"Fine, sir. You want to give your bag to Sergeant Lewis?"

"There are certain valuables in the bag."

"Yes, sir. We know, Father. That's why Sergeant Lewis has that Thompson hanging from his shoulder."

Welner somewhat reluctantly handed over the bag and allowed himself to be led to the parking lot and installed in the front seat of the ambulance. Lewis got behind the wheel and Cronley got in the back.

"We're going to drive from here to Kloster Grünau in a vehicle like this?" Welner asked. "It's in Bavaria, isn't it?"

"Yes, sir. It's in Bavaria. But, no, sir. We're going to fly to Kloster Grünau. Where we're headed now is to a little airport not far from here, where my Storch is parked."

"I'll take what comfort I can from knowing I am in the hands of God," Welner said. "I do not share — and you know I don't — the affection that you and Cletus and Hansel have for that ugly and dangerous little airplane."

"You and me both, Reverend," Sergeant Lewis said.

"If you don't mind, Sergeant, you may

refer to me as 'Father,' " Welner said.

"I'm a Born Again by Total Immersion Abyssinian Baptist," Lewis said. "Can I do that?"

"I think it will be all right with God, Sergeant," Welner said.

"Father, to clear the air a little, you can say anything you want to, personal or business, to Sergeant Lewis. Actually, that's the reason I brought him along with me. He's as close to Konstantin as anybody. Closer."

"Konstantin is the NKGB officer?"

"Konstantin Orlovsky. Yes, sir."

"I'll be delighted to hear what the sergeant has to say about him. But let me get this out of the way, first."

"Sir?"

"First, I was very sorry to hear about your loss of your wife."

"Thank you, sir."

"It was impossible for me to go to the United States with Cletus and the others. If I could have gone, I would have. I hope you understand."

"Yes, sir. I do."

"What I did do, Jim, was celebrate a mass for Marjorie in the Church of Our Lady of Pilar."

"That's the church by that cemetery downtown, in Recoleta?"

"Right. In which Cletus's father and others of his family have their last resting place."

"That was very kind of you."

"Not at all. How are you doing?"

"I don't know how to answer that."

"I had a thought on the airplane," the priest said. "Cletus told me how busy you have been here. I wondered if perhaps that's been a gift from God, a blessing in disguise, so to speak, taking your mind off your loss."

What took my mind off my loss, Father, was fucking a married woman.

And speaking of God, how the hell am I going to explain that despicable, inexcusable behavior to Saint Peter when I get to those pearly gates?

"That's an interesting thought, Father."

"We'll have more time to talk, I'm sure," the Jesuit said. "But right now, Sergeant Lewis, why don't we talk about the Russian?"

[Seven]

Commanding Officer's Quarters
Kloster Grünau
Schollbrunn, Bavaria
American Zone of Occupation, Germany

1425 8 November 1945

Father Welner and Staff Sergeant Lewis came into the room. Cronley, Gehlen, and Dunwiddie were sitting at the table.

"Orlovsky has accepted your kind invitation to lunch," the priest said. "But that's all I got out of him."

"Shall I get him, Captain?" Lewis asked.

"Fuck him," Cronley said.

"That's not very charitable, Jim," the priest said.

"I'm fresh out of charity so far as he's concerned," Cronley replied.

"What was your impression of him, Father?" Gehlen asked.

"I think that you're right, General. He is more than he appears to be, more than he wants us to think he is. I wouldn't be surprised if he is a more senior officer than a major."

"Can you tell us why?"

"He didn't say anything specific, if that's what you're asking. It's more his attitude."

"You mean his casual dismissal of the possibility that we're going to shoot him in the back of the head?" Cronley asked.

"I don't think he thinks that's going to happen," the priest said, then added, "Is it?"

"If we didn't really need the names of the people the NKGB has turned, I think I'd do it myself," Cronley said.

"I don't think you mean that, Jim. I hope you don't."

"I don't know if I do or not. But no. It's not on my agenda. Why do you think he doesn't care about that as a threat?"

"I had the feeling that he thinks his situation is about to change."

"Change how?"

"That he'll somehow be freed. Is there any possibility of that?"

"Absolutely none. If the general is right, and I think he is, he's a colonel or whatever. And you agree with that. And Sergeant Lewis agrees with that. Let's take it as a given."

Cronley looked between them, then went on: "What would you do if you were Major/Colonel/General Orlovsky's superior in the ranks of the NKGB and your hotshot screwed up and found himself in the hands of the Americans who didn't know he was a hotshot, but inevitably were going to find out?

"You'd try to bust him out, and failing that, to whack him. That's what you would do. That's what they are going to try to do. Now that I think of it, I'm surprised they haven't already tried. And that settles it."

"Settles what?" Dunwiddie asked.

Gehlen said: "Although they are not supposed to, I'm sure that some of my people have weapons. Especially those who, having turned, have to consider the possibility they may need them. And some of my people are highly skilled in that sort of thing. I'm afraid Jim is right. And I further suggest that if such an attempt will be made, it will take place before the move to the Pullach compound is complete."

"And that really settles it," Cronley said. "Konstantin is about to go to the Paris of South America."

"Involuntarily, you mean?" Gehlen asked thoughtfully.

"I don't think he's about to volunteer, do you?" Cronley replied. "Father, who flew the Connie from Buenos Aires?"

"Hansel," the priest said.

"Who the hell is Hansel?" Tiny asked.

"Former Major Hans-Peter Graf von Wachtstein, recipient of the Knight's Cross of the Iron Cross from the hands of Hitler himself," Cronley said. "Who by now is probably at 44-46 Beerenstrasse in Berlin."

"I'm lost," Tiny admitted.

"Father, I presume you brought identity documents and a passport for Señor Orlovsky?"

"Yes."

"Does anything have to be done to them?"

"Just the addition of a photograph and a name."

"There was a photograph of him on his forged German *Kennkarte*," Gehlen said. "And then Bischoff took some photos of him."

"We'll have to get Felix Dzerzhinsky's documents in order as soon as possible," Cronley said.

Gehlen laughed.

"Can you handle that, General?"

"Of course."

"That's what you're going to call him?" Tiny asked. "Why? It has some meaning?"

"Felix Dzerzhinsky was the founder of the Cheka," Cronley said.

"He was not a very nice man, Tiny," Gehlen said. "He said a lot of terrible things, but what most people remember was his hope that the bourgeoisie would drown in rivers of their own blood."

asked.

"Poor Felix, ill and delirious, will be strapped to a stretcher," Cronley said.

"And if he calls out for help in his delirium?" Tiny asked.

"He will also be wrapped in bandages like a mummy," Cronley said. "But I'd like to dope him, if I could figure out a way to do that."

"That can be arranged," Gehlen said. "I'll have a word with one of my physicians."

"You do that, please, General, while I get on the SIGABA," Cronley said, and then turned to Staff Sergeant Lewis. "I think you'll enjoy Buenos Aires, Lewis."

[Eight]

PRIORITY

TOP SECRET LINDBERGH

DUPLICATION FORBIDDEN

FROM VATICAN

657

NET

18 NOVEMBER 1945

ATTN HANSEL

TO TEX

1-URGENT REPEAT URGENT YOU AR
RANGE DEPARTURE FROM RHINE
MAIN 1600 9 NOVEMBER.

2-BE PREPARED TO ACCEPT JESUI
AND MEDICAL TECHNICIANS WH
WILL BE ACCOMPANYING ILL AN
PROBABLY UNCONSCIOUS PATIEN
BEING SENT TO BUENOS AIRE
FOR TREATMENT BY DOCTOR CLE
TUS.

3-ACKNOWLEDGE.

ALTARBOY

END

TOP SECRET LINDBERGH

658

[Nine]

Das Gasthaus
Kloster Grünau
Schollbrunn, Bavaria
American Zone of Occupation, Germany

1105 9 November 1945

Staff Sergeant Harold Lewis Jr. pulled open the door to the cell under the chapel and Staff Sergeant Petronius J. Clark, who was carrying a napkin-covered tray, entered ahead of him.

Both had brassards emblazoned with a red cross, identifying them as medics, around their right arms.

"Lunch, Konstantin," Lewis said. "A hot roast beef sandwich and French fries."

"Thank you very much, but I'm not really hungry."

Cronley entered the cell.

"I'd eat, if I were you," Cronley said. "It's going to be some time before you'll have the opportunity again."

Orlovsky didn't reply.

Father Welner entered the cell and leaned against the near wall.

"Bad news for you, I'm afraid, Orlovsky," Cronley said. "The game's over. By that I mean you can abandon hope that you're going to be sprung from durance vile."

"Am I supposed to know what that means?"

"You were winning. Now you're losing. You're good, very good. You even had General Gehlen going for a while. But it's over."

"What's this?" Orlovsky asked, pointing to the tray Sergeant Clark had put on a small table. "The hearty meal the condemned man gets before he's executed?"

"You're so good, Orlovsky," Cronley went on, "that I don't really know if you really would welcome a bullet in the back of the head, or whether that's just more of your bullshit."

"You are not going to be shot, Konstantin," Welner said. "I promise you that. What's going to happen to you is that you're being sent to Argentina."

Orlovsky looked at him with cold eyes. "You're pretty good yourself, Father. You almost had me convinced your sole interest in this was the salvation of my soul."

"Not my sole interest. I was, I am, also interested in the lives and souls of your wife and children. Presuming, of course, that you really have a family back in Russia."

"We should know that soon enough," Cronley said. "General Gehlen has already issued orders to see if there really is an Orlovsky family in Russia and, if there is — frankly, I wouldn't be surprised either way — to get them out of Holy Mother Russia and to Argentina."

"You would do that as a gesture of Christian charity, right?" Orlovsky asked sarcastically.

"No," Cronley said sharply. "If there is a Mrs. Orlovsky, and if we get her to Argentina, maybe she can talk some sense into you. But enough of this. Time flies. Last chance to eat your lunch, Major Orlovsky. Or is it Colonel Orlovsky?"

Orlovsky didn't reply.

"Okay, Sergeant Clark," Cronley said.

The enormous non-com wrapped his arms around Orlovsky.

"Doctor!" Cronley called.

A slight German in a white coat, who looked undernourished, came into the room.

"I need his buttocks," he said in heavily accented English.

Sergeant Clark bent Orlovsky over the small table, knocking the food tray off in the process.

Gehlen's doctor inserted — stabbed — a hypodermic needle into Orlovsky's buttocks, and then slowly emptied it into him.

Orlovsky almost instantly went limp.

"Do you wish that I bandage him now?" the doctor asked.

"Might as well do it now."

As he wrapped Orlovsky's head in white gauze, eventually covering everything but his eyes and his nostrils, the doctor explained what Lewis could expect and what he was to do.

"He will start to regain consciousness in approximately three to four hours, depending on his natural resistance to the narcotic. The sign of this will be the fluttering of his eyes. His eye*lids*. You will then inject him again. I have prepared ten hypodermic needles for that purpose. You understand?"

"Got it," Lewis said.

The doctor then wrapped Orlovsky's hands with gauze and put them in two slings across his chest.

"The greatest risk to his well-being will be during the flight to Frankfurt in the Storch. As soon as possible, get him into a horizontal position. If there are signs of distress, get him on his feet and walk him around."

"Got it," Lewis said.

"Okay, let's get this show on the road," Cronley ordered.

Staff Sergeant Clark, without apparent effort, scooped the Russian up in his arms.

Cronley had an off-the-wall thought: *He looks like a bridegroom carrying his bride to the nuptial bed.*

Ten minutes later the Storch carrying Cronley, Father Welner, and Orlovsky broke ground. The second Storch, carrying Kurt Schröder and Sergeants Lewis and Clark stuffed in the back, lifted off thirty seconds later.

[Ten]

Rhine-Main USAF Base
Frankfurt am Main
American Zone, Occupied Germany

1550 9 November 1945

Captain Hans-Peter von Wachtstein of South American Airways was standing at the foot of the stairway to the passenger compartment of the *Ciudad de Mendoza* when two former ambulances rolled up to it. Standing with him was Major Johansen, the assistant base provost marshal, and a handful of military policemen, two of them lieutenants.

Cronley was glad to see Major Johansen, whom he had telephoned when they had landed at Eschborn and asked to meet him at the plane. Getting Orlovsky and Father Welner onto the plane wasn't going to be a problem. Getting Sergeants Clark and Lewis onto the Constellation wasn't either, but since they had no orders or travel documents, getting them to stay on the plane was likely to be difficult. He thought Major Johansen might prove helpful if he couldn't bluff his way with his CIC credentials.

"Captain von Wachtstein," Cronley greeted him. "Nice to see you again, sir."

Hansel played along.

"Mr. Cronley. How are you?"

"Major, I see you've already met Captain von Wachtstein."

"We've been chatting," Johansen said. "How've you been, Cronley?"

"Overworked and underpaid."

"Sounds familiar," Johansen said.

Father Welner joined them.

"What we're going to need for the patient, Captain von Wachtstein," the Jesuit said, "is someplace where he can be placed horizontally. Where he can rest. I think there's a spot immediately behind the cockpit?"

"Can he climb that?" von Wachtstein said, pointing to a narrow ladder leading to the door in the fuselage immediately behind the cockpit.

"He's unconscious," Cronley said.

"Who is this patient?" Major Johansen asked.

I'm glad he's asking that question, not one of his lieutenants.

It was smart of me to think of calling him.

And now the other shoe will drop.

"Show Major Johansen your passport, Father Welner," Cronley said as he handed Dzerzhinsky's Vatican passport to him.

"Russian, huh?" Johansen said. "That name is vaguely familiar."

That's the other damned shoe dropping!

You had to be a smart-ass with Dzerzhinsky's name, didn't you?

"Of Russian ancestry, obviously," Welner said. "But now he's a citizen of Vatican City."

"So I see," Johansen said, handing both passports to the priest.

Sergeants Clark and Lewis appeared, with an unconscious Orlovsky strapped securely to a stretcher.

"There is a bed for our patient in a small area behind the cockpit," Cronley said, pointing. "Captain von Wachtstein will suggest the best way to get him there."

After a moment's thought, Hansel said, "If you two could carry him up the passenger stairway, and then down the aisle . . ."

"Not a problem, sir," Sergeant Clark said.

He bent over the stretcher, unfastened the

buckles, picked Dzerzhinsky up, and then, cradling him in his arms, walked without apparent effort up the passenger stairway. Lewis followed.

"Sturdy fellow, isn't he?" Major Johansen observed.

"Well, that's it," Cronley said. "Thank you for waiting, Captain von Wachtstein."

"Happy to oblige."

"When you get close to Buenos Aires, it might be a good idea to call ahead to have an ambulance and a stretcher waiting."

"I can do that."

"Have a nice flight," Cronley finally said. "You, too, Father Welner."

"I'm sure it will be less stressful than my last flight. God bless you, Jim."

He then started up the stairway.

Von Wachtstein shook Cronley's hand, and then Major Johansen's, and started toward the crew ladder.

"Captain," one of the MP lieutenants said. "Don't forget those two medics you have onboard."

"They're going," Cronley said.

"Sir, I didn't see any passports or travel orders," the lieutenant said to Major Johansen.

Johansen looked at Cronley. Cronley turned so that only Johansen could see his face, and put his finger in front of his lips.

Johansen looked at him for a long moment.

"Not a problem, Stewart," Johansen said. "It's an intelligence matter. You didn't see those medics get on that airplane. I'll explain later."

"Yes, sir."

Both sets of stairs were pulled away, and the doors closed.

There came the sound of engines starting, as Cronley shook Major Johansen's hand and then walked toward the ambulances.

[Eleven]

Park Hotel
Wiesenhüttenplatz 28-38
Frankfurt am Main
American Zone, Occupied Germany

1705 9 November 1945

Cronley took a healthy sip of his double Dewar's scotch whisky — to which, he decided, he was most certainly entitled — and went through his mental To Do list.

The major item — Orlovsky — was off the list obviously. So was the potential problem of someone questioning Kurt Schröder's right to fly a U.S. Army Storch. He had flown back to Kloster Grünau immediately after dropping off Clark and Lewis at Eschborn. The ambulances would return to Kloster Grünau in the morning, after picking up Cronley at the hotel and then driving him to Eschborn to pick up his Storch.

Only two things remained to be done, he concluded, and the sooner he did them the better.

"Hand me that telephone, please, Sergeant," he said to the American non-com supervising the bar. The bartenders and waiters were German.

"It's for official use only, sir," the bartender said somewhat righteously.

"Is that so? Hand it to me, please."

The phone was reluctantly slid across the bar to him.

"Munich Military 4474," Cronley ordered into the receiver.

When that order had been passed along and the phone in Munich was ringing, Cronley extended it to the sergeant, who put it to his ear.

The sergeant heard, clearly, and Cronley less so, "Twenty-third CIC, Special Agent Hessinger speaking, sir."

"Okay, Sergeant?" Cronley asked, gesturing for the handset to be returned to him.

The sergeant did not reply as he did so.

"This is Special Agent Hoover, Special Agent Hessinger," Cronley said. "The package is on the way as of 1515 hours. Please advise Colonel Norwich and Sergeant Gaucho immediately."

"Yes, sir," Hessinger said.

"I should be in Rome about noon tomorrow, weather permitting."

"Yes, sir. Be advised your friends from Washington are still looking for you."

"How kind of them. Please give them my best regards and tell them I'm making every effort to fit them into my busy schedule."

"Yes, sir."

"Nice to talk to you, Special Agent Hessinger."

"And to you, sir."

Cronley put the handset in its cradle, then slid the telephone back across the bar.

"Thank you so much, Sergeant."

If the FBI had tapped Hessinger's phone — and if Hessinger thought they had, it was ninety-nine percent certain they had — it wouldn't take them long to figure out that Special Agent Hoover was Captain James D. Cronley Jr. giving them the finger. It might take them a little longer to conclude that Colonel Norwich was First Sergeant Chauncey Dunwiddie and even longer to decide that Sergeant Gaucho was Lieutenant Colonel Cletus Frade, USMCR, but eventually they would.

It didn't matter. Fat Freddy understood that he was now to go out to the Pullach compound to get on the SIGABA and send an URGENT to Tex that von Wachtstein was on his way to Buenos Aires with Orlovsky and the Jesuit — who would explain everything — as of three-fifteen Frankfurt time. Dunwiddie would get a copy of that message, plus one of his own, telling him that Cronley would be back at Kloster Grünau at noon tomorrow. The FBI could not tap the SIGABA.

That the FBI would eventually catch up with him was a given. But they didn't know where he was right now, which would give him time to deal with the last item on the To Do list. That item was spelled Schumann, Mrs. Rachel.

Cronley drained his Dewar's and ordered another.

And then I will go to my room and call Mrs. Rachel Schumann.

As he crossed the lobby of the hotel toward the elevator bank, Cronley saw something he hadn't noticed before. There was a Class VI store. For reasons he couldn't even guess, the Army classified hard liquor as

Class VI supplies, and the places that sold such spirits to officers as Class VI stores.

He bought a quart bottle of Haig & Haig scotch whisky and took it to his room, sampling its contents before picking up the telephone to call Rachel.

Rachel answered on the third ring.

"If you can't talk, say 'wrong number' and hang up."

"I've been waiting and waiting to hear from you."

"Well, I've been busy. Rachel, I don't have your Leica."

"I know that, sweetheart. Where are you?"

"In the Park Hotel. You know, by the Frankfurt Hauptbahnhof?"

"What are you doing there?"

"Well, it was too late for me to fly home, so I'm spending the night here. Rachel, we have to talk."

"What are you doing in Frankfurt?"

"Actually, what I was doing was putting that Russian you're always asking about on an airplane."

Now, that wasn't smart. Why the hell did you tell her that?

What the hell. It doesn't matter. Orlovsky's gone.

"You put him on an airplane? What was

671

that all about?"

"If I told you, I would have to kill you."

"Have you been drinking, Jimmy?"

"What gave you that idea? Rachel, we have to talk."

"What room are you in?"

He had to look at the telephone to get the room number.

"Four-oh-seven."

"I'll be there in thirty minutes."

"Can't we just talk on the phone? What's the colonel going to think when he comes home for supper and you're gone?"

"I'll be there in thirty minutes." She chuckled. "And don't start without me, baby."

Then she hung up.

Cronley thought he might as well have another little taste while he was waiting for her.

[Twelve]

Room 407, Park Hotel
Wiesenhüttenplatz 28-38
Frankfurt am Main
American Zone, Occupied Germany

0905 10 November 1945

The telephone rang, and when Cronley answered it, he was told that his ride was waiting for him.

"Be right down," he said, and hung up.

Rachel was nowhere in sight.

What the hell did I expect?

She had to go home to her husband and the kiddies.

As he dressed, he tried to recall how well he had done in his attempt to get out of the affair as gracefully as possible.

If ending an affair means the cessation of sexual activity between the participants, I am still up to my ears — well over my ears — in this one.

Rachel had her tongue down my throat and her hand on my wang no more than sixty seconds after she appeared at the door.

But, despite that, she had not been as anxious to get nailed as she was to hear "finally" about the Russian. I had to tell her about Orlovsky before I could get her to take her underpants off.

Did I tell her too much?

Probably. Both before Nailing One, and before Nailing Two, as she was still interested in the Russian after Nailing One and brought the subject up again. Satisfying her female curiosity was the price of Nailing Two.

But what's the difference? She can't tell anybody, not even her husband. If she did that, he would want to know why I told her, and she certainly didn't want to open that subject up for discussion.

I don't remember much of what happened — anything that happened — after Nailing Two. I must have passed out.

Did I wake up later and see that she was gone? Did that happen, or am I just supposing it did?

What I am going to have to do is admit I failed to end the affair because I was a little drunk and thinking with my dick.

Ending the affair now goes on the Que Será Será list beside the FBI finally catching up with me.

Five minutes after his phone rang, he was on the sidewalk outside the hotel, getting into an ambulance.

[Thirteen]

Commanding Officer's Quarters
Kloster Grünau
Schollbrunn, Bavaria
American Zone of Occupation, Germany

1920 10 November 1945

First Sergeant Dunwiddie pushed open the door to Cronley's room without knocking. Cronley was asleep in bed and did not wake, although he was usually a very light sleeper.

674

Dunwiddie, none too gently, shook his shoulder.

"If that printout is to tell me Konstantin is safe in Buenos Aires, you are forgiven," Cronley said when he opened his eyes.

"Not exactly, Jim," Dunwiddie said as he handed the SIGABA printout to him.

"What the hell?" Jimmy said as he began to read:

```
PRIORITY

TOP SECRET LINDBERGH

DUPLICATION FORBIDDEN

FROM MOSES

VIA VINT HILL TANGO NET

1505 GREENWICH 10 NOVEMBER 1945

TO VATICAN ATTN ALTARBOY

SHARE WITH GEHLEN ONLY

    1-CONVOY UNDER PROTECTION BIS
      CARRYING ORLOVSKY ATTACKED
      BY SOME KIND OF ROCKETS AND
      MACHINE GUN FIRE SHORTLY
```

AFTER DEPARTING JORGE FRADE
FOR BUENOS AIRES.

2-THREE KNOWN DEAD INCLUDING
ONE OF YOUR SERGEANTS AND
SEVERAL OTHERS WOUNDED SOME
SERIOUSLY.

3-TEX SENDS BEGIN QUOTE AL-
TARBOY THEY KNEW WHEN AND
WHERE WE WOULD BE. WHOLE
PLAN OBVIOUSLY KNOWN TO
NKGB. ASK GEHLEN TO FIND OUT
SOURCE OF BREACH AND DO NOT
REPEAT DO NOT GET IN HIS
WAY. END QUOTE

4-TEX PRESENTLY WITH WOUNDED
IN ARGENTINE MILITARY HOSPI-
TAL.

5-MORE TO FOLLOW.

MOSES

END

TOP SECRET LINDBERGH

"Who is Moses?" Dunwiddie asked.

676

"Sergeant Stein. Ashton's Number Two. I guess he went to Buenos Aires after Ashton got himself run over. Rockets? What the hell?"

"And machine-gun fire."

"Where's the general?"

"Taking a walk. I sent a jeep after him."

"What the hell is going on?"

"I don't have a clue."

General Gehlen and a second SIGABA printout arrived together about five minutes later. Cronley handed him the first message as he read the second:

PRIORITY

TOP SECRET LINDBERGH

DUPLICATION FORBIDDEN

FROM MOSES

VIA VINT HILL TANGO NET

1515 GREENWICH 10 NOVEMBER 1945

TO VATICAN ATTN ALTARBOY

SHARE WITH GEHLEN ONLY

677

1-TEX SENDS BEGIN QUOTE

A-REGRET INFORM YOU STAFF SERGEANT HAROLD LEWIS JR. DIED OF WOUNDS RECEIVED IN ATTACK AT 1405 THIS DATE.

B-STAFF SERGEANT PETRONIUS J. CLARK SUFFERED SEVERE INJURIES AND BURNS AND IS IN CRITICAL CONDITION.

C-REV KURT WELNER, SJ, SUFFERED BROKEN SHOULDER AND SOME BURNS BUT WILL SHORTLY BE ABLE TO LEAVE THE HOSPITAL.

D-MAJOR KONSTANTIN ORLOVSKY SUFFERED MULTIPLE INJURIES AND BURNS AND IS NOT EXPECTED TO LIVE. E-MORE TO FOLLOW.

END QUOTE

MOSES

END

TOP SECRET LINDBERGH

"Who is Moses?" General Gehlen asked.

Cronley told him.

"Does that 'share with Gehlen' line mean Tiny is to be excluded from our conversations?"

"Well, if that's what Colonel Frade meant, fuck him. Tiny is not going to be excluded from anything."

"Good," Gehlen said. "Then I suggest, while we're waiting to hear more from Colonel Frade, how our security has been so completely breached."

[Fourteen]

1920 10 November 1945

```
PRIORITY

TOP SECRET LINDBERGH

DUPLICATION FORBIDDEN

FROM TEX

VIA VINT HILL TANGO NET

1705 GREENWICH 10 NOVEMBER 1945

TO VATICAN ATTN ALTARBOY
```

1-GENERAL MARTIN, TWO OF WHOSE
MEN DIED IN THE ATTACK AND
SEVEN OF WHOSE MEN WERE
INJURED IN ONE WAY OR AN-
OTHER, OFFERS THE FOLLOWING
SCENARIO WITH WHICH I CON-
CUR:

A-THE ATTACK WAS PROFESSION-
ALLY PLANNED AND EXECUTED
BY PERSONS FULLY FAMILIAR
WITH THE FACTS, IE, THAT OR-
LOVSKY WAS THE SICK MAN ON
THE AIRCRAFT.

B-IDENTIFICATION OF TWO OF THE
FOUR ATTACKER CORPSES AS
PARAGUAYAN CRIMINALS IS
CONSISTENT WITH KNOWN PRAC-
TICES OF NAZIS DURING AND
AFTER THE WAR TO USE CON-
TRACT ASSASSINS, WITH ONE
IMPORTANT EXCEPTION. NAZIS
ALWAYS LEFT SOME INDICATION
AT CRIME SCENE THAT THEY
WERE RESPONSIBLE FOR THE
CRIME. NO SUCH MARKER WITH
THIS ATTACK.

C-CONSIDERING THIS, AND NA-
TIONALITY OF SICK MAN ON THE
AIRCRAFT, THIS POINTS TO THE
SOVIET UNION. IT IS POSSIBLE
THAT USE OF GERMAN PANZER-
FAUST 60-MM ROCKETS ALSO
SUGGESTS IT WAS HOPED THE
GERMANS WOULD BE BLAMED FOR
THE ASSAULT. IT IS NOTED
THAT SOVIET UNION IS IN
TALKS WITH THE ARGENTINE
GOVERNMENT REGARDING RE-
ESTABLISHMENT OF DIPLOMATIC
RELATIONS.

D-IT IS UNLIKELY PERPETRATORS
WILL EVER BE KNOWN TO THE
POINT WHERE CHARGES COULD
BE DRAWN.

2-FOREGOING MAKES DISCOVERY
OF THE CAUSE OF BREACH IN
OUR SECURITY EVEN MORE IM-
PORTANT. EXPEND ALL EFFORTS
TO FIND THE SOURCE OF LEAK.

TEX

END

TOP SECRET LINDBERGH

Cronley suddenly felt clammy and sick to his stomach, and it took a great effort not to throw up. He knew who the source of the leak was. He did not mention this to either Gehlen or Dunwiddie. He was far too deeply shamed.

He waited until after the next message came in. That was two hours later.

He was later to recall that those two hours were the worst in his life.

```
PRIORITY

TOP SECRET LINDBERGH

DUPLICATION FORBIDDEN

FROM TEX

VIA VINT HILL TANGO NET

1910 GREENWICH 10 NOVEMBER 1945

TO VATICAN ATTN ALTARBOY

SHARE WITH GEHLEN ONLY

   1. AT THE SUGGESTION OF FATHER
      WELNER, ORLOVSKY WAS LED TO
      BELIEVE THAT HIS INJURIES
```

WERE PROBABLY FATAL. FATHER
WELNER ARRANGED FOR A PRIEST
OF THE RUSSIAN ORTHODOX
FAITH, WHOM HE KNOWS TO BE
ANTI-COMMUNIST, TO VISIT OR-
LOVSKY ON HIS DEATHBED TO
ADMINISTER THE LAST RITES.

2. AFTER A BRIEF CONVERSATION
WITH THIS CLERIC, ORLOVSKY
DECLARED THAT

A. HIS REAL NAME IS SERGIE
LIKHAREV AND HE HOLDS RANK
OF COLONEL IN NKGB.

B. HIS WIFE, NATALIA, AND SONS,
SERGIE AND PAVEL, RESIDE AT
NEVSKY PROSPEKT 114 LENIN-
GRAD.

C. HE FURTHER STATED THAT WHEN
HE ENTERED KLOSTER GRUNAU
HE WAS IN CONTACT WITH
FORMER OBERSTLEUTNANT GUN-
THER VON PLAT AND FORMER
MAJOR KURT BOSS, AND THAT HE
WISHED THIS INFORMATION
RELAYED VIA CAPTAIN CRONLEY
TO GENERAL GEHLEN.

3. NONE OF THE FOREGOING SHOULD
   DIMINISH IN ANY WAY ANY OF
   YOUR EFFORTS TO UNCOVER THE
   LEAKER.

TEX

END

TOP SECRET LINDBERGH

After reading the **SIGABA** printout, Cronley decided that the time to confess had arrived.

He struggled to find his voice, then in a quiet monotone said, "Tiny, would you mind leaving me alone with the general for a couple of minutes?"

"Why? I thought you said I wasn't going to be excluded from anything." He paused. "Wait. You sonofabitch! You think I'm the one with the loose mouth?"

"No. I know you're not. I am."

"What?"

"After the plane left yesterday, I went to the Park Hotel. Mrs. Rachel Schumann joined me there."

"You're referring to Colonel Schumann's wife? The IG's wife?" Gehlen asked.

Cronley nodded.

684

"What was that all about? Her camera?" Tiny asked.

"At the time, I thought she came there to get laid . . ."

"By you?" Tiny asked incredulously.

"By me. I have been fucking her ever since I came back from the States. Until about an hour ago, I thought it was my manly charm. Now I think she's a fucking Russian spy."

"You're really out of your mind, you know that? That woman a Russian spy? Maybe the colonel's one, too, huh? Maybe they work as a team. Jesus, Jimmy! What the hell have you been drinking? Or smoking?"

"Did it ever strike you as a little odd, Tiny," Gehlen asked, "that Colonel Schumann, the day Jim shot up his car, was here at all? What was the inspector general of Counterintelligence doing here, on this back road in the country? Why was he so insistent on coming in, when it would have been so much easier for him to return to Frankfurt and have General Greene order that he be admitted? That happened, you might recall, not before, but a day or two after Sergeant Tedworth arrested Colonel Likharev."

"Who?" Tiny asked. "Oh."

"We will soon know if that is actually his name. He fooled us for a while. I have the feeling he has not fooled Father Welner or

Colonel Frade."

"Sir, you're saying that you believe Cronley?"

"Let's hear the rest of the story of his romance with Mrs. Schumann, and then we can ask ourselves the question again."

"You are one dumb sonofabitch, Captain, sir," Dunwiddie said, shaking his head, when Cronley had finished relating the romance.

"Everything fits, Tiny," Gehlen said. And then chuckled. "It destroys poor Jim's picture of himself as being as irresistible as Errol Flynn. But it all makes sense."

"So, what happens now?" Tiny asked.

"In the morning, I fly to Frankfurt and tell Colonel Mattingly," Cronley said.

"No. That's out of the question," Gehlen said.

"Excuse me, General?"

"Think that through, Jim. If you are correct, and I think you are, the Schumanns have thought their exposure through and come up with a plan to deal with it. Those plans range from outright denial to flight. The latter we cannot afford."

"And the alternative?" Cronley asked.

"You're under orders from Colonel Frade not to get in my way," Gehlen said. "Why don't you just follow them?"

"What are your plans for your officers, the ones Likharev says are the ones he turned?" Tiny asked. "Actually, how do you know those are the real traitors, that from his deathbed Likharev isn't going to get two Good Germans whacked, and get us to do it?"

" '*Us* to do it'?" Gehlen said. "They're my responsibility, Tiny. Not yours."

"*Ours,* General," Dunwiddie insisted. "I wouldn't mind whacking them myself, but I'd have to be sure they are indeed trying to sink everybody else."

"And I would like to shoot Colonel Schumann and his wife," Cronley said. "So why don't I do that first, and then go tell Mattingly why I did it?"

"Now you're acting immaturely," Gehlen said. "Think that through, Jim. For one thing, Colonel Mattingly doesn't like you. He would be prone to think you shot her after a lovers' quarrel. We have no proof —"

"Except what happened just now in Buenos Aires," Cronley interrupted.

"Not only have we no proof of what happened there, but we couldn't tell anybody about it if we did," Gehlen said patiently, and then asked, "What good would it do anybody for you to go to the stockade or the hangman?"

Cronley didn't reply.

"Insofar as whether von Plat and Boss are traitors — and I think they are — Konrad Bischoff can determine that. Actually, he's proposed their names to me already. And I think we should be able to learn what we need to know about Mrs. Likharev and the children in Leningrad in no more than a week or so. I want to be very careful. Getting them out is going to be risky."

"You're still going to try that?" Tiny asked.

"I think it would be very useful to everybody if Sergei Likharev felt indebted to us because we reunited him with his family."

"Yeah," Tiny said.

"I'm a big boy . . ." Cronley began.

"I wouldn't take a vote on that right now, Captain, sir," Tiny said.

". . . I know I fucked up big time. And I'm willing to take my lumps for that. But . . ."

"But what, Jim?" Gehlen asked.

"The way I'm hearing this, I'm not going to get any lumps. I'm not to tell Clete or Mattingly, not even, for Christ's sake, Fat Freddy. It doesn't seem fair."

"I'm going to say this just once, so pay close attention," Gehlen said. "I regard the greatest threat to what we're trying to do

688

here as coming not from the Soviets but from those intelligence types from the Pentagon who will shortly be moving into the Pullach compound.

"I know how to deal with the Reds. I do not know how to deal with your Pentagon. You, Tiny, are close to General White. Jim had those captain's bars he rarely wears pinned on his shoulders by President Truman. You two, with friends in high places, and who believe in what we're doing here, are going to be my defense against the Pentagon. I need the both of you."

"Jesus," Tiny breathed.

"And now, if you'll excuse me, I'm going to find Konrad Bischoff and suggest he have a chat with Boss and von Plat."

As a Pavlovian reflex, both Cronley and Dunwiddie popped to their feet and came to attention when Gehlen stood.

When he had left the room, Dunwiddie said: "You know he's going to whack those two."

"And Colonel and Mrs. Schumann."

"Does that bother you?"

"Her, no. She's responsible for Lewis and the others getting killed. Him, I don't know."

"They call what he is 'an accessory before the fact.' "

"I wonder how he's going to do it," Cronley said.

"Wonder, but don't ask."

"I brought a bottle of Haig & Haig from Frankfurt. I don't suppose you'd be interested in a little taste?"

"I thought you would never ask," Dunwiddie said.

[Fifteen]

On December 21, 1945, the front page of the *Stars and Stripes,* the Army of Occupation's newspaper, reported with black borders the tragic death of General George S. Patton. He had been injured in an automobile accident on December 9.

A short article on page eleven of the same edition reported the tragic death in Hoechst, outside Frankfurt, of Lieutenant Colonel and Mrs. Anthony Schumann. A fiery explosion, apparently caused by a cooking gas leak, had totally destroyed their home. Fortunately, the story concluded, the Schumanns' two children were not at home when the explosion occurred.

[Sixteen]

On December 28, 1945, First Sergeant Chauncey L. Dunwiddie, Company C, 203rd Tank Destroyer Battalion, duty station with XXIIIrd CIC Detachment, was discharged for the convenience of the government for the purpose of accepting a commission.

On December 29, 1945, Captain Chauncey L. Dunwiddie, Cavalry, Detail Military Intelligence, having reported upon active duty, was assigned to the XXIIIrd CIC Detachment. No travel involved.

[Seventeen]

On January 1, 1946, President Harry S Truman signed an Executive Order that established the United States Central Intelligence Directorate, and named Rear Admiral Sidney W. Souers, USN, as director.

[Eighteen]

On January 2, 1946, Paragraph 3, General Order #1 Headquarters War Department (Classified Secret) ordered that Captains J. D. Cronley Jr. and C. L. Dunwiddie be transferred from XXIIIrd CIC Detachment to the United States Central Intelligence Directorate with duty station Pullach, Germany. No travel involved.

ABOUT THE AUTHORS

W.E.B. Griffin is the author of six bestselling series: The Corps, Brotherhood of War, Badge of Honor, Men at War, Honor Bound, and Presidential Agent. He has been invested into the orders of St. George of the U.S. Armor Association and St. Michael of the Army Aviation Association of America, and is a life member of the U.S. Special Operations Association; Gaston-Lee Post 5660, Veterans of Foreign Wars; the American Legion, China Post #1 in Exile; the Police Chiefs Association of Southeastern Pennsylvania, Southern New Jersey, and the State of Delaware; the National Rifle Association; the Office of Strategic Services (OSS) Society; and the Flat Earth Society (Pensacola, Florida, and Buenos Aires, Argentina, chapters). He is an honorary life member of the U.S. Army Otter-Caribou Association, the U.S. Army Special Forces Association, the U.S. Marine Raider Association, and the USMC Combat Correspondents Association. Griffin lives in Alabama and Argentina.

William E. Butterworth IV has been an editor and writer for more than twenty-five years, and has worked closely with his father for a decade on the editing and writing of the Griffin books. He is coauthor of the bestselling novels *Hazardous Duty, The Last Witness, Empire and Honor, The Spymasters, The Saboteurs, The Double Agents, Death and Honor, The Traffickers, The Honor of Spies, The Vigilantes, The Outlaws, Victory and Honor,* and *Covert Warriors.* He is a member of the Sons of the American Legion, China Post #1 in Exile, and of the Office of Strategic Services (OSS) Society; and a life member of the National Rifle Association and the Texas Rifle Association. He lives in Texas.

The employees of Thorndike Press hope you have enjoyed this Large Print book. All our Thorndike, Wheeler, and Kennebec Large Print titles are designed for easy reading, and all our books are made to last. Other Thorndike Press Large Print books are available at your library, through selected bookstores, or directly from us.

For information about titles, please call:
  (800) 223-1244

or visit our Web site at:
  http://gale.cengage.com/thorndike

To share your comments, please write:
  Publisher
  Thorndike Press
  10 Water St., Suite 310
  Waterville, ME 04901